STACEY LEA reined her horse at the Cliff to study the tall figure looking out over the water. The intruder disturbed her. She instinctively pulled the reins for a quick get-away, but it was too late; he'd already turned. Her hands were clammy as they tightened on the riding crop, more to steady herself than to defend.

"You're trespassin', sir. This is Culberson land, and that's a Culberson view."

Even as she spoke, he'd started walking toward her, taking in every bit from her faded jeans and scuffed boots to her well-worn suede jacket and mussed hair. Still without speaking, he helped her down and at the same time drew her close.

"If you were my woman, I wouldn't let you out of my sight."

Flippantly she replied, "I always thought I was." With this Stacey Lea stopped thinking, threw her arms around his neck and melded herself closer into him as his mouth reached into hers.

BACKSTAGE AT THE WHITE HOUSE

A NOVEL

BY

JEAN CANDLISH KELCHNER

To Pamela —
It's a pleasure to autograph
my book for Lorraine's daughter.
Very best,
Jean Kelchner

authorHOUSE®

AuthorHouse™
1663 Liberty Drive, Suite 200
Bloomington, IN 47403
www.authorhouse.com
Phone: 1-800-839-8640

First published by AuthorHouse 3/17/2008

ISBN: 978-1-4343-5686-4 (e)
ISBN: 978-1-4343-5687-1 (sc)
ISBN: 978-1-4343-5685-7 (hc)

Library of Congress Control Number: 2007909962

Printed in the United States of America
Bloomington, Indiana

This book is printed on acid-free paper.

Special thanks to my editor, Marie Kuszewski.

To Nancy Holland, who always believed in this book and me,
and
To the "First Woman President".

"No! No!" said the Queen.
"Sentence first — verdict afterwards."

Lewis Carroll, *Alice in Wonderland*, 1865

THE BEGINNING OF THE END

Randal looked out the window at the busy street alive with anticipation of the day's historic event. Yesterday's snowstorm had disappeared and the sun was shining, a good omen. Yes, but the sun was bright on the snow, and she knew she would squint. She smiled, thinking that a man would never have thought of that.

Our minds do work differently, but then, that had been the major thrust of the campaign—that difference. They'd had their chance, eons of it, and the country, like the world, was one big mess. Now, it was their time; it was time for a woman to clean house. She didn't mind the analogy; she was a woman and that's what women do.

Randal's thoughts again drifted to the glistening outdoors. People want to see you; they have a right to see you, Aunt Stace had advised— no sunglasses and no floppy brims. She loved sunglasses! They were such good places to hide, especially from those intrusive cameras that always hounded her. She'd have worn them to her father's funeral, no matter what Aunt Stace might have said, but there had been no sun to excuse them; it had rained that day.

She sighed, regretting that her father was not here to see this day. He had known the likely outcome for he'd died only two days before elections, his heart no longer heeding his will. Still, it seemed unfair that he had not seen the dream realized. A tear slid down her cheek, and Eli. "Oh, Eli," she whispered softly, "I hope you know how much I miss you, that I'd chuck it all for just one more night with you!"

Well, that was dramatic! She exclaimed to herself, wondering where such a declaration had popped from as she got herself back on course.

Yes, Eli would always be a regret; there wasn't a day that she didn't think of him, but she knew she wouldn't change a thing. It's simply an irrefutable fact that one can't have it all, and she had made her choice a long time ago. She couldn't imagine herself a professor's wife on some vine-covered campus. No, she liked where she was and she'd worked hard to get here. Still, it had all started after one of those nights that was now only memory.

"And where do you think you're going, slipping off without a word, shameless wench!" As he spoke, he reached out and pulled her down, an easy mark since she'd just leaned over to press a light goodbye kiss on his forehead.

"You've been playing cat; you were awake all the time."

"Just a short time. I didn't want you to know because I love watching you dress."

Randal blushed.

"I left you a note," she responded, reaching over, getting it off the bed-stand and putting it on the pillow beside him. "I didn't want to wake you."

"Well, I'm awake now and refuse to let you leave me on a Sunday morning. You should know better; it's our favorite time."

The bed smelled like sex, good sex, and she knew from the way he'd begun to caress her breast that he was interested in more, not that she wouldn't have also liked to stretch out for a lazy morning next to him.

"No, Eli, I can't; in fact, I'm going to be late even now," she said firmly, pulling away with difficulty and straightening her clothes while he read the note.

"Ah, the Aunts," he responded raising a scruffy eyebrow. "Now, I know why you didn't tell me last night."

"Yes, because we'd have argued; it would've spoiled our night, and our nights are too precious to do that." She leaned against him for a deliberate kiss.

"And our Sunday mornings, too. Randal,…"

"Shush!" she commanded, putting her finger gently to his lips. "Read *Hamlet* or ah, *King Lear,* whatever Shakespearean scholars do when they're turned on. I have to go; they're all there."

"And I'm here."

"Please, Eli!"

"I shall read *Othello*, Act V, Scene ii, while you're gone, my luv, for Othello knew how to deal with unfaithful women."

"Desdemona was not unfaithful and neither am I," Randal snapped. "You can hardly call visiting my mother and her friends being unfaithful to you."

"But I'd not want to test you if you had to choose."

"Try me," she challenged, knowing he wouldn't. "Besides, if you want to quote *Othello*, you'll have to marry me first." She closed the door before he could respond.

Randal smiled the same smile of over twenty-five years ago when she had gotten into her car and pointed it towards Fairmont and the old plantation houses along the Mississippi. It wasn't often that she got the last word with Eli.

They had met during her last year of law school at Harvard, when he was guesting for the year from Oxford where he taught English Literature. Word of him spread quickly and even if she'd had time to take his class, it was doubtful she'd have gotten in. It was a large graduate lecture class filled to capacity, but she'd leaned into a back corner when she could get away.

His deep Scottish voice was mesmerizing by itself but add to it a tall frame with broad shoulders, a scruffy salt and pepper Roman beard and marvelously intelligent twinkling eyes set underneath a thick craggy salt and pepper brow, and he was absolutely irresistible. Every woman in class hung on his every word, and she was sure it wasn't necessarily for the content, no matter how interesting he could be. Dr. Elias Abraham Fergusson exuded charm, but she hadn't realized how much until that day in the law library. She had been seriously involved with her laptop when his voice had penetrated her concentration.

"I like the way your brow creases when you're intense."

"How long have you been watching it?" she snapped without thinking. Looking up, an embarrassed flush began to color her face. His twinkling eyes, with those marvelous creases and brow framing them, bathed her. She knew exactly then that she was in love with him, and the flush increased in her cheeks because she knew that he knew it too. For a moment, she wished that she could turn invisible and slink away, have *Star Trek's* Scottie beam her up, or that she had simply pulled the covers back over her head that morning. But all that was just for a moment. The fact was, she was right where she wanted to be, right where she wanted to be for the rest of her life.

He didn't answer her question. "I've seen you visit my class, stand in a back corner, half in the shadows, and then swiftly slip away sometimes before I've finished. I don't allow that."

"I would've taken it if I'd had time, but I'm in my last year of law school and…"

"What's your name?" he asked, interrupting.

"Randal Fairmont."

"That soft accent places you south of the Mason-Dixon."

"Mississippi," she obliged, "Fairmont, Mississippi."

"A city named after you?"

"No, only a small town founded by my ancestors. I had nothing to do with it."

"Fairmont? Sounds familiar?"

"It could be. My dad was Senate Majority Leader during the Forbes Administration, and I have a brother in the Senate and one in Congress now. I come from a long line of public servants. It's what the Fairmonts do."

"And what do you plan to do?" he responded, seemingly unimpressed.

"Why, I plan to be president," she answered flippantly.

How quickly memories make the time fly, Randal noted, looking at her watch and allowing the present only a momentary entrance into her far-away thoughts. She was still back there, turning her car into the oak-lined drive at Oak Cliff Plantation and watching the fine old antebellum mansion that had been in the Culberson family forever come gradually into view.

"They're all waitin' for ya," a small boy said as he eagerly opened her car door in front of the mansion's fine ionic pillars. "They've been waitin' for ya a long time, Missy Randal," he continued in a serious voice, making it clear that he was glad he wasn't the one that had kept those formidable creatures inside waiting.

"It won't hurt 'em to wait a little once in awhile," she responded, sliding into the lazy Mississippi idiom as she gave him a big hug. "Besides, ah heard your grandma once say that most people spend their lives waitin'—waitin' fo' the mail, waitin' in lines, waitin' fo' the light to change, waitin' fo' the doctor, and finally, waitin' fo' the good lawd to take 'em home. Why, ah bet you've been out heah waitin' fo' me for a long time. No, it won't hurt 'em waitin' a bit."

She did enjoy applying such remarks to her mother and the Aunts whose privileged lives had spoiled them to such mundane things as waiting, but, for that matter, even Willy's grandmother didn't do much of it.

"How's ya' Ma, Willy?"

She had grown up with Willy's mother just as her mother and Aunt Stacey Lea had grown up with Willy's grandmother. Willy's family was as much a part of Oak Cliff as Aunt Stace's and perhaps loved it even more because they'd always taken care of it. The first of their blood had come as slaves and had stayed on to grow wealthy as partners in the horse business with Aunt Stace's father, Mister Wylie. But no matter how much money they made, they'd always taken care of the Culberson's. *It was their God-given duty*, Willy's grandmother always said. She'd tried to make her children understand, but most of them were gone from here now, successfully building their own lives.

"My Ma's fine," he answered. "She sez fo' you ta come see her 'fore ya leave."

"Sure will; you tell her."

"Randal, will you please stop your chattin' and get in here. We've been waitin' forevah," her mother called.

"Comin' Sue Ann," she called back, giving Willy a communal wink.

"And don't call me by my first name," her mother scolded as they hugged warmly. "Here, let me look at you. I've a feelin' that you're gonna be a bit difficult today," she added, eyeing her up and down.

"That depends, Mama, that depends."

They were in the library at the large oak table that filled the center of the room. Aunt Stacey Lea sat at the left end, which meant that the left end was the head of the table. She was always at the head. Even a round table had its head when she was present. To her right sat Aunt Sarah and to her left, Auntie Bev. The empty seat was at the far end, the foot. That would be her seat and to her right was her mother and to her left was Aunt Ellie.

Seating was very important in the group, and she took note that the arrangement was different today. Normally it would be reversed, with Aunt Ellie and her mother sitting to the right and left of Stacey Lea. After making the rounds and giving each of them a cheerful kiss, she took her seat, not apologizing for being late. If they intended to be different today, then so would she.

"How are you, Randal, my dear?" Aunt Stace inquired, as they all looked her way.

"I'm fine, and I think it's best to announce right now, before this meeting gets started, that I plan to get married."

"You could at least have allowed me time to offer you tea or a glass of wine before dropping such a bomb," Aunt Stace chided.

"What do you mean, a bomb?" Aunt Sarah asked vaguely, as usual void of a sense of humor.

"What it means, dear," the head of the table answered, gently taking her friend's hand, "is that Randal is putting us on notice, whether we like it or not, that she intends to marry a man twice her age and half J…"

"Why don't you just say it, Stacey Lea, for we all know Elias Fergusson is half Jew. Well, I'm whole Jew and that hasn't seemed to matter all these years."

"I know, Beverly, and you know that isn't what I mean. I just mean that it's going to be tough enough making Randal the first woman president, much less the first woman president with a half-Jewish husband."

"Yes, we've never had a half Jewish president."

"It won't make Randal a Jew simply because she marries one, Sarah, especially a half of one," Ellie, the voice of reason consoled. Everyone always consoled Sarah for she was gently made.

"Stop it, all of you," her mother commanded, standing as she pounded her fist on the table, her face livid. "Randal's my daughter, and she and I have been open to the proposal that she become the first woman president of this great land. Every step of her education's been taken toward this end, and she's been most co-operative, but she's not your puppet, and I'll not allow you to attempt to dictate her heart. If she loves Elias Fergusson and wants to marry him then that's that. If you don't like it, she and I will leave this table and you can find somebody else to manipulate."

"That was nicely said, Sue Ann," Sarah praised glowingly.

"Oh, sit down, Sue Ann," Stacey Lea snapped. "You know very well we don't consider Randal in any way a puppet, nor do we wish to manipulate her. If there's one thing that's important, it's that she be her own person. We want the first woman president to take her place in history as a great leader, a great president. That aspiration could hardly be possible with a mush-melon! All I mean is that it does present greater complications. It would've been much easier if she'd fallen in love with the, well…the boy next door type."

"Like you did, Stacey Lea?" Bev drawled. "Unfortunately, not everyone has a Forrest Thornton next door and we could hardly expect Randal to fall in love with one of those sweet little crew-cut things, or even someone like that nice little man Margaret Thatcher married."

"Please leave Forrest out of this, Beverly, and do try to control your tart tongue. So, Randal, Eli's finally popped the question? I didn't know if the two of you would ever get past the age barrier."

"He didn't and we haven't. He'll sleep with me, is even willing to stay in the States because of me, but he still thinks he's too old for me, and he's not twice my age, Aunt Stace, as you well know, only fifteen years."

"Sounds to me just an excuse, a safety net. Some men are perennial bachelors and use any recourse at their disposal to stay that way," Beverly observed, as always ready to demonstrate that she was an authority on men.

"I hate to be 'an I told you so', but I told you a long time ago that you can't make it too easy for a man to get what he wants. Men are by nature promiscuous," her mother said.

"I know, Mama, I know," Randal responded impatiently, "but there's more to it than that. It's this president thing and all of you."

"Us? Why, we've been nothing if not gracious to him."

"That's not what I mean and you know it. It's this pact we have."

"I can see where that would be a problem with a man like Eli Fergusson," Ellie speculated.

"Absolutely, besides being a hard-headed Scotsmen, he's also not but a few steps removed from 'the little woman in the kitchen' syndrome."

"How does he treat your being district attorney in these parts?" Ellie asked, "I know it takes a lot of your time."

"He tolerates it; besides, he doesn't really know how much time I spend at work. With him at Harvard and me in Mississippi, our time together's limited."

"That's like the arrangement I had with Charlie, and it didn't work," Aunt Sarah remarked as everyone looked up, for she never mentioned Charlie; even though her failed marriage was the reason she'd given for always wearing black.

"Yes, there's a lot at work against us, but I love him and he loves me. I'm not going to love anybody else nor am I going to have time."

"But I don't understand, Randal. If he hasn't agreed to marry you, then how are you going to marry him?" Aunt Stace questioned slowly.

"Because I decided to take matters into my own hands."

"And?" They asked in unison, followed by a great hush.

"And, I'm pregnant."

"Oh no," cried Sarah, flopping back into her chair, "a half-Jew president is better than an unwed mother one."

"Please, Sarah," Stacey Lea pleaded, annoyance apparent now in her voice, "this isn't the time to fall apart. Let us simply sit back and digest Randal's condition and work through it."

"Does Eli know?" her mother asked.

"Not yet."

"How far along are you?"

"Just missed. Took one of those home tests."

"I don't suppose…?" Bev started to inquire.

"Don't even think it. I want this baby. Besides, it's time."

"Do you want it more that being president?" Sarah could ask some ridiculous questions, but often they were quite perceptive.

"No, but I want her as much."

"Her?"

"That's just because I want a her."

With that, Randal was forgotten as the five of them began to consider strategy and possible problems that might arise. At no time was there any criticism of her or the *Murphy Law* position that she'd placed in their path. Perhaps because they'd become used to the fact that anything that could go wrong would, but also, she knew they respected her and considered it her decision. She liked that and looked with tenderness at these women who'd been her mentors for as many years as she had memories.

Stacey Leanne Culberson Forbes, wife of Goodman Palmer Forbes had been a very popular First Lady before returning to her childhood home. She and the ex-president hadn't divorced, but they rarely saw one another and it was rumored that he lived with a woman in Chicago where he spent his time developing his Presidential Library. Her mother and Aunt Stace had been friends forever, and her father had even introduced Palmer Forbes to his future wife, besides being Forbes' best friend and confidant during most of the years Forbes was president.

Beverly Jean Abelson had been appointed to her husband's Senate seat from New York after his sudden death; a heart attack it was said, but there were still lots of hush-hush rumors surrounding it. Now, she held her office firmly on her own; how firmly would be tested after President DeLucca, who had succeeded Palmer Forbes, completed his second term. There was going to be a big ruckus when he divorced his wife so that he could marry Auntie Bev, but they were determined to spend their golden years together. The group accepted it as meant-to-be; Aunt Ellie called it Karma.

Sarah Winthrop had been a distinguished and powerful Senator from Massachusetts. Then, one day, she'd held a press conference, resigned her post and retired to her family's huge nineteenth century mansion in Boston's Back Bay. She rarely went out, an eccentric recluse like her mother before her, and when at home, she wore widow's black just like Queen Victoria even to the little lace head covers. Still Aunt Sarah had lots of money and used it generously to promote *The Cause*.

Eleanor Fanny Farmer had worn many hats at the White House when Aunt Stace had been First Lady. Now she was a Federal Court Judge, and it was already decided that eventually she would be the first woman Chief Justice of the Supreme Court and better still the first African American one. She was the youngest of the group, in her forties, while the others were at various stages of the next two decades.

Randal smiled watching them. She felt loved and part of a great thing. How fortunate she was! She would be President of the United States some day, and Aunt Ellie would be there to swear her in when it was time. She had her own true love, was having his baby, and they'd all live happily ever after. Everything was right with her world.

That was the way she had felt watching them; now, as she rode back to Natchez and Eli, she wasn't as sure. She knew she had to tell him that afternoon, and she also knew his bloody temper would soar before it allowed the rational man inside to come through. There was no question that the rest of the day would be hell.

"Would you please repeat what you just said?" he asked slowly, his brow deeply furrowed, his voice stiff and controlled.

"I said that I'm going to run for the State Legislature."

"You know very well that's not the part I mean, the last part of that sentence."

"Oh, you mean the 'I'm pregnant' part?"

"How could that have happened? We were always careful."

"No, Eli. I was careful, that was my responsibility, and I decided that I didn't want to be careful anymore. It isn't as if I haven't told you many times how much I wanted us to have a baby."

"True, but I'd not agreed. This was your decision, yours alone, and you had no right to make it by yourself. You tricked me! You're a conniving witch and I'll have no part of it. You and *The Aunts* will have to get through this without me. How could you do this to us and the love we've shared?"

She did not answer for she refused to get into a shouting match with him. Besides, he didn't give her time to reply while he ranted at her and threw his clothes into a bag, planning to go back to Scotland and never return. He'd gotten almost out the door when he stopped and turned.

"When are you due?" he asked.

"It's very early, almost eight months left."

"And you're sure?"

"Yes."

"I guess it's time to put you to that test."

"Don't, please."

"Will you go back with me, live the life of a professor's wife?"

"You know I can't do that."

"Oh, but you can. All you have to do is pack a bag, get on a plane with me, and never look back."

"And then you'd make an honest woman of me, and we'd live happily ever after?"

"Does that sound so bad?" he asked with those melodious tones as he came back into the room and pulled her down on the sofa beside him.

"A little vine-covered cottage with a picket fence?"

"Stone wall, in Scotland we have lots of stone walls."

"And that'd be exactly what it would be for me, a wall. That's not my reality and that's not whom you fell in love with."

"Shit, bloody shit," he responded, and they made love well into the night.

The subject didn't rise again until the wee hours of the morning over bacon and eggs.

"And what does the *governing body* have to say about your proposed consort having a Jewish mother?"

"That's irrelevant, but does that mean you're going to marry me?"

"Do I have any choice? You seduced me, used me, got yourself pregnant, and now I must do the honorable thing. Hasn't that been man's fate since Eve?"

"Seriously, Eli, you know me well enough to know that this isn't a trap. You can walk out that door if that's what you want to do, but yes, I expect you to marry me. It's your child too, and you can't be too surprised because it's been a subject of contention between us. You love me too much, and I love you too much to let that love stagnate. It was time to take us to another level."

"It's a two-way street, Randal, as trite as that may sound. I should have had something to say about that next level."

"Would you? Have you ever considered my needs in this relationship?"

"What a thing to say!"

"Is it?"

They didn't speak for awhile, both concentrating on their eggs.

"All right, Randal. I'll admit that I'd have stayed content with the way things were. I understand why you forced my hand with the baby, and I'll admit that the idea of becoming a father isn't unpleasant to me. It's just that goddamn agenda of yours."

"I know. Eli, but it's as much me as you are."

"It's not going to work, you know. I won't be able to sit in the back row."

"If the time comes when you can't take it anymore.... It really won't change much. You'll still be teaching at Harvard and I'll be down here, a commuter romance becomes a commuter marriage, that's all." She took his hand as her eyes filled with happy tears.

Randal turned from the window that was filled with the glaring sun on snow. It always made her sad to think of Eli; he was her one big failure. They'd lasted almost six years before he'd packed his bags and returned to the ivy covered manor house in Scotland overlooking the North Sea, which had been the only home he knew. He lived an idyllic life teaching at St Andrew's and occasionally coming out with a new scholarly work. Once in a while he'd show up for a visit, but mostly, their twins would have to visit him. And sometimes, when things got too much for her, she'd wound up on his doorstep, always gently taken in. "God, Eli," she whispered, "how much I need you with me today."

He had announced his departure when she'd been running her successful campaign for Governor of Mississippi, explaining that the painful notoriety he was experiencing as her Consort had begun to affect his life at Harvard and was intolerable. Most men, he argued, would have trouble with such a role. Added to this was the fact, he said, that he disliked politics and abhorred politicians, which meant, she assumed, she had to be included in some of that.

She had thought that he'd eventually come around, but he'd never understood her mission or her tremendous pride at being the *chosen one*. He had never understood that today would not have happened at all if it were not for those five great ladies and others like them whom Eli called the *governing body.*

Once upon a time, a long time ago when there'd been only one woman in the United States Senate, Sarah Winthrop, they'd taken things into their own hands. Yes, *once upon a time...*

Randal picked up the small Moroccan leather bound book that she would carry with her today. "My God," she chuckled, "if the whole story of those early days was only known, she knew it'd make a first-rate-best-seller."

CHAPTER ONE

ONCE UPON A TIME ✦✦✦

Goodman Palmer Forbes approached the fish-tank. His tall, taut body was enveloped in a long hooded robe. With only the diffused light cast from the newly awakened waters, the shadows of early morning made him appear an apparition from centuries past.

But Goodman Palmer Forbes was not an ancient mystic. His tri-colored robe was the red, white, and blue of the country he had led with great popularity over the past five years. On the back was appliquéd in gold the presidential seal intertwined with his initials, a design he had created himself, and scattered over the plush field of velvet were exactly fifty stars.

Forbes' colorful and patriotic garb did not, however, keep him from enjoying a mental analogy with the past—the ancient high priest making sacrifice to the sea. On the contrary, he found it most appropriate, for the ritual he performed on the tenth day of each month was as secret as those ancient ones. He had always liked secrets, playing little games. This was one of his finest, and today would be his finest performance, for today, she'd been gone exactly one year.

He allowed his mind to digress. God, he was clever! The media had dramatically detailed his mother's last rites from her last words to her final resting-place, and his sorrow had been duly noted. How difficult it had been to look pained in front of that abortion of a monument she'd designed, no less an embarrassment than she had been to him all his life.

But he'd been good, even great! If he hadn't chosen politics, he would surely have garnered laurels in the theatre. But then, what was the political arena, no more than a stage and quality of performance seemed to have little bearing on success. Hadn't a recent predecessor actually prepared for his role in dubious *B* movies? Never, however, had the man given a performance such as he had at his mother's tomb.

She'd planned it all, down to the last detail. So like her to leave nothing to chance or to him. No doubt there'd been one of those goddamned lists, this one probably entitled *The Ten Commandments of Dying*. It'd always been ten. She had even managed to die on the tenth, almost as if she had made some pact with God, like Moses had.

Her final ten, he was confident, ended with *Last Words to Son*. He had often wondered what she would've done if he'd been away. Would she have postponed her departure just to leave him with the chant that he despised, that she had used at all the wrong times to ridicule him and make him her child? *Be a good man, Goodman,* were recorded as her last words when he was already a great and powerful man, a leader of men. He recalled the little rhyme that had haunted him all his life.

> Be a good boy,
> Be a Good-man.
> If mother can't see you,
> Remember, God can.

The anger and indignation in him exploded as aloud, he screeched, "Well, Judith Anne Goodman Forbes, I have my own rhyme, and when the last of these monthly rituals is completed, I'll be rid of you forever!"

He raised his arms and opened the wide-mouthed brass urn he held in his hands. Removing a pinch of powdery substance, he sprinkled it into the tank, intoning,

> Ashes to Ashes,
> Dust to Dust,
> If your son won't have you,
> Then the fishies must.

After securely locking away all vestiges of his early morning ceremonial charade, Forbes replaced the key and chain around his neck and, bidding a fond farewell to his aquatic conspirators, walked briskly across to his dressing room. Taking time only to don his suit jacket, straighten his tie, and receive back a look of smug satisfaction from his mirror, President Forbes opened the adjoining door and confidently strode into his wife's apartment.

"Good morning, my dear, are you ready to go in for breakfast?"

Stacey Lea Forbes turned from her mirror and greeted her husband with a pleasant smile. She was a meticulously groomed golden blonde beauty whom detractors had dubbed *Stacey Doll* claiming her comparison to the long popular *Barbie*, uncanny. Still, her unemotionally perfect exterior had done much to make the Forbeses a most popular pair, and the White House a place synonymous with gracious hospitality the world over.

In fact, the President's wife was the consummate First Lady, a fact the nation and the world appreciated. She did not stand out nor did she blend in; she did not have strong views, but made pretty little speeches; she did not meddle nor did she manipulate; she said all the right things at all the right times and did all the right things at all the right times; she was dutiful but never subservient; she always had a warm smile but was properly distant, and she gave wonderful teas and luncheons—those little women things that were read about in every detail by her adoring public. Today was one of them.

"Oh, there you are, Palmer darlin'. I've ordered some toast and coffee sent up. Have just a few more things to do before the luncheon," she said as she extended her cheek for the customary morning kiss.

"No, Stacey Lea, you know I expect you to eat breakfast with me. It's often the only time our day crosses. Besides, my mother always said it's the most important meal of the day."

A little frown closed her well-pruned brows as she marveled at how Mother Forbes had become an authority on just about everything since her death. She couldn't recall his ever quoting her before.

"And," he continued in a cajoling voice, "how'd it look to the staff if we didn't begin our day together? They'd think we'd had a spat."

He took her arm and gently steered her through her sitting room and toward their breakfast room, unflagging in his verbal prodding, "Now, that's a good girl, but you always do what's best, and see, Coleman has breakfast ready for you."

The First Lady gritted her teeth as she sat down and glanced at her plate. That Coleman! He knew she was having an important luncheon today, and he knew she'd only ordered dry toast and coffee for breakfast. The man was detestable, and his dark, sullen manner gave her the creeps! Why did Palmer insist on keeping him on? He'd been around a lot longer than any other house-staff member and certainly a lot longer than many of the previous tenants!

"Palmer, I'll have to be rolled up and down the stairs if I start eating big breakfasts like this and then big lunches on top of them. I'll send this back and…"

"Eat your breakfast, Stacey Lea," he responded firmly. "This luncheon's beginning to annoy me. It's all you talk about—luncheon, luncheon, luncheon. Frankly, I'll be glad when it's over and we can get back to normal around here."

Stacey Lea opened her mouth to retort among other things that she had never known anything to be normal around here when she noted that her irritable husband had evidently finished with the subject for he had picked up the *Washington Post* and begun to scan the front page.

"Jesus Christ!" he exclaimed, slamming his coffee cup down and splashing the brown liquid over an immaculate damask cloth. "That God-damned Winthrop bitch made the front page again! She'd better learn to keep her fuckin' mouth shut!"

"Palmer, listen to you, and look what you've done. You shouldn't read the newspaper at breakfast if it's going to upset you so much. Coleman, where are you? Coleman!"

"Yes, madam?" The voice came softly from right behind her.

"Do mop up that spill before it spreads," she responded, thinking to herself that she wished she had the nerve to throw her coffee right into his sneaky face.

Forbes did not answer but returned to his meal as he congratulated himself for marrying a woman who knew her place and caused him no political embarrassment. Not like that Winthrop bitch. Senator Sarah Winthrop of Massachusetts, *Lady Sarah,* they called her. Those damn New Englanders kept sending her back, but then, they'd always voted strange up there.

The news item in the *Post* that had triggered Forbes' outrage was a quote from a speech Sarah Winthrop had given the day prior at an AMA Convention in Atlantic City.

I believe that if men suffered through menopause there would be floods of government grants to remedy it. No, to cure it, once and for all! And yet, there's only one foundation in this country dedicated to the study of this problem, The Forbes Foundation for Women, founded by our beloved President's own mother....

My God, he fumed, the bitch has dragged out that business again about his mother's hobby, her real love! How humiliating that his name was linked to it! Especially,... Forbes mental diatribe was interrupted by the soft approach of Coleman, carrying a telephone.

"Pardon me, sir, there's a call on your personal line from Senator Fairmont. I thought you might want to take it."

"Thank you, Coleman. Good morning, Beau."

"Good-mornin', Goodie. Have you seen the mornin' papers? I can't believe they put her on the front page. Right there, Winthrop, Momma, and the Foundation." Fairmont's tone was strained.

"Yes, Beau, I've seen it. Something will have to be done." Forbes was annoyed. He couldn't seem to break Beau from calling him by the childhood nickname that he despised, *Goodie Two Shoes* as a child, *Goodie-Goodie* in prep school. Beau Fairmont would never seem to let him forget it.

"Frankly, I don't understand why you've let Stacey Lea invite her to that luncheon today. They're pretty chummy, you know. Wouldn't think you'd want your wife around her so much. You never can tell what..."

"She's coming here today?"

"You mean you didn't know? Maybe you better start takin' a good look at your wife's guest lists. Sue Ann told me last week that Stacey Lea had invited Winthrop to the luncheon, and you know my wife would know. I wondered then why you let her do that."

"I didn't, but I'll handle it now." Forbes returned the phone to Coleman as he directed a scowl at the bent head across the table that had suddenly developed an intense appetite.

Only a careful observer, and Palmer Forbes was not that where his wife was concerned, would have sensed the change in Stacey Lea, for it was hardly perceptible. The First Lady had been well schooled in the art of southern hospitality, and early on, had learned to mask her real feelings and thoughts; so much so, the veneer that coated her exterior was seldom penetrated. The few scars that had been dealt her were hidden away so deep in her secret self that only she was capable of conjuring them up, if that should ever be her intention. She had also learned early on how to handle her husband, which included when not to do so. Consequently, there were rare confrontations between them, and when there were, she preferred to be the confronted.

Preparing for the possibility of just such a situation that very moment, Stacey Lea had indelibly stamped the poached egg on her plate into her memory forever as she waited for Palmer's words and tone. Once she had tested the force of her husband's attack, she would, as usual, know how to proceed. One thing she knew for sure, Sarah would attend her luncheon no matter what.

"Stacey Lea, you didn't tell me that Sarah Winthrop was having lunch here today," he coldly confronted.

"Why Palmer, whatevah do you mean?" she responded, conjuring up the soft accent of her southern heritage to smooth and cajole the air between them. "You know perfectly well that ah planned this luncheon weeks ago. Ah even discussed the menu with you. When we discussed the guest list ah assumed you knew."

"Is Sarah Winthrop coming or not?"

"Yes, Palmer darlin', ah invited her. After all, she's a Senator, and the only woman one. How would it look if ah passed her ovah? Ah couldn't very well invite her husband to my Ladies Luncheon now, could ah? Besides, think of it this way, if she gets involved in my little *ole* cause, maybe she'll stop pesterin' you so much. Anyhow, I showed you the guest list, and she was on it. You're always so busy, I ..."

The First Lady adeptly turned on the tears causing the President to assume that most masculine of all husbandly burdens—guilt.

Knowing that she'd won, Stacey Lea decided to add a bit more for good measure. Besides she was now enjoying herself. "Ah am so sorry," she sobbed, "if ah had only realized how displeased you'd be, I'd nevah have..."

"There, there, dear, it's all right."   Palmer had come around the table and was patting her gently on the head while thinking that it really didn't matter so much for he'd take care of Winthrop in due time. Besides, he was interested in keeping his wife in a good mood; she'd owe him tonight.   "I know you didn't mean any harm.   You always do the right thing.   It's all right."

But was it all right?

Senator Beaufort Randal Fairmont put down the phone, wondering if Forbes had perhaps underestimated his wife.   Stacey Lea was rooted in many generations of southern belles, perfect,   gracious ladies who could make you think there was nothing in their pretty heads but frilly dresses, comfortable homes, and the desire to please their men-folk. They were forever soft, sweet, and content until crossed or riled and then God help you, if he could.   He'd kept his wife foaling.   With kids in the house, Sue Ann hadn't had time to get into much mischief, but Stacey Lea…?

He had known Stacey Lea Culberson all her life and had even introduced her to Goodie.   She'd always been strong-willed and always gotten her way.   On the other hand, Stacey Lea had changed since she'd married, settled down.   She had a lot of responsibility now and handled it well.   She'd be foolish to listen to Sarah Winthrop's meanderings. Besides, Goodie could handle her.   Hadn't he already handled the changes at the Foundation smoothly?   She'd been totally unsuspecting. Yes, Goodie could handle his wife.   There wasn't much he couldn't handle.

Senator Fairmont probably knew Forbes better than anyone did, for their friendship dated back to the Virginia prep school they'd both attended.

Beau took to Goodie early on; the Fairmonts had always had an uncanny ability to direct, at least abet, their destinies.   Forbes, on the other hand, had secretly been flattered to be allowed into the aristocratic Fairmont circle. It was one of the oldest and most powerful families in Mississippi. Beau liked to brag that Mississippi had always had a Fairmont, and the Fairmonts had always had a Beaufort.

When Beau had come along, most of the Fairmonts lived in and around the town that bore their name. The old Plantation House was a highlight on the fashionable Delta-Bottom Ante-Bellum House Tour, with the family opening it up once a year in early spring for a grand ball whose guest list made one automatically genuflect.

Public service was taken for granted by the Fairmont male and a Fairmont name on the ballot in Mississippi was a routine occurrence. The family accumulated governors, senators, ambassadors and sundry public office holders as easily as they accumulated fortunes. Yes, Mississippi was proud of its Fairmonts, and its Fairmonts were very proud.

They had served without interruption in the Senate for over a century, and Beau was in his third term, now as the powerful Majority Leader, a job he relished. His relationship to the President hadn't hurt, but it had its price. Here he was again involved in one of Goodie's secrets. If it ever leaked, he knew the Fairmont name wouldn't be worth much, but it was too late now.

There had been a time when Goodie's secret games had been fun, added a little zest to life. They hadn't really hurt anyone. He'd been proud to be included. Now...

With a big, sad sigh, Beau Fairmont took his hand off the telephone where it was still resting, stood up and focused his mind on the important business of the day.

CHAPTER TWO

THE LADIES LUNCHEON

Jacqueline Kennedy beautified the White House; Lady Bird Johnson beautified the highways; Pat Nixon tried, but failed, to beautify her husband; while Betty Ford's causes were more personally revealing as she exhorted women to breast examinations and fellow alcoholics to seek help.

By the time Stacey Lea Forbes became First Lady, most of the good causes had been taken—War on Poverty, Just say NO, Adopt a Child, the homeless, literacy, Children's Rights, mental illness…. She'd had a difficult time finding and adopting a popular cause, but she'd done it, and in so doing, she had raised the consciousness of patriotic, virtuous, moral Americans in all fifty states. WIPE OUT WASTE—not nuclear waste, toxic waste or even human waste, but simple, everyday sinful waste. The trashcans of America had once been filled with treasures, but not any more. With WOW leading the battle, mottoes like *Waste not, Want not; Haste Makes Waste,* and even *A Stitch in Time* had become household expressions.

Today, these re-vitalized slogans were delicately engraved on programs and place-cards in a room where staunch supporters of WOW were being charmingly entertained by the First Lady.

"...and again, Ladies, I thank each of you for your sincere dedication to my cause. My husband wanted me to thank you for him too. He was sorry when he realized he had to go to Chicago for some *ole* VFW Convention today and miss stopping in. Palmer's been wonderful about this campaign. As many of you know, he even gave me the idea for WOW when we were watching television one night and this commercial came on where someone was wiping up a spill with a paper towel. Palmer said it reminded him of that *Rosie Woman* he used to watch when he was a kid. He said that if he'd been President then, *I swear, Stacey Lea, I'd have had her arrested for littering!* We came up with *Wipe Out Waste* right then and there."

Stacey Lea continued to regale her audience with presidential anecdotes and other delightful small talk until the finish of equally delightful low calorie desserts. Then, after the presentation of awards for exceptional service and numerous other thank yous, the First Lady concluded by turning to her special assistant, "And I must say a special thank you to Ellie who did such a wonderful job in making today so grand for all of us. Without her help, I don't believe this day would have been possible. You all know Ellie."

With that, Eleanor Fanny Farmer took over. She had never yet missed a cue, and she'd been aware for awhile now that her boss was beginning to find the whole thing a bit tiring.

Ellie had an instinctive ability to anticipate Stacey Lea's needs. This had existed from the beginning, when they had met in that storefront South Chicago campaign headquarters during Palmer Forbes' second run for Governor.

"I understand you've been doing a wonderful job down here for my husband, Mizz Farmer," Stacey Lea commented in her most charming *we're-running-for-office* voice. "Have you ever done this kind of thing before?"

"No, ma'am," Ellie answered as their eyes met, "but if I'd known how interesting it would be, I'd have started a long time ago."

"Then you've been bit by the bug, my dear. I do feel for you because you can take it from me that once bitten, you become its slave for life."

"Hold it!" Ellie responded laughing, "I don't think the skin's been broken yet, but I've always been interested in serving in government."

For as long as she could remember she'd felt she had such a destiny. She'd never played dolls, house, doctor, all the things her friends liked. No, she had wanted to play Supreme Court, Senate, even Executive Branch. She'd known all the members—Secretary of State, Secretary of Treasury, Secretary of Defense, and could reel them off along with their duties, but she had always insisted on being President. Pretty soon, no one would play with her being the big shot all the time, so she'd played alone.

This had made life lonely, for even though she had lots of acquaintances, she could honestly say that there had never been one real friend. The closest to a real friend she'd ever had was Darryl Harding, a struggling PHD candidate she had been living with almost since the day she had arrived to work on her doctorate at the University of Chicago. Their mutual quest was in itself a bond, but even though they had good times together and great sex, she knew their relationship couldn't go anyplace. No, Ellie had this restless feeling that she was waiting, that her life was one long ellipsis and the monotony of all those dots with no exclamation points was getting harder and harder to accept.

But here she sat looking up into the eyes of the wife of the Governor of Illinois and feeling all that was now behind her. The magnetism was strong and immediate. It was as if they were drawn by something deep within, innate, a product of their pasts and even their ancestors' pasts. She knew Stacey Lea felt it too, but it was something too new for either of them to know how to react. They floundered.

"What're you planning to do when this campaign's over next week?" Stacey Lea asked, as a small frown began to work its way across her brow.

"Complete what I've started. I'm working here mainly to gain information for my doctoral thesis in Political Science."

"I know we've never met," Stacey Lea blurted, the frown deepening across her brow.

"Not in this lifetime," Ellie replied.

"Do you believe in such things?"

"Of course, don't you?"

"I don't know. I really don't know."

With that, Stacey Lea had turned and walked away. They didn't speak again that day. While Stacey Lea made a quick retreat, Ellie, more open to it all, quietly and warily, waited.

Eleanor Fanny Farmer was the product of southern sharecroppers. Named for Eleanor Roosevelt, whom her mother had long admired, the Fanny was tucked into the middle when her father humorously gifted his wife with a box of Fanny Farmer chocolates in honor of his daughter's birth. A keen intelligence complimented by an astute, perceptive, and determined nature enabled her to become the first black valedictorian of a rural County High School in Arkansas and graduate *magna cum laude* three years later from a State University.

Heading north with a degree in Journalism, she entered Fordham University Law School. When she'd finished, she could have had her pick from most of the powerful and prestigious law firms in the country, but she wasn't interested. She knew that somewhere there were bigger things to do.

When she met Stacey Lea, Ellie had only a final bit of research left for her dissertation titled *The Massa-Slave Syndrome*. The Civil War may have put *Massa* in the *cold, cold ground,* but she'd found that its choking tentacles had continued to afflict the black spirit right through the twentieth century. It had been a giant boa, like the evil of the Garden, slithering through the ages and constricting creative impulse, prosperity, even peace for the black American.

Perfectly timed to complete her work was the re-election campaign of Goodman Palmer Forbes. Here was the opportunity to show the bright future her community had carved from its past, to allay the nagging doubts that her research had produced. But no, the more she looked with keen, critical eyes at the future, the more repugnant she found the past. She was weary of the subject, and she wondered if her work could serve any good purpose.

Unfortunately or fortunately, she was never to know. The next week, Stacey Lea returned to the small campaign headquarters in South Chicago, and Ellie left with her. She left the University and Darryl. Ellie had found her Karma.

As a queen would dismiss her subjects, so the First Lady bid *adieu* to her contented guests; and as a queen has her trusted attendants, so the First Lady had her own intimate inner circle. It was this coterie who retired to Stacey Lea's sitting room after the luncheon.

Shoes off, belts loosened, drinks poured, their conversation was definitely off the record.

"WOW, thank God that's over!"

"WOW, what a cause!"

"WOW, I'll drink to that!"

"At least you can hold it. Did you see Didi Clark? I swear, I thought she was gonna keel right over into the punch bowl."

"Didi was swaying because her heels were too high."

"And so was Didi."

This elite sorority was not above a bit of gossip. It was a firmly established social craft with which Stacey Lea felt familiar and comfortable. With the exception of Sue Ann Fairmont, whose breeding and background were similar to her own, the others came from roots so alien that it was remarkable they'd ever connected, let alone given rise to close and loyal friendships.

"All right, Bev, let's hear all about Howie's latest guilt trip. You were flashing that consolation prize all through lunch," Stacey Lea inquired eagerly.

Fingering the three-carat ruby pendant, Bev replied, "Poor Howie, guilt trip is right. His shrew of a mother is always badgering him to visit her; he feels guilty if he doesn't go and guilty if he leaves me."

"However, any woman would love the way Howie does his penance," responded Sue Ann.

"Yes, I'll agree with that," Bev answered. "And he'll probably come back this time with the matching earrings. Wasn't it Shakespeare who said *Conscience doth make cowards of us all*? Fortunately, Howie always takes the cowardly way."

"I don't think that's what Shakespeare meant, Beverly," Sarah corrected.

"Well, that's only because he didn't know Howie." Bev raised her somewhat depleted Scotch and toasted, "Here's to conscience, long may it waver." Her full rich laugh dominated the room, but then, she had a natural ability to consume any setting.

At present, she had draped herself around a plush Federalist chaise whose rich curves complimented her own. Her hair at eighteen had been black with touches of gray, at forty-three the condition was reversed. It was made of that kinky stuff bestowed by her Hebrew ancestors and considered a curse or blessing, depending on the recipient. Most of the time, she wore it loose around her shoulders where it appeared lightly starched. For the luncheon, it had been pulled into a low bun at her nape, but parts, as if having wills of their own, rejected restraint—a condition totally in keeping with their mistress.

If one looked closely, a few light freckles were discernible across the bridge of her nose, but first one had to get past long lashes icing marvelous cat-like green eyes. Her complexion was pale but lightly tanned, and today she had swathed it in a soft wool dress that had a tendency to cling while at the same time hang loose. Its rich mauve found companion in the oleander petals of the chaise's lush print.

The chaise's fabric had been designed especially for the First Lady, and with it, splashes of magnolias, hibiscus, and sundry other botanical species indigenous to the South were picked up in the other upholstered pieces as well as the wallpaper and drapes. Beverly had once remarked that the room made her hay fever act up. Nevertheless, the woman often described in the press as Junoesque was lounging Camillesque on what had become known to the five as *Bev's Chaise.*

In fact, each had her place in this order, for like most creatures, their habits had drawn them to the same positions often enough to endow each with squatter's rights, a respected mode of ownership for civilized people since the pioneers. Stacey Lea always sat alone on the middle cushion of the Federalist sofa where, as hostess, she could reign over the small but ample tea table in front of her. The upholstered pattern of her throne combined Bev's oleanders with magnolias, their leaves and flowers intertwining. The magnolia print was the sole occupant of the two-wingback chairs pushed away from each end of the table. The one to Stacey Lea's right belonged to Sue Ann Fairmont, the wife of Senator Beaufort Randal Fairmont and Stacey Lea's childhood friend; the one to Stacey Lea's left belonged to Senator Sarah Winthrop of Massachusetts.

Bev's chaise was slanted away on the opposite right so that the configuration became a circle broken only by Ellie who moved her straight chair in and out as her duties warranted. It was the chair from Stacey Lea's little Queen Anne desk which she had brought from home. The seat and back were done in fine needlepoint with cotton bolls scattered over a blue background. It was much prized by the First Lady because her mother had done the design and all the work herself.

Ellie preferred to sit away from the circle at the desk. Not only was it near the telephone and the door, it was also where she felt more at ease She might be Stacey Lea's closest confidante, but she wasn't one of them. At no time was this more apparent to her than during these sessions, for she was unfamiliar with the lighthearted banter the group found so amusing, which when Bev was around invariably became a bit tart and spicy.

"Tell me, Sarah, how did Charlie measure you for that saddle? Charlie sure knows how to give a woman a good ride!"

The women dissolved into shrieks of laughter at their clever pleasure over Sarah's gift on her fifty-fifth birthday. Charlie Baynes, the big lovable Texan who had finally *broke* Lady Sarah, had also provided the group with material for some of their juiciest banter.

Sarah, as usual oblivious to the humor, responded, "I don't understand what's so funny about my saddle. It was a wonderful gift, and I love it! A Texas saddle is just as fine a ride as an English one, but a little bigger and, of course, harder."

This, of course, renewed the shrieks of laughter and caused Sarah to recede in confusion.

"I swear, Sarah," Beverly whooped, "when God was giving out senses of humor, you must have been rambling around in that big old mausoleum you call home because he sure didn't find you. Will someone please explain to Sarah what's so funny?"

"Well, my birthday's coming up soon," Stacey Lea inserted, sympathetic to Sarah's discomfort. "I wonder what little gift Palmer's planning on for me?"

"Maybe he'll buy you a piranha and set you up with your own little fish tank," suggested Sue Ann.

"That would be adorable," goaded Bev, "then the two of you could have your tanks monogrammed *His* and *Hers*."

Ellie was the only one in the room to notice Stacey Lea straighten up at this. The man was peculiar, especially when it came to those fish, but her loyalty to Stacey Lea over-rode her dislike of the President. She was surprised that Sue Ann and Bev were so insensitive, especially Sue Ann.

But Sue Ann pursued, "My mama always said *Little boys, little toys; big boys, bigger toys.* Maybe with Goodie it's *foolish boys, foolish toys.*"

"I'm not amused," Stacey Lea responded coldly. "I don't know why you've chosen to pick on my husband, *your* president. Besides, lots of people have fish tanks, and I'll bet lots of people have piranhas swimming 'round in them."

"I agree. We have a fish-tank at the ranch, and Charlie and I find it peaceful watching those little things swim around."

"Oh, spare me your attempts at domesticity, Sarah," Beverly moaned, obviously not intimidated by Stacey Lea's annoyance, even though she did change the subject. "I want to hear about Charlie's trip to Japan. I've never been there. Tell me, is it true about those Geisha houses? Do they really give blow jobs in the hot tubs?"

"For godsake, Beverly," Stacey Lea snapped. "Why don't you freshen your drink, or better still, take a cold shower?"

"I have to leave soon. It's Randal's twenty-first birthday and we're havin' a family party." Sue Ann remarked, looking at her watch.

"Another birthday?" Bev drawled. "Seems as though somebody was always getting born at your house, Sue Ann."

"Only three, Beverly, but I guess that seems like quite a brood to you since you don't have any."

"Brood?" pondered Bev, "then what does that make you, Sue Ann, the brood mare?"

"What's with you today, Beverly?" Stacey Lea snapped. "I've never seen you so ornery. Sue Ann has a real cute family, and it's the perfect size. Palmer and I never had time for children, but now, I'm kinda sorry, especially when I see all the hub-bub at Sue Ann's."

"Hub-bub?" Sue Ann laughed. "On special occasions, it's more like chaos."

Sarah added her voice as if to settle the matter. "No, Stacey Lea's right. My life has certainly been enriched by Charlie's family."

But that did not settle it, and if anyone had been the slightest bit wary at that moment, she would have noticed the strain developing in Beverly's voice. "You know, Sarah, people like you always make me feel like throwin' up, and you did too 'til I knew you better—silver spoon, Rhodes scholar, successful career, and then adorable Charlie and his ready-made family. I'd love to read your horoscope. The planets must've been in perfect harmony. Mine," Bev sighed, "must've been hitting each other."

"Look who's talking about silver spoons," Sarah returned warmly. "Park Avenue certainly fairs well with Boston's Back Bay in anybody's address book, and Howard's no slouch. You're just out of sorts because he's visiting Mama."

"Rebecca Abelson, the epitome of Jewish mamas. I don't think any woman would've been good enough for her Howie, least of all me, and I have no doubt that she continues to draw breath only to spite me."

"Really, Bev," Stacey Lea scolded, "your tongue is pure vinegar today. What a terrible thing to say with the poor woman bed-ridden the way she is. Now, let's change the subject. I want to talk about that cute Marsha Marshall, even the name's cute. Don't you think Senator Marshall took himself the cutest little *ole* chile bride? The dirty old geezer!"

Before anyone could react to this well-intended shift back to the festive mood with which the little party had started, Bev exploded.

"Is *cute* the only word they taught you in Mis-sa-sip-pee, Stacey Lea? *Cute* family, *cute* bride, *cute* name—why, ah bet you even go to *cute* funerals. Here's a good one: Wasn't that a *cute* earthquake in Mexico last week? And what about that story in the newspaper yesterday where that banker murdered his daughter? Wasn't that *cute*? And how 'bout that teenager who died last week from a back-street abortion. Ah really bet you thought that was *cute*. But no, you wouldn't even have read about that 'cause I'm sure your cute little *ole* Palmer told you that'd be bad, and Stacey Lea doesn't want to be a bad girl."

Beverly stood up, none too steady, and waving her glass, continued, "And how've we spent our day? I'll tell you—WOWING THE WORLD! WOW! What an inane bit of time waster. Perhaps next year we could make a quilt, king-size, of course." Then she turned to face the speechless Stacey Lea, but before addressing her, took another gulp from her glass, splashing a bit as she did. "And milady, if it's true that your husband suggested your great purpose, or shall we say *busy work*, then I suggest that perhaps the acronym was already functioning on another level. W.O.W.! WIPE OUT WOMEN! Yes, that's what it is, but frankly, Scarlett, you don't seem to give a damn! And frankly, Scarlett," Bev's shoulders drooped ever so slightly as she added, "neither do I."

With this, Beverly Jean Abelson put down her almost empty glass, picked up her shoes and, with less grace than usual, departed. Outside the closed door, she paused, feeling remorse for her outburst. She wanted to turn back, but she was suddenly enveloped in an almost suffocating fear and with it a premonition that there was no turning back, that her life would never be the same. God, she wished Howard were home, but maybe it was better that he wasn't, give her face another day. She may have fooled the girls, but Howard was too observant

After what seemed a very long time, the stunned silence maintained by the four remaining women was broken by Sarah who, in New England practical, attempted to bring some sanity to her friend's appalling performance. "We all know that Bev has an acid tongue, but this isn't like her. Something must be wrong."

"That's enough, Sarah." All eyes turned to Stacey Lea whose tone brooked no other response. Sitting ramrod straight, hands folded in her lap, her countenance matched her tone—formidable, controlled and unreadable. "Beverly, in her typical style, has exploded a few scurrilous bombs before leaving, and, it seems, the three of you to clean up the debris. No pun intended on my *busy work.*"

Only Sue Ann had seen her friend this way before. She knew, when triggered, Stacey Lea could erupt with the quickness and fury of a summer storm. "Now, Stace," she soothed, "we all know Bev exaggerates. What you're doing is good. We're a wasteful nation and developin' awareness of this is certainly preferable to, uh, uh, Ladybird's beautifyin' the highways!"

"How can you say mine's preferable?" Stacey Lea responded coldly. "Picking up highway trash was Ladybird's busy work and just picking up plain old trash is mine."

"Stacey Lea," Sarah soothed, "please, you're turning words around. No one means anything like that, least of all, Bev. Obviously, she's upset about something, and she had too much to drink and got into one of her moods. She'll say anything that comes to her mind then. You know how she dramatizes things anyway."

"Maybe, but what concerns me is that I don't hear any of you convincingly disagreeing with her."

There was no response.

"That's what I thought." After a weighty pause, Stacey Lea proceeded, "Let me make a few things clear. I'm not as naive as you obviously seem to believe. I've interpreted my role as I see it to be. I'm from a proud, distinguished Southern American family, and I'll not be a source of laughter or patrimony. If, as Beverly insinuated, there's something goin' on here against women that made her use the name of my cause the way she did, and you know about it, I want to know about it too, and right now."

"There may be something in what Beverly implied, but there's no proof to give you. It's more complicated than that."

"There's enough proof that maybe it's time Stacey Lea and the rest of us took a good hard look at it," disagreed Ellie, to the surprise of all. "What's happened to women all over the country in politics, law, business, medicine too? What's happened to women—period, and black women, forget it. Let's start with Congress, only two women left on the Hill with you."

"Yes," Sarah admitted with some reluctance, "and Catherine Osborne's getting senile and won't be back next year. Alma Tyler, well, her son was just picked up on drug charges which will probably drive her to retire."

"Strange the way things keep befalling women in prominent places," Ellie continued. "No one says anything, but they're getting scared to be there, and I can't blame them."

"This isn't proof, Ellie. It only indicates that women are changing their focus back to the kitchen! We can't refute that no matter how suspicious we might be."

"When I was a girl, I believed I could be anything I wanted to be. I had visions of being on the Supreme Court, even President. I realized, however, even before I met Stacey Lea that those dreams were no longer possible. It's unfair!" exclaimed Ellie, her eyes ablaze with indignation.

"Fair has absolutely nothing to do with it!" Sarah responded passionately as she rose to her feet. "Oh, if we could but have a fair fight! How I'd love to throw down the gauntlet; bear high the standard; ride my gallant steed through the lines of those dastardly bastards!" Sarah's eyes had become glazed. Even Ellie was forgotten now as Sarah charged recklessly across some field of conflict that only she had entry. Then, suddenly, her courageous effort collapsed as abruptly as it had begun, and sitting, she continued with a sigh of defeat.

"My file swells with evidence of foul play but all without support. And if we could prove our case, where would we take it? The courts have become nothing more than tools of the administration, a fact that would sadden our forebears. One cannot fight a pervasive and insidious evil that will not show itself."

"Are you, of all people, giving up?" Ellie asked, surprised.

"Charlie wants me to," Sarah answered, shaking her head. "He wants me to quit and stay in Texas where he can keep me safe. There was also a suspicious incident last week with Charlie Junior that disturbs us both. I have no right to jeopardize his family. Charlie was in an absolute rage after my statements before the AMA yesterday. I don't blame him, but I felt I owed it to Sandra Ackerman. Her death disturbs me."

"Yes, Dr. Ackerman's death was too sudden and too timely, coming just three days before she was to announce the results of the Foundation's ten year study."

At this, Stacey Lea bristled, "If your other suspicions or no more valid than those regarding Sandy, then you have vivid imaginations, indeed. As you know, Mother Forbes made me a trustee of the Foundation almost a year before she died. I've seen the official report and am satisfied that Sandy injected herself with that serum she believed would end menopausal problems for women forever. It surely did, for her. She was a brilliant woman, but as Palmer observed, she must've been overcome by her own zealousness. I'll be happy to get the report for both of you if you want to review the facts."

"You want to talk about facts, well, I'll tell you a few. The only place men want women today is not the kitchen but in bed, and that's probably the only place they've ever wanted 'em.!" Sue Ann, enveloping Bev's chaise had obviously been drinking up the nearby liquor supply along with the conversation.

"My God, Sue Ann, you're…"

"And I'll tell you another fact. That Dr. Vonder—uh, Von delbagarten?"

"Vondergraven, Doctor Claude Vondergraven," Stacey Lea corrected firmly with exasperation reflected in her voice.

"Yes, him. Well, he likes his women in bed too, even made a pass at me. Guess he figured Beau being the way he is that I must be lonesome."

"Not Dr. Vondergraven! I can't believe that!" exclaimed Stacey Lea.

"Just because you were always belle of the ball doesn't mean I didn't have my share of suitors, Stacey Lea." Sue Ann replied in kind.

Sue Ann would never be asked to play the femme fatale, the love goddess, the home wrecker—come to think of it, why is the latter always a woman's role? No, Sue Ann, as much as she despised it, could be best described as pretty and cute, the girl next door, the type June Allyson made popular back in the forties. She had soft curly, blond hair that bounced when she walked. It framed a softly rounded peaches and cream face that held sparkling bright blue eyes that could easily spark. The rest of her was also softly rounded for which she was constantly starting new diets and trying new spas. A bit plump was, it seemed, her lot in life.

"You know I didn't mean that!" Stacey Lea snapped. "It's just that he's so reserved and distinguished. I can't imagine his doing such a thing and especially to a Senator's wife. When was it, and what did he say?"

Sue Ann had now enthralled the floor.

"It was at that reception in Chicago several weeks ago when he took over for Dr. Ackerman. We were talking by the punch bowl and all of a sudden he said, *How would you like an enriching experience?* Well, I figured that he was into seances or something, he's so strange, so I told him that it sounded intriguin'. Then he said in a second-rate Dracula voice, *I know how to make you feel things you never thought possible.* With that the light dawned so I decided to lead him on a bit. I told him that he struck me as a man who did everything well; he probably knew a lot about women. *Oh yes,* he said preening, *I must admit that I do.* With that I replied, 'Then you must know that you are about to make this one fart, and I did!'"

While the others were doubled up with laughter, Sue Ann began to dance unsteadily around the room, her drink splashing. Of course, once they'd caught their breaths, they had to know what happened next.

"How would I know? I'd quickly walked away leaving only a faint aroma." With this, she prissed around inside the circle adding visual impact to their already sidesplitting mind's eye.

The laughter continued until abruptly stopped by a change in Sue Ann's voice.

"He's a nasty man, Stacey Lea, I feel it. I don't trust him."

"His credentials are impeccable, and his report on Sandy was thorough. All the trustees are impressed with his professionalism."

"And those credentials, Stacey Lea, were they checked?" inquired Ellie quietly.

"Damn! What's going on here? Are you all askin' me to question my own husband? Palmer recommended him!"

As she said it, she knew. They all knew. No one spoke. There was nothing to say. It was an awkward silence, the kind that makes one wish to be elsewhere but not knowing how to get there.

"Goddamnit, Stacey Leanne Culberson," scolded Sue Ann, "when are you gonna get your head out of your ass! I know ya blood, honey. I also know that when your Momma-in-law made you a trustee she told you that she'd taken every precaution to keep her son from meddlin' in her affairs. I guess she had her reasons. But you'll have to deal with your own conscience on that one. As for my husband, at least, I recognize him for what he is—the biggest womanizer in the U.S. Senate, and that's sayin' a lot. Furthermore, I believe there's much more to what's been said today than any of us know, and I guess I've felt that way for some time. Big boys, big toys, hurtful things are happening and if Palmer's involved, Beau's only a step behind."

Sue Ann's voice had choked and softened along the way; now she stopped for one big sigh before concluding. "As for me, I'm tired, tired of the sham, the forgivin' and the ignorin'. I don't know what I'm gonna do yet, but I know I can't go back to this mornin'. As for you, well, if you can stay in that cocoon after today, then, honey, you're a changeling for sure."

With that, Sue Ann put on her shoes, straightened her dress and brushed her hand through her hair before requesting Ellie to call down and have her car sent around.

To her receding back, Ellie heeded her request and a concerned Stacey Lea asked, "You're not driving yourself, are you, Sue Ann?"

Sue Ann only turned her head for an exit line. "Shame! Senator Fairmont's wife drive herself home from the White House? What would the world be comin' to."

They were three exhausted women; the day had seen to that.

Stacey Lea, always the perfect hostess, recognized that their fatigue must be equal to her own and ordered up some hot tea and a little snack, "…for this has often been the perfect prescription when I've needed that little extra surge of energy to get through a long day of campaignin' or some equally trying experience."

Without further ado she continued, "Now that the more emotional members of this gathering have departed, we must do a bit of serious talking. Perhaps, however, we better stay away from Bev's chaise. I swear, it must be possessed." Her attempt at levity was acknowledged with smiles, but at the same time, the three looked at the object charily.

"First, Sandra Ackerman, why does her death disturb you, Sarah?"

Sarah's response evaded the question. "You know, Stacey Lea, the expression *Ignorance is bliss* is often the best policy for certainly what you don't know won't hurt you. (Sarah was the source of much lampooning in the press for her chronic use of clichés and sayings. One critic had actually suggested that she must have memorized *Poor Richard's Almanac*.) "In any case, there is nothing you could do about it, that is, if there were anything that needed to be done and I'm not sure . . ."

Cutting Sarah's ramblings short, Stacey Lea turned to Ellie. "Well, Eleanor Fanny, is this it?"

They shared a moment of silent communication before Ellie affirmed, "I believe it's time," as if the two women knew that a time would come but had never given it voice or known what it would be.

Sarah watched the drama before her. The motionless response that followed Ellie's reply seemed to generate an energy that removed Sarah even further from the two women, but at the same time, held her fast, as two skilled performers can hold their audience to a suspenseful conclusion.

As if on cue, they turned toward Sarah, and Stacey Lea spoke.

"Sarah, I appreciate your obvious concern for my feelings, and I understand your reticence to speak frankly when such talk could possibly implicate my husband who's also president. But Pandora's box has already been opened. We couldn't close it now if we would." Stacey Lea paused and smiled kindly as if to give Sarah time to digest her words.

"Grandma Culberson always told me that you need to give a man a long leash, plenty of room to play, but when he gets out of hand then it's time to pull it in, no matter how hard you have to pull or how short you have to keep it. My allegiance is to my husband and our responsible and honorable position. I've never taken either lightly. If Palmer's intentionally using his power to do wrong, then he must be stopped; if Palmer used me to get his way for some unethical purpose with the Foundation, then he's misused me, and that I'll not tolerate. Serious accusations have been made or implied. I must weigh their worth. If I judge Palmer guilty, then he'll be my responsibility, mine alone. I trust, now that my position is clear, that you'll feel at ease to speak freely."

But Sarah wasn't at all at ease with the recent turn of events. Granted, the range of emotions displayed this afternoon had surely had their awkward moments, but that could be understood. Even

Beverly's irrational outburst could, she knew, be understood given the facts. And Sarah needed to understand.

She probably couldn't explain exactly why a push of a button brought figures to her video screen, why a blossom preceded an apple, or exactly why her car moved, but she knew there were reasonable explanations. Added to this, she admired the empiricist Hume, the pragmatist Paine, and even felt a kinship with Mr. Spock of the classic TV series *Star Trek* who kept insisting that things be logical.

Yes, practical, logical Sarah was not comfortable with the past few moments in this still turbulent atmosphere. She knew that what she'd witnessed between Stacey Lea and Ellie was not within her reality, and she felt an intruder—like one who has come upon two lovers at the height of their passion. On top of this, she had just been privy to a melodramatic little speech in which she was told by a woman only slightly taller and definitely softer than her own five foot three inch wiry frame, that if her husband had been a bad boy, she'd see to him. And this husband that she would see to was president of the most powerful nation in the world and enjoyed unparalleled personal popularity. Bev had said it well when she'd suggested the king-sized quilt, for there was already a wave afloat to give Goodman Palmer Forbes a third term— yes, a man who could be king. Thank God, she had a disciplined mind and could reason things out. For a moment there, she'd almost believed her hostess.

Sarah looked over at Stacey Lea and Ellie waiting patiently for her to think things through. A tap intruded and Ellie responded, returning to place the tea tray between them before resuming a position beside Stacey Lea. No one spoke. All activity had ceased as if simple things like drinking tea and eating little sandwiches would never again take place until she, Sarah, had spoken.

The burden was overwhelming, but she understood everything now. The chaise wasn't possessed; she had, like Alice, fallen through a rabbit hole, where she'd entered some crazy world where everything was awry. She didn't like it here; she wanted her world back; she wanted Charlie!

Sarah jumped up, opened her mouth to express hurried farewells, and stated without hesitation, "I believe Sandra Ackerman was murdered."

The words were magical, as if the whole afternoon had been in preparation for this moment. The tension that had been building since Bev started it all was suddenly gone. In its place were sounds of life that had previously been absent, at least, unnoticed, a dog barking, an occasional horn, the mantle clock chiming five, and the sound of Stacey Lea pouring tea.

"Sarah, would you prefer lemon or cream?"

"Lemon, please," Sarah replied as she slowly slumped down into her chair.

Stacey Lea quickly began her best tea cart chatter. "Sarah, do try one of these little egg salads. Cook does make marvelous egg salad with olives. I do love it that way, reminds me of home."

The joy of small talk turned a rather quickly put together afternoon tea into a rare feast. The three women, needing to prolong the refreshing interlude, discussed the merits of ripe over green olives as well as pimento cheese over egg salad, which Sarah observed had to be Stacey Lea's influence since pimento cheese was a southern sandwich filler.

Such are the pleasures of afternoon tea that they raised their cups in toast to the British for this glorious civilized tradition. Stacey Lea, her magnanimity overflowing, considered abandoning her cause and espousing this sacred ritual instead, so that all women could experience its delights and rejuvenating powers. She considered designing dainty tea sets in red, white, and blue with stars, and Sarah proposed that she'd draft legislation making *Afternoon Tea* the great American pastime for women and, perhaps, some men.

But, Ellie cautioned, men must be required to pass a pinkie test. To which the three collaborators raised their pinkies a bit higher, reveling in their sparkling wits.

"And if it doesn't catch on," Stacey Lea stated emphatically, stiffening her back, "well, it's at least my idea and far more to my taste than WOW!"

She had said it, and with it they had come full circle. Their journey, which seemed like days, had taken only a few short hours, but the weary travelers were refreshed and ready to take on the concerns at hand. Without voicing it, they knew themselves as committed conspirators, and the tone was serious as they got down to business.

It was almost eight when Ellie showed Sarah out. She returned to find that Stacey Lea had not moved. The lengthening shadows of twilight were now the product of a full moon that exposed Stacey Lea's folded hands but not her face.

"You know, Ellie, this whole thing's beginning to sound like a *B* movie, a bad one," analyzed Stacey Lea from the darkness.

"I know what you mean, but when you see Sarah's file tomorrow, maybe you can get hold of things. For now, get some rest. I think we're both drained. You sure you don't want me to order you something to eat before I go?"

"No, thank you. Do you think Coleman saw Sarah leave?"

"Yes, he was there, as always."

"I guess you're right. I must be tired. Even Coleman doesn't rile me tonight."

After Ellie had left, Stacey Lea walked over to her window and confronted the dancing lights that flickered around and about the great House. She thought about Bev over there somewhere. She wasn't angry with her anymore, for she recognized that Bev had only been the catalyst for what had been building for sometime. Besides, Ellie had pointed out that she'd noticed a bruise underneath Bev's make-up. Now she was worried about her; something *was* wrong. In fact, everything seemed wrong, or maybe, for the first time in a long time, it was beginning to seem right.

Stacey Lea might enjoy and certainly prefer the light gossip with which the afternoon had begun; she might prefer to remain aloof from confrontations or controversial subjects; she might, as Bev suggested, prefer not to care, to feel, to become involved, but she did give a damn.

A superficial coating covered several hundred years of solid southern breeding, genes that when forced to respond did so with an inner strength and courage equal to and perhaps more rigid and unswerving than that consistently attributed to the Puritan heritage of Sarah Winthrop.

Unlike Bev, Stacey Lea had no premonitions or fears that her life would never be the same, for she was sure it wouldn't. The knowledge was slowly filling her with new life in anticipation.

She walked through the bedroom to the door connecting her husband's rooms.

"Tonight, Palmer, darlin'," she stated aloud, "you'll have to pleasure yourself 'cause this 'good little woman' has needs, and tonight, she needs to be alone."

The First Lady turned the lock.

CHAPTER THREE

BEVERLY'S DILEMMA

In her exclusive Highgate penthouse looking down on Washington and overlooking the Potomac, Bev Abelson also needed tonight alone.

She had just curled up with a glass of wine and a recent best seller when her private phone intruded. "Damn," she vocalized her annoyance. She was sure it was Howard, but she didn't even want to talk to him tonight. He'd ask her about the luncheon, and she'd have to tell him how badly she had behaved.

She couldn't blame Stacey Lea or any of them if they didn't forgive her. What made her do some of the things she did was even hard for her to understand, but when Howard went to New York, she seemed to get herself into the biggest messes. If Howard would stay home, maybe, she could be good.

Oh well, she'd broken it off and hopefully that would be that. If he would let her go, she swore, she'd never again get involved. She wasn't quite sure how it had all gotten started anyway. With a sign of resignation, she reached for the cause of her irritation and greeted the caller.

"Hello, gorgeous," came the intimate response. "I said, *hello*. What's the matter? Cat got your tongue? I know I leave the ladies speechless, but where's your manners, doll?"

"I didn't expect to hear from you." Her eyes were closed, her voice barely audible. "I thought you were already back in California."

"Had to postpone my return. Have an important meeting tomorrow, so I thought I'd settle in for the night with a cool drink and somethin' sweet for dessert. I couldn't think of anything sweeter than you, so how's about hurryin' your sweet little ass on down here?"

"No, no more. I told you that last night, and I meant it. I never want to see you again." She took a deep breath, determined to deal with him. "No man has ever laid a hand on me before, and no man ever will again. Find yourself someone else to beat on."

Bev quietly replaced the receiver. She should have slammed it down—that was her style, but her anger was tempered by a new feeling she was having trouble dealing with, fear. She also had the feeling that it was going to get worse before it got better. He didn't care anything about her; she was sure of that, but he wasn't going to let her go until he was ready; she was pretty sure of that too.

Bev stared at the phone, hating it, hating him. Of course, it rang again. She tried to ignore it, to outlast it, but it rang and rang, and frustrated, she picked up the receiver. He wasted no time.

"Listen, you Jew bitch, don't you ever hang up on me. Nobody hangs up on me! Now, you get your tail down here right now, or you'll be sorry, and so will your precious Howie!"

"Don't threaten me. I'm going to tell Howard myself. I'm sorry I ever got involved with you. You're a vile, detestable man!"

"But at least I'm a man, which is more than I can say for poor Howie. I hear he never could get it up for you. Shall I tell you what else I hear, Mizz Abelson?"

"I have no idea what you're talking about," Beverly replied blankly, thinking, *dear God, he couldn't know about that!*

"Oh, I think you do," Earle smirked. "And unless you want the world to hear about Howie's dirty little secret, you'd better be real nice to me. Now get down here right now."

The line went dead, and so did the remaining sparks that had once flashed in Bev. How long she sat staring at the instrument that had caused her despair is hard to say, but at some point she began to breathe again, pulled from her stupor by another intrusion from the vile thing.

"PLEASE HANG UP. YOUR PARTY HAS DISCONNECTED. PLEASE HANG UP. YOUR PARTY HAS—" She hurled the contamination across the room, killing forever the dehumanized sound of modern technology that had polluted the air. In its place, another sound, a distant one, slowly reached her ears. It was a moaning, wailing, gut-rending cry, "No, oh please no." She slid limply and helplessly to the floor.

Beverly Jean Abelson had always insisted on making life hard for herself. From the moment she had clawed and kicked herself screaming from her mother's womb, she'd felt obliged to continue the process. Perhaps if the lives of children of women past their prime were studied, one would find they all share eccentric behavior patterns; nonetheless, we do know that these children are invariably extremes—extremely bright or extremely simple, and Beverly's mother never failed to boast that when amniocenteses proved she was carrying a healthy girl, she knew that she would be an extraordinary child touched by God.

Since the only other times Bev had heard her mother use the name of God was in vain, she quickly deduced that her mother's feelings for her fell in the same nugatory category. Here she was thrown slap-dab into the midst of a prosperous self-contained little family unit that seemed to have little need or time for her. She was determined to make her presence felt.

In all fairness, her parents did recognize her destructive tendencies and did attempt to help. In fact, by the time she was nine, she'd already exhausted two analysts, five nannies, as well as two schools. If she were told don't, she did and vice versa. So by her early twenties, she was living a Bohemian lifestyle with a forty year old artist in Soho, and by her late twenties, she was back on her parents' doorstep, having made a botch of herself and her life. These parents who had a few years earlier washed their hands of their only daughter now took the matter of her future firmly in hand. Their remedy was Howard Abelson. She was hardly in a position to refuse.

She had been brought to her parents' portal by her latest lover, a starving actor named Stan. A backstage abortion that hadn't gone well had panicked Stan into doing one of the few responsible deeds of their relationship, whether or not self-serving. Nevertheless, as Beverly would later admit, it had worked out for the best, and she would thus be left with a warm spot for weak Stan, no matter his motives.

It was, without a doubt, the lowest point in Bev's tumultuous life. She'd been aware for some time that she was going nowhere, and in a family of achievers, it was evidently difficult not to feel the need, no matter how hard one might try not to care. She was also very depressed over the loss of her baby. Even though she still believed, maybe unjustly, that she was ill prepared to care for a new life, it affected her deeply. On top of this, the news that she'd lost future choices threw her into a depression that made her family fear for her sanity, even her life. A family meeting was called.

Beverly was watching from the window as her brother walked up the steps. Elaine, his wife, wasn't with him, so she knew it was not a social call; it was a summons. She'd known something was getting ready to happen. It always did when her mother silently went around shaking her head, but the dead-give-away was when her father started playing nothing but Beethoven on the piano. Beethoven always wore him out, but it had also always been his one escape when his world became even slightly atilt. She'd already noted how pale and worn he was becoming. She felt sorry for him and ashamed that she was the cause. He was so talented, so delicate, not of this world. His world was music and most of his life had been spent there. She understood why he had difficulty dealing with the menial things of life, with her. She even understood why Beethoven helped.

Beverly had always been in awe of her father. Aaron Rabin (the "owitz" had been dropped in his teens, not long after he had left Russia) had been a world renown pianist for some years before she was born. She could remember well how her mother would take her to concerts when she was small, and she'd gaze up at that distant star on the stage, hear the bravos and plaudits and always think to herself with wonder , , , *Could that possibly be my father? Did he beget me like all those begots that led to Abraham?* Then she'd look at her mother and wonder , , , *Did he beget me with her?* As she got older, the wonder of her begetting became . . . *Did they?* And after much consideration, she dismissed the subject by concluding that she'd been begotten from a sperm bank, or, at the very best, she was the product of artificial insemination. That her mother and father had coitused even once to beget her brother was beyond her realm of plausibility.

While her father was of moderate height and slender frame, her mother was almost six feet and ample. Everything she wore, and said, and did was large. Stella Ruben Rabin was forty-two and a third generation Park Avenue plastic surgeon with a prestigious patient list (some of it inherited) when she found out she was pregnant with Beverly. It was a shock. Everyone who knew her, including her husband and son, were surprised when she announced that she intended to go through with it. In fact, her husband enlisted the help of her two sisters in an attempt to dissuade her, and her son rebelled for the only time in his life, mortified that at nineteen he was to be presented with a baby sister. It seems that everyone was embarrassed but Stella.

Because there was so much opposition, Stella promised herself that she'd make sure that this child brought little change to their lives, at least to Aaron's. So she never complained, worked right through the first labor pains and was back on the job in seven days. Behind the scene, she helped arrange an extended concert tour for her husband so that he'd not be inclined to play Beethoven when confronted with those early frustrating days of adjustment, days that are inevitable when a new family member appears.

Her son presented no problem since he was more than pleased to stay at school where he was preparing to become the fourth generation Park Avenue plastic surgeon. She had also encouraged him to take his Spring break elsewhere, and given his frame of mind, he'd readily agreed.

On the ninth of March under the sign of Pisces, Stella quietly checked into a private room at Cornell Medical Center, had her baby and just as quietly returned home to her large Eastside brownstone. For three solid months, she nursed, bathed, changed, rocked, spent every free moment taking care of and loving her new daughter. She'd look back on those three months as the happiest time in her life. However, when her husband came home, Stella made sure life went on as before. That is, she tried. Beverly had other ideas.

The three of them had been down there over an hour before they sent for her. As she prepared herself for sentencing, she thought of the scene that would greet her when she got downstairs and opened the big double doors to the library.

It was a wonderful room, and she'd spent many wonderful pretend times there. She wouldn't let it intimidate her now. The rich dark English oak paneling and shelves surrounded thousands of books that literally went from floor to the twenty foot ceiling. She remembered that she used to tell her friends that there were a million books in that room, and they'd believed her—there were, if you were a child. A regal only slightly worn Kirman rug of rich deep plums had graced the floor since her mother was a child, and on it but near the small paned leaded windows was the massive oak desk. It had been made in England but traced to Rasputin. That was where her mother was sitting now, behind it in the oversized wing-back swivel of deep brown leather that had softened with age. It was truly a make-believe chair, for once you sank down deep into its dark recesses, you could be anyone you wanted to be or go anyplace you wanted to go. She'd taken many grand trips from its safe depths, with and without a book to guide her.

To each side of the desk were expansive Regency tub chairs of walnut, upholstered in deep burnished gold velvet with gilded lions' heads at the arms and gilded lions' paws holding up the front legs. One of these had been her throne many a rainy day when she'd ordered heads cut off and kingdoms destroyed. The lonely decisions of monarchs seemed compatible with those of a lonely little girl.

Her father would be sitting in the one to her mother's right, and Allan, her brother, would be in the other one. Papa would be distracted, eager to return to his Beethoven; Allan would be fidgety by now, afraid that Elaine would be getting angry because he'd been gone so long—he was such a milquetoast. And Mama would be sternly but patiently awaiting the arrival of the wayward child.

Beverly took a deep breath, straightened herself and raised her head high as both hands grasped the knobs to fling open the big doors. It was a grand entrance; they'd not cow her. She imagined herself Anne Boleyn as she walked directly to the chair of the accused. It was in the center facing her mother, a strong walnut corner chair attired in the same brown leather that graced the matriarchal chair behind the desk.

Her mother wasted no time.

"Beverly, we've been giving considerable thought to your future since you've been back with us these few weeks. What we're going to say will perhaps anger you, but in view of the circumstances of your sojourn, you owe us the right to be heard." She went on, assuming, as

usual, that that was that. "I'll not dwell on the circumstances except
to point out that your poor judgment not only almost killed you, but
made it impossible for you to ever bear a child. I'm sorry for that. If
you'd only come to me, I'd have helped you get a safe abortion—if you
were set on it. I feel that I must take part of the blame because you
didn't feel you could come to me."

Were those tears in her mother's eyes or only her own she was
looking through? Her mother swiveled her chair to face the windows
as her brother continued.

"The fact is, Beverly, your life is out of control, and you need some
stabilizing force in it. Now, I've a friend who needs a wife. I spoke…,
don't get up, hear me out." Her brother put out a restraining hand as
she instinctively started to rise. "I spoke to him about you because he's
always admired your beauty. He's interested in talking to you, that's
all."

"What kind of man can't get his own wife?"

"You'll have to hear that from him."

"I don't know. This is crazy."

Her brother reached over and put his hand on her arm. She looked
into his eyes. Was there warmth there?

"He's a good man, Beverly. He's warm and thoughtful, and he's
also successful. He'd take good care of you.

"Does he know about my latest fiasco?"

"Yes."

"Does he know I can't have children?" Her voice broke.

"Yes, I told him."

"You know him well, then?"

"Yes, he's about my age. We went to school together."

"Do I know him?"

"Yes, you do."

"Well, who's this knight that would come to the rescue of a fool such as I? He must be crazy, and you must wish him ill, if you wish someone like me on him."

"Don't be so hard on yourself."

Was her brother taking up for her?

"But I'm not going to tell you who he is until I'm sure you'll give it some serious consideration. It won't be easy for either of you, but if you go into this purposefully, it might work better than some of these so-called love marriages. Love doesn't make the world go 'round. I suppose you already know that."

Bev looked at her brother closely, seeing him for the first time. He looked a lot like her father, but he wasn't delicate, he was strong and he was good; he wasn't a milquetoast either. She looked at her mother who'd turned around now and was looking at her closely and kindly. She looked at her father who wasn't looking at her or anyone else. She knew that he was already back in his world, probably hearing Beethoven in his head. She hoped that it was something happier like *Fur Elise.* But even he was patiently waiting for her to think things through.

"All right. I've made a mess of things. I can't make any promises, but I'll give it a good try. I do owe you that for all the trouble I've been. I thank you." She was looking at her mother, but then she got up and went the few steps to give her brother an awkward kiss on the cheek. It was a first time thing. He, just as awkwardly, stood up and put his arms around her as the sobs rushed in making her 'Thank you, Allan' almost unintelligible.

They broke apart embarrassed by the newness of their relationship, and Allan Rabin immediately looked at his watch. His voice was husky when he spoke. "Unless there's anything else, I better head for home. Elaine is probably having a fit. I didn't tell her where I was going, and I don't intend to tell her about today." He looked at Beverly steadily to let her know that what had transpired would remain in this room.

After kissing his mother good by, he gave his sister a light kiss on the forehead, put his hand on her shoulder and commented, "Howard will be quite the envy. You're a handsome woman."

Beverly laughed. "Thank you, Allan. But I think you've forgotten something important. You haven't told me a thing about him, you know, about this Howard."

They laughed, even her father. Allan opened his mouth, but Stella beat him to it as she announced with no little pleasure. "It's Howard Abelson, Beverly, the Governor of New York."

Beverly let out a surprised gasp as a frown spread on her face. "You can't be serious? I would be nothing but a liability—my past, my personality. Certainly, I'm not suitable. What can you be thinking? What can he be thinking?"

Allan responded. "He knows what he's doing. People are open-minded today; besides, he won't be running again for over three years, and if there's any to-do, it will have died down. It's his decision."

"I don't know what to say."

"You've already said it. You've agreed to consider him, and he wants to consider you. That's all either of you will be doing at this stage. Leave it be." With this her brother turned and departed, concluding the issue.

Beverly followed him and her father toward the door of the room, just beginning to realize the significance this afternoon could have on the rest of her life. She was eager for some space, but her mother called her back.

"Beverly, I'd like to talk to you further, if you please."

Beverly thought to herself that it was just like her mother, never knowing when to leave things alone. She had to admit, however, that Stella had been quiet today.

"Mama, please. There's been so much for me to take in. I really need to be alone."

"You'll get your chance. I won't keep you long."

Beverly let her shoulders droop as she returned to her place, knowing from her mother's voice that further resistance would be futile.

There was a heavy silence in the room before Stella Ruben spoke. In fact, she'd turned her chair back to the windows while she gathered her words. Finally, she turned around and looked closely at her daughter. Beverly was tense; she could tell. Why had it always been so difficult for them? Stella took a deep breath and began, and her daughter was totally unprepared for what she had to say.

"They say that a love child is a special gift from God." She spoke slowly. "That she's generous, bold, and beautiful; that she holds herself proudly but not with vanity; that when she enters a room, it's filled with sunshine. You're my love child, Beverly, and you're all those things. No one wanted me to have you, so late in life. But I needed you, perhaps, more than you needed to be. I loved carrying you. I talked secretly to you all the time, even read to you. When you were born, I was so proud. For your first three months, I arranged it all, and I had you all to myself. It was wonderful. Then I let you go because I didn't think it was fair to your father.

Perhaps, I was wrong. Allan had always been self-sufficient. I thought you'd learn to be that way too. But you're different, so vulnerable. You've never made life easy for yourself. I don't know if Howard Abelson's going to be your answer, but I'm confident that someday you'll be at peace. You have to work at it, though, and I think it's time you started. You're my daughter, and I love you dearly. Never again must you feel you can't come home."

Beverly said nothing through it all. When her mother had finished, there was still nothing she could say; there'd been too many years of silence between them. She had, however, moved over to the great chair, and curling up beside it, had rested her head on her mother's knee. As Stella Ruben stroked her daughter's hair, they shared a silence filled with the harmony their lives together had eluded. Beverly couldn't help but be grateful to the marvelous chair that held so many of her childhood dreams. She knew now that it was truly magical.

The shadows of evening were beginning to collect in the room when they proceeded with their lives. As Beverly climbed the stairs to prepare for dinner, she noticed the sound of the piano for the first time. Her father was playing Mozart.

How long Bev had been curled up beside her bed was now a cause of concern. She knew for sure that he'd be angry, and he'd been angry enough on the phone. Throwing on a pair of slacks and a bulky sweater, she ran her hands through her hair as she dashed for the door. At the door she hesitated, turned back to the closet and pulled out her ankle-length black mink. She'd go down there proud, she thought, and maybe the coat would help. God knows, she needed all the help she could muster.

She didn't take the elevator but entered the stairwell for the three flights down to the *devil's den*. Her mind raced with her speed of descent. She thought of her mother, grateful that she'd never know what a mess she'd made of things after all. She thought of Howard's pearl-handled Lilliput that lay in the little secret drawer of the library desk that'd once belonged to Rasputin. She thought of Howard.

Bev stood looking at the door. She'd managed to get herself this far but was unable to go any further. He knew about Howard. How?

He knew, too, that she was standing there, and he threw open the door. She could feel his anger before she looked into his face. When she did, she saw those eyes. It'd been his eyes that had first attracted her, hypnotic blue. Now she saw them for what they were—possessed, pure evil, drawing everything in and down.

"Well, doll, for taking so long, you sure didn't get too dolled up. What're you standin' there for? Come in, and have a sip of my drink; it'll loosen you up."

When she spoke her voice seemed far away, almost as if it wasn't her at all. "What did you mean? On the phone?"

"Later, sweets, later. If you're real good tonight, I'll give you all the juicy details. But first, I've got somethin' juicy for you right here." He grabbed her hand and pulled it toward his crotch. "Feel this, it's ready for you. Nice and hard, just the way you like it."

She tried to pull her hand away, but his grip on her wrist only tightened. It hurt.

"Little girls should do what they're told." His clipped words caused her to stiffen, to prepare for the blow, but he toyed with her. With the fingers of his free hand, he held her face, turning it roughly to examine the bruise he'd left the night before.

"That's not so bad, darlin'. You should've seen by wife before she learned to obey." She could feel his hot breath. "Now, you're not one of those libbers who objects to the word *obey*, are you? After all, the Bible tells us…"

"Just tell me what you know about Howard!"

As swift and as vicious as the attack of a cobra, the blow knocked her to the floor.

Standing straddle her, he sneered down, "Let me put it this way, I know everything about you and your precious Howie. Want to know what happened to that guy who knocked you up? Or the quack who cut you up?"

Kneeling over her now, he put his hand in back of her neck and pulled her head up to look at her closely. "But you want to know about your Howie, don't you? About his visits to Mama, rather where he really goes. Want to see my file on his boyfriend, or would that be too much for you to swallow?"

Well, then," he added, as he quickly unzipped his pants, "swallow this!"

CHAPTER FOUR

THE NEXT MORNING ♦ ♦ ♦

The President swallowed a blob of poached egg and bit off a piece of buttered toast. He wasn't just irritated; his inner steam was enough to fry the egg and burn the toast before they reached their point of process and distribution. A man of strict personal routine, he had difficulty tolerating the slightest ripple of change to it. Even the morning's workout in the pool had failed to work him out of his black mood. In fact, Coleman's report that the Bunker was ready hadn't been greeted with the pleasure such news would usually receive.

The target of his displeasure was at her usual place quietly sipping her coffee. They'd not come in together nor had they spoken. In fact, her silent but seemingly undisturbed attitude only added fuel to his fury.

Usually finely tuned to her husband's moods, this morning, Stacey Lea was too preoccupied to notice that the President of the United States was about to throw a tantrum.

"Goddammit, Stacey Lea! What the hells gotten into you?" he shrieked, slamming the morning paper down and spilling his coffee all over a fresh damask cloth for the second morning in a row. "Every goddamn veteran is gonna be down our throats, that *ole* convention, indeed! Here I allowed you to have that silly luncheon and what do you do? It's that woman's fault. I should never have allowed you to invite that Winthrop bitch!"

"What are you talking about, Palmer? I don't understand." Stacey Lea's tone was testy, but her husband didn't notice or would probably not have cared if he had.

"Don't understand? Of course, you don't understand. And that's the point! You women get involved in things you don't understand and next thing you know there's a bloody mess! Let women get involved in politics and WHAM, there goes common sense, right out the window. You had your Bella Adzug with her crazy hats, and Imelda Marcos with her stupid shoes. You almost had a female vice-president, and Clinton's wife thinking she was! Thank God, sensible heads put a stop to all that. And I promise you this, that Winthrop bitch is not gonna do anymore damage because I intend to take care of her."

Stacey Lea rose quickly as she spoke, causing a balancing black stain on her side of the breakfast table.

"I won't listen to your ugly diatribe, Palmer. It's pure venom today. Furthermore, it's beyond me what Sarah Winthrop has to do with anything."

"I'll tell you what Sarah Winthrop has to do with everything! Just look at you, she's even got you taking up for her. All her silly ideas about women and their female complaints. She's as bad as my mother was. I'll bet she put you up to last night. Whose idea was it to lock me out of your bedroom? Huh? You've never done that before, and you better never do it again. I'll not have it!"

Stacey Lea was shaking with rage as she turned to leave, brushing past Coleman whose throat clearing sounded more like an *ah-men* than an *ah-hem*.

"Don't you leave when I'm talking to you. I command you to stay! I'm the man of this house and I'll have obedience! I am your husband! I AM YOUR PRESIDENT!"

Stacey Lea's throat released a sigh of relief as she stepped back into her rooms.

Silly luncheon, indeed!

Her face was still red but what had begun as embarrassment had now become an indication of her growing anger. "How dare he," she whispered aloud, "how dare he scold me about our sex life, or lack of it...and so loud! God only knows who heard. Certainly Coleman heard!" Her face got redder as her thoughts turned to Coleman. Cold-man, that's what he was. Wonder if he had a mother? Was a child? Had sex? Yuck! Surely he was spawned by the devil and brought up from earth's core full-grown just waiting for the day when he could make her life miserable. Cold as it was at earth's center, or was it hot? Sexless...hmm? Her focus turned to Palmer, and for the first time since her marriage, she allowed herself to think about their relationship.

Stacey Lea soon found herself lying across her bed—something she never did, and staring at the ceiling while she thought of the times she and Palmer had made love here. Made love...she wondered what that meant? Was it something you manufactured, like a car or a new dress? But then you had something when you finished making it? Strange expression. Is that what she and Palmer did? If they did then there had to be something left when they finished.

Did Palmer ever have anything left? God knows, she didn't. Perhaps there's more to making love, and if you didn't make anything you weren't doing it right; you were only playing like you were doing it like those mystery weekends where people played like they were part of a murder. Ceil Roberts was talking about one of those weekends at the luncheon yesterday. Was the luncheon only yesterday?

Stacey Lea closed her eyes and allowed her thoughts to drift back to that fateful luncheon; however, the meandering interlude ended abruptly as her eyes popped open at the same time that her mouth delivered a knowing smile. Yes, she'd figured it out? Marriage was nothing more than a game like those mystery weekends and just as full of deceit and confusion. At least, those weekends were short-lived and people weren't deluded; they knew them for what they were. Well, she knew marriage for what it was now, and she wasn't much interested in playing anymore. She was sure Palmer wasn't much interested either.

It was just that last night was *that* night. She'd figured that out too. The tenth of every month was an absolute must and had been for about a year now. She wasn't quite sure when it had all started but with it came changes in that boring routine of his. It was the one day of the month that he didn't swim, just stayed in his room longer, stayed with her longer too, and things were different between them, not better, she analyzed, just different.

The President's wife had an above average curiosity, but only to the point that it didn't impact her cushioned existence. First-rate antennae were quick to sense this danger level. Therefore, she'd given that day of each month that affected her some lively speculation but had stopped short of any active pursuit of knowledge. There was something strange about it, something she was absolutely sure was better not known. Perhaps it was time to know, but not today. There was enough to occupy her mind today.

With a sigh, Stacey Lea sat up and pushed one of the intercom buttons by her bed-stand.

Ellie had been waiting for Stacey Lea's summons for almost an hour. Still, when it came, it interrupted thoughts so distant that it took a few moments for her to return. Slowly, she reached over and touched the button to acknowledge.

"I'll be right up," she said, but she didn't get up immediately. Instead, she leaned back in her chair and stared down at the large manila envelope unopened on her desk.

When she did stand up, she did so, so abruptly that she almost knocked over her chair. Her eyes never left the envelope as she pulled herself to her full height, and that was considerable.

Ellie stood almost six feet tall and a little over in the low tapered heels she usually wore. Her bones were large, and since she was quite thin, her warm brown skin stretched tautly over them giving her an angular look. The consequence was that all her clothes seemed to hang as if still on hangers. That was the case with the nubby wool suit she had on today. It was a deep yellowish brown with a short jacket trimmed in brown leather piping and buttons. The brown blouse was so close to the color of her skin that the line of its high neck was hardly discernible as it reached up toward a finely shaped head partially covered with tightly packed black ancestral frizz. This framed large brown eyes held up by high cheek-bones; a long delicate nose led to full lips—not ancestrally thick, but full and so sensuous that they'd conjured up many pleasant interludes among members of the opposite sex.

At the moment, however, they were only a thin coral line above her chin as they reflected her troubled thoughts directed toward the light brown packet in the middle of her desk. Leaning over, she picked it up and quietly remarked, "Well, Mizz Forbes, if ever there was a time, it's now. I hope you have something here worth all that fuss. God knows, Stacey Lea can use a little help, even from the beyond."

With that, Ellie picked up her notebook, put the packet in it, and with a grace that would have been appreciated by a jungle feline, she turned and left her office.

"Sorry, I was a little slow responding this morning," Ellie remarked as, after a light tap, she entered Stacey Lea's sitting room, "you caught my thoughts somewhere else."

"That's all right. I've been the same way. Guess it's the day, or the day after."

"Did you get any rest last night? You look tired." Ellie observed, relieved that Stacey Lea had wasted no time referring to yesterday's unsettling developments. She had a tendency to postpone unpleasant things.

"I was restless, but I think my looks have more to do with the fact that Palmer and I just had an awful row, in front of Coleman too. He's in a super bad mood today, and it's all directed at me. It started with the paper quoting my saying something about Palmer being at that *ole* VFW Convention. He said we're gonna have all the veterans offended because of that. I swear, when you want the press to quote you accurately they don't, and when you make a little slip, you can be sure they'll be very accurate."

"I had an idea that little word would come back to haunt you," Ellie noted, nodding her head. "You never make slips like that."

"Thank goodness! I couldn't take a frequent dose of this morning," Stacey Lea responded as a slight frown traveled across her forehead. "Then Palmer got into a terrible tirade about women and how they make nothing but a mess in politics, and then he got on Sarah and swore he'd take care of her. I still don't know why."

"No, and that's what's so disturbing."

"I guess you're right," Stacey Lea sighed, "and I guess all of you are right that there's more to it. But is it wrong to want things to be back as they were?"

"No, but I don't believe that deep down you want that. Remember what you said about Pandora's box? Later this morning, we should receive the data from Senator Winthrop's file. In the meantime, I think you should take a look at this." Ellie handed Stacey Lea the large manila envelope that had caused her concern earlier that morning.

"What is it?" Stacey Lea inquired as she turned the packet, examining it but not opening it, and obviously not wanting to open it. Intuitively, she knew that this packet would alienate her even further from her pre-luncheon life, and she wasn't ready.

"This is from Mrs. Forbes. She put it in my care before she died, admonishing me to give it to you if you needed help. I figure, if you ever needed help, it's now."

The two women sat quietly on the sofa, for Ellie didn't move as Stacey Lea read and re-read. Finally, she placed the pages in her lap, looked at Ellie and inquired, "You don't have any idea what this is about?"

"No, not an inkling."

"When did Mother Forbes give this to you?"

"About six months before her death. Do you remember when she came here unexpectedly that last year of her life furious about that trumped up abortion raid at the Foundation?"

"Yes, she closeted herself with Palmer for the longest."

"Well, several months after that I got a call from her. She said she needed to see me, but she cautioned me that no one must know that I was coming. I had to take every precaution to see that I wasn't followed and I had to announce myself with a password."

"And did you?"

"Of course. Would you have disobeyed Mrs. Forbes?"

"Not I," Stacey Lea responded with mock terror. "I was scared to death of the woman. What was the password?"

"*Do you live by the Ten Commandments?* Very mysterious."

"After reading this legacy Mother Forbes has left me," Stacey Lea observed, looking down with distaste at the sheets of paper in her lap, "it's no mystery to me. In fact, the world has turned topsy-turvy, and I feel a bit like Alice must have felt in Wonderland. Ellie, I need to go home. Is it possible? I've got that big State dinner next week and…?"

"But this week's slow," Ellie interrupted, looking in her notebook. "Remember, we made it that way because of the luncheon. Next week's impossible. You have something every day, and the Chinese Delegation will be in on Wednesday. If you're going, you need to go now. That'll give you Friday and Saturday at home."

Ellie had responded quickly, understanding the seriousness of Stacey Lea's request.

"Palmer's not gonna like it," the First Lady acknowledged with a grimace. "But he called my luncheon silly. I intend he pay for that, and going home's a start!"

"You know he didn't mean it, Stace," Ellie responded, laughing. "Your program's good for the country. He knows that."

"I know it too, but it's also busy work. Give the First Lady a project to keep her busy. No one judges a First Lady by her *busy work*."

With this, Stacey Lea stood up, her mind already flowing toward the Mississippi.

CHAPTER FIVE

THE BUNKER BUDDIES ✦ ✦ ✦

Judge Earle Salvation Walker was having a leisure morning, a rare happening for him. As head of the Church Eternal, he was a busy and important man. He'd often remarked, "It isn't an easy job keeping my children on the straight and narrow, but God's told me that's what I have to do." So Earle traveled the world, his life dedicated to praising the Lord, and making sure everybody knew what God wanted.

Not that life was without its simple pleasures. He made sure of that. His work for the Lord needed diversion, and like a sailor, he had one in every port. He also had a luxurious jet to get him port-to-port and equally luxurious quarters at every stop in which he could pray and play. His flock took good care of him

Judge Earle, as his followers affectionately called him, had come along when a big part of this nation's Christians were floundering, looking for a church that could fill the void left by the fall of the big TV ministries. Some, in desperation, had even stuck with or gone back to their fallen leaders simply because they didn't know anything else to do. But it was never the same, the bloom was off the rose. It'd been a long dry spell. They were ripe, and Earle was ready.

Before he went about his Father's business, Earle enrolled in a small Baptist Seminary in North Carolina. It didn't take him long to realize there wasn't much they could teach him, so he didn't stay long. Still, when he left, he took with him a pretty little church musician named Carolyn, as his starry-eyed bride, and his first apostle, Harlan. Parker

His ministry grew rapidly. The strays of God—of which there were many—had immediately capitulated, followed by the fundamental factions in most of the established denominations, then splinter groups and whole churches in denominations of little central control, like the Baptist. On and on until now, in less than thirty years, Earle Walker had become one of the most powerful churchmen in the world, and his church, The Church Eternal, a modern day phenomenon.

Much of his success was attributed to his creative organizational abilities. Earle had realized right from the beginning that the emotional response he so easily achieved would weaken in the light of day. In other words, getting them was easy, keeping them was something else. So right after he reeled them in, others stepped in to give the new converts their proper places in the order. Indoctrination was swift and complete, and very few strays had been recorded. Earle ran a tight church.

He'd patterned his Church after IBM right down to his Blue Blazer Bible Brigade; however, he'd added some clever ideas of his own. Earle had set his Church up around three important biblical numbers—one, three, and twelve. For example, the Church in the United States was divided into three parts—the *Father, the Son, and the Holy Ghost;* each part of this triumvirate had twelve regions named after the twelve apostles; although he replaced Judas with Paul. Each region was then divided into districts named after the twelve minor prophets, and churches within each district were named after books of the Old Testament. Therefore, an Eternist from Kansas City would be The Son, Peter, Nahum and maybe, Church Genesis. And, of course, over it all was its designer, the GREAT ONE, Earle, himself.

The psychological effect was extraordinary. Eternists threw off their old identities and became absorbed in their new churchly ones. They adopted regional flags, flowers, symbols, etc. Miami, that is, The Holy Ghost, Matthew, Obadiah, even adopted a favorite fish, the dolphin. And Sunday School and Bible meetings were filled with color, symbol, and flower drills. Eternal fluency was a thing of which an Eternist was proud.

And to Harlan Parker, Earle had added eleven other handpicked apostles. Mindful of Judas, however, not only did they police each other, but he never let any one of them know too much. Only one, Harlan Parker, had ever been in his Washington condo. This was a particular favorite of his and so was Washington. He'd even thought of moving his world office here amidst all the intrigue and power. It stimulated him.

He'd awakened with a smile on his face and was still smiling when he stepped out of the shower. Not exactly a nice smile but the kind about which you can never be sure. Perhaps that helped produce the aura surrounding him. After all, hadn't *Mona Lisa* survived for centuries because of some mystic charm that began with a thin-lipped smile?

However, it wasn't Earle's smile that started it all. In fact, most of Earle was pretty ordinary. With 5'9" the average for an American male, Earle was 5'9" and a smidgen. His frame was also average, but it was finely coated with nicely developed muscular tissue. Earle had always taken good care of himself.

Under the bright lights of the white tiled and mirrored bathroom, Earle Walker's raven-black hair stood out in sharp contrast. He had a thick head of hair, not too curly and not too straight. There was a touch of gray at the temples—just the right touch, and it was doubtful that he would ever allow more, nor that he should. The gray also mixed with black to soften heavy brows that almost touched across a broad forehead. Both were needed to contain the feature that was without doubt the seat of his mystic charm, his eyes. They were neither gray, nor blue, nor black but had been called all three. At times, one could see ice in them—sharp shards that could pierce like lasers, at other times, fire—smoldering coals to a three-alarm uproar. They had the power to turn a man rigid, scare the soul right out of his body and give it back only when it was deemed ready for redemption. In fact, one of his close aides had sworn that he actually saw Walker stare at a table until it shook, collapsed, and decomposed to sawdust so fine that it was swept up and carried away in a dust pan.

At the moment, however, the seat of his mesmerizing power was unspectacular as Earle stood admiring himself in the bathroom mirrors. He'd had the whole room mirrored—even the ceiling, and it had turned out to be the perfect room for his favorite post-shower pastime, pumping iron.

Reaching under the cabinet, Earle Walker pushed a button that activated a humming response as many of the mirrors began to turn. He stepped back on the one black tile on an otherwise sterile white floor, and behold, a many faceted nude Earle appeared. Earle was using one of his sexiest, most captivating smiles as he went into a muscle-flexing routine for his make-believe, admiring throng. His muscles rippled impressively, and his routine was flawless. Sometimes he included another muscle, but this morning, that one was at rest; it'd had a busy night. Well, at forty-nine, it was natural for a man to slow down a bit.

His routine lasted exactly nine minutes. At the end, he spread his legs, bent forward and raised his arms back, up, and out in a sort of bicepual bow. Then he slowly raised his head and smiled. It was a sweet smile that filled the mirrored room and caused Earle to prolong his finale for a good thirty seconds.

Even before Walker returned himself to an upright position and re-positioned the mirrors, his focus was directed to the day ahead. He'd not allowed intrusion into his morning pleasure, but now, as he brushed his teeth, he allowed himself to hear his apostle, Harlan, fussing around in the bedroom.

Harlan Parker had arrived late that morning, just as Earle had requested. He could smell the sex in the room, and the woman—the same woman as the night before, he could always tell. In fact, her smell had been around for some time now. He didn't know who she was, nor did he care, for Parker was a realist. There was big money in religion, and he was with the best. He'd hitched his wagon to Earle Walker when he was nothing, and it had paid off. Life was good. In fact, the good life had added a good thirty pounds excess to his small frame, focused mainly in his mid-section. He had the look often associated with priests and nuns—carefree, wrinkle-free and well fed. If it weren't for the paunch and a shiny head with white fringe, one might consider him closer to forty than the fifty which he attained this day.

Yes, Harlan Parker had reached the half-century mark and was confident that something was being planned for his big day. He was upset to be stuck in Washington.

When the call came from the White House early yesterday afternoon, they'd been ready to leave for the airport. He knew as soon as he heard the voice that he might as well unpack. He didn't like the President's man. He hadn't liked him from the start, from the first time he'd heard his voice. Some people just did that to you right away. Coleman—he was that all right, as cold as a corpse. Wonder if he'd been given a party for his fiftieth? Had friends? Had relatives? Yuck, as his niece would say.

Granted, he was proud that Walker was part of such an elite group. They'd come a long way from the Seminary, but he couldn't help but be perturbed that this emergency meeting was messing up his special day. Besides, he was constipated, always was when he traveled. His mother used to say that you needed your own pot. That was sure true for him.

Harlan's mutterings were disturbed by the sound of Walker singing *Bringing in the Sheaves*, indicating that not only was he in a good mood, but he'd be out soon and wanting his coffee. He dashed to the kitchen to comply.

"Good morning, Brother Earle, I trust you had a good night's sleep?" Harlan greeted as he set a steaming mug of fresh brew on the counter.

"That I did, Brother Harlan, that I did. And you?"

"It was fine, but I'm ready to go home."

"We'll be headin' that way as soon as the meeting's over. Shouldn't last too long."

Naturally, he wants to go, Earle thought. He has to know something's planned for his big 5-0. He deserves it too, loyal since the beginning. Sometimes, however, he wondered about Harlan's motivation. He'd never quite figured out what made him tick, and then, there'd been that incident years ago when he'd taken Carolyn's side. Maybe that's why he felt a little wary of Harlan? Harlan had changed after that too; he'd gotten too nice. You couldn't completely trust someone who was too nice.

"I picked up some melon on the way over. Smells sweet. You want some for breakfast?"

"That'd be good, and give me some of that cereal, the kind I had yesterday, you know, the, ah, snap, crackle, and pop kind."

"All right. I put out your blue pinstripe. You look nice in it. Okay?"

"No, think I'll wear the gray, with a blue shirt."

Harlan's peeve became a huff as he made the switch. He knew Earle was being intentionally disagreeable. He didn't care what suit he wore; all his clothes were nice. Harlan had no idea what made Earle do this with him sometimes. Just happened for no reason at all.

The silence that followed the blue and gray conflict was not broken until Earle had almost finished his rice crispies.

"I'll take more coffee. Do you have everything taken care of for our departure?"

"Yes, Dan will be waiting with the plane from one on. Frank's downstairs now, waiting to alert us when Senator Fairmont arrives, and James Elmer's taking care of everything on the other end."

"Fine. I assume you've also arranged to have someone meet me when Fairmont drops me off at Dulles?"

"Yes, Nick Bell and I will be watching for the helicopter to touch down." Harlan, not sure of what had gotten into him, added a little discreet get-even. "I suppose His Eminence will be there?"

"Goddammit, Harlan," Earle exploded as he threw down his spoon, "you know how the very thought of that red-trimmed popinjay angers me! Get the hell out of here and do your work, and keep your fuckin' mouth closed."

The final charge in this scathing over-boil was delivered to Harlan's receding back. Fortunately that was the view, for if Earle Walker had seen the pleasure on his steadfast aide's face, Harlan Parker's eternal wings might have been permanently clipped.

Earle now glowered at the bowl with contents that had completely lost their ability to snap, crackle and pop. Harlan had spoiled his breakfast and his morning by bringing up that holier-than-thou son-of-a-bitch; he pouted. He never liked to think of him until he had to; it got him too upset. He wished he could get something on the pompous ass, so he could bring him down a peg or two, But the good Cardinal seemed beyond reproach and was probably more powerful than he was. That was a bitter pill, but Bishop had all the American Catholics *cowtailing* to him, even many outside the country as well. Kept them pretty much in line too, Earle sullenly credited. He was even being touted as the next Pope, although from the looks of things, that'd probably be a comedown.

Neither Earle Walker nor John Bishop would have ever admitted to being on the same wave-length, but this morning as one sat in his posh Washington Condo considering his most formidable rival, the other sat in his posh Madison Avenue residence involved in similar thoughts.

After reading the same sentence over at least five times, His Eminence put down the morning paper and allowed a frown to furrow his aristocratic brow. He wasn't happy about this meeting today. He knew why Forbes had called it. In fact, he'd been expecting it after reading Sarah Winthrop's front pager. He wished she'd stop shooting off her mouth, take it easy for awhile. She seemed determined to drive Forbes crazy. The irony of it was she didn't know it. Forbes was cool and collected about most things, but Winthrop got to him. He didn't like it. Emotions make people careless, and that could be dangerous.

That's why he despised that idiot Walker. You never knew what he might say when he got started on one of those stupid philippics of his. For the life of him, he'd never understand how that man had gotten so powerful, but he had built quite an organization—too emotional for his taste, mind you, but it seemed to be filling some primitive need in the masses. In fact, it was beginning to smack of cult, and Eternists were becoming obnoxious, like their leader.

Cardinal Bishop smiled thinking of the good Judge. He knew he made him uncomfortable; he was an expert at making people uncomfortable, making them squirm. In fact, he alone had restored the great Catholic Conscience to its rightful place in the forefront of Catholic thought and action. That's why the churches were full, the confessionals were full, and the coffers were full. That's why many considered him the greatest Catholic leader today, greater even than the Pope.

John Marion Bishop was born in upstate New York. His mother had been heiress to a canning fortune, mainly applesauce, which had led to quips early in his career such as *Saucy Seminarian* and *Apple of the Church's eye*. However, such fun poking quickly died out when greeted by Bishop's autocratic manner.

His father, if he'd actually had one, had faded away long ago. All he could remember was his mother, especially the many times he spent sleeping close in her arms, his head snuggled deep in her ample bosom. As he lay cradled there, she would recite to him, as if chanting a litany, the vision she'd had when he'd first moved within her. For the great herald of Christ, John the Baptist, no less, had appeared to her. He had told her that she would bear the Catholic Church a priest who would lead the Church back to its Counter-Reformation glory. With this, the prophet had reached out his hands and brought his cousin, Mary, into the vision. She'd actually placed her hands on the stomach of John Marion's mother and blest him in the womb. At that moment, his mother had named him after the two of them.

This wasn't a widely known story, and those who knew it only whispered it reverently to others who had the faith. The world was too profane to accept the truth of miracles and visions; on the other hand, even the most skeptical of the supernatural and the most critical of the Cardinal would be foolhardy not to pause when presented with the facts. Not only was the princely leader born on June 21st, the birthdate ascribed to John the Baptist, but his accomplishments were more than seemed humanly possible. His faithful considered him blessed, both heavenly inspired and supported. John Marion agreed.

He never doubted his destiny; therefore, he guided his flock with a firm hand, never questioned because he was never wrong. He was questioned once, back when he was first elevated to Bishop in upstate New York. Sister Margaret Fidelius of the Fallopian Sisters caused quite a fuss when he banned women from behind the altar rail. During an especially well-attended mass one Sunday morning, she'd rushed down the aisle, torn up part of the altar rail (she was a big, strong woman), and holding it above her head cried, "If women can't go behind the altar rail, then there will be no altar rail!" The new Bishop said nothing, but none that were there will ever forget the look of disdain he gave her as she was led away. She hasn't been heard from since. Good-natured jests followed her mysterious departure, placing her attached to a cement block at the bottom of the Erie Canal, but no one is quite sure what the Church does with its wayward offspring.

John Marion's rise up the ecclesiastical ladder was swift. He was a priest at twenty-three, a Monsignor at twenty-eight, and a Bishop at thirty-three. That was the year his hair turned white, and he had some difficulty with his role, at least the dignity part.

You see, Father Bishop had a nice ring to it, Monsignor Bishop resounded with dignity, but Bishop Bishop? If the red hat had not fit him so well, it would surely have toppled from the crushing weight of this coincidence of birth. Those bitten by the green-eyed monster were quick to point out that this condition alone was responsible for Bishop's elevation to Cardinal when he was only forty-two by a too kind Holy Father in Rome. This was unfair, however, for Cardinal Bishop had, as John the Baptist had prophesized, almost single-handedly returned the Church to its seventeenth century prestige and splendor, and the Holy Father had been shrewd to recognize Bishop's miraculous talent.

The Cardinal's breakfast thoughts had just shifted from the Bunker meeting to that shrewd Holy Father, another cause for concern. His official summonses to Rome were becoming much too frequent, and the *Old Man* was getting much too interested in his affairs. He didn't like it. Rome should have sense enough to let him alone. They got a good Peter Pence collection as well as just about anything else they wanted. Why couldn't they leave it at that? Jealously, that's all it was, but that could cause lots of problems. He had this unsettling feeling that they were looking for a way to move him out, exile him.

He didn't want to tangle with the Vatican; for now, his power was greater from within. That's why this irrational obsession Forbes had with Winthrop bothered him. If any of his involvement with Forbes and his schemes came out…well, that could mean schism. Bishop's mutinous thoughts were beginning to coagulate when interrupted by his aide, Monsignor Wordman.

"Your Eminence, I'm sorry to disturb you, but Bishop O'Donnell's on the line from Buffalo, and he won't take no for an answer. I don't want to cause a problem for you with him. What do you want me to do?"

"What I'd like for you to do is tell the Irish bastard to go to hell, but…tell him I'm on the toilet. Tell him that I'm also running late for a meeting, ah, with the mayor. Yes, that's a good touch, tell him I'm meeting the mayor and I'll get back to him later."

"He said it was urgent."

"It's always urgent with him. Last time, he just wanted to know what kind of wine we used in the Cathedral. I, of course, didn't know. Sometimes I wish he didn't admire me so much, but it's good to have adulators, even if they're idiots. Now, get rid of him, and I'll meet you in the office. We have time for a little work before I have to leave."

The Cardinal smiled as he watched Wordman depart. A man after his own heart. What would he do without him? Still, it wasn't good for anyone to be trusted with too much.

The Cardinal frowned as he thought of O'Donnell—didn't trust him at all, too nice. Never could trust anyone who was too nice. Tom O'Donnell might appear to kiss his ring, but he suspected that the man could easily be a Judas. He knew his hate of the Irish might be coloring the issue. With this thought, His Eminence did not leave but walked over to the window. Looking over the wintering Chancery garden, he remembered the one Irishman who made him curse all Irishmen.

He had been twelve years old when Danny Gallagher had come into his life. Nothing had been the same after that. At first, he'd liked him, that Irish charm, the soft boyish look with the red hair and freckles and the sparkling eyes, but his mother had become bewitched. Oh, he'd had that Irish gift of speech, the silken tongue, he'd give him that. That silly myth about Saint Patrick charming the snakes out of Ireland became plausible after you'd met *Danny Boy*, as his mother always called him.

Gallagher had come to their door selling vacuum cleaners and had never left. And he never again got to sleep close to his mother's breast; she never again told him the story of his great destiny; he never again sat at the head of the table, her little man, her champion. She had her Danny Boy.

His chaste, beautiful mother became a tramp under Gallagher's spell. (The Cardinal's face was becoming red as he remembered.) Sure they'd married, after he'd knocked her up, but that scrap of paper hadn't changed anything. She had still been Danny Boy's whore. They'd been insatiable.

He'd never forget the sound of their sin, the bed's rhythmical squeaking, gently at first then fast and hard, the giggling changing to squeals of pleasure; his grunts, like a pig, and the *Oh, Danny's*, the *Oh, God's*, even the name of God in their wicked pleasure.

The Cardinal quickly looked around at the open doorway as he realized his hands had instinctively reached down while he rhythmically swayed against the windowsill. Reaching over, he picked up the morning paper, a welcome camouflage against his imprudence, and proceeded with some chagrin to the closest bathroom to take his relief. He was annoyed with himself. What was wrong with him this morning? He knew better than to allow himself to think of their filthy mating except in his most secret times. It never ceased to arouse him, had for over fifty years now. He promised, as he had many times before, that he'd never let this happen again.

Nevertheless, after his private ritual was complete and he was heading toward his study, the look of pleasure belied his prior vexation.

Not all of it had to do with his recent libation, for he always enjoyed thinking of Gallagher's weak seed. He'd been soft, proved it time and again. Six girls in rapid succession. Never able to father a healthy son. They'd had one, only able to gasp through an hour, but the girls were hale and hearty. God, how they drove him crazy; the *Weak Seeds,* he called them to himself. Women were weak; his mother had proved that. Aristotle had called them *failed males,* a pleasant thought with which to begin the business of the day.

Forbes arrived early at the Bunker to observe his co-conspirators from behind a one-way glass. He was an advocate of people watching; you never know what you might find out. For example, he'd learned early on how much the Judge and the Cardinal despised one another. He enjoyed watching them parley, vie for attention, even seating. In fact, only a mastermind could have put this unlikely group together. He chuckled, quite pleased with himself.

Palmer's pleasure turned to irritation as he thought of his wife. Granted, he'd perhaps gone a little overboard this morning, but it was her fault for sitting there as if nothing had happened. She'd never locked her door against him. He'd even pounded. He should have broken it down; that's what he should've done. It wasn't the sex; frankly, sex wasn't that big a priority, but it was important last night, for it was all part of his routine on the day he exorcised his mother.

He'd planned her exorcism very carefully. He smiled as he thought what His Eminence might say if he knew all that water he'd been so flattered to bless for the La Paz Cathedral had wound up in his fish-tank. Holy water was supposed to have all sorts of miraculous powers. One dunk, even a little sprinkle, and man's sins were washed away. Well, a whole tank full should take care of his mother. He wasn't sure that the Cardinal's water was the best choice, but he guessed it was as good as any. He'd never been much impressed with these so-called holy men.

The President's thoughts were interrupted as Beau Fairmont arrived with Earle Walker in tow. Both headed straight to the bar where Coleman had set up a little *hors d'oeuvre* arrangement. He didn't need the intercom to know what they were ordering. Beau always drank bourbon and water, having this idiotic idea that it added to his image as a Southern gentleman. The only thing it was adding was extra inches to his middle. In fact, under this undisturbed scrutiny, he noted that Beau was looking a bit seedy. Oh, not his $1500 suit, but he was beginning to have that worn look that represented too much boozing and too much playing. Interesting…he'd never noticed it before.

Walker liked fancy drinks, the way he liked fancy women. Wonder who he was screwing in Washington since he'd dumped Didi Clark? Never left Highgate anymore. Somebody there? The Abelsons lived there. Wouldn't it be something if it were Howard Abelson's Bev? What would Stacey Lea think of her friend then?

Forbes filed away his possible discovery just as Coleman strained out Walker's *Margarita*. Coleman had everything running smoothly. What would he do without the man? Past presidents hadn't used him properly, wasted his talents. That's what Stacey Lea would have him do; she couldn't understand that Coleman was a man's man, that was all. If it hadn't been for Coleman, he'd never have known how late that troublemaker Winthrop had stayed last night, almost eight when she'd left.

Stacey Lea knew how much he hated the woman. Couldn't even trust his own wife anymore. Maybe she was going to get crazy like his mother had when she started the change? God, if that's it, he'd gladly send her home to her *dear* Daddy and her Muddy Mississippi. She'd sure been on a high horse this morning when she'd told him she was going home, totally out of character. She'd better come back repentant, or there'd be some changes made. Well, well, enter the Cardinal in all his pompous finery. The fun begins.

"Good day, Gentlemen," Cardinal Bishop greeted as he made an outward gesture with his hand, adding greater focus to his grand entrance. He was well known for his entrances. Tall and aristocratically thin, he had managed to acquire a bit of the pale, gaunt look of the suffering saints of El Greco. His thick white hair added to his stature, but his hands, ah, these were his crowning glory. They were long and tapered and flowed gracefully when he spoke, often making speech redundant. For the Cardinal's hands prayed, blessed, cajoled and charmed like the strings of a violin; unfortunately, they could also show disdain and wrath with the persistence and thunder of an overactive kettledrum. There were many who had felt those lyrical fingers tighten in absentia, for to brook his disfavor could mean banishment from his holy presence with the finality of God's to the fallen angel.

"Good day to you, Your Eminence," responded Beau, mustering as much enthusiasm as he could. The man was so superior acting; it wasn't easy to be comfortable with him. "Would you like a drink while we wait? Dr. Vondergraven is joining us today, and he seems to be running late."

The Cardinal put up his hand in an agitated motion.

"I thought we'd agreed that no others would be involved in these meetings?"

"That's true, but the President felt it was in all our best interest to have the doctor here today since he's active on the operative end of our plans."

"He managed to bungle the last one quite well."

"Maybe that's a good enough reason to have him here, find out what went wrong, right from the horse's mouth," Earle piped in. "Now, what's it you Catholics like to drink,…Virgin Marys? He chuckled as he chalked up the first point.

"The Mother of God is not one to jest about, even by those who haven't the faith to accept the Virgin Birth."

"I wouldn't call it faith; I'd call it wool, wool over the sheep's eyes." *Boy, I'm sharp tod*ay; Earle complimented himself.

The President complimented him too. In fact, he almost clapped his hands with glee as he listened to Earle best John Marion. Hadn't the Cardinal questioned his presidential judgment in bringing aboard Claude Vondergraven? Served him right.

For his part, Cardinal Bishop was nettled by the riposte of his usually quite inadequate opponent. After all, he'd just arrived and had not had time to don proper demeanor for a successful duel. Most ungentlemanly to take such advantage, like one firing at ten paces instead of taking the customary twenty. He had by far the better aim, proved it time and again, but he'd learned that sometimes it's better to ignore the gauntlet and rise above. He'd also learned to never turn the other cheek. .

As His Eminence haughtily ignored the bait and was about to take his first swallow of the bland but well-belted Bloody Mary Coleman had served, the object of his vexation arrived.

"I'm sorry to be late," apologized a breathless Dr. Claude Vondergraven as he smilingly rushed toward the bar, "had some plane problems, but I see our President hasn't arrived." Vondergraven breathed a sigh of relief. It was a proud day for him to be invited here. He didn't want to get off on a bad foot by being late, even if it hadn't been his fault.

"You're fine," Beau assured. "The President's here but working on some affairs of state. He'll join us shortly. Have you met Cardinal Bishop and Judge Walker?"

"No, this is an honor," Vondergraven responded as the men shook hands all around.

Watching the doctor's entrance, Forbes thought how much he reminded him of that *late* rabbit in *Alice in Wonderland*—silly man, bloated with self-importance. Look at him out there practically slobbering on everybody, bet his pants were wet.

"Tell me, Doctor, since you were there, what were the circumstances surrounding Dr. Ackerman's death?"

Before Vondergraven could respond to the Cardinal's pointed question, Forbes stepped into the room, interrupting any immediate confrontation on this touchy issue.

"Ah, good day, Gentlemen. Sorry I had to keep you waiting, but the burdens of office, you know. I was just informed that Congresswoman Tyler of California is resigning. Not official yet but true nevertheless. Now on that good note of our continuing success, let's have lunch. I, for one, am starved."

To the thoughtful observer, if such could have been the case, the convening of the three major participants was masterful, indeed. To the world, they were displayed as wary watchdogs of one another whose philosophies collided and sparked with continuous friction. But, gathered together at this table with neither head nor foot, their spirits communed with common purpose. Like those other knights of a round table, they met to make the world the way they believed it should be. If the dragons they fought were more their own than the world's, were they any less misguided than those knights of old? Did Gawain find the chalice? Did Arthur and Lancelot ever find peace? Is Camelot possible? Thoughts to ponder, for certainly these men believed in their cause and certainly they believed in themselves and their destinies as devoutly as did their predecessors. But mythological kingdoms do not aspire to reality, and beliefs that are out of touch with reality can only aspire to mythological kingdoms. The only survivors are those who leave fairy tales be. And today this fairy tale seemed to find its participants, for the first time, less confident of the happy ending.

They had met at the Bunker every three months for over three years to plan strategy, but this was the first emergency meeting and this in itself seemed to have made them circumspect. They had also had two of their plans go awry. Nothing like that had happened before. Was the pendulum swinging? *Had they gone too far?* Certainly, these questions were in the Cardinal's mind, the most cautious of the three. He was determined they desist for a time; however, convincing Palmer Forbes of this, given his hatred of Winthrop, was not going to be easy.

The Judge's alarm had not gone off; but he didn't like the fact that their orders had not been completed satisfactorily. He'd never been able to tolerate failure, and finding it, he was beginning to doubt the competency of their organization. Still, the challenge of officially taking on Winthrop might be too irresistible to deny.

For the President, his hatred of Winthrop clouded the vision he'd relied on so successfully throughout his political career. Her determined support of his mother's Foundation even after Ackerman's death was more than he could tolerate. He would not be denied her decline, but he was bothered. He couldn't put his finger on it, but things were just not right. Something inside always told him, like a little sick feeling in his stomach, an itchy nose or not being able to clear his throat. One thing he knew for sure, he wasn't having much fun today, not even when he'd been doing his eavesdropping. Everything had lost its edge. Even lunch wasn't as good. Coleman was serving his favorites, tuna noodle casserole and Caesar salad, but the taste buds just weren't with it today.

There had also been none of the usual competition by Bishop and Walker to sit at his right. To top it off, without Beau's bourbon bonded babble and Carl's nervous fawning, table talk would have been practically nil. Even Walker was more reserved. God, he didn't like change!

"Since we're running a little late today, let's get down to business during dessert. I called this meeting, as you may have guessed, because of Senator Winthrop and her continued attempts to direct attention to the Foundation. This, you must agree, cannot be allowed to continue, especially after Ackerman's death."

"I agree that it's not desirable," responded the Cardinal, "but neither was Ackerman's death. I had just inquired of Dr. Vondergraven some explanation of this unfortunate occurrence when you walked in, Mr. President. We've successfully used the serum in the past to neutralize extreme resistance without causing death. How did this one come off so disastrously?"

"One reason I asked Dr. Vondergraven here today was so that he could explain to you precisely what happened; however, let me remind you that we always knew something like this could happen. That it hadn't done so before never meant that the serum was safe against such conclusion. As you said, we've only used the serum in extreme cases where other tactics haven't been satisfactory. I remind you, our rate of success is quite good."

"Well, as far as I'm concerned," Earle jumped in, "Ackerman was a big Jewish cow whose passing's no big loss or big deal. It'll all die down shortly. She's better off than that Shipley woman in Wyoming who's a vegetable. Frankly, I'm more concerned that your handpicked task force messed up in Texas, Mr. President. Things like that could cause a real problem for us. The Baynes family have a lot of influence. We can't make mistakes when we're setting out to entrap them."

"Quite right, but I've interrogated my men and I am confident that no mistake was made. You know how efficient they are. The cocaine was planted, and the State Police stopped Baynes' son as scheduled. How the cocaine got out of his car, we don't know, but whoever found it doesn't know where it came from either. It's stalemate this time. I won't deny that this isn't a problem, for they've been alerted. Therefore, I propose we go right after Winthrop. She's a stubborn bitch, and our scheme probably wouldn't have stopped her anyhow. Got to get her and be done with it."

"I think," suggested Cardinal Bishop slowly, "we're getting ahead of ourselves. I still haven't gotten an answer to my question about Ackerman."

"Vondergraven," Forbes barked, "tell everyone what you told me."

"Well, Gentlemen, as you know, the serum quickly removes hormones causing almost immediate menopausal symptoms. The stronger the dose, the more extreme the symptoms, running the gamut from palpitations, hot flashes and a depressed psychological system to complete physical breakdowns, strokes and heart attacks of various magnitudes."

"We're familiar with this information," acknowledged the Cardinal. "You still haven't answered my question."

"Give him time!" The President snapped.

"Using a negative situation for positive results, I've had a fairly accurate idea of serum strength to weight since Senator Shipley's unfortunate reaction. It's, however, still pretty much a guessing game. A scientist must patiently keep records, sometimes a lifetime, and we're dealing with chemical combinations here that are basically untried. Not only is it impossible for me to examine and keep up with those who've been given my serum, but I've no way of getting a thorough physical work-up on our targets before administering it. Sometimes, a target may already have imbalances that aren't known. Finally, even if I had every test possible run and knew a target's history thoroughly, the serum's reaction is erratic and so is a female's physiology, especially in the over forty age group of our focus."

"You mean you don't know anymore about it than you did at the start?"

"I didn't say that, but there will always be intangibles that cannot be factored in. In Ackerman's case, she had an existing heart condition that any chemical shock would have triggered. I doubt if she had very long to live to start with, but we didn't know this."

You mean the woman was about to croak on her own?" Earle thundered. "How the hell…"

The President's face was getting red, but he didn't speak. The only other indication of his increased agitation was the fingers of his right hand drumming at erratic speeds on the dark mahogany tabletop. Black thoughts occupied his mind of dark, deep dungeons filled with ear-rending screams from those being torn apart on the rack or beaten until the flesh parted from their bones—the legitimate and proper punishments handed down to those who dared question the judgment and authority of their King. He wouldn't have batted an eye when, with just a raising of his hand, these pseudo-holy men were dragged off to similar fates. After all, Machiavelli had argued that a wise prince must use cruel punishments at times to keep his subjects united, and this had been proved true time and again. And time was being wasted with all this questioning, for he would have his way when all was said and done.

Senator Fairmont also didn't speak and hadn't done so since lunch had slipped from light to serious. Instead, he waved his arm for Coleman to get him a refill. He was probably less comfortable than anyone with this game of Goodie's. Oh, he'd been happy enough in the beginning to be part of it, but it had only started with some friendly persuasions, perfectly harmless. Now it was heavy. Things had gone sour, even at home.

After twenty-nine years of marriage, Sue Ann had moved him out, for no reason at all. She hadn't even played fair, catching him with his pants down. There he was just drying off after his morning shower and in she'd walked. *Beaufort, I'm moving you and your belongings into the green guest suite today. You may stay there, if you wish, until I decide what I want to do. For now, however, I want you to leave me alone. We won't talk or see each other anymore than we have to. Now that's all I'm gonna say on the subject right now."* Then out she went.

When he'd gotten some clothes on, he couldn't find her anyplace. Craziest thing! He knew Sue Ann when she meant business, and she meant business. That little jaw of hers was tight and her eyes were sparking. What was it all about? He wasn't even sleeping around now;

besides, all those other women had just been subsidies. He'd never been serious about any of them.

Beau's meanderings were brought back to the table by the sound of an angry presidential voice.

"Look, Gentleman! Dr. Vondergraven's explained to you that no medical records could be found on Sandra Ackerman indicating the severity of her heart problem. It's obvious that she didn't know or had diagnosed herself and was treating herself. What profits this conversation anyway? The situation cannot be reversed. Besides, we wanted to neutralize the Foundation, and her death has done just that. Also, we've effectively used her death to void her work. It's unfortunate that she died, but all in all, we've accomplished what we set out to do. We've always agreed that women are totally unpredictable and irresponsible. Has that changed? Hasn't our goal always been to remove women from places of authority so that we can keep this world in proper order? Has that changed? If so, tell me! If not, could we stop this wringing of hands and get down to business?"

Beau nodded his head in agreement on one point; women were certainly unpredictable.

"The point is…, " the Cardinal blustered.

"The point is Sarah Winthrop," the President interrupted. "The longer she keeps calling attention to the Foundation, the longer it'll live, and the longer before any of us can rest in peace over Ackerman's unfortunate demise."

Palmer Forbes was angry, really angry, maybe as angry as he'd been with his wife that morning, but he had control of it this time. One of his greatest strengths was that he never allowed his personal feelings to interfere with business. Politicians had to have thick skins. He hadn't gotten where he was losing his cool.

There he sat, his white knuckles on the tabletop, an outward manifestation of his inward condition. They were large knuckles on large hands attached to long arms. Forbes was tall, over 6'2", and lanky. An admiring writer had once described him as *Lincolnesque in stature*, referring also to an esoteric analogy. Literally, however, the comparison wasn't too far-fetched if you decapitated him, but from the neck up he was a total contrast.

Where Lincoln had dark, straight hair, Forbes had sandy with a gentle curl; where Lincoln had dark, heavy eyebrows, Forbes had light-brown and light-textured; where Lincoln had a long, craggy face, Forbes had a round soft one. In fact, Forbes was pretty, almost too pretty as has been said of many whose features have taken on those admired attributes often used in describing the more delicate other sex. His face was hairless; in fact, shaving was just a weekly sometimes stretched to a ten-day ritual, a condition to be envied by most men. Also to be envied was the superior condition of his skin that the lack of prickly hairs and abusive prods of the razor had left soft and youthful. He had those boyish qualities that most women want to mother, sitting on a frame that gained him dignity and stature. Obviously, this was a winning combination when even the Cardinal and the Judge were hesitant to push it too far.

"Now, Mr. President," the Cardinal placated, recognizing that previous tactics needed to be modified if any compromise were to be reached, "you've had time to digest the information Dr. Vondergraven's just presented; we haven't. Surely, you agree that we should consider all possible aspects of past deeds in order to improve our operation. Our communal goal remains the same, only after Ackerman, I feel a great urgency for caution."

"Well, I'm all for that," Walker chimed. "Winthrop's the biggest fish we've ever tried to fry. If we go after her, I want to be absolutely sure we'll be successful."

"And how do you propose to be absolutely sure?" Each word of the Cardinal's question dripped with sarcasm.

Earle's reply, if he had one, cannot be recorded since the Commander-in-Chief was determined that no more idle chatter, inane sparring, or nonsensical questioning would be allowed at his table. He'd been more than patient with his confederates, but sometimes he wondered why he bothered with them at all. He did all the major things in this little venture, and he took all the major risks. He'd hand-picked the highly secret governmental task force that did their bidding; he'd employed Claude Vondergraven and secured the funds for him to develop his serum; he'd conspired to get Vondergraven accepted at the Foundation; and he'd always planned the meetings, furnished the food, the transportation, even this highly secret meeting place.

Yes, the Bunker was another of his inspirations. Nestled deep in the Alleghenies in the western part of Maryland, it was obscured from civilization. It had been secretly built not far from Camp David, during the Eisenhower Administration, and was intended as a shelter for the First Family and as command headquarters in case of a nuclear attack. All but forgotten through the preceding administrations, Forbes had seen its possibilities. Naturally, he'd had to do some updating, and he had done it gradually and discreetly over the past four years. It had, however, been surprisingly modern considering when it was built, and it was large, large enough to function as a strategic headquarters and to house key personnel.

He liked to slip off when he visited Camp David and play with the mapping and radar screens in the huge two level war room. That's where they were now, the War Room. Very few knew that everything still functioned. He'd even had some sophisticated war games installed in the computers. Closed off in his isolated fortress, he held the fate of the world in his hands. His palms would sweat as he watched the blinking lights on the radar screens as the enemy came closer. He had to act, and he did without hesitation. If only the world could see his military prowess, his decisiveness at the helm. He'd have been a great war president.

Sometimes he brought discreet members of his administration to play with him, but he had just as much fun by himself. He didn't need others involved in his games to enjoy them—never had, and he didn't need these churchmen if they were going to be difficult.

"You know that I've asked you here to reach some decisions regarding Sarah Winthrop. I've always considered her the greatest threat to our work. You know where I stand, where I've always stood, but you've consistently vacillated when asked to agree to firm steps where she's concerned. Now, you can see how right I've been. She's powerful. When she speaks, she gets big media coverage. Her latest diatribe wasn't the first to call attention to the Foundation, but it was by far the most blatant and the most devious. No, she didn't mention Ackerman or her work. What she did was far worse, for she dramatized the need for research and emphasized the Foundation as the only place doing it, giving it unwarranted importance. That emotional appeal of hers is bringing all sorts of support to the place. Isn't that right, Doctor?"

"Yes, donations started coming in right after she spoke. Also, several women's magazines and a talk show had called before I left requesting interviews."

"You see? What did I tell you? She's a sly one, all right. The longer we let her go, the harder it's going to be to shut down that pet project of my mother's, and I will shut it down, believe me! Why, she even pulled my name in, calling attention to my biological connection. Hardly fair since I've never supported the thing. I only got involved after my mother's death and only then to get control. She's going to ruin all my efforts, and I'll not have it!"

With this final declaration, Palmer Forbes slammed his large ashen fist down on the hard table, causing everyone to take note of his angry red face as an effective reverberation resounded in the round room.

Cardinal Bishop was no fool; he knew further stalling would be useless. At this point, an objection might cause him to be on the outside; he didn't want that. His only concern now was to make sure the outcome of this meeting was decided rationally, and that was going to be tough enough with the President in his present condition and that fool Walker who was never rational.

"I agree, Mr. President, you've been right all along. Something will have to be done. For the life of me, I can't understand why she's developed such a thing for the Foundation. I know her mother left a sizable endowment to it, and Winthrop's the administrator of that endowment, but her obsessive interest is most peculiar."

"She's crazy, that's why, just plain crazy!" Earle's uncalled for and illogical response awarded him a look of unmitigated contempt from his soulful rival.

The President, however, agreed, adding, "The fact that Winthrop's mother was a generous benefactor must have something to do with Lady Sarah's dedication, and as you know, her mother was as crazy as a loon, lived alone in that big old house in Boston, never went out, never saw anybody. Thank God, my mother never got her mother on the board. Can you imagine what a mess that would've been?"

Taking a deep breath, Forbes continued.

"However, the reason for her attachment to the Foundation is irrelevant. She's trouble in everything she does. She's already trying to get more women involved with her. With that devious mind of hers, she could start putting some things together, and we can't have that now, can we? We must stop fooling around and attack her directly. Now let's make our plans so that we can call it a day."

Senator Fairmont did not break his silence throughout the planning stage. He'd remember later that he had felt an immense affection that afternoon toward bourbon and its solicitous nature. He'd known before he came today that any objections would be useless, and he knew that Winthrop had been asking for it for a long time. Teasing Goodie about Winthrop was one of his sadistic little pleasures, but he'd never wanted to hurt her. Besides, Winthrop was a challenge on the Hill. He respected her, and she and Sue Ann were friends. This was getting too close to home.

As for Palmer Forbes, he was pleased when the meeting ended, confident that their plans would run smoothly and would be successful. It'd turned out to be a pretty good day after all, he considered, as he waited for Coleman to fetch him an antihistamine. He'd never had such an itchy nose.

CHAPTER SIX

THE EVANGELIST

As his super supersonic rushed him to California, Earle Walker stretched out in the familiar and comfortable seat. He was hyper—always was after those meetings, partially because he was never quite comfortable at them, but Earle would never have admitted that, even to himself.

He took a sip of the cold Perrier with its twist of lemon, which he'd been balancing on the armrest, and activated his thoughts. He'd put the screws to Lady Sarah tonight, and he was pleased to be the first step in her imminent misfortune. What a coup! When she fell, the whole world would look back on tonight and remember his words, more proof that God spoke through him. With this he put down his drink, stretched and allowed his thoughts to turn backward and home.

Judgment Earle Salvation Walker was born in a small town in southwest Texas called Make-Up-Your-Mind. Story goes that some West Virginia miners packed up their families and took off to mine gold instead of coal during the California gold rush. They were ill-prepared and their leader, Tom Turner, got lost hunting for short-cuts more often than he got it right. Finally, they arrived at this spot up from the Rio Grande that looked quite green considering the barren waste they'd just been through. They were tired and disillusioned. Somehow gold didn't have the hypnotic ring it'd had when they had started out. Turner looked around and said he didn't believe any of them were ready to go back through those awful dust storms, west and north didn't look any better and below was Mexico. They sure didn't want to go there. He decided that they'd stay where they were until he could make-up-his-mind.

Everyday, their leader would climb one of the tallest of those big dry hills and look around; everyday, he'd come down shaking his head and wearing a frown. While his people awaited his decision, they built homes, a school, a church, a general store, and then a saloon opened. With it came a pretty little Mexican singer named Margarita, and old Tom stopped climbing the hill. He had made-up-his-mind.

By the time Little Earle came along, the town had a population of just under 3,000 plus a few who were resting awhile before they moved on. His father was the town barber, and both his parents were stalwart members of the community, Baptist and Democrat.

Morgan and Thelma Walker had spent much of their twenty years of marriage praying for and trying to produce an offspring. About the time that they had about given up and Thelma was about to dry-up, along came Earle. A miracle! At least that's what his father thought; his mother wasn't so sure.

Earle showed unusual talents quite early, talents his father called brilliant but his mother called no-good. By six, he had the remarkable ability to convince playmates that their prized possessions should be entrusted to his care. This was all right as long as those items were pet rocks, lizards and other things of little value; however, when expensive items like train sets, bicycles, and stereos began to show up in Little Earle's possession, something had to be done.

His mother demanded that he be whipped, insisting that the rod had been spared too long. His father couldn't see what all the fuss was about. "God, Thelma, don't you see what we've got here? The boy's brilliant. He'll be a rich and powerful man someday, mark my word. Why, he could be the greatest salesman in the whole state of Texas, even a lawyer, even Governor!"

His mother's expression did not change. Her blue-gray eyes crackled with ice as she reached for her yardstick and proceeded to break it across Earle's backside. The pain went straight to his gut and there it festered. He was eight years old.

Earle had his mother's eyes. During those early years, Thelma Walker was able to control her son with her pair, but each year it got harder. More and more often, those two pairs of eyes would lock and seemingly move some invisible barrier back and forth from her space to his space like two men arm wrestling. The confrontations became longer, and finally, when Earle was twelve, he won. He remembered it well. As for his mother, she sort of dried up after that from the inside out. Soon, she wasn't.

Rarely had a day passed that Earle Walker hadn't thought about the day he'd looked his mother down. God, how he hated her; even though she'd been in her grave nearly thirty years. She'd never trusted him, never believed in him, always stood in his way, or tried to. But he'd shown her, and he'd shown her that day because it was God's will. When you come right down to it, he smirked, his confrontation with his mother was the least significant thing that had happened to him that day, his own private little bonus.

He'd had a premonition when he woke up that Sunday morning that something big was going to happen. The feeling was stronger by the time he and his parents left for the big tent revival meeting held once a year out by Turner Hill. It was later in the day just as Saving Sammy was about to administer a little healing charge to Old Joe Clausen's bum knee that it happened. Without warning, a dust storm like you wouldn't believe hit the campground. The tent flapped and rose as the stakes loosened; chairs blew over and around, and people fell in clusters and mounds seeking protection.

The storm left as quickly as it had come, leaving behind some smaller dust covered hills like Turner's big one filled with people and things. They never found the tent or Old Joe Clausen, for that matter, but when the dust had cleared and was cleared from everybody's eyes, Behold! Right on top of Turner Hill, arms outstretched, holding a Bible, stood Earle.

Those who were there that day said there wasn't a speck of dust on him. Some even said they saw a pale glow around him, and others remembered other things. No one is quite sure now exactly what happened, but everybody agreed with Saving Sammy who immediately pronounced it a miracle. Earle Walker was God's chosen and God had encased him in a spiritual armor more real than that of God's holy crusaders of old. Through it all, Earle just stood there, holding out his Bible.

To witnesses that day and to his followers to this day, it's a story greater than Moses on the mountain, Daniel in the lion's den, Jonah in the whale, even Jesus in the desert. To Thelma Walker, it was the beginning of her end, for the harder she tried to get at the truth, the weaker she got. She never knew what happened, but there was one thing she always knew for sure—God had nothing to do with it. And to Earle, well, it was the day he got it all together.

He has told the story with charismatic eloquence many times in many versions until he probably doesn't know himself what really happened—if he ever did.

And today, as he sped toward Los Angeles, it was much in his mind, for today was her birthday, and he always had a big meeting on her birthday. It was also Harlan's birthday, another thing that bothered him about the man.

Maybe a little nap before tonight's show, Earle Walker considered, as his private helicopter whisked him from the L. A. airport to Eternal City. He'd made good time.

Moments later, the craft hung quietly atop the sprawling California community. This ordained pause was a standing order, for when Judge Earle returned home from his many duties, he enjoyed casting those cool blue eyes over his kingdom. Master of all he surveyed! He had built it from nothing, this desert oasis, and it, and everything in it, belonged to him.

He wasn't the first religious leader to establish his own kingdom here on earth, but he was the smartest. The others had been too soft. You had to organize and control; that's where the power was. It was easy, and much simpler than what those Catholics did with all that conscience nonsense.

The helicopter hovered in anticipation of the slightest gesture from its master, but Walker lingered. He knew they were directly over the great domed church, *The Father's Church,* which he had made sure was a foot larger all around than St. Peter's in Rome. Toward the south sat the monstrous religious theme park, the Garden of Paradise, and behind him were the condos and bandbox-size single homes that housed those fortunate enough to have acquired permanent residency. They stayed filled as did his two large hotels, The Tower of Babel and Jericho, for the Eternists' idea of eternal life, here on earth, that is, was to live in Eternal City. Far to the east, he could see there was already activity at Eternal Stadium where he would speak tonight. He smiled as his nod launched the plane's gentle descent.

"Don't just stand there, Carolyn. Come in and close the door." The voice oozed with sickening sweetness.

Carolyn Walker did as she was told but did not move further. Instead, she stood quietly in the darkened room, waiting as her eyes gradually adjusted to reveal the shadowy outline of the voice's source.

She hated this room, secretly calling it the *devil's den*. She hated the man it belonged to, too.

The silence was far more deadly than speech, and she was well aware of what it often meant. She quickly explained that she hadn't intended to upset him.

"I thought you'd come with Harlan directly to his surprise party. I planned to meet you there. I thought I was doing the right thing, after all, Harlan's been with us from the beginning, uh, I wish you could have seen him; Earle. He was so pleased. It's his fiftieth, you know. No one ever pays much attention to his birthday since it's also your mother's. But this time, his fiftieth, I thought…"

"Shut up, Carolyn, and come here," his voice interrupted as it reached around her.

"Please, Earle," she pleaded, as she instinctively stepped back toward the door. She wondered if she dare attempt to flee, but the thought was violently thrust from her head as he quickly breached the distance between them to ram the whole of his body into her with powerful force. Slammed against the heavy oak door, his hard body held her pinned. She hurt all over; in fact, she had no doubt that if he stood back, she would crumble to the floor, her bones now no more than flimsy fitted pieces of a jigsaw puzzle. He brought the rough cowhide belt over her head and around her neck. Its feel was familiar.

"I've told you not to think. I've told you to do what you're told. Now, what've I told you that you must always do?"

Walker's voice was cold and controlled, as he spoke, holding the belt tighter.

She answered with difficulty, "Be here when you get home."

"There," he purred, nastily, as he loosened the belt ever so slightly, "you knew all along what a good little wife was supposed to do, but you disobeyed me. You know I can't allow that."

His body remained formidable and silent against her. He had perfect control. Even that hurtful part, which could swell to sizes that made her feel as if she'd surely be ripped apart, only did so at his bidding. He was getting it ready now, for the thing was rising and swelling against her, already bullying her. She waited.

"Now, you know what I must do. Take off your clothes," he said in a matter-of-fact tone, giving her room to maneuver her hands while at the same time pressing the instrument of his finale closer. It was always the last thing he did.

"No," she responded firmly. After all, whatever was going to happen would happen anyway. She'd not help him, no more.

He ordered her again, his tone only slightly shriller.

"No," she replied again, her tone ever so slightly stronger.

"I told this Jew Bitch I fucked last night that you always did what you were told. Oh, well, Jesus gave Peter three chances. Do you deny me a third time, bitch!"

"I deny you a hundred times!" she answered, forcefully.

Earle responded quickly, but so did Carolyn. As he relaxed his hold so that he could rip off her blouse, she managed to push him off balance and make a dash for their connecting bedroom door. Even though, he captured her fleeing wrist and spun her around, she came swinging, hitting him hard and full on the face. It was only by a nose, as the expression goes, that the contest was decided. For Earle Walker's powerful hand hit his wife's jaw just a split second before her foot would have made contact with his groin. One can only wonder at what might have happened if Carolyn had gotten there first. What trauma would Earle have experienced with such a jolt to his manhood? In fact, how would the world have reacted to a neutered Earle? But this is only fruitless conjecture. Carolyn had put up a good fight, but she could fight no more.

With all the energy she had left, she prayed. She prayed intently through the cowhide belt's brutal assault, and she prayed more intently through her husband's painful finale. She didn't stop praying until he laid her unkindly on her own bed, and then she paused only to whisper, "I'll be avenged," she promised. "God will punish you."

"And what're you gonna have God do, Carolyn," he chuckled, "turn me into a block of salt?"

Walker turned to leave, but then turned back when he reached their connecting door.

"By the way, Carolyn, I'll excuse you from my mother's birthday celebration tonight. After all, you've already celebrated *one* birthday today. I trust it was worth it."

As Earle closed the door behind him, Carolyn whispered fiercely, "Vengeance is mine, saith the Lord!"

The lights dimmed and a hush fell on the throngs that overflowed the great stadium in Southern California. Emotions were already soaring, effectively primed by thirty-three musicians and ninety-nine singers. The expectant crowd had been skillfully brought from a rousing participation in hand clapping and hallelujahs to the point where hardly a dry eye remained. Now, except for an occasional nervous cough, all was hushed as a dim spot followed the lone, solemn figure across to the podium.

Soft lights gently rose to illuminate a stage banked with flowers and strategically placed potted palms highlighted by a giant cross in the center back. A perfect setting for the elegant figure clad in a Gucci black silk suit and black snakeskin shoes handcrafted by an Italian artisan called simply Leonardo. The only hint of gaudiness was a large diamond which, enlivened by the lights, danced on the wearer's right pinkie.

Earle Walker silently surveyed his audience. "Thank you, Lord," he said quietly, "there'll be a big haul tonight. I'll see to that."

In a soft but resonant voice he began. "My dearly beloved in Christ, I'm compelled tonight to speak of myself. Most of you've heard it all before, and for that I beg your indulgence. Tonight, you see, I'm filled with many memories, so many happy ones that are now tinged with sadness, for today's the birthday of my dear, departed mother."

Even though most of them knew this, a gasp of sympathy and anticipation ran through the congregated.

Earle's voice quivered, "How I miss the love and inspiration of that saintly woman. What can replace a mother's love?"

'Amen' could be heard from various points around him.

"Yes, my friends," His voice began to rise, and he began to pace back and forth like a caged tiger. "I speak of Mother. M-O-T-H-E-R! NOT THOSE WOMEN WHO DUMP THEIR CHILDREN ANYPLACE THEY CAN TO PURSUE CAREERS. NOT THOSE WOMEN WHO DUMP THEIR CHILDREN ANYPLACE THEY CAN TO PURSUE THE ALMIGHTY DOLLAR. NOT THOSE WOMEN WHO SPEND TIME AT COUNTRY CLUBS, SPAS AND BEAUTY PARLORS CONSUMED BY THEIR VANITY, AND—!"

Judge Earle's charge ended so abruptly that the intakes of breaths by his faithful made a cynical observer wonder if the Santa Ana winds which blew these canyons without warning had just decided to pay a visit.

Walking slowly to the front of the stage, Walker placed himself so that he'd be perfectly centered in the TV cameras which flashed his larger-than-life image to four enormous screens high around Eternal Stadium. The agony was unbearable as, surrounded by Earle, the listeners hung.

When he again spoke, his voice was cold and deliberate, filled with disdain. "And not those women who involve themselves in public service like Congresswoman Tyler, from this very state, whose son was picked up on drug charges last week. Where was she when her son needed her?"

The 'amens' now like gentle waves began to ripple through the sea of devouts.

"And not those women like the eminent Senator from Massachusetts, Sarah Winthrop Baynes, who cloaks her desire for fame and power under the guise of helping the less fortunate, which is most of us."

The intimacy with which he had ended his slanderous accusations had made his listeners co-conspirators. It was an effective ploy that had never failed him. He was good at it, and soon he'd have them just where he wanted them.

"Lady Sarah and Women's Rights...hmm, Women's Rights? The way I understand it, that means the same rights as men. Now does that make sense? God didn't make 'em like men." He chuckled. "I think we all know that."

That had done it; he was content now; the rest would be a piece of cake.

"Oh, I have malefactors and critics, even in this very congregation, who'd call me male chauvinist pig and worse!"

From the sea of revived humanity came tidal waves of denial.

"No, it's true, but that's all right because I know from whence it comes. I've fought the forces of evil too long, since that day on the mountain when I was only twelve years old and God came to me. He told me it wasn't gonna be easy. He told me there'd be those whose hearts were made of stone, unmoved by His word and unmovable. But, you *know*, you who have been born again in Christ, you know that I only speak God's word."

There was silence as Earle slowly walked to the podium, which held a large, gold Bible.

"Read with me, if you will." he said calmly to his Bible wielding congregation. "Genesis, the first book, the beginning, Chapter 3: Verse 16." He waited for everyone to catch up, then he read.

> To the woman he said: I will multiply thy sorrows, and
> thy conceptions. In sorrow shalt thou bring forth
> children, and thou shalt be under thy husband's power,
> and he shall have dominion over thee.

"There it is, not my word, God's word! No, it's not easy! It's not easy to follow the word of God, but we must remember that this world wasn't meant to be easy. He told us it wouldn't be easy. It's a valley of sorrow, our trial, the place we prepare for our judgment day, and we must be strong. We must obey God's word, and it'll keep us strong. Praise the Lord! Keep your Bible by your side, my friends in Christ, for the devil's all around us, and anyone or anything that tries to keep us from doing God's will has been SENT BY THE DEVIL. PRAISE THE LORD!"

"AND SENATOR SARAH WINTHROP AND HER WOMEN'S RIGHTS...? Well, if she's gettin' in the way of us doin' God's word, then she can only be one thing—the handmaid of the devil. YES, BROTHERS AND SISTERS, SHE'S THE HANDMAID OF THE DEVIL, AND WE CAST HER OUT! JUST AS WE CAST OUT THE DEVIL! PRAISE THE LORD!"

By this time, Judge Earle had stripped down to the bare essentials. His pretty silk jacket had been thrown back to the top of the piano; his tie was still sort of on but it was loosened and askew of the open collar; his shirt sleeves were rolled up, and there was no question that this was serious business. He was working so hard that there didn't seem to be a dry spot on him. A steady stream of water poured from his head to be caught in front by those heavy brows which laden to capacity appeared doubled, giving him a diabolical look. In fact, with those watertight eyebrows and a head flattened from its wetness on the top but sticking up on the sides, he looked strangely like the old Beelzebub he was always trying to cast out.

Not, however, to the frenzied faithful. At this point, he could've told them to jump off the Garden of Eden monorail and not a one would have hesitated. That is, if a mesmerized chant of *Cast her out!* coupled with *Praise the Lord!* can be taken as any indication of their fervor. In fact, it even took Earle nearly twenty-seven minutes before he got them settled down enough so that he could continue. In the meantime, the band played, the singers sang, and Earle's twelve apostles and their Blue Blazered helpers weaved their way through the tumultuous throng tendering an offering basket in one hand and comfort in the other.

During this forced but anticipated interlude, the television cameras switched to a pre-recorded plea by Earle's wife, Carolyn, for worldwide support of his ministry. This was followed by a presentation of gifts from the ministry's gift shops which sold everything from bookmarks with Earle's face to a gold pendant, shaped like a cross and topped off by a tiny Earle in relief at its side. This was the hot item, at present, and came in many price ranges. The better ones began at one hundred dollars for a gold-plated with only a minuscule diamond chip glinting on Earle's pinkie to five thousand for an eighteen carat with diamond chips adorning the message and outlining the cross. Even more elaborate ones could be custom-made.

As Cardinal Bishop watched the Eternists hawk their wares that night, he thought how silly all this religion business could get. Were Catholics any better with their medals, cards, and statues, many sent through the mail unsolicited? Begrudgingly, he acknowledged that his house, in this respect, was decidedly made of glass, albeit stained. Earle Walker, however, was a different story.

He had tuned in because he knew Walker was going to take on Sarah Winthrop tonight. Watching him, you could almost believe that he did have a direct line to God. He *was* convincing, as if he believed every word he was saying himself. Little did Cardinal Bishop know that he'd stumbled on the most important ingredient of Walker's success, for Earle Walker did believe everything he said.

And by the time all the *cast them outs* had subsided enough for Earle to continue, he was getting annoyed that the plain old truth caused such commotion. It'd been a long day, and it was going to be an even longer night because he still had lots to do. Besides, his face hurt where Carolyn had managed to land one. He didn't know what had come over her, but she sure wouldn't try that again. He'd fixed her ass, still…he paused, his core twitching from its sated memory.

"Now, I want you to listen real close to what I have to say because I'd never steer you wrong. You don't have time to worry about Sarah Winthrop. God'll take care of her. In fact, that's what he told me just this afternoon. He said, 'Earle, you have to worry about your people. Warn 'em but leave Sarah Winthrop to me.' That's what He said, and that's what we're gonna do."

"But what we're gonna do here tonight, right now, is dedicate and re-dedicate ourselves to God's word. And it's gonna be extra special because we're gonna do it on my dear mother's birthday. A holy woman, she was. Yes, my friends, she was older like Elizabeth, the mother of John the Baptist, and like her, she'd already given up ever having a child when I came along. My birth was not easy for her, but…."

Earle's voice trailed on, warm and intimate, as he enjoyed the John the Baptist analogy. He'd used it a lot and always on his mother's birthday. He went on to note that, like John's mother, his had also had a vision. A messenger from God had come to his mother in a dream and told her about him, even before she'd been to a doctor. The messenger had told her to name him *Salvation* no matter what anyone said, and she had, just as the good Lord had commanded. (Earl had evidently forgotten that his mother's maiden name had been Sylvester, but why should he remember something so insignificant, when everything he said was the truth.)

"Yes, my friends in Christ, she accepted God's messenger just as she always accepted God's word in the Holy Bible. She never wavered, and this is what you must do, women of the Church Eternal. God's written word tells you that you must *bring forth children and be under thy husband's power, and he shall have dominion over thee*. I'm gonna stay right here all night if I have to, just to make sure I bless your affirmations personally."

It was a long night, almost three a.m., before Earle finished. And to his credit, he never wavered; he was as enthusiastic with the last as he'd been with the first.

The next morning over 20,000 women quit their jobs to stay home with their families. It's hard to say what the number had risen to by week's end.

Meanwhile, back at the ranch, Charlie Baynes was wavering. He'd watched Earle Walker's attack on his wife last night, and he was worried. Walker had mentioned her from time to time in the past, but never had he gone after her so viciously. Why now? Then his son finding that cocaine in his car. Where'd it come from? Who'd tipped off the police? Were they connected? Alma Tyler's son had found drugs in his car. Was that connected? Baynes was a cautious man. Nothing made sense, and until it did, they had to be careful. But Sarah had made that speech the other day...

He wished Sarah would leave Washington. It'd been all right for awhile, but he was getting tired of having a commuter marriage; besides, he had no control long distance if something went wrong. Did he have the right to insist Sarah leave? He knew how important her career was to her. That was one of the things he loved about her—that dander she could work-up over issues, her dedication.

Lot different from Lettie. Lettie's dedication had been to him, him and the kids. They'd never spent a night apart, except when she went to the hospital to have another baby. Six of 'em they'd raised together, and then she'd died, so sudden, only forty-nine. Those next six years had been lonely, even with the kids. Then he'd met Sarah.

He wasn't the kind of man that could live without a woman. Not many men could. Women seemed to get along a lot better without men than men did without women. He needed a full time wife and Sarah wasn't that. In fact, he'd spent more nights alone these past eight years than he'd spent with Sarah. But did he want her here all the time?

She'd been acting real strange lately. Baynes' muddled thoughts were interrupted when his wife walked in from her morning ride.

"Good-morning, dear," Sarah greeted as she bent over to kiss her husband. "It's a beautiful morning. I'll never cease to be amazed by the sounds and smells of mornings here. Everything heavy with dew, capturing the smell of hay mixed with alfalfa and all sorts of botanical specimens indigenous to this area. Then the soft sounds of the cows beginning to wake, stretching like…"

"Sarah, you do have a quaint way with words," her husband interrupted, "and usually just listening to your attempts to describe Texas turns me on, but this morning, we have more serious business to discuss, and you know it. I suspect the oration you were just getting into was actually the beginning of a filibuster."

"I stand guilty as charged, but can't I at least have breakfast before we discuss Earle Walker? He's tough to take on an empty stomach."

"All right, but afterward, you're gonna have to face his venom. I taped it for you."

"I'm not going to watch him. I can't stand the man!" Sarah retorted stiffly, turning pale.

"Yes, you are. His attack on you last night was plain vicious. He's a Texas sidewinder and just as ruthless. He had everyone riled up about you last night. Making you the focus of his diatribe is something new. I don't like it, and I don't think we can ignore it."

"Sticks and stones may break my bones, my dear, but words will never hurt me," Sarah chanted, hoping to tease her way out of what she feared would turn into a corner.

"I'm not sure you're the only bones at stake here," he replied stiffly.

Looking at her husband's concerned, determined face, she capitulated. "Oh, very well, I can see your mind is made up, and I'll get no peace until I listen to the idiot. I've lost my appetite anyway.

Let me get some coffee, and we'll go into the study and watch as Judge Earle passes his judgment on me."

Charlie Baynes ignored the annoyance in his wife's voice just grateful that he'd won the beginning round. There was no moving Sarah once she'd made up her mind, and she had always had her mind made up about Earle Walker. For her to watch him now could only mean that she was wavering too.

He got up and up, filling the room, for Baynes was a big man, over a head taller than his wife and large. Each of his sixty-three years had added girth until now his expansion tended to overwhelm many who could look him in the eye. In cowboy boots, which he always wore, and a ten-gallon hat, he was in size and style a credit to his State. But now, still in robe and slippers, his head of thinning sandy-gray hair framed a face strained with concern, and Baynes filled the room less, as if, stripped of his vestments, he was divested of those parts that contained his essence.

As Sarah Baynes settled down on the big, brown leather sofa and placed her cup on the wagon wheel cocktail table in front of her, Charlie Baynes leaned back beside her and put his feet up. He then flipped the remote that triggered their morning viewing. They didn't speak, and Sarah's coffee got cold.

When Sarah left for Washington Sunday night, she'd promised Charlie that she'd give serious consideration to leaving the Senate. She had never thought she'd do that, resign her responsibility and desert those who depended on her, but Walker and those people chanting *Cast her out!* had dismayed her.

At the Dallas Airport and now on the plane, she found herself looking around to see if anyone was looking at her. Usually, she liked being recognized, but not tonight. This sea of strangers became a sea of enemies. She could hear their silence; its cadence pulsated through her again and again, repeating over and over, *Cast her out! Cast her out! Cast her out!* She was afraid. She was also afraid of losing Charlie.

Charlie was worried about his kids; she was too. She'd never forgive herself if something happened to one of them because of her. Charlie would never forgive her either, and she knew he was getting weary of their long-distanced marriage. She couldn't blame him. He deserved a better wife, someone who'd stay with him and take care of him the way Lettie had. He talked of her more and more lately, and she didn't think she did well by comparison.

She was glad she hadn't told Charlie about Stacey Lea and the file; he would really have been upset. What if Stacey Lee confronted Palmer with the file she'd given her? Why did Palmer Forbes hate her so much? And Walker? What had she done to them? If she didn't know better, she might think they were working together, but they were a totally unlikely twosome.

With these two powerful men against her, she felt vulnerable. Maybe her mother had been right, just stay in Boston and let the rest of the world go by. It was beginning to appeal to her more and more.

Little did Sarah know as the plane took her swiftly back to the nation's capital that it really didn't matter what she decided or what she'd promised Charlie. Her world had spun out of her control.

CHAPTER SEVEN

MISSISSIPPI MUD ♦ ♦ ♦

Stacey Lea reined her horse at the Cliff to study the tall figure looking out over the water. The intruder disturbed her. She instinctively pulled the reins for a quick get-away, but it was too late; he'd already turned. Her hands were clammy as they tightened on the riding crop, more to steady herself than to defend.

"You're trespassin', sir. This is Culberson land, and that's a Culberson view."

Even as she spoke, he'd started walking toward her, taking in every bit from her faded jeans and scuffed boots to her well-worn suede jacket and mussed hair. Still without speaking, he helped her down and at the same time drew her close.

"If you were my woman, I wouldn't let you out of my sight."

Flippantly she replied, "I always thought I was." With this Stacey Lea stopped thinking, threw her arms around his neck and melded herself closer into him as his mouth reached into hers.

They were that way a long time. When they parted, both aware they needed a moment, he took Prissy over to tether at a bush near his own horse, and she took her turn looking out over the water.

While returning, he chided, "You're late, Stace. I've been here since sunrise."

"You bastard! It took some illogical thinkin' to come at all. Besides, one of the first lessons I learned in bein' a lady was not to appear too eager."

They settled down on a bench in front of the octagonal gazebo they'd met at so frequently since they were children. It stood on a Mississippi River phenomenon, Culberson Cliff, which rose almost eighty feet above the river but tapered back to its more natural bank less than fifty feet either way. Before the War Between the States, the Culberson's had maintained an American flag here, then a Confederate one, as a promise to boatmen that they'd soon be in Natchez. A shelter, now a fancy gazebo, had been added about the same time and lots of stories could be told about the spying that went on and the important messages that were sent from Culberson Cliff.

"Sorry 'bout your wife."

"Yes, she suffered bad."

"Were you happy?"

"Yes," he again affirmed but not with the same conviction.

"Did you ever think of me?" Her question was almost child-like and completely void of guile, a matter-of-fact kind of question by one fairly sure of the answer or at least sure of not being hurt.

"You know I did."

"No, but I always hoped you did, and that it…. Did you ever think of the night we, uh, the night of your Daddy's funeral?"

"Yes, and the last time too, the time I came back with Emilie."

"God! How you hurt me, Forrest. You broke my heart. I shut it up after that 'cause nobody was ever gonna do that to me again. It hurt too much."

"I'm sorry. I didn't know."

"You didn't want to know."

"Christ sakes, Stace! I was going on thirty and…"

"You were twenty-eight."

"And you were fresh out of high school. I remember when you were born."

"And I remember the first time you shaved, and no one could tell. What does that matter?"

She'd had the last word and there was silence. A barge had almost disappeared down-river before he responded.

"It scared the hell out of me. The passion between us that night came from nowhere."

"It was always there. You just never recognized it or allowed yourself to." She was up now, looking away.

"Well, I couldn't handle it. Christ, I'd always been like your big brother. It seemed sinful."

She twirled around. "Not to me, not ever to me!" she avowed.

"Well, it was to me; it was too sudden. I had too many feelings on me then, and I couldn't reconcile 'em, so I ran." Was it her or the memory of it all that was making him feel defensive?

"Just like that. You were a fool, Forrest Thornton, and a coward too. I'd have made you so happy. We could've made beautiful babies, raised cotton and horses, stayed right here where we both belong, combined our lands…grown old together." She paused, the emotion spent except for a deep sigh as she sat again, looking around. "I've always loved this place, but it's unsettlin' here since Momma died. Sometimes I find myself resentin' Momma choosin' here, spoilin' it for me. Isn't that awful?"

"No," he assured. "I know what you mean."

Stacey Lea went on, encouraged by his support. "You know," she glanced back, "we found her horse just where you put mine. I've reconstructed it so many times. I know exactly what she did. Did you know it's exactly forty-one steps from the horse to the edge? I know she took them calmly, never stopping, just took that forty-second one right off. We couldn't find her."

Stacey Lea had gotten up again and was walking toward the edge. The river flowed gently below, a dark spot edging the rocky cliff, an ominous indication of its murky depth.

"Finally, three days later Big Muddy just spit her up no more than thirty feet from where she jumped, still on Culberson land."

"Stace, goddammit, move away from there!"

"I'm all right. Do you think her spirit's still here?"

"I don't believe in such things."

"I don't know. I've heard that restless spirits stay where they left 'til they satisfy nature. Momma didn't even leave a note; she didn't even say good-by. That's unnatural."

"I'm not surprised. Your mother was always high-strung, and she was getting strange before I left. I wondered what Travis' death would do to her."

"She never was able to handle that."

"He was hers."

"But so was I. Do you think I could get like that?"

"No, you're like your father. You're strong."

She hesitated before replying, "I hope so. I have need to be, especially now."

Before he could question her, she rushed on. "I've tried lots of times to conjure her up." Stacey Lea went closer to the edge, spread her arms out and delivered an incantation. "Virginia Leanne Stacey Culberson, I call you. This is your blood, your daughter. Please, Momma, I want to help you find peace."

After a pause, she turned to find Forrest close behind her, finding it difficult to find peace with her so near the edge. She looked at him. "One time I felt this freezing chill—in mid-summer, and I knew she was comin', but it just swept through me and was gone. Do you think…?"

"I think," he interrupted as he pulled her back, "that you're gonna get us both killed."

"What happened to the romantic in you?" Her mood teased as she moved away. "I can see the headlines now, *First Lady and Childhood Lover Plunge to a Muddy Mississippi Death.* Juicy? Why, we'd pleasure the world's readin' for years. All the sordid details would come out until we finally mellowed into one of those great lover pairs like Abelard and Heloise. No, more like Tristan and Isolde or Romeo and Juliet, mostly fiction." She was getting into it now, but he wasn't playing.

"What's got you so bothered?"

His response quieted her. God, she thought, how well he knew her, even after nearly thirty years. Stacey Lea put her hand up and touched the side of his face lightly as she looked long into his eyes. "You've weathered well, Forrest, just as I knew you would, like fine leather."

"And you haven't changed at all, just all woman now. I was afraid you might've turned into that perfect First Lady the rest of the world knows. Palmer's *little woman* always standing sort of behind him like he's king. Thank God, you're still here."

"But I'm not. This is the fantasy, the other, that's the real me now." With that, Stacey Lea pulled herself back into her proper place and started walking toward her horse. He went to help her on.

"Tomorrow morning?" he suggested.

"No, no more. You know, Forrest darling, I should hate you for denying me, and I did, for awhile, but I think I always knew that it was what you had to do and that I had something else to do. I can't say it's what I want, but I'm sure now that I'm where I'm suppose to be, and whatever I have to do, I'm gonna be able to do it. Thanks for that." She leaned down and kissed him on the forehead before she left.

His frown followed her, not understanding a bit of it.

"Here, Mista Wylie, you put this blanket 'round your legs. There's a real chill in the air this mornin', and you could catch your death 'fore Stacey Lea gets back from her ride. No tellin' how long she's gonna be gone. Won't you at least come inside?"

"No, I'll wait here. I didn't see anything of her after she got home yesterday, with her in that tree so long and then in her room the rest of the time. I'm gonna at least make her sit and eat breakfast with me. I'll have a little more of that great coffee of yours while I'm waitin' though?"

"No, you don't. You know what the doctor said. I'll let you have a little more with your breakfast, but that's it. I sliced into that big ham Preston brought home from Kentucky his last trip. Tastes real good, and I made red-eye gravy and hot biscuits. Those biscuits are already having trouble stayin' hot. Stacey Lea probably won't eat much anyway. The mood she's in this time, she may not eat at all."

"Yes, she will. I'll see to that."

Annie Burnham gave a sigh and shrugged her shoulders as she went back into the house. She'd known before she went out that it would do no good. She supposed Stacey Lea was going to see Forrest Thornton, and she knew Mister Wylie thought so too. Sad, that hadn't worked out. Well, there'd been enough crying over that spilt milk. Funny how someone goes away for a long time, and when they come back, all the memories and all the feelings that you thought you'd gotten rid of were just tucked away someplace waiting to come back too. She'd seen the truth of that in the look on Stacey Lea's face when her daddy had told her Forrest was home to stay. Poor baby, that on top of whatever was frettin' her so much now.

She loved Mister Wylie and Stacey Lea. All she'd ever wanted to do was stay here and take care of them. She didn't think her children would ever understand how she felt, but she didn't care; it was her life. They'd had it pretty good, anyway. All four of them had gone to college, and Mister Wylie had paid and was still paying for Clifford. He'd insisted she go too, but she'd hated it. Oak Cliff Plantation, the Culbersons, and horses were her only passions then, so Mister Wylie had finally given in. He'd said that once she'd learned something about something, he'd let her come home. So he'd sent her to Kentucky to learn all about good horseflesh. That's where she'd met her other passion—Preston—and then she hadn't bothered to learn much more about horses. She didn't have to with Preston knowing so much.

Annie smiled, daydreaming about her husband. He still made her feel all light and giddy, even after thirty years together. Stacey Lea said they were this perfect match. That everybody's part of a puzzle that has to find its just right fit. Most people spend their lives restlessly searching, but she and Preston were the lucky ones. They were sure that—a fine home and family, and success.

The three of them, she, Mister Wylie and Preston, had made Oak Cliff Stables one of the best. They were partners, but her kids still thought she wasn't much more than the slave her ancestors had been. They didn't understand that there are some people born on this earth to take care of others and some born to be taken care of. That's it pure and simple, and Mister Wylie and Stacey Lea were her responsibility.

Annie looked out at the old man sitting in the porch rocker. He reminded her more and more of his Papa. He used to sit in that same chair, rocking and waiting. Her mother used to tell her that Mister Wylie Sr. was waiting for the Grim Reaper and that his rocking was his way of trying to reach him quicker. He'd died in that chair. One morning he'd just stopped rocking. Seemed sometimes like his son was trying to do the same thing. Today, however, his rocking had nothing to do with the Grim Reaper. Stacey Lea did that for him.

Wylie Culberson had too much on his mind to meet his Maker today. His girl was home and she had troubles. He'd suspected, when she'd called, that she was coming home more to think than to see him. A few years ago, that might have bothered him, but now that he was declining, it was reassuring to know that she had the place, the river, and her tree to depend on.

The Pondrin' Tree. He looked out at the great live oak that sat on the River side of the house about sixty feet down. Its fine arms, that spread out over thirty feet all around, were hung low with Spanish moss. You always knew the weather was warm and damp when you started seeing Spanish moss, and sitting less than two hundred feet from the warm Mississippi, Stacey Leanne's tree was blanketed with it. Like all its kin, its knobby roots were mostly above ground, and they spread out and up like giant tentacles determined to be as splendid as the branches they fed. His grandfather used to tell him that oak tree roots were the most prideful part of an oak tree. They sat right there above ground to remind everybody that the giant above them was mostly their creation.

He could see her out there playing, and it wasn't his oldness making him see the past. She'd left her childhood there.

"Mista Wylie, Mista Wylie, you come quick! Momma said for me to get you quick!"

Annie had run the nearly half mile to the stables, quite sure that Stacey Lea's life depended on it.

"Slow down, girl. What's wrong?"

"Mizz Virginia, she's out at the tree."

That's all it took to make Wylie Culberson take off so rapidly that his twelve-year old messenger was left still breathless, her story not completely told. He was getting more and more concerned with his wife's rages, especially since they seemed to be directed more and more at their daughter. When he got to the house, he didn't bother parking, just rode right over the grass to the tree. There was already a congregation from the house—his mother and father, Annie's mother and father—but they were standing around helplessly as Virginia's shrill voice was directed toward Stacey Leanne.

"What's this all about?"

"Well, it's about time you got heah," Virginia snapped as she waved a hand in anger at the small girl standing firmly between her and the tree. "I came out heah and very politely asked her to let Travis play with her this afternoon, and she refused. She'd made him leave earlier, and Travis was devastated. Travis has just as much right in that tree as she has. There's no reason for her to be so stubborn. You've got this child spoiled rotten."

Stacey Leanne's stance was pure defiance. With her feet firmly planted, arms folded, and chin high and tight, he knew that he'd have to drag his daughter away before Travis would get into that playhouse. Even though he knew it was wrong, he couldn't help being proud of this eight-year-old seed of his for demanding her rights at any cost. She was his daughter, all right, and Travis was Virginia's son. He looked at the slender little boy clinging to his mother's leg, waiting for her to get his way.

"Travis is five years old, and old enough to find his own place. We've already agreed that this is Stacey Leanne's playhouse, and no one's allowed in unless she invites."

"You agreed, I didn't."

"C'mon now, Ginny. You know Stacey Leanne plays with Travis a lot. Why, I saw them out here this morning."

"That's not the point. The point is she refuses him entrance sometimes, and she has to be asked all the time. She hurts his feelin's. Besides, this time she put him out and says that he can nevah come back."

"Is this true?" Wylie Culberson asked his daughter.

"Yes." Stacey Leanne responded firmly, looking him right in the eye.

"Why?"

"Ask Travis."

"I'm askin' you."

Stacey Leanne did not reply at first, but turned and raised up the mossy curtains that hid the tree's secrets. The contents were in total disarray—her little table and chairs were overturned, some of the dishes were broken, her dress-up clothes were strewn all over the ground, her art work had been pulled-down and torn-up—her much loved playhouse had been vandalized in a most hateful way.

"We were gonna have a tea party, Daddy. Annie was comin', and we were even having little sandwiches—pimento cheese and egg salad with olives. You know how ah love 'em; Travis does too. Annie was helpin' me bring things down, but when we got here, he was breakin' my dishes. What Travis did was wrong, and he'll not come back in evah again. If he does, I'll kill him."

"You see? You see what an ugly, mean child we've got? Why, ah bet she'd do it." Virginia's voice got shriller as she clung tighter to Travis who clung tighter to her.

"Be quiet, Virginia. You know Stacey Leanne doesn't mean that, but how can you take Travis' side when he did such an ugly thing?"

Without waiting for what he knew would be an irrational response, he commanded, "Travis, you tell your sister you're sorry, and then you get in there and clean it all up to her satisfaction. Then, the four of us are gonna sit down and thrash this thing out. Now get busy."

"No! It's my playhouse, and it must be my justice. Travis did it on purpose, and he's not sorry. Ah won't have him tell me he is when he isn't."

Stacey Leanne shook her head resolutely before she leaned toward her brother. Raising her hands to form claws and putting on her scariest face, she threatened, "And you, Travis Samuel Culberson, if ah evah catch you neah my tree again, I'm gonna claw your eyes out and while the blood's spurtin' all over you, I'm gonna drag you down and throw you in Big Muddy. She'll know what to do with you."

The screaming and crying that followed were enough to bring him gratefully back, but it was more the mention of the river. He never could stay long away from Her; She sustained him; Stacey Leanne was the same. Even now, she had the helicopter bring her up-river from

Natchez, so she could breathe in the sights and sounds of Her before she got home.

He looked out at the expansive surface that rippled quietly in the early morning sun. Just like a woman She was, all cool and calm outside but underneath mysterious and unpredictable, full of changing currents and whirlpools that were constantly brewing and boiling. Big Momma spread wide, all wet and warm and waiting. Never could take Her for granted, and many a fool had died trying. A man could sink into Her and never be seen again. That's what he wanted to do, and Stacey Leanne had promised she'd take his ashes to the Cliff and let him go. Wonder if Virginia would be there, as his daughter believed? He'd had a hard enough time living with her in this world; however, if she should be waiting, he'd make his peace; at least, he'd try. Wouldn't be long now, he figured, even though he still cut a pretty good figure.

Wylie Samuel Culberson had good genes and good breeding. His hair was still thick but the color had aged with him to become as white as the magnolias that blossomed all around his patriarchal estate. His back was as ramrod straight as in his youth, his skin firm and lightly tanned, and his blue eyes were lively. All in all, he looked much younger than his eighty-two years, for the only indication of his growing frailty was the cane at his side. This was more by accident than age, but it had idled him considerably and was beginning to take a toll. He'd been almost eighty when his horse had stepped in a rabbit hole and toppled. They'd both been lamed, but the horse had been shot. As Culberson felt the vitality waning with his forced inactivity, he'd often wondered if that wouldn't have been the more humane action for him too.

Culberson had lived a life unique to Southern gentility. The club was small and criteria restrictive. You could be a WASP, wealthy, even famous, but if you couldn't trace your blood back to strong Southern roots, you'd have a better chance of becoming a member of the British Royal family than getting in. In other words, there was only one stipulation for membership—birth. Most Southerners understood this, and life went on very much as it always had, everybody staying about where they belonged. Even the influx of northerners had done little to change the reality of the Deep South. Fact of the matter was, most southerners didn't really like outsiders, especially Yankees. The Great War they'd fought against them was still too deeply rooted in their psyches. Still, they tolerated them and their money, and Yankees kept coming lured by warmer climes, slower paces and Southern hospitality, never catching on to the fact that Southern hospitality was nothing more than a game, a game of manners.

Annie Burnham, holding a mug of steaming coffee, gently nudged Culberson awake, "Well, if you won't come in, I guess I'll have to give you some more coffee just to keep you warm inside. You want a little bourbon with it?"

"No, not on an empty stomach. She won't be much longer now. Why don't you stop fussin' over me and sit down and talk awhile? I was thinkin' about the Tree. Do you remember the day it got named?"

"Like yesterday," Annie responded as she sat down next to him. "It was the day your poor Momma died. Lawd, she suffered so. That last week when we knew she was goin' was a bad time for all of us, but for Stacey Lea… well, she was always huddled in some dark corner never far away from her Granny. Seemed to resent the sun, as if it weren't right for it to shine when there was so much gloom."

"That was tough on her. She worshiped Momma, the only momma she'd really ever had with her own mother favoring Travis so. Then, right after Momma died, she disappeared. You found her, right?"

"Yes, she was so grieved, she wouldn't answer. I'd been out to *The Tree* once, so when I went back, I took a flashlight. I knew she had to be there someplace. She was always out at that tree. I shined the light up."

"Stacey Leanne, what're you doin' up there? You're gonna get yourself killed, besides you got everybody scared to death. Your Daddy don't need to worry 'bout you right now."

"I need to be by myself, and this is the only place I can do that. Tell Daddy, he'll understand. Now go way and leave me be. I've been up here lots of times."

"How old was she then? It's clear to me, but I can't place her age?" Wylie Culberson was enjoying going back. Seemed lately that he spent more and more time there.

"She was ten," stated Annie emphatically. "I remember 'cause I'd just started to high school."

"She was a stubborn one," Culberson chuckled. "I couldn't budge her either, but she was hurtin' so I couldn't get too upset with her. Wonder how long she'd been goin' up that tree?"

"I 'spect at least a couple of years. No one bothered her out there after that big flare-up when Travis broke it up. He never went near that tree again and Mizz Virginia didn't either. Did you know Stacey Lea never fixed that place up after that?"

"What do you mean?"

"Well, she invited me in for tea ever' once in awhile, but it wasn't the same. The play clothes were gone, the dolls were gone, everything was gone but her table and chairs and some books and colorin' things. I think when Travis wrecked her playhouse he sort of wrecked her childhood, and she shut it up."

"She nevah could tolerate injustice."

"No, and no one could ever take advantage of her twice. Besides, ah think he'd spoiled it for childhood things, so she turned it into the place she took growin' up things. She could close those mossy curtains, climb up high off the earth and shut out the world 'til she could deal with it. Still does, and for some unanswerable reason that I've pondered, it seems perfectly natural for Stacey Leanne, a grown woman, even wife of the President of the United States, to climb up in a tree and sit there for hours while she sorts things out. If anyone else did it, we'd send for the white coats."

"You're right, when you put it that way," Wylie Culberson laughed, "but everyone needs a special place where no one else'll intrude. When we don't or don't take the time to sort things out, that's when the white coats have to be called. I used to get in my old motor boat and go up-river to a little inlet. Good catfish there and I'd sit and fish and think. Never took anyone else with me, and if I hadn't had that spot, I might've beat Virginia off the Cliff. Papa first showed it to me. He used to go there, and then when he got too old he'd sit right here, where I am now. Life doesn't seem to change much from one generation to the next."

"I remember him sittin' here."

"Yes, and I remember how it used to fascinate Stacey Lea that no one was allowed to bother Papa when he was ponderin' here" Wylie Culberson's thoughts again drifted back and inward.

"Now, Stacey Leanne, I know how upset you are over your Granny's death, but you had us pretty worried. Besides, you're too little to be climbin' that high. You must've been up near twenty feet. What if you slipped?"

"That's my tree, Daddy. It'd never hurt me. I've been goin' up there for a long time. The limbs are like steps all the way up, and there's a seat big enough for me to curl up into, cozy like a sweet-pea in a pod. The tree made it for me. Come and see."

"It doesn't matter. I'd still worry about you going up there, and why didn't you answer when we were callin'?"

"I was pondrin'."

"You were what?"

"I was pondrin'. Grandpapa sits on the porch in his rocker, and he won't answer, and no one's allowed to bother him 'cause we know he's pondrin'. Well, my place to do my pondrin' is in the tree, and no one can intrude when you're pondrin'. Isn't that right?"

"Mista Wylie, I think I hear Preston's truck. I'll go see."

Annie jumped up and hurried toward the door. It wouldn't take her long to reach the front since the front door was directly opposite the backdoor or vice versa with no impediment. To avoid confusion, they'd forever called the door opening to the Mississippi the River Door and the one to the circular driveway the Other Door. Both entrances were exactly alike, with the same modest Ionic pillars holding up porches that stretched from one end to the other of the great upstairs and overhung to form the roof for the downstairs porches. The foyer separating the two doors was the narrowest part of the house since it was built to function as a breezeway to pick up what little motion might be around on some of the murkiest of Delta days. It also functioned as the most trafficked area since it held the main staircase and separated the cooking and eating from the entertaining and relaxing. Oak Cliff Plantation House was one of the grand and historic remnants of a once too prideful south, and Annie cared for it with the same devotion she had for its proprietors, recognizing that they all shared with the great house an intricate counterpoint going back generations.

"Stacey Lea, your Daddy's been sittin' out on that porch for…"

"Leave me be, Annie, and get your man some hot coffee for bringin' me up from the stable," commanded Stacey Lea as she rushed past her scolder, brushing a kiss on her cheek as she did.

"Daddy, you know better than to sit out here all this time. What'd I do if you got sick and also knowing that it was my fault. I'm truly sorry that I was gone so long." Stacey Lea had reached her arms around the back of the rocker and nestled her cheek against her father's as she spoke. "Now, come on and let's eat. I'm starved, and I'll bet you are too. I'll just take time to wash my hands."

When she reached the kitchen, Annie was already serving breakfast at the heavy oak table that had long served for preparing as well as eating.

"Umm, that smells good!" Stacey Lea announced sniffing the air.

"Ham and Grits, biscuits and gravy—Mississippi heaven must be made of such," Stacey Lea exclaimed. "I feel like a big dunkin' egg this morning, Annie. I'll make it, if you want?"

Annie didn't respond as she walked toward the stove.

Stacey Lea, following her, reached out and tried to pinch Annie's nose. "I'm surprised your nose wasn't snipped off long ago for puttin' it in everybody else's business the way you do!"

Annie dodged as she grabbed a big wooden spoon off the counter and held it threateningly.

"You try that again, and I'll swat you with this, girl, hard too. I've done it before."

"Stop your silliness, both of you!" The humor in her father's voice belied the gruffness of his words, "Now get back over here and sit down, Stacey Leanne. You probably can't cook anymore anyway the way you've been waited on so much these past years. I'd like to eat in peace."

"Then you should've eaten before I got back from my ride," Stacey Lea huffed as she reseated.

"Well?" Annie questioned, turning from the stove with her hands on her ample hips, the spatula still in hand.

"Forrest was waiting for me at the Cliff, just like always."

"That's what I figured," Annie responded, nodding her head in the way one smugly does when one has anticipated the answer.

"God, he's gorgeous! But then, he always was. He's not as tall as Palmer, but he makes you feel he is, takes up more space with those broad shoulders."

"How do you like his beard?"

"It's marvelous, so masculine and very sexy. His hair's thinned enough on top that it's the perfect addition, and those touches of gray are very dignified. What's that beard called, Daddy? I know that cute little one you wear is called a chin-warmer, but...?"

"I suppose most of them could be called chin-warmers," Wylie Culberson laughed. "Mine's a chin-curtain or neck-warmer. I've heard it called a slugger too. Forrest's is Roman. His father wore one. Never realized how much he looked like his father until he grew that beard."

"Here comes a couple of those Secret Service men again," announced Annie, looking out the window. "I think you drive 'em crazy when you're down here and won't allow 'em any closer than that house we had to build for them."

"They aren't supposed to intrude."

"They're only doin' their job," her father chided.

"No, they aren't supposed to bother me when I'm home. You don't know what it's like always being under spyin' eyes." She got up abruptly, pushing her chair back in a frustrated manner. "Now, let me go get rid of my shadows."

Stacey Lea dropped the lacy curtains behind her shutting out most of the light. She stood still for a moment, breathing deeply. The aura of her that was contained in this place never ceased to overwhelm her. She'd left so much here—the tears of a little girl when her grandmother had died and the tears of a young woman when Forrest had denied her. Over there was the sadness she'd suffered when her mother had jumped off the Cliff; next to it were the lingering regrets she'd felt that night Travis was killed in the motorcycle crash.

She guessed everybody had regrets about something they didn't do when it's too late. It always seemed too late for her and Travis. There were a lot of too lates in here. She'd left them in the tree because she couldn't carry all of them around. With a sigh, Stacey Lea began to climb her old friend.

She nestled in, pulling her legs up to her as she closed her eyes and allowed the serenity of her place to flow through her. There were no secrets between them; everything she was, was here. Enveloped in its protective arms, she rested.

She didn't know how long she'd been that way, but her legs were stiff and aching when she abruptly awoke. It was just a dream, a nightmare, she assured herself. Then why was the turbulence of it still here, filling her place and making her feel unwelcome?

Gasping, Stacey Lea scrambled rapidly down the tree and out from its always benevolent curtain that now moved and twisted around her attempting to hold her fast. A storm was brewing but she'd weathered many a one from within its benign embrace. It wasn't the storm that had changed the atmosphere inside the Pondrin' Tree. Disturbed and confused, she dashed toward the consoling lights of her ancestral home.

"Hello, Casey, I thought for a minute there you weren't gonna take my call."

"It's wonderful to hear your voice, Stacey Lea. It's been a long time."

"Yes, it has. I need to see you."

Stacey Lea's tone was brusque.

"I don't see how that's possible right now. We're dreadfully busy at the office, and I…"

"I'm home, and I've made a plane reservation for you for seven a.m. tomorrow on Southern's Flight 103. It's all paid for, and you can pick up your ticket at the airport. You'll be met there by…."

"Hold it a minute. Have you lost your mind? I have no intention of coming to Mississippi tomorrow."

"Let me put it this way, Casey. Either you meet me tomorrow down here secretly, or I'll come into Nashville to see you on my way back to Washington. You know what a hullabaloo my stop-ins cause, all the reporters and such. That's up to you, but one way or the other, I'll see you tomorrow."

There was a long pause before Casey Bartholomew yielded.

After the click, Stacey Lea listened to the empty phone for a few moments before she sighed and dialed her next number.

"Forrest, I need a favor."

Stacey Lea's last call was to Ellie. It was a long call, and by the time they'd finished, shadows had deepened, and Annie was waiting dinner.

The next morning brought rain and an early call from Palmer. His voice was curt.

"Good morning, dear. I expected you to be the one calling and before this, especially after the way you left."

"I don't think the way I left was my fault."

"Let's don't start again."

"I believe you brought it up."

"I've missed you."

"I've missed you, too," she responded, her voice now softer. "It's unsettlin' when we have problems, but we have one where Senator Winthrop's concerned. Your opposition to her frustrates me; it also places me in an awkward position, for you see, I've asked her to be on the Board of WOW."

"You know how I feel about her."

"Yes, but I don't understand why. And she can give my cause a lot of prestige; she can enhance my endeavors. You know, Palmer, you're such a special President that I want to be special too. I believe WOW offers me that opportunity. I want to show that the woman behind the man in the White House can make a difference. I want to do the kinds of things women do best and be an example to other women in the country, even the world."

"You've already done that, Stacey Lea. Everybody praises you as the perfect First Lady."

"Yes, I know. I'm grateful that I've been that for you, but I want to be more. I see in this *Cause* of mine an opportunity to leave something lasting behind when we leave the White House. You helped me find a cause, now, help me perpetuate it? I never could do anything without your help. I do depend on you so."

"All right, Stacey Lea," he relented. "I'll support your cause. I'll even do my best to get an appropriation for WOW. But in return, I want things just like they've always been with us. And I never want you to lock the door between us again."

"I promise. I'm truly sorry about that. I don't know what came over me. You know, my duties to you have always been my A-one top priority. No matter what happens, taking care of you will always come first. I promise."

"Very well. When you get home, we'll see what we can do."

"I'm ever so grateful to you, Palmer, darlin'. Why, I'm surely the luckiest woman in the world!"

"Perhaps when you get home, we can have a nice little dinner, just the two of us?"

"I can hardly wait. I'll come back early, ah promise."

"Until then."

"'Til then, Palmer, darlin'. Oh, and I'm gonna speak to Ellie, and tell her I want a Board Meeting planned for WOW the first of the week. Sarah Winthrop will have to be invited because she's on the Board. You do understand, don't you?"

His mind already moving ahead to the little *tete à tete* he'd be enjoying later with his wife, he didn't even slightly bristle at the second mention of his adversary's name.

Stacey Lea sighed deeply as she hung up the receiver, the tension visibly leaving her body. That'd been easy. You could sure get more with honey. Here she'd mended her marital fences—nearly that is, gotten her way about Sarah, and started WOW on the two-faced journey she'd decided it would take. Strangely, she felt few pangs of conscience for using Palmer. Well, why should she? Palmer had used her wrongly, and it looked like a lot of other people too. She'd not allow it. She was his wife, his helpmate, and if he'd allowed himself to go astray of his duties, then it was up to her to set him back on the right course.

"Yes, Palmer darling," Stacey Lea whispered to the silent phone, "taking care of you is my A-one top priority."

Stacey Lea huddled down in the back seat of Preston's large cabbed pick-up and considered how two heads were better than one, at least in this case.

"Annie, have you seen my riding slicker?"

"It's down here in the River closet, but you aren't plannin' to go out in this mess are you? It's rainin' cats and dogs!"

"I have to," Stacey Lea answered as she arrived in the kitchen from the back stairs, which emptied there. *"I have to go to Thornhill. An old friend's meeting me there. It's secret, and if I drive, I'll alert my shadows, for sure."*

"Well, you'll be sick if you ride in this. Won't be good for Prissy either. You know she's gettin' old."

"I thought of that. I could take another horse, unless you have a better idea."

"As a matter-of-fact I have," Annie had responded, smiling smugly, as she assured Stacey Lea that her husband went over to Thornhill Stables lots of times. *There'd be nothing untoward about it.*

Stacey Lea had almost an hour's wait before her host and guest arrived.

"I thought something awful must have happened. Let me look at you, Casey? It's been ages." Stacey Lea said as she reached up to hug the big woman, not an easy chore since she was over six feet and large in other respects."

It's good to see you too, Stacey Lea," Casey Bartholomew responded stiffly before turning to Forrest. "Thank you, Forrest, I enjoyed your company."

"My pleasure," he responded as he flamboyantly handed Stacey Lea a wet magnolia branch with a twinkle in his eye.

Stacey Lea blushed, remembering their telephone conversation yesterday.

"I didn't know if you'd recognize each other after so many years, so I told Casey that you'd be carrying a magnolia branch."

"Really Stace, wouldn't something normal like a carnation, or a rose do?"

"Yes, but I had to make a quick decision, and I wasn't sure you'd find any of the normal things early on a Sunday morning, and magnolia branches are all around your place."

"How big do you want this magnolia branch to be?" he asked with laughter in his voice.

"Stop it, Forrest. Sounds silly to me too, now, but it was the first thing I could think of, and I sure don't want to call her back."

The door had hardly closed behind their host before Casey began her obviously prepared statement.

"Stacey Lea, you know how I feel about coming here. When you called me after I dropped out of the gubernatorial race, I told you that I just wanted to get back into private practice with my husband and spend the rest of the time raising my children. I've not regretted that decision."

"I know better."

"You don't know better! You have no right to badger me this way. You even blackmailed me to get me down here."

"No, I didn't. Most people'd be flattered to have the First Lady stop her big *ole* plane just to see them, but you'd rather make a miserable trip in miserable weather just to keep from being seen with me. Why?"

Casey floundered.

"I didn't want to put you out, that's all."

"Oh, spare me, Casey. I may seem to act brainless sometimes, but you know full well, I'm not."

"I don't know why you have such a hard time believin' me."

"Because once a politician always a politician, and you were born with the malady, my dear. Your family's served Tennessee ever' bit as long as the Fairmonts have Mississippi. You only went to law school 'cause you knew it was the best steppin'-stone to a grand political career. You've been preparin' since summer camp. In college, you ran for everything and won because you're a natural. Now, let's get the bull out of this conversation and get down to business."

Casey collapsed into the big wing chair as if she'd been punctured. She didn't know exactly what to make of Stacey Lea or this meeting, but she had an idea the jury was back and she had lost.

"The first thing we're gonna do is swear an oath. Some things will be said here today that must not leave this room, at least, for now. I'll swear too. Do you cross your heart and hope to die?"

"Cross my heart and hope to die?"

"I know how it sounds. Usually oaths are on the Bible, but it seems to me that those are so common anymore that people don't take them as seriously as they should. I've never heard of anyone breaking a *cross your heart and hope to die* swear."

"All right," Casey sighed, accepting the inevitable. "Cross my heart and hope to die."

As she spoke, Casey brought her hand up and made the sign to her heart that was necessary to make it take.

"Good. Now it's my turn."

Casey couldn't believe it, but as Stacey Lea ritually crossed her heart, a new feeling started in hers, a good feeling.

"I'm gonna be brief because you have a plane to catch, and I've a lot to do before I go back to Washington. I have a mountain of circumstantial evidence that there's a conspiracy going on in this country against women, especially women in public office. I need to know why you dropped out of the gubernatorial race last year, Casey, you had it won."

"I told you, Stacey Lea. My family needed me!"

The First Lady paid no attention as she continued, "This is very important. You have to know an enemy's tactics. I figure we're gonna have to fight fire with fire, and I know you have somethin' important to tell me."

"Are you tellin' me that you intend to fight?"

"Yes."

"That could be dangerous."

"Then there *is* something?"

Casey again floundered before she responded.

"Maybe, but it might hit close to home."

"Oh, I've already decided that Palmer's involved, if that's what's botherin' you. In all fairness, however, women have let it happen. We don't stick together, but that's a conversation for another time. Tell me your story, Casey. I've no intention of lettin' you go until you do."

"That's what I figured," Casey responded with a still reluctant sigh. "You were always determined to get your way, but…"

"Casey!" Stacey Lea demanded impatiently.

"Oh, hell!" Casey surrendered. "I've been wantin' to tell somebody for so long; it might as well be you."

As they settled back in their chairs, a tap at the door announced Caana, the Thornton's long-time cook, with a pot of steaming coffee, hot buttered biscuits and homemade muscadine jelly.

Casey, whose ample figure was proof of her love of such things hardly glanced at the tray's contents in her eagerness to tell her story.

"Back in October in the heat of campaigning, two FBI agents came to me and asked for my help. They said that a wealthy Colombian named Tomas Martinez was tryin' to bribe officials in some of the Southern states in order to set up new drug routes to the North. They believed that he'd be approaching me soon since I'd surely be the next governor of Tennessee. They asked if I'd be willin' to cooperate in a plan to trap him. I agreed."

"Did they mention any of these other Southern officials?"

"No, and I didn't ask. They were, however, very convincing. After all, what reason would I have not to believe them?"

"True. Proceed."

"It wasn't more than a week before this Martinez called me, and we set up a meeting in my suite at the Hotel Peabody in Memphis which I'd allowed the agents to bug."

"Come in, Señor Martinez."

"Thank you, Congresswoman Bartholomew. I have heard good things of you and I have looked forward to meeting you."

"He was very formal and shy. I had to encourage him."

"I didn't know I had admirers in Colombia. What have you been hearing?"

"That you are a woman of your word. That when you make a promise, you never back down. Everyone and every nation need a friend like that."

"You flatter me, Señor. Sit down over here, please. Could I get you a drink?"

"Yes, thank you. I'll have a Coke, if you have it."

"Certainly. Coca-Cola is one of the prides of the South. Its home office is in Atlanta, and the original recipe's locked up in a safe there right now with only a few people at one time ever knowin' the full formula."

"I did not know that, but I do know that Colombia furnishes many of the cocoa beans that make it possible."

"I hadn't thought of that."

"Yes, the coca plant is a versatile and important product for my country."

"You can imagine how my heart was pounding, Stacey Lea. In fact, it threw me into a hot flash, and my face, I'm sure, turned beet red. I feared he'd notice my distress, but he showed no signs. He was a cool one."

"I think I'd have been struck dumb. You were very brave, Casey. So, . . ." Stacey Lea encouraged, eager to hear the rest.

"So, before I knew it, I'd accepted a briefcase with $100,000 in it for my campaign and a promise of more when I became governor and cooperated with their plans. We were shaking hands to seal the bargain when the FBI barged in."

"*Congresswoman Bartholomew, you are under arrest for accepting a bribe. You have the right to remain silent....*"

"*There's some terrible mistake here. I've done nothing wrong. In fact, I've been helping your people. Just get your agents Carl Sixbey and Tony Garcia. They'll explain it to you.*"

"It was then that an Agent named Harold Curtis came in, told me he was in charge of the operation and asked me to come into the bedroom with him so that we could talk privately.

"*Thank you, I knew someone would understand. I was proud to help, but I really got a scare when your men barged in accusin' me.*"

"*Don't misunderstand. I don't believe that crazy story you were telling when I came in, and no one else will either. What were those agents' names?*"

"*Tony Garcia and Carl Sixbey, and I assure you, they exist. Sixbey is a large black man, about my height, and Garcia is short, about five-seven, and he has a scar on his upper lip. Perhaps they're using other names? I could look at pictures? I'd know them anywhere.*"

"*Does that make any sense? Why would FBI men planning a set-up with you use phony names?*"

"*I tell you, I . . .*"

"*No, I'll tell you. You've been caught, ma'am, and you're in serious trouble. If I had my way, you'd be booked and this whole ugly mess sent right to the papers so that everyone could know your true colors, but it's not my call. It seems that you have friends in high places.*"

"*What do you mean?*"

"What I mean is that I was told to let you go. I was also told to tell you to lay low the next few days until the evidence has been examined and a decision made about you. You'll be contacted."

"By whom?"

"I don't know; that's out of my hands. But I suggest that you take a little rest from your campaigning until this is straightened out. Understand?"

"How did you ever bear up under such a burden?" Stacey Lea exclaimed as she reached over to hug Casey."

"Then you believe me?"

"Of course, I believe you. You're about the most honest person in this whole world and one of the best. Who'd do such a horrendous thing to you?"

"I don't know, and I've been too frightened and ashamed to try to find out, even if I could."

"You have nothing to be ashamed of."

"I know, but they make you think you do. It seems you're guilty anymore until proven innocent. Many people's lives have been destroyed from just being arrested, especially when it's the Feds. They're powerful, and they don't necessarily use that power prudently. They like to push people around. I had too much to lose, and it wouldn't have been fair to my family to let them suffer on my account."

"Did you tell Bryant?"

"No, not even him. He's never understood why I dropped out of the race, but I think he sort of likes the results—my being around more, you know."

"Well, I can certainly understand why you dropped out."

"I didn't drop out then. I dropped out when I was advised to, when I was contacted."

Casey had finished her revelation hesitantly, raising her hand, as a signal to her friend that the information she would now impart should Stacey Lea ask the next obvious question would be more intimidating that anything she'd said prior.

Stacey Lea understood the warning but did not hesitate.

"Who contacted you, Casey"

"Stacey Lea, it was Beau, our old friend, Beau Fairmont."

Stacey Lea's voice reached out to a source she could not see. "Forrest, where are you? Call Preston at the stables for me, please. I've got to get back, and you have to get Casey back to the airport."

"He's in the kitchen with me having lunch," the source responded. "Before you go, I want to talk to you a minute, though."

"I don't have a minute and neither do you."

"You'll have to find it," Forrest insisted as he drew her into the dining room, "because I want to know what you're up to. Why all this secrecy?"

"I don't know what you mean."

"You know exactly what I mean—secret meeting, coming over hidden in the back of a truck. C'mon, Stace, don't play games with me."

"Your privileged attitude with me is as annoying as hell. You come back into my life after years of silence, and you expect to take over, to walk right in. I tell you right now, just mind your own business and stay out of my life. It's got no room for you."

"I beg your pardon. I'm spending all day Sunday playing host and taxi for you, and you say it's none of my business? Furthermore, if you think I'm going to fall for your little diversionary tirade and get in an argument with you so you can huff out, you better think again." Forrest had grabbed her arm and turned her roughly to face him as she had attempted just that. "You haven't changed one bit. You're still a bossy bitch with as many tricks as Pandora—a true descendant of Eve. Maybe that's why I left, for some peace."

"You only left because I was too much woman for you then, and I tell you this, I'm too much woman for you now!"

"That did it!" His kiss was rough and hard, and she felt as if she'd surely suffocate if he didn't let her go soon. Then as the kiss got gentler and his hands began to caress, the thought of suffocation seemed to her a merciful end.

When the last vestiges of sanity finally parted them, they both had difficulty putting anything into words, not knowing if words would help or hurt this unsure ground that formed the course on which they'd been thrown. Stacey Lea had big tears streaming down her face, and Forrest, who, like most men, had a smaller reservoir, was still obviously shaken.

"I'm sorry, I didn't think," he stated quietly.

"You never did," she reproached, and equally as quietly added, "Don't ever do that again. My life's complicated enough right now. I certainly don't need you muddyin' it up more. You're right. There's a lot going on, but I can't discuss it. You must respect that. If I could, I'd tell you. I promise, no more games. Please, trust me?"

"You better get going," Forrest responded, gruffly, after only a slight hesitation, "and Casey and I better get started to the airport."

"Thank you," she said, touching his arm as he turned to leave.

This time, he did not respond.

"One more thing, Casey," the First Lady asked as her old friend got into her rain gear and prepared to leave. "Is there anything else you can tell me about those so-called FBI men?" What about the Colombian, for example? Did you read anything about his goin' to trial, anything like that?"

"No. At the time, I just wanted to forget it, but I've looked back more and more lately and less and less makes sense. Like, what did happen to the Columbian? He simply vanished. And everything was just too slick—their pat statements, Curtis' timing, as if they all had scripts but me. And then there's Beau. It might have been awkward for him, but there was something missing."

"Was Beau sweatin'?"

"Like he was about to meet his Maker."

"Beau always sweats like that when he's uncomfortable. Yes, there's something rotten here, but we need some solid proof."

"Well, I've racked my brain over it. But Beau was right when he said that you sometimes only dig yourself in deeper when you start digging around."

"You can also find the worm that will catch the fish."

"That's true too. Maybe if I'd told you this when I withdrew from the Governor's race...?"

"Don't even think about that, honey. I wasn't ready. You know, Casey, you used to draw pretty well. Think you could draw any of those men who treated you so badly?"

"I can try. I'll certainly never forget them, at least, the two who first contacted me. That last one, Harold Curtis, who told me to go home, is rather blurry; I was so upset by then."

"And Señor Martinez?"

"Yes, I can sure draw him."

"Good. Get them done as soon as possible and send them to Ellie. We're going to find those scoundrels."

"I've dreamed about that, but what are we gonna do when we get them?"

"Oh, maybe we'll gorge out their eyes, cut off their ears, and pull out their tongues, that way they can *see no evil, hear no evil, and speak no evil.* They won't be worth much for schemin' and spyin' after that."

"Stacey Lea," Casey replied, laughing heartily, "your imagination's as big as it was when we were kids, and you're just as devilish. But I'm surprised at you; you forgot their peckers."

"Why, shame on me for forgettin' them! We'll certainly have to snip them off if we wanta be assured that they'll *do no evil.*"

When the First Lady started back to Washington late that day, she did so eagerly. She'd not felt such excitement in years. She had gone back to her source only two days ago, and it had not failed her. She knew the doubts and fears she'd brought home weren't entirely gone, but she was sure now that when they got too heavy again, she could come home and make things better.

Stacey Lea had brought home the sadness and disillusionment she'd felt over Palmer and their marriage and tucked it away in the Pondrin' Tree. She'd left it all there so that she was free to move forward.

Yes, she would make a difference. Not the way Palmer thought, but it didn't matter what he thought anymore. He'd had his chance and he'd misused it; she would not. She had found her destiny, she would pursue it, and she would win.

Stacey Lea put her head back, closed her eyes and allowed her thoughts to drift back to those last few minutes with Casey and the promise she'd made.

"Seriously, Casey, I don't know what we'll do with them yet, but I promise, we'll find them, and we'll take care of them. I suspect you aren't the only one who's been hurt by their intrigues."

"I hadn't thought about it that way."

"Yes, and it's also imperative that we find them, so we can see where they lead. If they're really federal agents used in this contemptible manner, then that's a terrible abuse of power."

"I hadn't thought about that either. Here I was so wrapped up in my own problems that I didn't see the bigger picture."

What was the bigger picture? And how was she going to find it? She didn't know the first thing about covert stuff, she admitted, thinking back to the so-obvious magnolia branch. How was she going to find some secret, evil men who certainly didn't want to be found? Well, she'd promised. Somehow, she'd find a way. She had Ellie and her friends to help her, and Casey.

She was tired, she acknowledged, and she had Palmer to deal with tonight. After all, there was nothing she could do about anything right now. Stacey Lea eagerly released her worries and doubts with one big satisfying sigh before drifting off to sleep.

The pilot's voice on the intercom roused the First Lady. She repaired her make-up and straightened her hair and clothes so that all was in place before returning to her seat for landing. Looking down at the twinkling lights of Washington, she considered the fact that some of those lights belonged to her borrowed home. Ellie was at one of them, Palmer waiting at another, and Coleman? Yes, Coleman was at one of those lights. She wondered which one? If she only knew, she'd reach down right now and snuff it out. A smiled cracked her well-groomed veneer. The *Stacey Doll* was back.

CHAPTER EIGHT

A NEW MORNING

Taking time only to don his suit jacket, straighten his tie, and receive back a look of smug satisfaction from his mirror, President Forbes opened the adjoining door and confidently strode into his wife's apartment.

"Good morning, my dear, are you ready to go in for breakfast?" Leaning over to kiss her extended cheek, he added softly, "or should I say, my tiger?"

Stacey Lea blushed, and then blushed more, realizing she was blushing. What a silly thing to do, she thought.

"Good morning, Palmer darlin'. I'm just trying to get this hair of mine in some condition to join you. Thank goodness, Gus'll be here soon. I don't know when I've needed his services more."

"You look just fine, and we're going to have to hurry if I have any time for breakfast with you at all. I have to be at the UN with the Chinese Delegation at two, and I've lots to take care of before then."

"Well, as long as *you* think I look all right, that's all that matters."

"You know, Stacey Lea," Palmer said intimately as they walked toward the small dining room, "maybe we should have more arguments if making up is going to be so much fun."

"Maybe we will if you don't help me promptly with my ideas for WOW," the First Lady responded, assuming a phony pout. "I don't feel I have any time to spare to do all the things I want to do. Good morning, Coleman."

"Good morning, Madam. Good morning, Sir, I hope you slept well?"

"Good morning to you, Coleman. That I did, that I surely did," the President responded in a tone filled with unsubtle innuendo, "and I'm starved."

Coleman was flustered by the presidential response and more than slightly annoyed. He loved the camaraderie he always shared with his Commander-in-Chief at these intimate little breakfasts. The First Bitch, as he privately called her, could not begin to understand how important these meetings were for them. Their breakfast by-play went right over her head. This morning, however, he seemed to be the one left out, and he didn't like it.

"You know, Stacey Lea, I was thinking…"

"Oops! Oh, I hope I haven't scalded you, Coleman. The coffee's boilin'. How clumsy I am, and all over your nice white sleeve, too. I've just ruined it. Here, let me help you wipe it off."

"I'm all right, Madam," Coleman responded as he flinched away when she tried to help. "I can take care of it. I'll get Thomas to serve you while I change."

The fact was he could hardly wait to get out of there. This morning wasn't going well, and she'd done it on purpose; he was sure of that. She'd be sorry, he promised as he retreated. He would not retreat again.

"Oh, I do hope I haven't upset Coleman? I'm really a klutz this morning." Palmer was too absorbed in eating and reading to notice the little smile Stacey Lea delivered with her words.

"He'll be all right. Now, are you ready to talk?" Palmer asked as he folded his paper to the side of his plate, fully aware that his wife was always ready for discourse. "I don't have much time, but I was thinking that you could get your swap program idea started immediately by making D.C. the model. Start right here right now. You have enough money for that, don't you?"

"I suppose so, but it takes so long for those pilot programs to prove themselves. I'd rather bungle a little all over the country and do some good than have a perfect little program goin' in one place. I don't have time for trials anyway. We could be out of office before it got off the ground, and somebody else could get credit for all my labors."

Palmer laughed at his wife's logic and winked confidentially as he assured, "We may be here longer than that; I rather fancy the place. Besides, I didn't mean you had to wait until all the kinks were worked out. I just wanted you to know that I think it's a good idea, and you have my approval to start. You may even start planning on a larger scale, but it's going to take me a little time to get you the money you'll need, especially with the holidays coming. Only thoughts on Capitol Hill now are recess and home!"

"Oh, this is just grand!" Stacey Lea responded bringing her hands to her breast in pleasure. "You're so good to me, Palmer. I truly don't deserve it the way I act sometimes."

"My dear," he comforted, as he came around the table and patted her shoulder, "don't be so hard on yourself. No one's perfect. Besides, I was a bit hard on you the other day. Now, give me a big kiss; I have to be on my way. Remember, I'll be eating dinner at the UN and remember also our little bargain when you get so busy with your project—I STILL COME FIRST. Which reminds me, I would appreciate it if you would hands-on the state dinner we're hosting for the Chinese on Wednesday. They're always better when you add that woman's touch."

"I have every intention of doing just that. After all, we've a reputation to uphold. Now you run along and have a good day, dear. I've got loads to do."

To her husband's receding back, Stacey Lea had Thomas fill her cup as she evaluated the hours since she'd returned to the White House. She could spare a moment's dawdle.

Yes, Palmer, darling, you're certainly going to come first. They were right back on course with their marriage, as if nothing had happened. Actually, things were better. Palmer reminded her of the Cheshire Cat this morning, so pleased with himself and her, that he'd actually ignored Coleman. She was learning to be quite deceitful, and it evidently took lots of deceit. She'd always known all the little tricks for getting her way, but she'd also thought there were limits. Now, after twenty-four years of marriage, she was beginning to realize that anything was possible. It was all in how you played the game, and that's what it was, just a game.

Was it the Catholics or those Eternists who believed that if you thought something sinful and took pleasure in it, it was the same as doing it? If that were true, she was a real sinner this morning. Maybe that was why she'd blushed so when Palmer had referred to it. Adulteress—a big letter "*A*" was burning deep in her breast—harlot, strumpet, bawd, courtesan. Courtesan, she liked that one. There was an air of elegance surrounding it. On the other hand, she liked bawd too. Being a bawd sounded like fun. Wonder if bawds played like they were with someone else when they did it? Wonder if Palmer ever played like he was with someone else? Well, if he had last night then she hoped he stuck with it because last night hadn't been bad at all. Wonder if she'd blush the next time she saw Forrest?

"Madam, could I get you anything else?"

"Yes, as a matter of fact," Stacey Lea responded, slowly coming back, "you can get me a big, hot pot of coffee and ask Ms. Farmer to join me here."

"I've been on pins and needles waiting for your summons!" Ellie announced as she bolted in. "We've got a busy day. Gus will be here in less than thirty minutes, and all the week's plans to discuss . . . "

"Don't chide. I'm in the middle of my metamorphosis." Stacey Lea announced, before continuing. "It's good to see you, Ellie. Sit down and we'll talk here awhile. Thomas, please get Ms. Farmer a cup."

"Where's Coleman?" Ellie quizzed.

"I did such a dreadful thing. I was so clumsy this morning; I spilt burnin' coffee all over his sleeve. Just ruined his jacket, and Lord knows how much discomfort I may've caused him. He went to change, but he's been gone so long maybe he had to get treated."

"That's terrible! I'll check on him later for you. See if there's anything I can do."

"That's good of you, Ellie," Stacey Lea responded seriously, adding, "Thank you, Thomas, that'll be all. We won't be needing anything else, so you're excused."

Stacey Lea watched Thomas comply with her request and waited a discreet moment before she allowed herself to look at Ellie, knowing that the moment she did they'd be unable to contain their silent levity.

"My God, how I would've loved to have been here. What did he do?" Ellie exhaled vigorously as she collapsed almost off the chair.

"He retreated like a whipped dog, but he'll be back to fight another day. If he didn't know then, he's figured out now that I've declared war, and he'll be ready next time."

"Seems to me, you have enough to think about without picking a fight with Coleman."

"No, I believe that he's a bad influence on Palmer. He feeds his dark side, and he has to go. Now, enough about Coleman. Did you speak to Alma Tyler?"

"Yes, and she's on hold waiting for your call. I don't know if you can talk her out of resigning, though. This drug charge against her son isn't the first scare she's had. She's also very upset about the way

Earle Walker came out against her last week—right in her own home state. He's very powerful. She said that after his scathing sermon Thursday night, she'd have had trouble getting a seat on a bus much less in Congress."

"That man's vile! He's been ugly in the past about Sarah too, hasn't he?"

"That's not the half of it. Sarah was his main target on Thursday. He's never been so vicious, and he had all his people chanting 'cast her out' right there along side the devil."

"Is she coming today?"

"Yes, I set things up just the way you wanted. Sue Ann at one, Sarah and Beverly at two, but I don't know about Beverly. She wouldn't commit herself. She has a nerve considering how ugly she was to you. I don't know if I could forgive her the way you have."

"You're loyal, Ellie, but you were the one taking up for her last week. You pointed out that she was hiding a bruise at the luncheon. That had to affect the way she was acting, and she was picking a fight with everyone, not just me. Besides, I need Bev and I like her brash honesty. Don't forget, she's the one who opened this can of worms. She started it and she's gonna be there at the finish.

"My God, Stacey Leanne Culberson, what've you done to your hair?" shrieked Sue Ann Fairmont from the just opened door. "I bet Palmer had a tizzy. I know how he hates change."

"That's just what Ellie said. Both of you act as if it's the eighth wonder of the world."

"Well, it is. I haven't seen you change your hair in over twenty years. Now, stand up and turn around. I want to get a good look 'cause this is a once-in-a-lifetime event."

Stacey Lea stood and modeled her new hairdo. One would think that Gus had shaved her head from the comments, when he'd just cut off an ever so small amount. Remarkable what a few added curls and flips in different directions could do.

So remarkable was her transformation that the nation's beauty salons would be besieged for the next two weeks with women in search of this new look. They'd not find it, however, since the First Lady's hair was only an exclamation point to the change emanating from within. Sue Ann's considered response made Stacey Lea emanate more.

"You're gorgeous, honey, absolutely stunning. It's taken ten years off. What did Palmer say?"

"He hasn't seen it, and he'll probably have a fit. It had to be done, however. It's part of the new me."

"What do you mean by that?"

"I mean I need a new hairdo to fit my new mission in life, and we need to get started."

"What's this *we* stuff if it's your mission?"

"Just as you predicted before your grand departure last week, there *is* some high level plottin' going on against women, and we have to do something about it."

"Why we?"

"Come on, Sue Ann, you said yourself that you were worried and planned to do something. Now's your chance."

"I only planned to deal with my own little world."

"That won't do it. Once you've read some of Sarah's files, you're going to agree, especially after I tell you about my conversation with Casey Bartholomew on Sunday, but you'll have to swear that you'll keep it to yourself."

"I swear. God, I haven't seen her in ages."

"Cross your heart and hope to die?"

"This must be serious," Sue Ann exclaimed, her demeanor changing. Such an oath was not one to be taken lightly. She still held secrets from her childhood that she'd guard with her life even though they didn't seem that important anymore. Therefore, Sue Ann was very serious as she crossed her heart and took the solemn oath. "Cross my heart and hope to die; Stick a needle in my eye."

"You don't have to use that last part. It's gory."

"Well, it's part of it, and as far as I'm concerned, the swear's no good without it."

"Oh, all right," Stacey Lea responded with a hint of exasperation. "Now, back to Casey. I got her to tell me why she dropped out of the gubernatorial race last year, and it turns out that she was forced out."

"Forced?"

Stacey Lea told Casey's story with few embellishments. After all, it was frightening enough just as it happened.

"Poor thing. It must've been horrible. Who contacted her with a deal?"

"That's where you come in. It was Beau."

"Shit!"

"Yes, and he was sweatin'."

"That bastard! I'm gonna leave him now for sure."

"That's exactly what you're not gonna do."

"What do you mean?"

"I mean that he's your responsibility, and you're going to have to take care of him. Besides, keeping an eye on Beau will help us keep an eye on the whole situation."

"You mean you want me to spy on my own husband?"

"That's exactly what I mean."

"Well, what're you gonna do if you have this little chore for me? You know as well as I do that Beau was only doing what Palmer told him to do."

"Yes, I know. I'm not asking you to do anything that I don't plan to do myself. I'll take care of Palmer, but Beau's yours. I won't clean your house."

"Look, Stace, I've already moved Beau into another bedroom, and I won't talk to him. I really don't know what else I can do?"

"Honey, you've been kowtowing to him for years. You've given him a good home, raised three children almost by yourself, and done all the proper things for a politician's wife. Meanwhile, Beau has slept around and done just about anything he's wanted to do. I know he's been good to you in lots of ways, that it's been better than lots of marriages, but maybe it's time you took control. Maybe Beau's out of control? Have you thought of that? In that case, it's your duty to set him back on the right track, and just maybe it's payback time too?"

"You're tougher than I am; you always were. You just have to call it up."

"Sue Ann, I believe you can do anything you set your mind to do. You want me to count you out? You want to run away from your duties to you husband, your family, even to your country? Are you going to be able to live with all that?"

"You don't have to put it that way."

"There's no other way to put it. Frankly, I think you're more ready than you realize. Your after-luncheon special was most tellin'."

Sue Ann gave a big sigh that revealed more than any words would have. Everything Stacey Lea had said was true. She knew that she'd been arriving at this point; her friend had only accelerated the journey. Actually, she had a few surprises for Stacey Lea, but she'd save them for awhile.

"What did Beau say to Casey?"

"He told her that Palmer was going to cover everything up for her, but it would be necessary for her to give up any dreams of a political career. At the time, she was just grateful to be able to protect her family and her name, but the more she thinks about it, the more it bothers her."

"Shit, how could he do that to Casey? He knows she's as honest as the day is long, a real good person. She would've been a good governor. That's why he was sweatin', 'cause he knew. He knows as well as I do that Casey Bartholomew would never have taken a bribe." Then after a pause and a sigh, she held out her hand. "I guess you better let me see Sarah's file."

Sue Ann curled up in her magnolia-covered chair and began to read, and Stacey Lea started making some notes in an old school notebook she'd taken from her room at home. She confidently checked off Sue Ann, drew a line through Beau, and brushed up on items under Sarah's name, adding Earle Walker. Neither spoke again until the door opened and Ellie entered with Sarah.

"Good Afternoon, Ladies," Sarah greeted primly, before she noticed. "Stacey Lea, you've changed your hair? It's stunning!"

"It's her new look to go with her new mission," pronounced Sue Ann flatly, looking up.

"New mission?"

"Yes, Stacey Lea's decided that there's a big conspiracy goin' on against women and that we're gonna jump on our white chargers and save the nation."

"Well," responded Sarah, throwing an anxious look at Stacey Lea, "that, uh, that's very interesting."

"I thought you'd be more enthusiastic than that!" Stacey Lea exclaimed.

"If you ask me," Sue Ann butted in again, always talkative when she got nervous, "if our men are involved in any hanky-panky against women, it's because they don't have enough to keep them busy. As you would point out, Sarah, *idle hands are a devil's workshop.*"

"Idle minds," corrected Sarah, laughing "and certainly true, but there are many national and international problems, enough to keep us all busy for lifetimes—like world hunger, balance of trade, the environment, equality, the ozone layer, unemployment. I could go on and on the rest of the afternoon."

"But that's just what I mean—the kinds of problems. For example, last week the Senate spent the whole week debatin' whether to make apple pie the national dessert, and they still didn't decide."

"That might sound minor, but it's not an issue to take too lightly," censured Sarah. "It's like a tax—once you get it in, it's hard to get it out. For example, in the nineteen eighties, they made the rose our national flower without much ado. If I'd been there, I'd have caucused, filibustered, even been dragged away in chains before I'd have let us get that mistake in the records."

"Why? It's a pretty flower and smells good too."

"I agree, but it has a long history with England. Today's ruling family has the Windsor Rose as a symbol, then there was the *War of the Roses* fought between the families of York, with their symbol the White Rose, and Lancaster, with their symbol the Red Rose. We have copied the English enough throughout our history. The great Senate Orator Everett Dirkson must have turned over in his grave. It would have been much wiser to choose the marigold as he proposed back in the sixties. At least, we'd have been original."

"They stink!" Sue Ann sullenly retorted already finding Sarah's rhetoric tiresome. "And the reason they didn't pay much attention to roses or marigolds was probably because they had something more interesting to do."

"Sue Ann does have a point," Stacey Lea agreed. "I felt last month as if we were all part of some big Pillsbury Bake-off. The last straw, I think, was when Jim Terry from Ohio marched right onto the Senate floor dressed like a Chocolate Chip Cookie."

"That seemed to be the last straw for everybody," laughed Ellie, "because that's when they tabled the thing. Another spell like that and we'll welcome an international incident."

"That's it," cried Sue Ann, "that's what we need, a juicy little war. When you think about it, a little conflict once in awhile does men good, keeps the adrenaline flowin'."

"I never heard anything so ridiculous," scoffed Sarah. "As General William Tecumseh Sherman said during the Civil War, *War is hell.*"

"He said that because he made the South burn like Hell. He was a pyromaniac." Sue Ann responded, bristling. Most good Southerners bristled at Sherman's name.

"Come to think of it, our men-folk may need rough-housing and little wars the way they need sex. What was that play, the old Greek one, where the women withheld sex until the men stopped warrin'?"

"That was *Lysistrata* by Aristophanes," Sarah informed, "and I agree that there's something to all you say. The idea's not original. The German philosopher Immanuel Kant wrote that *with men, the state of nature is not a state of peace, but war,* but even so, all this discussion is purely academic. There's no war on the horizon, and we certainly aren't going to start one or withhold sex, for that matter."

"Why can't we start one?" Sue Ann maliciously teased. She was finding Sarah downright pompous today, and she was sick of her quotes. "I suggest Central or South America. They're always squabbling down there. A little meddling might be all it'd take, and Lord knows, we know how to do that."

"This is absurd!" Sarah protested, her eyes beginning to bulge. 'Look what happened when George W. Bush decided he wanted to start a little war!"

"No, not our southern neighbors, Sue Ann," Stacey Lea responded, ignoring Sarah. "Their leaders have always been unpredictable. Either they surrender right away which wouldn't help us at all, or they head for those jungles they have down there. The first way, all we get out of it is taking on their national debt, and the second way, they've become ours before we thrash them out."

"The first bit of logic I've heard this afternoon," pronounced Sarah.

"Now, I propose the Middle East," Stacey Lea went on, still ignoring Sarah. "They trust us even less over there and hate . . . "

Sarah interrupted, her face red with anger and astonishment. "I can't believe you, Stacey Lea! Have you so quickly forgotten 9-11, that disastrous war in Iraq, and . . . ."

"I propose the Japanese," Ellie quickly inserted, not wanting to go down those cheerless roads. "We could probably get lots of sympathy if we attacked them because there are still ill feelings over World War II. And the way they've invested in this country, why, we wouldn't have to go far. Don't they own the Mayflower Hotel, right down the street?"

"A sneak attack on the Mayflower. And I, as Commandress-In-Chief will lead the charge!" Stacey Lea rose, dramatically spreading her arms. "Our forefathers would be pleased, wouldn't they, Sarah?"

"Maybe," Sarah replied, finally catching on, "but if we're going to go to all that trouble, let's make a statement. Attack snooty France. We could take apart that awful Eiffel Tower and teach them a much-needed lesson at the same time. They wouldn't be here today if it hadn't been for us during World War II, and they've never paid us back, not one single dime for all our generous aid. I'd like to see them eat crow."

"Or a slice of American *tarte au pomme!*" Sue Ann blurted incoherently as the four of them collapsed with delight.

This was the scene Beverly Abelson found when she arrived. She'd planned her entrance carefully, hoping that it would be dramatic enough to give her a little edge. After all, she didn't have an explanation for her bad behavior last week, at least, not one she could confide. But her timing was lousy for she arrived totally unnoticed.

"Well, I thought this was some kind of serious meeting, secretive too," Bev remarked peevishly, her presence creating a more sobering effect than she had thought possible.

She had dressed herself from neck to just above ankles in clingy black, the skirt molding her in a gentle flare, with the long sleeves and high neck leaving what flesh that was left exposed to function as accessory. Even her head was clothed in a large floppy black felt hat that mostly shadowed her face. Its black mink trim was partner to the lots of coat she was dragging after her on the floor.

"I'm too busy for frivolity," she snapped, but then bellowed in amazement, "My God, Stacey Lea, what've you done to your hair?"

Howard Abelson, sitting in his study at the heavy oak desk that could be traced back to Rasputin, ran his hand over his balding head in frustration. Across from him sat a burly man in a dark suit that looked every bit the Private Investigator he was.

"Like I said, Senator, if your wife's having an affair, he has to be invisible or right under your nose. I've found no suspicious occasion in the two months I've had her under surveillance."

"Did you pursue that?"

"What, invisible?"

"No, of course not. Under my nose."

"As a matter of fact, I did. I've had the elevator from your floor watched over a month, and it always comes all the way down."

"And other tenants? Have you checked them out?"

"Yes sir. This is pure speculation, mind you, but there's a tenant three floors under you that was having an affair with another Washington wife. That's been over for about three months, and he hasn't taken up with anyone else, as far as I know."

"Who is it?"

"Earle Walker, the Evangelist."

"Interesting, but what led you to consider him?"

"Well, he had an affair with Rep. Rueben Clark's wife, Didi. He's had lots of women, but no one in Washington lately. Not like him."

"Is he here now?"

"No sir, he left last Thursday."

Howard Abelson sat quietly for a moment before making a decision. "I want you to find out everything you can about Walker. If, as you say, he's had lots of women, find out how he's treated them. I want intimate stuff. Also, I want to know the exact dates he's visited us in the past three months. We'll meet again when you get the information. In the meantime, continue to watch Mrs. Abelson."

Long after the detective left, Howard Abelson remained at the desk in a pensive mood. He'd never feel comfortable spying on his wife. Fortunately, he hadn't had to very often. She'd been quite faithful given the circumstances surrounding their marriage. Only two affairs that he knew of, and one of them, he believed had been no more than a dalliance that had gone awry. Beverly was good at making things go awry for herself. Her mother had warned him about that before they'd married. He'd tried to watch over her, but with Paddy dying, he'd had to spend a lot of time in New York lately. He was letting her down. Could Walker be the one? Someone was abusing her, but it wasn't like her to put up with it.

Abelson's thoughts turned back. He could still get that panicky feeling he'd had that Sunday morning walking across Park with Allan to the big Rabin townhouse. His palms started sweating just thinking about it. He had been so nervous that he'd nearly backed out. He recalled that he had felt as if he were on his way to a duel, and he hadn't chosen the weapons. Beverly would never marry him.

"How are you feeling?"

Beverly turned and looked him straight in the eye. He hadn't realized how sensitive the question was, or it would have gone unasked. They'd already discussed the weather and her family's health, and it had only been another polite inquiry to keep things going. Not to Bev. He could see the hurt in her eyes. He'd always thought of her as strong and invincible like those great Jewesses of the TaNaK, but she wasn't. She looked so vulnerable that he swore then and there to protect her always.

"Howard, I've really made a mess of things. Seems that's all I ever do. I can't understand how you might want to get involved with the likes of me? I can only bring you trouble."

"You let me worry about that. I'm old enough to know what I'm doing. But I can see you still have a lot of healing to do. Let me help. Let me visit you, take you out, uh, be your, uh., escort?" He blushed. "I'm afraid I'm not very good at this."

"I think you're charming, old-fashioned, but charming."

His blush deepened under her smiling gaze.

"All right, Howard, I'd be honored to be courted by you, but don't say you haven't been warned." Beverly laughed that husky laugh he would learn to love before adding, "What shall we do first?" There was a bit of gaiety in her question that immediately raised his spirits and gave him confidence. She was willing!

The pencil in his hand snapped with the pressure of his emotion as he remembered. Abelson reached inside the front of the desk and opened a small secret compartment, revealing a very small pearl-handled revolver. He didn't touch it, but his stare was formidable as he reaffirmed his vow to protect his wife no matter what.

"All right," Beverly sighed from her flowered chaise as she yawned, stretched and tried to sound more casual than her insides felt, "I've agreed to be part of whatever we're getting ourselves into. I've even taken that stupid little kid swear without much objection. Now, can't we just have a drink and relax? Besides, we all have our next assignments. As Sarah would say, *Rome wasn't built in a day."*

"I've been misquoted enough without your putting words in my mouth, Beverly," snapped Sarah peevishly.

"You two stop it," Stacey Lea commanded. "I don't know what's got you so uptight this afternoon, Sarah. I do know, however, that you all have a lot to digest, but we must get organized if we want to get Casey elected."

"Digest!" cried Sue Ann; "I've had nothing to digest all day!"

"That's not my fault," Stacey Lea snapped. "If you wouldn't try to skip meals, Sue Ann, you wouldn't be so hungry all the time."

"I wasn't tryin' to skip. You usually have so much to snack on; I didn't want to eat twice. How did I know you were gonna be so filled with purpose that social amenities would be *cast to the wind.*"

Stacey Lea's stern focus crumbled as her friend brought her arm up and out in dramatic interpretation of her final words.

"Very well, I suppose we could all use a little refreshments. Ellie, would you mind ordering something? If you want a drink, Beverly, you're free to help yourself."

"I think I will; in fact, I'll make everybody a drink if Ellie promises not to order egg salad or pimento cheese. I've had enough of that to last me a lifetime. How about a little kosher ham?"

"I thought you liked egg salad and pimento cheese?" Stacey Lea challenged, defensively.

"I did in the beginning, but there are limits. I didn't know that would be all I'd get."

"That's not true!" Stacey Lea denied, hotly.

"Mrs. Abelson is just baiting you, Stacey Lea," Ellie laughed, reaching for the intercom, "but frankly, a change of menu does sound welcome. Docs it have to be kosher ham?"

"I think it's about time you called me Beverly, Ellie, especially, if we're going to be partners-in-crime or vigilantes together or whatever it is Stacey Lea's making us."

"That goes for me, too. No more Senator Winthrop, Ellie, just plain Sarah."

"You're far from plain, Sarah luv," soothed Beverly, hoping a bit of flattery would make amends for prior sparring.

"That's all I want to be. Life's gotten too complicated." Sarah sighed as tears slid slowly down her cheeks.

"What the hell's wrong with you?" Beverly blurted in her normal tactless manner.

"Here, Sarah dear," Sue Ann soothed, "here, take my hanky, it's fresh this morning."

"I'm sorry, I'm so sorry," Sarah, said softly, her face partially buried in Sue Ann's handkerchief. "You see, after Earle Walker's awful sermon about me last week, Charlie made me promise to be quiet. I even promised that I would consider leaving Washington. Now, everybody's decided to do something, and I've promised I won't. If I break my word to Charlie, it'll ruin my marriage. What am I supposed to do?"

"Really, Sarah," consoled Sue Ann, "I'm sure no one would expect you to choose between your marriage and some unexplainable sense of duty. Isn't that right, Stacey Lea?"

"No, that's not right. We're all in this together to the end. However,..."

"That's ridiculous!" interrupted Sue Ann.

"You're serious, aren't you?" drawled Beverly sarcastically. "Sounds like we're supposed to be like the three musketeers. *All for one and one for all.* Women don't do those silly camaraderie things."

"It's about time they did," snapped Stacey Lea. "Maybe we'd have had a more equitable past, and maybe we wouldn't be in the mess we're in today. For example, have you considered how the past might read if poor Martha Mitchell had had somewhere to turn?"

"What does she have to do with it?" quizzed Sue Ann."

"That poor woman lived a nightmare that certainly had a lot to do with her death. No one would listen to her. She was deserted by all of us, and she's just one case."

"Casey didn't have anyplace to turn either," Ellie added. "She had to carry her terrible situation all alone too."

"That's because women don't network. They don't even take up for each other."

"We understand what you're saying, Stacey Lea, but I for one will have nothing to do with damaging Sarah's marriage," Sue Ann insisted.

"That's exactly the trouble with us, we let other things get in our way; especially we let men get in the way. Do they let us get in theirs? You all know the answer to that. As for Sarah, she's been compiling evidence because she sees unjust and sinister actions. Now's her chance to right wrong, and if her marriage is her only sacrifice, then perhaps she'll be fortunate. Do you think there's no risk to what we do? This is no frivolous little game we enter. We're in this together—together we're strong, and we've all sworn that we'll stay together no matter what the sacrifice or the consequence to our comfortable little worlds. That, my friends, is my interpretation of our *kid swear*, and I expect it to be yours. We'll do whatever we must to succeed. Do you understand?"

They understood perfectly. Stacey Lea's eyes were bright, her face red with passion, her breath short, but at the same time her voice was cold and controlled. There was no question what she meant, and there was no question that life as they knew it had ceased to be. It was a discomforting moment.

Stacey Lea, who'd risen during her impassioned speech, returned to the middle of her sofa before continuing, "Now, as I was going to say, Sarah, before I was interrupted, I do agree with Charlie that you may be in danger and that you should keep a low profile for the time being. That's why you've been given some very discreet assignments. No speeches, no great visibility, just quietly make your contacts. Charlie will be none the wiser, and as time goes by, you can work to bring him 'round."

"But I've never lied to Charlie," replied Sarah still not convinced.

"Well, there's a first time for everything," snapped Stacey Lea. She was disappointed. Sarah was not as strong as she had thought, and except for Ellie, she could see that she didn't have the complete commitment she wanted from Beverly and Sue Ann.

"Your support and compassion for Sarah is commendable; however, I can't help but resent that there seems to be none for me. I'm not askin' Sarah to conspire against her husband the way I'm gonna have to mine. Do you think this is easy for me?"

Stacey Lea stood up, by now in a rage, and directed her finger coldly toward the door. "All right, I release you from your swears. Go, all of you, just go. Ellie and I'll do this without you. Go home to your safe little worlds and stay out of my way. I don't need spineless friends!"

She stood frozen with her arm pointing in command. It was quiet as she waited.

"God, I'm starved! Do you think all this covert stuff is going to affect my appetite? That's the one thing that would make me leave, for sure," moaned Beverly as she lazily unfolded from the chaise and started toward the liquor cabinet, adding, "Ellie, I thought you were gonna order something to eat? I'm so hungry, I believe I could even enjoy pimento cheese."

The laughter that followed was even shared by Sarah as the tears dried on her face. However, the sobriety of the moment was not totally alleviated until Sue Ann innocently questioned, "I know, Stacey Lea, that Margaret Mitchell died before her time in that car accident, but I swear I didn't know she'd had such a rough life. Why, I thought she was the toast of Atlanta society after she wrote *Gone with the Wind*."

It took a moment for everyone to comprehend, but when they did, the level of merriment was greater than Sue Ann had caused with her French Apple Pie.

Beverly was the first to speak but not from a desire to illuminate. "You know, Sue Ann, you're proof positive that you can take the girl out of the South, but you can't take the South out of the girl."

"I'm afraid, Sue Ann, that you've inadvertently confused your Mitchells," Sarah enlightened. "Margaret Mitchell was the toast of Atlanta society and did meet an untimely death in an automobile accident, but Martha Mitchell, the one Stacey Lea was referring to, was the wife of Nixon's Attorney General. John Mitchell. She met her untimely Waterloo with Watergate."

Sue Ann was relieved to see the food arrive.

John Marion stretched and smiled as he lay watching the large buxom woman sitting at the dresser. He loved watching her brush and braid her hair. That wonderful Rubenesque figure he had admired when they had first met had changed little over the years. He wished he could take her down to New York with him, but that was too risky. It had been all right to have her as his housekeeper when he had been an obscure Upstate Bishop, but he was too big now. In fact, it was getting risky to be with her at all.

"You know, Johnny, your mother, bless her poor soul, is getting weaker. I'm gonna hate to see her go, but I guess what worries me most is how we're going to see one another after she does."

"Don't you worry about that. I'll find a way. Come on back to bed for a few minutes, and we'll talk."

"No, you know we won't talk," she laughed, "and the house is beginning to wake. I must get dressed and see to things."

"Come on. You can come here for a few minutes. While I was watching you do your hair, I was thinking about that first time we met. You don't look any different."

"Oh, go on," she laughed again, as she let her robe drop and brought herself across the bed to curl up comfortably near him, persuaded. "That was over thirty years ago. I was just a young scared widow needing a job, and . .why, you hardly had a gray hair then, but so dignified." She reached up and stroked the side of his face familiarly.

Familiarly, he twisted over her and took one large succulent breast in his hand before responding warmly, looking into her eyes, "Had you ever thought, Claire love, that maybe you put them there?" Moving his mouth down, he gently traced around her nipple with his tongue before sucking, slowly at first.

"I swear, Johnny, I've never seen you so lustful and me lovin' it so," she gasped as she gave herself in to the moment.

The moment was only a satisfying memory now as Claire quietly watched the long black limousine pull away. A frown had settled on her brow as she thought of how often she'd stood here, watching the same scene that only changed with the seasons. Last time, she recalled, it had been a bit blustery and cloudy with the last leaves of autumn blowing like they were trying to escape from the harsh winter ahead; winters were always harsh here. Now, a light snow was falling, and what leaves that hadn't gotten away would likely be covered until spring.

Was she like those leaves, trapped by her love for Johnny and her own fear of whatever else might be out there? Change—most people didn't like change. They sat in the same pews, ate the same foods, got up at the same time, went to bed at the same time, watched the same television shows, slept with the same man…Claire sighed.

Albert, she'd probably still be living on a farm, sleeping with Albert if he hadn't gotten killed. So young and handsome he'd been, a rough lover, new at it, both of them. Would she have lots of kids now? Would her hands be rough, her body worn? That's what she'd thought life would be for her, but Johnny had needed a housekeeper. It was only going to be temporary.

"I understand you were recently widowed. I'm sorry."

"Thank you. Yes, my husband was killed hunting rabbit. We'd only been married about three months." She felt uncomfortable under his piercing gaze. The interview had not been going well.

"Hasenpfeffer?"

"What?"

"Hasenpfeffer, that's a rich rabbit stew, isn't it, a favorite of the German community?"

"Ach, yes, it is."

"Can you make Hasenpfeffer?"

"I make good Hasenpfeffer." She beamed as she began to talk about her culinary accomplishments. She would learn with time that he had a knack for making people comfortable, and just the opposite, too, when that suited him. *"I use a recipe that came over from the old country with my family, but I've a few little tricks of my own that have improved it, so everyone tells me,"* she modestly added, lowering her eyes. *"The secret is the sauce. It must have a hearty dry wine, and of course, it must always be thickened with the rabbit's blood, otherwise, it's flat. It was Albert's favorite, my husband, Albert."*

"Would it be too painful for you to make some for me, since it was your husband's favorite dish? I wouldn't want to upset you."

"Not at all. I don't hold with that kind of thinking." Her reply was so eager that she blushed.

"Good. I was hoping you would say that. Suppose you come here next Tuesday and make your Hasenpfeffer? We can talk more then."

She'd come Tuesday and made her *Hasenpfeffer* and served it with red cabbage and potato dumplings. She'd stayed on to make her *Sauerbraten*, her *Wienerschnitzel*, her *Spatzl*—he loved her *spatzl,* and all those wonderful German desserts like her *streusels* and *kuchens,* and even the *streuselkuchen* that delighted him so.

Claire chuckled, thinking that she had certainly proved that the way to a man's heart was his stomach. At least, it had been for Johnny. For awhile, he'd even put a little weight on those bones when she had been able to cook all the time for him. Those had been wonderful days when he'd been the Bishop here. She'd almost felt as if they were married. Maybe they would have been too, if Catholics weren't so hardheaded, expecting their priests to be normal men without doing normal things. She'd been good for Johnny, and he'd been all the better priest because of her. She was sure of that. Now, he was going to cast her out. She was sure of that too. He might not be ready to admit it, but once his mother died, he'd stop coming to Buffalo.

Except for those few stolen moments when he came home to visit his mother, there was no time for them anymore. Sure, things were good when they were together but that was less and less, and sometimes lately she got the feeling that she was just habit with him that he could easily break. And he looked bad. His work was wearing him out, making him lose touch with important things—like her. He needed her more than he realized, and she needed him. "No, Johnny, We've been together too many years. I won't let you discard me now," Claire whispered as she gave her deepest sigh yet before turning from the window and the outdoors. Her heart was heavy these days, heavier than it had ever been.

"Our afternoon repast is delicious!" announced Sue Ann, glad the conversation had moved away from Margaret and Martha Mitchell. "I must call down and let the chef know how pleased we are. I swear, none of us'll be able to touch another bite for the rest of the day."

Sue Ann's praise of the midday feast was well-deserved. It was as if the chef was tired of pimento cheese and egg salad too, for Ellie's request had brought from the kitchen a large silver platter centered with cold roast chicken and surrounded by vegetables and cheeses. A smaller companion platter held a chafing dish of chocolate fondue, accompanied by plump, deep-red strawberries. It delighted the eye, and as Sue Ann pointed out, was more healthy than fattening if one just ever so lightly dipped the tip of one's strawberry into the warm brown cream.

"I propose *Women Of Worth*," stated Sarah as she reached over to pour herself a cup of tea, "or *Women Of Worthiness*."

"That sounds more like where we're from, you know, like the Women of Worthiness, Mississippi. What's that silly town in Texas that awful Earle Walker is from?" asked Sue Ann busily dunking a strawberry deeper than she'd advised.

"That's Make-up-your-Mind and I see-what-you-mean," answered Sarah, undaunted that her latest contribution had been spurned. She was having fun. She liked word games, and the challenge of selecting an appropriate name for their new and very secret organization within WOW had become a lighter more pleasant side of the afternoon's agenda. In fact, even Beverly had thrown herself into the matter.

"How about mauve as our color? It isn't worn much, so when we see it, we can be pretty sure that she's one of us. Besides, I love to wear it. I could really get into this thing if we use mauve."

"Beverly, we aren't ready for colors yet. We have to decide on our name first. I know it's taking longer because we have to use the same acronym as my *busy work*, but we agreed that it makes sense. Our dedication to WOW is going to take on a whole new perspective."

"My goodness, Stacey Lea, you're still bugged by that *busy work* thing. Let it go. Besides, I have a good one. How about *Women Of Wisteria?*"

"For godsake, Sue Ann, what does wisteria have to do with anything?" bellowed Beverly. "I suppose you're going to tell us that it was the flower for some Greek Goddess or the theme for one of those cotillions you used to go to. This one you really have to explain."

"I don't have to explain anything," snapped Sue Ann, still stinging from Bev's Margaret Mitchell comment. "I like wisteria, besides it's prettier than mauve and more feminine than your *Warriors Of Washington!*"

"All right, both of you, stop it. In all honesty, however, I do agree with Beverly, Sue Ann. *Women Of Wisteria* has no significance to our cause. Let me go over the list. Most of them have been rejected out of hand, but perhaps we've missed something. *Women Of Worth.*"

"That has no significance for us either."

"All right, *Women On Women.*"

"That's not bad, but didn't someone say that there was already an organization with that name?"

"I said it, but I'm not sure. We could save it and check if we don't decide on another."

"Okay, we'll do that. How about, *With Other Women?*"

"Personally, I like that one best, and it isn't mine."

"All right, we'll save that one too. Now, *Warriors Of Washington*."

"Too local and too militant."

"Then that would also eliminate *Watchdogs Of Washington?*"

"Yes, and *Women On Warpath*."

"Agreed. But what about *Watchdogs Of Women?*"

"I don't know about the rest of you, but I don't like being called a watchdog, maybe, *Watchers Of Women?*"

"That sounds like a Peeping Tom Club."

"We do have *Watchful Of Women* to consider."

"What about *Women On Watch?*" Ellie proffered quietly, having made no contribution until now.

Her suggestion was greeted with a moment of reflection before Beverly responded with enthusiasm, "That's it! That's it exactly. *Women On Watch* and mauve will be our color. Now, what else do we need?"

"Not so fast. Everyone has to agree. What do you say, shall we be *Women On Watch?*"

All nodded.

"Then it's settled. We are officially *Women On Watch*. Now let's get our color decided for Bev's sake. Frankly, Beverly has a good argument for mauve. Not only do you rarely see women in it, but men never, except a touch in a tie now and then. Does anyone else have a suggestion?"

It took them a good hour to agree on all those important traditional features that would give identity and permanence to their new sisterhood. Sue Ann was stubbornly resolute against mauve, pointing out with some logic that it was not the easiest color to wear. She was only persuaded when the group agreed on Wisteria as their flower or vine as Beverly caustically noted.

Perhaps the most difficult tasks were selecting their password and sign. After all, the selection of words and signals that would alert the kindred spirit but cause not even the raising of a brow to the most wary of adversaries was no easy feat. Certainly, Mother Forbes' *Do you believe in the Ten Commandments?* would not fit easily into most conversations, and beeping one's nose or dinging one's ear, even scratching one's head was undignified at best.

Finally, after deciding on their password and deciding they were unable to decide on a sign at this time, they agreed that enough monumental decisions had been made for one day. To go further under their present exhausted state might be self-defeating.

"I swear," exclaimed Sue Ann, "it's too bad you don't lose as much weight exercising the brain as you do exercising the body. I believe I'd have lost a good ten pounds this afternoon."

"It's a proven fact that mental exercise is more tiring than physical," supported Sarah.

"I agree, enough is enough," Stacey Lea announced closing her notebook.

"Haven't you forgotten something, Stace?" Ellie nudged quietly. "Why don't I order up a cold bottle of champagne to toast this very productive meeting, and while we're waiting, Stacey Lea can tell you about her vision."

"It was only a dream I had, a bad dream. Ellie has this weird idea that I've a supernatural gift of divining. Quite absurd."

"Well, absurd or not, my curiosity's aroused," Bev announced, "besides, after such a decision making day, a glass of champagne sounds good."

All agreed that a glass of champagne was their due. Each woman held a silent hope that those marvelous little bubbles might communicate some of its long pent-up energy to relieve their own exhaustion; besides, who could possibly leave without hearing about Stacey Lea's vision. They waited, their eyes turned to her.

"Very well," Stacey Lea surrendered, flashing an annoyed look at Ellie, "but I assure you, this is a waste of time!"

"When I was home last weekend, I was sitting in my special thinking place when I dozed. I saw five men sitting at a table—a round table, and Coleman was standing by Palmer. Palmer was facing me and Beau had his back to me. The other three men were not easily discernible because they had their faces turned toward Palmer, and there was a gray haze over the whole scene. What I could see clearly were the hands of two of them. The one on Palmer's right had a drink in front of him, and when he picked it up, I saw a large sparkling diamond on his pinkie; the one on Palmer's left wore a robe like the cassock of a priest and his hands were long, tapered and graceful. All around them, whirling and flashing in and out, were women's faces, unhappy faces, some in pain, some with tears. I could hear their moans. . . . . "

"The right pinkie?"

"What?"

"The man on Palmer's right. The diamond was on his right pinkie?"

"Yes, that would be the hand closest to me in the dream."

"Earle Walker wears a large diamond on his right pinkie."

"How on earth would you know that?" exclaimed Sue Ann.

"I just do, that's all," snapped Beverly, surprised she had proffered such information.

"Beverly's right," supported Sarah. "I recall seeing it sparkle in the camera's lights when I watched that diatribe of his last week."

"Then you see how absurd my dream was. Palmer would never be caught with Earle Walker."

"I don't know about that," Sue Ann stated, smiling, knowingly. "It so happens that Beau picked up Earle Walker last Thursday morning at his condo. He has a condo where you live, Beverly. But I suppose you know that."

"How would I know something like that? I wouldn't associate with such riffraff!"

"Really, Bev, he's much too famous, and you're much too nosy not to know, especially when you know about his pinkie. You could even be the reason Walker dropped Didi Clark."

"You nasty little bitch! I'm going. I don't have to stay here and get insulted like that."

"No, you don't, but you're not going either," Stacey Lea reacted, grabbing Beverly's arm. "Sue Ann, I don't know why you'd say such an ugly thing, but you should be ashamed of yourself!"

"I'm sorry, Beverly. Truly, I am. I don't know what came over me. I'd be offended too if anyone coupled me with that awful Earle Walker, even teasin'."

Beverly was more frightened than offended. Sue Ann had innocently blundered into the truth, and she'd over-reacted. They might all think about it later. Well, what if they did? These were her friends, weren't they? Maybe she should tell them? Maybe they could help her? No, to tell them would lead to Howard and his secret lover, Paddy Monaghan? God, she was glad he was finally dead.

"How do you know Beau picked up Walker, Sue Ann?"

"Because I've been having Beau followed for a coon's age now. He picked up Earl Walker at Highgate, they went to the heliport at the Capitol, and then they went off in a helicopter together. They were gone about four hours, and when Beau returned, Walker wasn't with him but that awful doctor, uh, Vondergrat…"

"Vondergraven."

"Yes, him. He was."

"Could Vondergraven have been the fifth man in your vision, Stacey Lea?" Bev asked.

"Dream," the First Lady correctly sharply.

"Well, could he?"

"I don't know; I guess he could."

"Seems to me," considered Sue Ann, "if Beau can be seen with Walker then the possibility of Palmer having something to do with him too isn't that outrageous."

"Logical deduction," agreed Sarah.

"Hold it, all of you," Stacey Lea demanded. "I can't believe that you're taking this crazy dream of mine seriously. Even if there might be some coincidences in it, we cannot begin our grand design on such flimsy footage."

"I understand how you feel, Stacey Lea," acknowledged Sarah. "I'm not much for visions either, but I agree with Ellie, we can't dismiss yours out-of-hand. Think about it! Walker's recent attacks on Alma Tyler, his vitriolic attacks on me, his preaching that women belong at home. His rhetoric has consistently attempted to control the position of women in our society. I'd say that he's a logical and formidable candidate for this conspiracy and since your vision ties them together…"

"And it doesn't take any great effort to know who that priest with the eloquent hands is. That has to be the distinguished John Marion Cardinal Bishop from my home state. He's as bad as Walker, just more sophisticated and subtle," Beverly announced.

"Yes," Ellie agreed, "and as I told Stacey Lea, whether one believes in visions or not, hers has gifted us with interesting avenues to pursue, directions we'd hardly have considered on our own."

"Absolutely," chimed Sarah. "There's no question that we'd have had enormous difficulty placing these men together, knowing their public images and adverse philosophies. A brilliant collaboration! It took great imagination!"

"That does it!" the First Lady exclaimed. "Walker with Palmer is absurd enough, but Walker with Bishop and then both of them with Palmer? Ridiculous!

"Diabolic, if you ask me," Sue Ann corrected. "Think about it. Where was Palmer last Thursday?"

"I can answer that," responded Ellie. "He left shortly after Stacey Lea—by helicopter, and he took Coleman with him."

"Wonder where they went?"

All eyes searched Stacey Lea's face.

"To that," she responded as she flopped down on the sofa, conceding defeat, "I have no clue."

The champagne arrived as each began to quietly fit together the puzzle that was Stacey Lea's vision. Agreeing that it needed more thought and brighter minds than they'd been left with today, they allowed the effervescence of the champagne to permeate their farewells. Their glasses touched with a bright clinking sound as they quietly and in unison pronounced for the first time their motto and their promise.

"All for one and one for all."

It was a moment that each would remember always.

Ellie worked late that night in the little study off her bedroom. Painstakingly, she transcribed the copious notes she'd taken during today's momentous events. She wrote them out carefully in the beautiful Moroccan leather bound notebook her father had given her over four years ago. It was his last gift, and she treasured it. Sometimes she'd take it out to feel its burgundy softness and fill her lungs with its marvelous aroma. She'd never thought she would use it. It was much too grand, but now, its time had come.

She recalled Stacey Lea's exact words this afternoon.

"WOW will continue to wipe out waste, but underneath we're going to make it a strong support group for women so that what happened to Casey won't happen to others. We're going to make it a networking so strong that women will never again fear to follow their destinies, and anyone who tries to stop us will feel our retribution."

Having always had a sense of history, she recognized, perhaps more than the others, the importance of today. They'd changed this afternoon. They now had a common purpose, a common bond; they were united, and she knew they'd stay that way, and others would join them. It was for them that she'd carefully keep a record. Dutifully, Ellie recorded the secret name, their color, their flower, their motto, but the password, no, it was much too secret.

Ellie finished her first entry and went to bed.

CHAPTER NINE

DUTY CALLS

"I do love all this!" Stacey Lea looked around her, her eyes absorbing and holding all the sparkle and elegance a State Dinner at the White House could realize.

She glanced to the front of the reception line where her husband stood by General Chen, the newly appointed Chinese Premier. Palmer's exquisite in formal attire, so debonair. They did make a grand pair. It was their destiny. Damn you, Palmer! Why did you have to spoil it?

"Mildred, darling, how marvelous; it's been forever." Stacey Lea exclaimed, warmly. "Madame Chen, let me introduce our most illustrious Supreme Court Justice, Mildred Dillard. Most illustrious," she emphasized, "because Justice Dillard is absolutely the only one sitting up there of our variety, and we women must stick together, you know." The last part was delivered with the most intimate of the First Lady's smiles and even included a little wink to further draw both women under her spell.

Madame Chen had succumbed soon after her arrival earlier that day. Full surrender had occurred when she saw Stacey Lea in the gift she'd brought her. To think that she was partially responsible for this delight to the eyes filled her heart with joy. She vowed to buy her secretary, Poyee, an especially nice gift for choosing so well. The ivory silk brocade with its scattering of pearls went well with her hostess' warm blonde hair and lightly tanned skin. And Madame Forbes wore the slender Mandarin style almost as well as she did herself. Yes, she would indeed buy Poyee a nice gift.

On the other hand, Stacey Lea's profuse and confidential greeting left Mildred Dillard somewhat wary. She was well aware that, to many, she was a disappointment and, to most, she was of little consequence. Not that she'd ever been treated rudely by the First Lady, she just hadn't been paid much attention to at all. Hence, that lavish introduction was unexpected and bode something, of that, she felt sure. She'd long ago learned that one must be alert to even breeze-shifts in this microcosm called Washington. She was a pragmatist. If she'd not been the voice many women would have liked, it was because she was a pragmatist. Where had all the grandstands gotten Sarah Winthrop and that endless procession that had preceded her? No, she was playing the game the only way it could be played.

Before the evening was over, Her Honor had even more reason to feel circumspect. The First Lady had invited her to one of her little private luncheons.

"Dinner was excellent tonight, Stacey Lea. It's a grand evening, and I can hardly wait to see Terry Drake dance. He's ever' bit as sophisticated as Fred Astaire in those old movies. And you look absolutely stunning, between your hair and that gorgeous gown. Are those pearls real, you think?" Sue Ann rattled on but was careful to deliver her question to the side.

"I'm sure they are. Madame Chen, Senator Fairmont's wife was just admiring my attire. I can't tell you enough how much I'm enjoying wearing this magnificent gown. It's so grand, I intend that it be in the Smithsonian someday, or maybe I'll save it for my husband's presidential library. People will come from all over to view it. I'm sure of that."

The Premier's wife nodded and preened but before she could respond, Stacey Lea changed the subject.

"Sue Ann, I'm eager to know if you've talked to Martha?"

"Who?" Sue Ann blurted, flustered.

Stacey Lea scolded as she explained to Madame Chen and the others around her that this mutual friend, Martha, was quite ill. "However, we're working on her recovery. You know, Sue Ann, Senator Abelson's wife might know how she is. Why don't you go ask her before we settle down for the evening's entertainment?"

Stacey Lea put her hand under Sue Ann's elbow nudging her slightly toward Beverly who was involved in a small cluster about ten feet away. As she did so, she stated quietly, "You didn't handle that well, honey."

"I wasn't expecting it. That was mean."

"That's the point of a password, to identify ourselves without letting everybody else know. You think somebody's gonna come up and say she has a password for you? You need practice. Run along and practice on Bev."

"I bet she'll be caught off guard too," snapped Sue Ann as she huffed away.

Entering the Abelson's little circle, she couldn't resist taking a miniature but subtle snipe at Bev's gown, especially now that Stacey Lea had gotten her in such a bad mood.

"You look stunning in mauve, Bev. No wonder you have so much of it. It's not an easy color to wear, you know. Most of us stay away from it like the plague. In fact, I find the color pure oppressive."

Beverly looked down at Sue Ann through lazy eyelids, ignoring the gibe but accepting the compliment.

"Thank you, luv. What a nice thing to say. By the way, do you know how Martha is?"

Sue Ann said nothing just turned on her heels and went to find Beau. She wanted to go home; her evening was ruined.

By the end of the following week, Sue Ann had received a large bundle from Bev with the note, *Luv, saw this and thought of you. Enough for the whole family!* Inside was a huge bolt of fabric covered with enormous bluish-purple wisteria blossoms, their vines running every which way. She vowed to get even.

"I do believe this was one of our finest parties, and I'm still high with the wonder of it," Stacey Lea exclaimed as she and Palmer ascended the steps to their private quarters.

"I agree. It was a huge success. Chen will be hard put to top us when we visit them in the spring. You did a splendid job," praised Palmer, squeezing his wife's arm.

"No, we did a splendid job. It takes the two of us, and we're very good together," Stacey Lea corrected as they were brought to a standstill in front of a large hall mirror. They stood there for a moment assessing and admiring the elegant couple that stared back at them.

"Care for a nightcap, dahlin'?" Stacey Lea drawled as she reached for a nearby door, her door, and twisted the knob.

"An excellent idea," Palmer responded as he closed the door behind him and took Stacey Lea into his arms. "Perhaps you had something else on your mind too?"

"A nightcap can mean lots of things," she replied, looking up into his eyes as inviting as she possibly could.

"I don't think you've ever looked so beautiful to me."

"Then you must be over that little snit about my hair?"

"I am, this time, but don't do it again without consulting me first. You know how I hate change."

"Very well, dear, I promise, but I must say that if a woman changin' her hair style can cause that much ruckus, then it was high time. A woman's not supposed to be too predictable. I bet my grandmother is turnin' over in her grave with me forgettin' such an important lesson."

Stacey Lea chuckled as she started undoing Palmer's stiff collar.

"Now you get that *ole* jacket off and get comfortable while I get us that little drink. You want brandy, don't you?"

"Yes. By the way, I understand Forrest Thornton is back at his place, Thornhill, isn't it?"

Stacey Lea was glad her back was turned for that one. Of course, he knew it was Thornhill, but any mention of Forrest had always seemed taboo. They had never discussed him.

She was pouring the warm liquid, her back still turned, when she replied, "Yes, he's back. He's back to stay, so he says."

She smiled. That was just the right answer. If he knew she'd seen Forrest, she'd acknowledged it, and if he didn't know, she could easily say that Daddy had told her. On the other hand, if he should know that she'd seen Forrest, what else did he know? Casey? Her smile turned to a frown. Palmer was good at asking and doing the unexpected. Sometimes she forgot what an adversary he could be. For that matter, had she ever really thought of her husband as an adversary? Well, Stacey Lea, you're now playing with the pros, and you better get yourself into condition.

With that in mind, she replaced the smile on her face and returned. Casually handing her husband his glass, she clinked hers to his and toasted, "Here's to us."

"To us," he responded never removing his eyes from hers.

"So, why all this sudden interest in Forrest Thornton, dear? You've never shown any before."

"He wasn't around, and he was attached. It wasn't a lesson from your grandmother, Stacey Lea, but I learned a long time ago, on my own, that one never underestimates anyone. Thornton was your old beau, and I do believe you had it pretty bad at one time. He's back and unattached, and you didn't tell me."

"But I'm attached. What should I have done, rushed back to warn you about someone who's had no significance in my life for over a quarter of a century? It was irrelevant, but can't say I'm not pleased to see what looks like a little of the green-eyed monster in you. That's a new facet. But tell me, dear, how did you know he was back?"

"Because," Palmer said as he took their snifters and placed them on a table, "as I said before, I never underestimate anyone. I have always known exactly where Thornton was and exactly what Thornton was doing."

He reached around and began unzipping his wife's gown; she, relieved that he didn't know about Casey, kicked off her shoes, and smiled at her husband's bravado. It was good to be assured that she wasn't included in Palmer's *anyone.* Yes, it was good to be underestimated. It would have boggled his mind to know that his *good little wife* harbored villainous thoughts this night.

Later as she looked at Palmer sleeping peacefully beside her, she thought about how she'd lured her very own husband into her boudoir, planning to deceive him. She felt scarlet; especially now since things were better between them.

Maybe they could turn things around together? Maybe she wouldn't have to spy on him or use his mother's commandments; they might not work anyway? Stop it, Stacey Lea, Palmer may come out of that sound sleep at any time, and the deed must be done.

She reached underneath the bed, feeling the frame. Finding nothing there, she ran her hand up and down the bottom of it as far as she could reach. He stirred; she froze. Calm down, she told herself, take a deep breath and think. Reaching down, she felt the carpet underneath where she had stuck it and quickly found the flat lump of clay. With a quiet sigh of thanksgiving, she turned toward her husband. He was now lying toward her, half on his back with the key hanging to his side invitingly, almost on the sheet. Swiftly, she pressed the key into the soft clay. Removing it gently, she carefully polished the key with the sheet to make sure no telltale clay was left.

The deed is done, she acknowledged as she turned and opened her bed-stand drawer to deposit the casted clay. Yes, the dastardly deed is done.

She felt nauseous and began to shiver to the point that she became afraid she might wake her husband. He stirred and pulled her into his arms as if sensing her trauma. Big tears filled her eyes. How many times she would have liked for him to feel her need, but not now, not when she'd just committed such treachery. Stacey Lea moved herself away, but she didn't sleep.

At least, that's what she thought until she found Palmer shaking her, and she heard herself screaming. It was strange, as if her voice were detached, working independently, entreating over and over, "No, No! Not the tree! Not the tree!"

"Stacey Lea, for godsake, what's wrong with you?"

"What? I woke you?"

"Yes, and probably the whole nation. You must've had a very bad dream. You're even clammy. What could you possibly have dreamed to make you this upset?"

"I don't know," she reacted, shaking her head in bewilderment.

"Well, I'm fully awake now, and since it's already early morning, I think I'll go for my swim," he responded, dismissing the subject. "I have an early day, in any case, starting with a seven o'clock staff meeting. Why don't you sleep in? Thank God, we only have lunch left with the Chens before seeing them to their plane. I'm beginning to find them tiresome."

Palmer gave her a light kiss on the forehead before he left, and Stacey Lea gave him a contented smile, indicating how much she looked forward to the few hours of rest that now lay ahead. But as soon as he was off, a deep frown furrowed her forehead. She got up, put on her robe, and grabbed the cotton boll afghan her grandmother had made. Going to her sitting room, she curled up on Bev's oleander covered chaise. It was only then that she allowed her dream to return but this time to her conscious mind. It was as vivid as a remembered dream can be.

She was in a giant courtroom that looked like the General Assembly, and all the seats, even in the gallery, were filled. Everybody was pointing at her and screaming. There was so much noise she couldn't tell what. Then a gavel fell like thunder, and with it a voice resonated throughout, "Order in this court, or I'll put you out!"

Her eyes found the voice, though she knew it before she looked, Coleman, so neat in his white steward's jacket, except for the one sleeve spotted with a large brown coffee stain. His eyes were full of hatred as they caught hers. Holding out his arm, he pulled his sleeve up slowly to reveal roasted flesh falling from the bone. The putrefied smell of it was suffocating.

"See, See what you did? You burned me and you ruined my coat! I can't get it out!"

With that, Coleman ran around the courtroom showing everybody and screeching over and over, "See? She ruined my coat and I can't get it out!" People began to stand and turn their thumbs down as they picked up the chant, "She ruined his coat and he can't get it out! Off with her head! Off with her head!"

The gavel fell loudly for the second time and her eyes traveled up in search of it. It was very large and made a loud noise, loud enough to be heard around the world. There was no other sound now as her eyes slowly traced the hand on the gavel up through the black robe to the face of her husband. Her judge, she guessed, since she was the only one standing before the bench, and her arms were shackled behind her, even her ankles were shackled. Did he think she'd run? She was a Culberson, and a Culberson would never run.

He looked silly in a powdered wig, slightly askew. If she hadn't been in chains, she might have straightened it for him. Too bad, let him look silly. He had no business judging her.

"Why am I here?" she asked boldly, her voice echoing strangely.

"Did you hear her? Did you hear her ask why she's here?" Palmer shrieked in a high, unnatural voice. "She doesn't know why she's here!"

As he spoke, Palmer looked to his right and then to his left. She followed to find that her husband wasn't her only judge. To his right sat the Evangelist, Earle Walker, in a yellow robe. She recognized him now. Just like in her vision, he had that big diamond on his pinkie. It twinkled brightly as he pounded rapidly with a gavel as small as Palmer's was large. On the left of Palmer sat haughty Cardinal Bishop dressed in a scarlet robe. The Cardinal had a little gavel too. He beat more slowly but just as persistently as the Evangelist. They had, along with the rabble, picked up Palmer's chant, "SHE DOESN'T KNOW WHY SHE'S HERE!"

Stacey Lea literally shook herself free, threw off the afghan, and stood up, barefoot in the cool morning air. The stillness that comes with the dawn filled her with thoughts of home. She was always out riding by this time when she was home. She loved the muffled sound of her horse's hooves as they buffeted the fresh heady dew always found early morn near Big Muddy. The soft feel of the air and the sweet smell of it made her hug herself with longing. She thought of that last time home when she'd met Forrest in that same early morn. Forrest, she'd not allowed herself to think of him. He had to be, just as she'd told Palmer, only part of the past.

Stacey Lea, too agitated to sit, wrapped herself in the afghan again and began to walk around the room. Judge Earle, they called him. Well, this was the closest he'd ever come to being a real judge, and this was only a dream. Up there in that powdered wig, he didn't look any more dignified than he did standing on a stage crying for sinners, or money. And that pompous Cardinal was much too pretentious not to have some skeleton in one of his closets. Hmmm....?

Stacey Lea's mood became speculative as she curled back up in the chaise, determined to see her dream through to its end....

"Whew!" she gasped, as she threw off the afghan for the second time, clammy from the hot flames lapping up around her. Guilty! They'd all said guilty. And Earle Walker had rallied the mob with *Burn her at the stake!*

At first, she'd felt a little sorry for Palmer just as she always had for Pontius Pilate. It never seemed to her that the crowd ever gave him much choice either, but when Palmer's gavel fell for the third time, she saw how much she'd misjudged his obvious quandary. It wasn't over whether to burn her, but where? Palmer had arrived at an ingenious conclusion, and the glee in his countenance, askewed wig and all, showed that he knew it.

"Stacey Leanne Culberson Forbes, you have been found guilty, I sentence you to be taken immediately to the place of execution which I will now signify." Standing up, he turned to Coleman and commanded, "Tie her to the Pondrin' Tree, and BURN THEM BOTH TO A CRISP!"

The First Lady shivered and pulled the afghan around her Indian style. Horrifying thoughts were now filling her. Are you mean, truly mean, Palmer? Is this man of my dreams closer to the real you than the one I've known for over twenty-five years? She felt as if she'd just slept with a stranger. Did anyone ever know anyone? Were lots of couples strangers like she and Palmer? Perhaps your mother does know best; perhaps your mother is right about you. The evidence is becoming weighty. Just the fact that you've secretly allied yourself to those awful churchmen is enough to make me sure you're up to no good.

Then, Stacey Lea took a step back. Doubt crowded in. Did she have the right to condemn her husband on supernatural things like visions and dreams? If she did, she was no better than Palmer was when he'd pronounced her guilty. What had been his reason? Surely not the coffee stain. No one had ever said, but then, one never remembers every little detail of a dream.

She walked over to her smallish Queen Anne desk and picked up the picture of that grand day of Palmer's first inauguration. She remembered how proud she'd been to stand and hold the Bible as her husband was sworn in as President of the United States. She'd sworn too, silently, but she'd sworn too. Her thoughts began to race as she looked long at that momentous day.

Finally, her thoughts quieted as they came together. "Guilty," she whispered. Then again louder, "Goodman Palmer Forbes, I find you guilty." Stacey Lea raised the picture above her head with both hands, then, forcefully, brought it down against her desk, shattering the glass and frame as well as ripping its contents.

"You're up early," Ellie commented as she briskly strode in with Thomas slightly out of breath behind her carrying a breakfast tray. He'd placed it on the table in front of Stacey Lea and left before she responded.

"Yes, it wasn't a good night. I had a terrible dream."

"You know, Stacey Lea, you should never take your dreams lightly, not with your gift."

"So you keep telling me, but if I have a gift for the supernatural, so do you."

"Whatever I have you brought out. What I wouldn't give to know when we were together before and whose fault it was that we didn't complete our destiny together then."

"How many times have we had this discussion?" Stacey Lea sighed before continuing with a mischievous twinkle in her eyes. "Maybe, just maybe, if we come through this mess not too scarred, I'll go to my Pondrin' Tree and use all my powers to conjure up, at least, one of those past lives. That is, if I have any of these so-called powers left. I'm going to need ever' bit to get us through the days ahead."

"I'm not worried about that."

"Ellie, what would I do without you?

"Well, you don't have to, besides you have good friends to support you."

"They're still untried."

"They're stronger than you give them credit."

"Maybe, all but Sarah."

"I'm concerned about her too." As Ellie spoke, she automatically looked towards Sarah's magnolia covered chair, a momentary thought running through her that it wasn't right to discuss Sarah this way when she was not here to defend herself. Her eyes traveled past the chair where they caught glints from the sundered picture.

"Is that broken glass around your desk?"

"It's my shattered past. I plan to put all the pieces in that magnificent ivory box that the Shah of Iran gave me. I'm going to keep them as a reminder of the morning's events."

"You better let me pick them up. You might get cut and how'd that look, the First Lady covered with Band-Aids."

"It's too late, I'm already cut, nothing bad, however." Stacey Lea raised the sleeves of her robe to show some small lesions.

"That was a crazy thing to do. You could've blinded yourself."

"Well, I didn't. C'mon, let's clean that mess up together, and I'll tell you my dream."

Stacey Lea told her dream carefully, remembering parts that she hadn't remembered earlier.

"Did you see Dr. Vondergraven?"

"No, but Beau was there. He was the jury—all twelve members. And Palmer was also the Prosecutor and the Accuser. He was everywhere, and Mildred Dillard was there. I hadn't remembered that until this minute…and she was on my side."

"I'm not sure about her."

"I know, but I have this strong feeling that she'll be a powerful friend. We'll know for sure when she comes to lunch on Monday."

"I'd be more inclined to share your confidence if you were better at interpreting these things. You really need…"

"Don't start that again. You know full well that someone in my position would be inviting all sorts of scandal if it got out that I was seeing psychics and such. Remember all that ruckus when it got out that Nancy Reagan was consulting an astrologer? No, that's not for me. I'll admit that the dream in my tree may have some significance, but this last one was caused by pure guilt."

With that, Stacey Lea went to her bedroom and returned with the small piece of indented clay. "This represents my first act of treason against my marriage," she said, laying it gently on her desk, while she removed a brown envelope from the desk drawer. "And the second act of treason is gonna be this. Yes, it's the packet from Mother Forbes. I told you then that I'd have to think on it. I have, now it's your turn."

After putting it in Ellie's lap, Stacey Lea turned and walked again to her bedroom. Ellie was left alone to ponder the mysterious contents that she herself had guarded with such diligence since the death of the President's mother.

"Well, what do you think?" Stacey Lea asked, returning and turning around to model her new gently fitted long jacketed suit.

"It's unbelievable," Ellie responded, very intent.

"'Not that, I mean me," Stacey Lea corrected, turning again. She was as monochrome as one can be, honey-colored from the tips of her toes to the top of her head. Only her jacket was a deeper richer shade of her all over hue. The effect was splendid.

"You look marvelous," Ellie responded with admiration, "but it's hard to come out of what I've just read."

"I don't want you to. Let's get to it."

"Mrs. Forbes has accused her son of terrible things here."

"Yes, I know. I wondered, at first, if she was pure crazy, but I don't think so. Take, for example, her accusation that Palmer sent a team of FBI men to go through her records under the ruse that the Foundation was only a front for illegal abortions. Do you remember that?"

"Yes, in fact, it wasn't long after that she sent for me and gave me this packet."

"It was the only time Mother Forbes ever visited us unannounced. She stormed in and spent ages behind closed doors with Palmer. Before she left, she asked me to serve on the board of the Foundation. Actually, she didn't ask, she told me."

"What did the President say?"

"He didn't like it at first, then, he did a complete turn around, said it was about time his mother recognized my worth. I was never sure that was her reason. When she left, she said a strange thing, *Stacey Lea, sometimes things aren't as they seem. Be prepared.*"

"She must've been a Girl Scout when she was young."

"Be serious, Ellie."

"Serious? Are we going to be serious about this?"

"We have no choice. I believe the Foundation plays an important role in Palmer's actions, and it is important to our investigation. For example, the day of the luncheon, Palmer exploded over a published excerpt of that speech Sarah gave at the AMA Convention. She'd made reference to the Foundation. Was it that reference that bothered him? Beau called, and I'm positive that it had to do with that speech, 'cause when Palmer got off the phone, he confronted me about inviting Sarah to the luncheon."

"And it was also right after that that Earle Walker made his vicious attack on Sarah."

"And right before that attack, Walker went someplace with Beau in a helicopter and Palmer and Coleman went someplace in one too."

"And Senator Fairmont returned with Dr. Vondergraven."

"And Dr. Vondergraven puts us right back at the Foundation. You know, I can't remember one unfortunate incident at the Foundation after Mother Forbes' unexpected visit. Do you remember how they were always having something happen, like they were jinxed—a little fire, vandalism and the ugly graffiti on the walls of the lab, the telephones going dead, all sorts of crazy things?"

"But what's your point?"

"That she had some way of getting Palmer to do her bidding. The FBI pulled out with an apology almost before she left here, and Palmer would hardly speak to her when they'd finished, as if he were pouting. Maybe he'd been bested? He doesn't like to lose. If she were able to control him, which I've never seen anybody do, then maybe there's something to what she's advised me to do here. I can't ignore it"

"It's crazy."

"Sure it is, but if Palmer is doing what we think he is, and if his cronies are who we think they are, isn't that crazier? Maybe we need to look at this whole conspiracy, along with my dream, as part of some other place, a *once upon a time* place. That might put it in perspective, and make it easier to fight. Besides, I'm figuring that Mother Forbes may've known her son better than I know my husband."

"You make sense, well, some kind of sense, I guess." Ellis frowned as she added, "But it is still confusing."

"I know. Here we have grown men in very responsible positions doing malicious things to women for no other reason than that they're women, and women planning to fight back through a secret club organized like something from their childhood, and these women have gotten their most important information through a vision. Now, to top it off, the First Lady's planning to control her husband, President of the United States, no less, through a plan concocted by his mother who's been in her grave over a year, and…"

"Enough!" Ellie cried, putting her hands out. "Do me a favor. Don't ever put this to anybody else in that unique simplistic manner of yours. Some things are better not put into words."

"Oh my, look at the time. We'll have to hurry. I have a few things that we still need to go through."

"We have a lot of correspondences to go through."

"I don't have time. Any invitations, just accept what you must and decline what you can. I'm too busy right now to get bogged down in all that First Lady stuff."

"Perhaps if some of that First Lady stuff took you to places you wouldn't have reason to go otherwise, you could get a lot of things done for WOW first hand."

"That's a good thought. I guess we should look at each invite in a different way."

"What do you want me to do with these?" Ellie asked holding out Mother Forbes' papers.

"Find someone who can forge her handwriting."

"Since *Nine* is the only one written in, don't you have enough of those she filled in herself to last awhile?"

"Yes, but I believe *Number Nine* should be directly related to what's going on now if it has any chance of working. I think Mother Forbes felt that way too, since she left so many blank ones."

"I see what you mean," Ellie agreed, shaking her head as she looked through the sheets again. "That's a strange little child poem at the end. To think that for his whole childhood, President Forbes lived by a set of daily Ten Commandments with that poem always the last one. That in itself could make a person crazy."

"Or dependent. That's what we want. We want Palmer dependent on me the way Mother Forbes claims he was on her. If *Be a good boy/be a Good-man* does it then we can count our blessings. Let's face it, how can it hurt him? Drive him mad?"

"I don't know,…"

"Don't get soft on me. I've already grappled with this. It scares hell out of me that my husband may be controlled by something like this. I almost hope it doesn't work, but if it does, then he must need it."

"When are you going to need them?"

"Not until we return from our visit to Germany and France. I don't think it's logical to start now with Thanksgiving on top of us and our trip on top of that. Besides, this trip will give me a chance to work on Palmer. If ever I wanted him unsuspectin', thinkin' me his *good little woman*, it's now."

As Stacey Lea started toward the door, her mind was already jumping past this final luncheon with the Chinese Delegation to pleasant anticipation of going home for the holiday and the state visits that followed.

"You know, Palmer, I don't know why if the Senate can take an extended holiday recess, the Executive Branch can't, at least, free up its schedule enough to enjoy a little breathing room 'round Thanksgiving."

"You wouldn't care, Stacey Lea, if our busy commitments weren't taking away from your time in your *dear* Mississippi."

"Seems to me you always plan so there'll be very little time in *my dear* Mississippi."

"As wife of the President, you have duties too."

"Don't throw up my duties to me. I spend a lot of time in Washington and every place else doing my duty; so around my favorite holiday, I'd like the luxury of doing exactly what I want to do."

"That puts us right back to what I said before."

"No, it doesn't. You make it sound as if I'd prefer to stay in Mississippi. I like being First Lady, and I take it seriously. When you took your oath of office, I stood right there and whispered it with you. Do you ever think of the words of that oath? The responsibility is frightening."

"You can't run a country with oaths, my dear. Idealism is foolish and impractical. Just look what happened when Jimmy Carter was president. How did we get involved in a conversation like this, anyway? Don't worry your pretty little head with oaths."

Palmer gave his wife a consoling pat on the knee while Stacey Lea took a deep breath and held it, positive that its emission would steam-up the air.

He must surely believe I have nothing in my pretty little head. She was in a bad mood, and his smug condescending manner made it worse. It had been an awful week. To start, Palmer had insisted that they spend the weekend at Camp David, and she hated Camp David.

They were going to relax, he told her, away from the phones and everybody else, for as soon as they got back, they'd be on a treadmill preparing for their trip. At least, they hadn't taken Coleman, and she did have to admit that she'd gotten a lot of thinking done with Mother Nature that she wouldn't have if they'd stayed at the White House. She'd planned her whole meeting with Mildred Dillard, and it had gone very well. Even Ellie had had to admit that.

Everything else since Camp David was a blur of trying on clothes, being poked and stuck with pins, and last minute fittings. She would have welcomed her old faded jeans and worn leather jacket that were hanging in her closet at home, but no chance she'd have time to wear them. Here it was already Thanksgiving Morn, and they had to go back tonight. She might as well have had Annie send her a turkey sandwich by express with all the time she'd have to enjoy her favorite dinner. She probably wouldn't even have it digested before they took off for Germany. Palmer had done it this time, and she knew Palmer had done it on purpose.

He hated her home, even though Mississippi had given him overwhelming support in both elections. But it wasn't Mississippi he hated, it was Oak Cliff—Oak Cliff and everything about it, including her father. She and Daddy were close, and she understood more than ever why he couldn't appreciate their relationship, given that strange one he'd had with his mother, and his father never coming back from Viet Nam.

However, one thing she promised herself as their helicopter set down, *I will return here to live, and by hook or by crook, Palmer Forbes, you'll return with me.*

Stacey Lea was right. When they started back to Washington, her dinner was still in her throat, clogging her entire system. The whole thing had been a disaster. Her father had been stiff, her husband had been stiffer, and on top of that, Annie's brood had been so boisterous they'd even gotten to her. She wasn't used to being around children, and Annie had seven grandchildren—three of them new this year.

Then came the real topper.

"Daddy, you should know better than to invite Forrest over here with Palmer comin'. You've only antagonized him," she scolded, when she got a moment alone with her father.

"Well, he antagonizes me. Comin' down just for the day. You know this is my favorite holiday, and I like it to be relaxed and special"

"Not everything can be the way you like it all the time. How do you think I feel? It's my favorite holiday too. It's awkward for me with Forrest here."

"It was only last minute. I got so annoyed when you said you could only come for the day that..."

"It's okay," she said, giving him a loving squeeze. "But, remember, the more Palmer hates to come down here, the more I'm gonna have to stay away. With Christmas comin', I was hoping to make a case for a long holiday here since this one had to be cut so short. You may've hurt that considerably."

"He's never interfered with your visits before. I don't want him here anyway. He sulks."

"Well, I can't leave him Christmas, you know that! And you're doing a fine job of sulkin' yourself!"

Her father clammed up, didn't say another word. She looked over to find Palmer staring at a football game on television when he didn't like sports. Forrest had evidently gone off to the kitchen to find someone to talk to, and she was getting a splitting headache. It was the very worst Thanksgiving she'd ever spent, and she offered thanks when it came to an end.

"Stacey Lea," Palmer called, "We're going to have to get on our way. Start making your farewells."

She still had her headache when they left the next morning for Germany.

CHAPTER TEN

THINGS ARE NOT ALWAYS AS THEY SEEM

President and Mrs. Forbes gala state visits to Germany and then to France received worldwide media coverage. Every small detail was absorbed by one and all everywhere, and citizens of the United States basked in the plaudits and prominence their stellar representatives received wherever they went and whatever they did. They were the perfect couple.

Cynical observers occasionally tried to suggest that it was impossible for any two human beings to be quite so perfect as Palmer and Stacey Lea Forbes seemed to be, but only a few, a very few could quietly acknowledge with authority that things definitely are not always as they seem.

Ellie had had any number of occasions these past few weeks to remember that particular admonition of the President's mother. One case in point was Mildred Dillard. Stacey Lea had insisted that she also attend the quiet luncheon scheduled with the Supreme Court Justice. It had been awkward at first.

They were three southern women, Stacey Lea pointed out, with her from Mississippi, Her Honor from East Texas, and Ellie from Arkansas.

This alone gave them a common bond, a shared center in which they could meet. Her Honor agreed that such an hypothesis was valid. As women, and then again as southern women, they certainly had two remarkably cogent grounds for a communal position. However, they were half way through their Tuna Nicoise before Stacey Lea got down to business.

"I understand, Mildred, that in your early days as a lawyer you were a pure women libber. Trying all sorts of cases for the cause."

"One never quite loses one's past. Yes, as I look back, those were brash days." Their guest chuckled uncomfortably.

"You were also a Pro-Choice advocate, weren't you? Got yourself in a few little scrapes?"

"I don't understand the direction of this discussion, Stacey Lea. That was a long time ago, and as Disraeli wrote, *Youth is a Blunder.*"

"*Middle-age is Struggle; Old Age is Regret.*" Ellie was pleased that she could complete the quote. People didn't quote Disraeli that much, but he was one of her favorites.

Stacey Lea was pleased too and promptly gave Ellie a look of quiet approval.

"That's an interesting quote," Stacey Lea noted. "I'm going to remember that, let's see, *Youth is a Blunder; Middle-age is . . uh?*"

"*Struggle.*" Ellie prompted.

"Yes, *Struggle, and Old Age is Regret.* I certainly hope my regrets are not abundant. I'd hate to spend my old age in too much regretting. Wouldn't you, Mildred?"

"I'm in that third stage now, Stacey Lea, and I've few regrets except perhaps those blunders of youth when my energies were so misdirected."

"You mean to tell me that that activist fire of your youth has been totally put out?" Stacey Lea pressed with an impish lightness.

Mildred Dillard looked at her challenger closely not knowing how she should answer this last question in this strange turn of conversation.

She'd fully expected to be asked to be involved in some area of Stacey Lea's project, WOW, and she'd prepared her polite excuses prior. It was a good cause, but she was already over-burdened with her own work; besides, she was intent on writing her memoirs. She simply didn't have time, but that didn't seem to be it at all.

Stacey Lea's countenance belied the lightness of her question. Her look was intent, her body poised forward, taut and controlled. Mildred looked at Ellie only to find the same air about her. In fact, the atmosphere was still and heavy as if something in it too was waiting. She looked back at Stacey Lea and this time stared searchingly into her eyes. Windows to the truth, she believed that. She'd looked in lots of eyes in her years on the Bench. They spoke truer than words. Justice Dillard made her decision, choosing her words carefully.

"I'm a pragmatist, ladies. In Texas there's a saying, not very feminine but it gets right to the point—*only a fool keeps pissin' in the wind.*"

"But Mildred," Stacey Lea responded slowly, "what about that Irish saying, what if the *wind were at your back?*"

It hadn't taken Justice Dillard long to capitulate after that, reflected Ellie. In fact, she'd even taken that *kid swear*, as Beverly called it, with great solemnity. Mildred, as they both now called her, suspected more than either had realized. Who she suspected to be at the bottom or top of it all, whichever way one preferred to look at it, was not discussed, nor did Stacey Lea mention her vision. As Stacey Lea noted later, a Supreme Court Justice would have learned to base decisions on facts; a mention of visions and such might have dampened her enthusiasm, might even have scared her off.

Mildred, like Sarah earlier, had cautioned that their evidence was circumstantial at this time and, given its nature, could probably never be otherwise, but, she also agreed that there was too much to ignore. She'd left with her assignments, many proposed by herself, and the pictures Casey had drawn of her conspirators. Mildred Dillard's connections in the Justice Department were going to be invaluable, no doubt about that, and there was no doubt either that things are not always as they seem.

Mildred Dillard was thinking much the same thing as she poured her third cup of coffee and stared carefully at Stacey Lea and Palmer Forbes' picture on the front page of the morning paper. Here Stacey Lea was attending a gala performance of Igor Stravinsky's *Le Sacre Du Printemps* at the Paris Opera House and looking every bit the perfect appendage, when in reality…what was reality anyway? Was what she saw before her reality? Not if what she had seen in Stacey Lea's eyes last week was real. Was Palmer Forbes all that met the eye? She'd give anything to look deep into his; however, even if she got the chance, she doubted he'd hold them still enough for her to get a good look. That was always a suspicious signal. Wonder if Stacey Lea suspected her husband? She tended to think she did, for when she'd suggested last week that there might be some involvement in these audacious schemes against women at the very highest social and political levels, Stacey Lea had promptly replied that she was prepared for anything at this point. Her *nothing would surprise her* was ponderous with meaning.

The plan was a good one. There would be no marches and campaigns to attempt to manipulate public opinion; and there would be no petitions to the courts, no lawsuits or angry accusations; besides, the law moved too slowly and wouldn't be their friend anyway. No, they would do exactly what their enemies were doing—work behind the scenes. They'd fight fire with fire. She felt a familiar fire in her that she'd not felt for a very long time.

Mildred Dillard's thoughts were interrupted by the arrival of a visitor who strode in familiarly and unannounced.

"I told your new maid that I was in a hurry and would announce myself, that you wouldn't mind."

"That's all right, Faye, Mr. Berger's an old friend," Mildred assured, as her new maid also appeared, a look of concern on her face since she wasn't allowed to do the proper thing.

"But since you're here, get Mr. Berger a cup. You'll have some coffee, won't you, Jake?"

"Need you ask?" Jake Berger replied as he reached down to receive a welcoming hug and kiss before seating himself beside her at the table.

"How's Elyse?"

"Fine. She sends her love. She'd like you to come to dinner soon. It's been too long. Since James' death, you've become a recluse."

"The adjustment to widowhood hasn't been an easy one, not for me. I've coped by working until I'm too tired to think, much less be sociable. I'll give Elyse a call soon, I promise."

"I'm going to hold you to that. However, this request of yours was highly irregular. I may not want to be seen with you if you're getting yourself into something that's none of your business."

Berger's remarks were made lightly, but a scowl of concern appeared across his forehead.

"Don't worry about me. What did you find?"

"The drawings are good and I believe I have identified two of the men. They're agents, all right. Carl Sixbey is Agent Craig Summers and Tony Garcia is Agent Anthony Marconi. However, their files are classified. At that point, I left them alone. I counsel you to do the same."

"Interesting. Do you know where they're based?"

"No, but I did find that they were cut out of Department control at about the same time, a little over three years ago. That would seem to indicate that they're working together. Want to tell me what this is all about?"

"I would prefer not to," Mildred Dillard announced slowly, stressing each word.

"Replied Bartleby the Scrivener!" Berger's remittent memory responded quickly, causing them both to laugh with an intimacy only possible for those who've shared special moments and times.

"My God," he continued, "I haven't thought that old Melville quote in years. You always used it when your mind was made up and further discussion was fruitless. Is that the case here?"

"Yes."

"Well, I guess that's that. You know, Millie, reaching back for that quote along with that look in your eyes, conjures up a lot of memories for me of a determined young woman I thought was gone forever."

"I thought so too."

"I'm not sure how I feel since I'm not sure what you're up to, but I guess you're old enough and seasoned enough to know what you're doing." As he spoke, Berger removed a manila envelope from his briefcase and placed it on the table. "Here are your drawings back along with file pictures of the two agents and what information I could get."

"Thanks for your help."

"And remember, I'm still around. Deputy Attorney Generals may not have the prestige of a Supreme Court Justice, but there are things I can do that you can't."

"And you did. Give my love to Elyse."

As Jake Berger saw himself out, his thoughts were full of Mildred Dillard Parsons. He envied that old fire he saw in her. How he'd loved her in those early days when they'd both thought they could change the world. Maybe anything was worth getting that spark back, believing in something again, believing that you could still make a difference. He knew that was what Millie was thinking. He'd thought she had lost that fire forever, but it must have just been smoldering, waiting.

Mildred was more than smoldering as she watched her old friend leave. The very idea, using government employees for such dirty work, and it was hardly something that could be bared! But it would be stopped she promised as she poured herself another cup of coffee. Picking up the envelope Berger had left, Dillard walked purposely to her office.

She had to tug hard at the desk drawer where she'd stored all the cards and letters received after James' death. She honestly did not believe one more slender card could be fitted into the bulging collection, and this wasn't all. So many strangers throughout the country had reached out to her in her grief, but most of those she'd discarded after acknowledging. She'd kept a few that were especially nice, but for the most part, she'd kept only those that validated the significance of their life together. Somehow, that had seemed very important at the time, but it was a sad drawer, she considered, as she began her searching. She guessed she should be rid of it. She would one day, one day soon.

It took her almost fifteen minutes to find the envelope she wanted. By that time, she'd begun to get impatient. Yes, perhaps it was time to be rid of all this. *Time*, as Emily Dickinson had written, *for sweeping up the heart, and putting love away.* James would not have approved of this new challenge in her life, anyway. He'd liked to play it safe. Could he have talked her out of it, kept her in the *status quo*? Maybe, but he wasn't here; she was, and it was time for her.

With almost a frantic vitality, Mildred Dillard removed the drawer and emptied its contents into a nearby wastebasket. Opening up the one saved card, she dialed the telephone number that had been the object of her search.

"Janet Cuéves, this is Mildred Dillard."

"Justice Dillard, what a wonderful surprise! I've thought of you often since your husband's death. You two had such a wonderful marriage; I know it must be difficult for you now."

"Yes, it's been difficult, but life must go on. I was surprised when I got your letter to find that you'd retired. You were a born investigator, such good work you did for the Bureau. I thought you would be there forever."

"Me too, but things change. I'd been promoted to a desk job almost three years before I left. They wouldn't give me field assignments anymore, so when they offered me an early pension, I took it before I bored myself to death. I've started a little agency of my own down here, the kind of thing old Feds do, *Cuéves, Tracer of Lost Persons.* I'm happy enough."

"I've some work for you, Janet, some important and secret work. It will take you away from Miami and your agency. I need you."

Before Mildred Dillard left for Miami, she gave her new maid the day off, that is, after she had her empty the wastebasket. With Janet Cuéves' help, no one ever suspected that the only female member of the Supreme Court left her home that day, but then, things are not always as they seem.

Senator Beaufort Randal Fairmont was thinking about the same thing as he finished his morning paper and breakfast at about the same time. He'd decided that Sue Ann was never going to speak to him again, but all of a sudden this last weekend, she'd started talking, and now, this morning, she had suggested he move back into their bedroom. He didn't know why he was being welcomed back, but he'd never been able to figure out why she'd moved him out in the first place. One thing he did know, he wasn't one to look a gift horse in the mouth, as the expression goes. Yes, all was getting right with his world again.

Beau took another look at the glamorous Forbeses, staring back at him from the front page of the *Washington Post.* Things were pretty good in the good old U.S.A. too, he assessed, and Goodie and Stacey Lea were doing a great job spreading the news. They made a perfect pair, and it had been he who had introduced them. His pleasant thoughts were interrupted as Sue Ann bounced into the room.

"Beau, you'll never guess who I just spoke with on the telephone," she rattled on, not expecting a guess. "Evelyn Rodgers, that's right, Evelyn Rodgers from Tennessee, and she told me some excitin' news. She told me that Casey Bartholomew is gettin' ready to run for the seat her husband is vacatin' in the Senate next year. Isn't that grand? It'll be wonderful to have Casey here, and she's sure to win—she always wins. I'll never understand why she dropped out of that Governor's race last year. She had it cold, and she would've made a good Governor too."

"Hold on now. Are you sure of this?" The Senator's eyes began to bulge as he returned his coffee cup to its saucer slowly.

"Of course, Evelyn Rodgers told me. I'm gonna get right on the phone and tell Casey how excited we are. You can talk to her too."

"Wait a minute. You . . uh, you wouldn't want to call Casey and embarrass yourself if she isn't, and I can't believe that she is."

"Why on earth not?"

"Well, uh, the way she retired was decidedly definite. She made it very clear that she was choosing family over politics, forevah."

"Oh, bull, you know as well as I do that you politicians are just big bags of wind shifts. You say what fits your situation and needs at the moment. No one takes what any of you say seriously."

"That's not true. Shame on you for thinking that of me, your own husband."

"Beau, dahlin', be real. Just because I'm a woman and have spent most of my life raisin' three children, doesn't mean I don't know somethin' about what goes on. Now, do you want to speak to Casey when I call her or not?"

"Not so fast. How do you know Evelyn Rodgers is right?"

"Because she got it right from the horse's mouth, that's how. Casey told her, herself!"

"I tell you right now I don't believe that Casey Bartholomew is going to run for the Senate."

"I don't know how you can be so sure. Maybe you know something I don't?"

"No, . uh, it's pure intuition, that's all."

"That's a woman's domain."

"Gut feelin' then. Is that better?"

At this point, the tempers of both husband and wife were heading toward a catastrophic confrontation which neither wanted. Beau certainly didn't want it because he was just getting back into his own bed; besides, a pleasant, uncomplicated home-life was essential to a man's well-being, especially one with the monstrous responsibilities that had been his lot to assume. If he occasionally strayed from the fires of home, it was only to relieve the enormous tension that sometimes developed in one forced to make earth-shaking decisions day-in and day-out. Sue Ann needed to understand this need and address it. He was beginning to feel like a horny priest must feel, and he was surely praying just as hard for deliverance. Here he was with his penance seemingly ending when Casey Bartholomew stepped in his way. Damn her!

Damn him! Sue Ann was thinking as she attempted to control a desire to throw her now cold coffee right into his smug face. He doesn't care about Casey. All he cares about is his own comfort. There was a time when he wouldn't have reacted this way. What's happened to him? What's happened to us? All he seems to want is to save his ass, and she was getting to the point that all she wanted was to kick it all the way down Capital Hill. As Stacey Lea said, maybe it was payback time, and maybe he *was* her responsibility. She was beginning to feel right about it, but it was going to be slow—make him squirm—so he'd remember. She did not intend to do things like this the rest of her life.

"Beaufort, it's beyond me what we're getting ready to argue about. Why would Casey Bartholomew planning to run for office cause us to quarrel, especially now that things are getting better between us? Besides, she isn't even from our state."

"I agree, sweetheart," Beau sighed relieved, as he reached over to pat her hand. "I'm sorry if I couldn't get as excited as you. After thinking about it, maybe it wouldn't hurt to give Casey a call. Find out just what she did tell Evelyn Rodgers. There may not be anything to get excited about. You know how gossip is—like that whisperin' game we used to play as children? Evelyn Rodgers isn't the most reliable source, anyway, even if she is talking about the seat her husband is vacatin', you know that."

When Senator Fairmont left the house that morning, a radical change had taken place in the status of his *good ole U.S.A.* Casey Bartholomew had confirmed to Sue Ann that she was going to run for the Senate, and he was concerned for her. He was still ashamed of the part he'd already played in her life, but it had been the only thing he could do. Why wouldn't she just stay put? He didn't want her hurt anymore. All hell was going to break loose when Goodie found out, and he was going to be right in the middle of it.

He felt tired; the early morning's euphoria had left him drained. Yes, he was tired, he admitted, tired of trying to live up to everything a Fairmont should live up to, tired of trying to please everybody but himself, tired of doing anything he had to in order to hold on, tired of being Palmer Forbes' boy. Yes, that most of all.

Sue Ann watched her husband leave the house that morning, not a happy man. She could always tell his state of being from the set of his shoulders. *Poor Beaufort!* She had wished him a good day and had even given him a little peck on the cheek. She did feel sorry for him; she couldn't help it.

Stop it, Sue Ann Davis, she told herself, you can't allow yourself to get sentimental! Has Beaufort felt sorry for Casey? Has he been sorry all the times he's pulled down somebody else's panties? You better take my advice and have a good day, Beaufort Fairmont, because it may be the best you'll have for a long time. Sue Ann picked up the phone and firmly pushed redial.

They didn't talk long, just long enough for Sue Ann to tell Casey that her husband had taken the news badly.

"Yes, honey, the fat's in the fire. Now, you get that war chest ready, and remember, you're not alone. It's *all for one and one for all* or *one for all and all for one*, whatever the dang thing is. Anyway, Stacey Lea will be back tomorrow.

CHAPTER ELEVEN

THE SENATOR SECEDES

Stacey Lea was over the Atlantic on her way home when the call came from Ellie.

"Stace, all hell's broken loose here with Sarah. You'll be hearing it on the news, but I thought I better prepare you. I know you can't talk, so just say anything in response while I talk."

"Oh, we're fine, Ellie, tired but fine. How are you doing?"

"Sarah called a press conference in Boston this morning and blasted not only Earle Walker but Cardinal Bishop."

"Oh, that's too bad."

"And she looked a sight. Her hair all mussed, her clothes not neat, not prim Sarah at all, and her speech was wild, so were her eyes, but you'll see for yourself on the news."

"I understand how you feel. Even though it doesn't sound like much, now that your mama's older and your daddy's gone, you worry more. You get on a plane right this minute and go see her."

"You want me to go see Sarah?"

"Yes, and don't you worry about a thing, but be sure and call me. I'll be anxious to know how she is."

Stacey Lea didn't have to wait long to find out for herself. Palmer had tuned in to the twelve o'clock news while she was on the phone, and she put down the receiver just in time to hear.

And furthermore, my Sisters in this great Country, you must awaken to the fact that churchmen like Evangelist Earle Walker and John Marion Cardinal Bishop have far too long used the Bible to justify their own misguided and self-serving desires to shackle and control us. Robert Green Ingersoll, the great orator and lawyer wrote in 1877 that "as long as woman regards the Bible as the charter of her rights, she will be the slave of man. The Bible was not written by a woman. Within its pages there is nothing but humiliation and shame for her."

"Senator Winthrop," the newscaster continued, "went on to warn that there is an evil afoot determined to remove women from every major role of leadership in this country. She wasn't specific about this but obviously filled with emotion when she cautioned that women must band together if they are to survive as free individuals. Her twenty-minute speech was sprinkled with well-chosen quotes and sayings that have become synonymous with her quaint New England style. At the end, she cautioned the Churchmen and any others who are conspiring against women in this country to remember the words of Abigail Adams, wife of John Adams, the second President of the United States."

(The camera panned again to Sarah)

"If particular care and attention is not paid to the ladies, we are determined to foment a rebellion, and will not hold ourselves bound by any laws in which we have no voice or representation."

"As you can see, the Senator was overcome by the end of her statement. What precipitated her dramatic remarks at this particular time is not clear; however, she has long been the target of religious groups, especially the Eternists and their dynamic leader, Judge Earle Salvation Walker, who do not agree with her forceful stand on women's rights. Elsewhere in the news…"

Stacey Lea did not hear the *elsewhere* and neither did her husband.

"You see, you see how crazy that friend of yours is? She's as nutty as a fruitcake. Put her away with *Poor Richard's Almanac* and *Bartlett's Book of Quotes*, and she'd be perfectly happy and so would this world she keeps talking about. It's about time something was done to shut her up where she won't cause any more trouble or slander people the way she does."

"She hardly slandered innocent people. You know yourself that she's been the object of terrible diatribes from the mouth of that Earle Walker. You don't like him either."

"No, I don't, but that doesn't mean I go around ranting and raving about him. If I took off on everybody I don't like, we'd never be where we are. How she keeps getting elected is beyond me, but Massachusetts has always had a peculiar constituency. Remember, my dear, you always get more with honey, but I think you know that the way you manage me," he teased as he reached over and touched her breast with a new familiarity.

Thank you for reminding me, Palmer. Stacey Lea silently recognized that she'd been getting ready to take up for Sarah, no matter the consequence, and it could've been dear. She'd worked hard to develop this new intimacy they had. She couldn't afford to damage it no matter how upset she might be over Sarah.

Sarah? She sat back and closed her eyes. Had this *evil afoot* gotten to her? Otherwise, she should know that just mentioning *an evil afoot* jeopardized their work, and mentioning Walker and Cardinal Bishop together was even worse. She couldn't go off on her own.

Stacey Lea's thought process was interrupted by Palmer talking quietly on the phone. She concentrated on his voice.

"You mean you had nothing to do with it? She did this entirely on her own? How marvelous! I always knew she wasn't wired properly. Perhaps we should see each other. I'll be in touch."

"Who was that, dear?" Stacey Lea asked sluggishly as she stretched.

"Oh, just a little business I remembered. Thought I'd take care of it while you were dozing. Hope I didn't wake you?"

"No, but I'm surprised I dozed. Weren't we talking?"

"Yes, we were talking about honey, and I'd just started thinking that you have sweeter places." He was smiling as he reached over and began to open her blouse.

"Palmer, whatever's come over you? We're going to be coming onto home shores any minute now, and I was just getting ready to tidy up for our arrival. Palmer!"

"I was also thinking that we haven't ever had sex on a plane. In fact, I wonder if anyone has ever had sex on the presidential plane?"

"It does conjure up some fascinatin' images," Stacey Lea giggled. "I've an idea that we could be the first, but we're gonna have to save that exciting record breaking experience for another time. I'm sure there's not enough time to break that record properly at this moment."

"You seem to be forgetting that I'm President of the United States and I can do anything I want," Palmer declared as he reached over and pushed a button on the intercom.

"How long until we set down?"

"About thirty minutes, Sir. I was just getting ready to alert you."

"I want you to revise your flight plan so that we don't touch down for exactly one hour."

"Uh, where do you want me to go?"

"I don't know, just don't land. Oh, and Colonel Thompson, be sure that no one disturbs me for any reason. Understand?"

"Yes Sir! One hour!"

But Colonel Thompson did not understand, nor did the staff members and reporters in the fore compartment, nor the staff members and reporters in the accompanying plane, nor the reception committee and band awaiting their triumphant return. Nor did anyone else any place else as the news flashed worldwide.

The country went on alert, the world went on hold, and for one full hour a concerned populous waited as the President of the United States and his First Lady engaged in a mile-high, rip-roaring fuck.

"I still can't believe that Palmer actually suggested you go see Sarah," Sue Ann stated for the fourth time since Stacey Lea had called her last night to announce that she, Sue Ann and Beverly were going to see Sarah the next morning at Palmer's suggestion.

"I think it's about time you adjusted to that reality, honey, since we're pointed in that direction and at least a mile-high already."

Her reply made her think of her and Palmer's little romp yesterday when they had officially joined that so-called *Mile-High Club*. Wonder if Bev and Sue Ann were members? What a delicious secret something like this was. There they were, flying over God knows where, Air Force Two flying right along with them, everybody waiting, and the country even going on alert—they found this out later. She couldn't believe Palmer could be so naughty. What was it that was so much fun about being naughty? She hadn't had to think of Forrest once to get excited. She'd felt absolutely bawdy, and she blushed remembering.

"Where are you, Stacey Lea? Here I've been talking away about Beau's reaction yesterday when I told him about Casey, only to find Bev sleepin' and your thoughts so far away that you might as well be. All this wasted energy talkin' to the wall."

"I'm not asleep," responded Bev lazily, "I've heard every word you've said, but I make it a practice never to get up before ten, it's barbaric. Besides, I need to keep my eyes closed as much as possible to ward off bags."

"You Jewish women do pamper yourselves. I bet if you stopped, at least fifty percent of the beauty salons and spas in this country would go bankrupt, and you don't represent that much of the population."

"You have a nerve, the money you've spent on spas trying to lose weight."

"Stop it! This baiting and bickering has got to stop. Remember, it's a*ll for one and one for all.* We may've already lost Sarah and that's bad enough."

"We won't lose Sarah," Sue Ann corrected, "she just, well, she just must've had a bad day."

"We surely can't be encouraged after Ellie's report," Bev responded, as she sat up and leaned over toward Sue Ann. "You've got a real good heart, Sue Ann, but you're going to have to harden it a little for some of these things we're going to have to do. As for us, Stacey Lea's right. We have to get along better. You may think I've an acid tongue, but yours is pretty tart too, underneath all that sugar. I apology for baiting and bickering with you, and I want us to get along in the future. What do you say?"

"Thank you, Beverly. I don't know if I could've been that big." Sue Ann was stunned and unprepared; her response was automatic.

"Maybe I wouldn't have been last week, but I've been doing a lot of thinking since our last meeting. I've also decided to tell you both something. I not only know Earle Walker, but I've been having an affair with him for sometime now."

There, it was out. Beverly breathed a sigh of relief, and since the two women staring at her seemed incapable of response, she continued, "I know you can't imagine how I could take up with the likes of him, but you can't imagine what he was like in the beginning. He absolutely mesmerized me. Those eyes of his…anyway, he came along at a time when Howard was away a lot, and I was feeling pretty sorry for myself. I'm not making excuses; I'm just trying to explain."

"You don't have to, honey," Sue Ann comforted. "Look at what a huge following he's developed. He's got to have some powerful aura about him, and I've heard some strange stories about those eyes. Lots of people claim they have a life of their own."

"I know this much—they're pure evil, concentrated evil."

"I can't imagine you continuing to see somebody when you feel this way," observed Stacey Lea.

"He won't let me go."

"Has he threatened to tell Howard?"

"I wish that were all. No, I'm afraid of what he'll do to Howard. He knows something about him that he'll reveal if I'm not at his beck and call."

"Could whatever he has on Howard be that bad, to continue such a relationship? Howard has one of the finest reputations in the Senate. He couldn't be easily brought down. Perhaps you should let Howard decide," proposed Stacey Lea.

"No, I can't take that chance, and I won't have Howard put in that position. What Walker knows isn't that bad, but he also knows how to twist it and make it vile, and he would. He'd do it right in front of his big following—the way he did Sarah, and you know how people like to believe the worst. It would destroy Howard. He's a good man and a good senator, and he doesn't deserve to be hurt. I won't be his destruction."

"Walker's ugly to you too, isn't he, Bev?" Stacey Lea asked gently. Bev's bottom lip began to quiver, and she gulped back a lump before she could reply.

"I'm scared to death of him. Look, I hadn't planned on sleeping with him; it just happened. I know I talk a lot about sex, but it's mostly talk. He calls me his *Jew Bitch.*

"What a vile man!" Sue Ann exclaimed, furiously.

"Yes, he is, and I'm not so sure that in that twisted mind of his I haven't become a symbol for the whole Jewish nation, and he has me paying for what he calls the sins of Zion. More than once he's said, *Vengeance in mine, saith the Lord,* before he…"

"Before he what?" blurted a mesmerized Sue Ann.

"Sue Ann!" admonished Stacey Lea.

Surprisingly, Bev laughed that deep, husky laugh that was so appealing. "That's all right; we needed a little levity. I was beginning to feel sorry for myself. My mother always told me that I was my own worse enemy. She said that if I worked as hard on positive things as I did to make life hard for myself, I'd be a successful woman."

An intercom announcement that they'd be setting down in fifteen minutes, caused all three to direct their focus to straightening their clothes and hair and repairing any minor make-up damage that may have occurred on this revealing flight between Washington and Boston.

"My God, I look terrible," grumbled Bev. "I can't get off looking like this."

"Don't be silly, you look wonderful, as always," assured Stacey Lea. "Besides, no one is gonna see you. Air Force Junior isn't landing at the main terminal, and a limousine will be waiting to whisk us directly away to Sarah. We'll hardly see a soul."

That's exactly what happened, and as the small motorcade discreetly wound its way to the snobbish Back Bay Snowden Estate, the three friends agreed that along with Ellie, they would put their heads together for a satisfactory solution to Bev's dreadful problem. For the moment, however, they would put even that aside in order to give full attention to Senator Sarah Snowden Winthrop Baynes, the reason for their sad mission.

As their car started up the long driveway to the great nineteenth century mansion that Sarah called home, Stacey Lea thought of Sarah's remarks regarding her maternal family seat. She'd called it her fortress against any kind of storm. Whenever she felt besieged, she would come here, where from behind its thick granite walls nothing, not even words, could penetrate. It was certainly formidable, a virtual Bastille. The infamous Bastille of Paris had once been a home—someone's castle, before it had become a prison, and she concluded that a fortress and a prison were much the same, depending on one's point of view.

A shiver ran up her spine as the huge, cold mass loomed closer. It seemed to hold little solace, the kind we all need. Yes, this could easily become Sarah's *Bastille* if she didn't hurry to escape, tear it down quickly and frantically as the French had done theirs.

"This is sure an imposin' place," stated Sue Ann. "Not much to my taste, mind you, and far too big. I don't know why Sarah's held on to it. I say she should give it to the Historic Trust, let them worry with it, and just visit it now and then. That's what the Fairmonts did with their big old place, and it's smaller than this. Can you imagine growing up here? No wonder she loves it in Texas."

"Be sure you don't mention Texas," Bev warned. "You don't want to set her off. As for me, I find the house quite impressive, and those two little guesthouses attached to the big house are delightful. They're perfect replicas. I understand there are some marvelous Corinthian columns on the other side, facing the water."

"I believe one of those little twin houses contains a pool, built later," Stacey Lea noted. "Sarah's mother insisted on swimming everyday, and Sarah took up the habit. Maybe we'll get a tour before we leave. Look, there's Ellie waiting on the steps."

"Am I glad to see you!" Ellie announced eagerly as she hugged Stacey Lea. "I can't believe he let you come. How did you manage it?"

"I didn't. He suggested it, adding that he wants me to call him as soon as I find how Sarah's doing. He's very concerned." Stacey Lea winked at Ellie as they moved away from the car and outsider ears. "A clever ploy on his part, for what better way to learn her status than through me. And the whole world will find it such a grand gesture, sending his wife on this errand of mercy."

"That *is* clever, you know."

"I'd never accuse my husband of not being clever, but this time, he's more thoughtful than he realizes. It plays right into our hands. I'm going to make good use of this private time. How's she today? Any better?"

"I'm afraid not. Her break-up with her husband along with her strong sense of responsibility have her all mixed up, at least, I think that's it. Frankly, I'm a bit confused. She talks more about the past and her mother than her marriage or her constituency. Well, let's not stand out here. You can see for yourself."

Ellie guided them through the door into the large domed foyer.

"Sarah will meet us in the library. She's gone to the kitchen to see how lunch is coming."

Almost before they could reach the large open double-doors to a very large room with well-stocked bookshelves, Sarah was behind them.

"How nice of you to visit me. I've often wanted to have you here, and I've ordered a grand luncheon, Massachusetts' style, in honor of the occasion! As you can see," Sarah continued, guiding them into the room, "I've also put our cozy sitting arrangement right here near the fire. Stacey Lea, you sit in the middle of the sofa, as usual; Sue Ann, there's your wingback and here's mine, and Beverly, I had this plush velvet chaise brought in from the solarium, especially for you. The only thing I can't decide is where to put Ellie. Your sitting room, Stacey Lea, is much smaller than this room. If I put her back near the wall, she'll be too far away."

"Ellie can sit here on the sofa by me," Stacey Lea responded, quickly, patting the cushion beside her. "Ellie's my right hand so what better place for her to sit than here by me on my right."

"That's perfect," Sarah agreed, after a short pause. "In fact, she should have been there all along."

The five women sat stiffly, well aware that this was not going to be one of their shoes-off, hair-down, belt-letting sessions.

Sue Ann looked toward Beverly. In fact, they were all looking toward Beverly, for Beverly was the only one who could ask what had to be asked. She was the one with the tactless tongue. Besides, Beverly had always been closer to Sarah than anyone else here.

Beverly knew what they were thinking, but this wasn't the time to ask blunt questions. Stacey Lea had that special gift with words, she should do it, but Stacey Lea was looking at her too. And Sue Ann's lips were pursed, waiting, as if she were determined to keep her mouth tightly closed until the matter was resolved.

Beverly looked at Sarah sitting rigidly in her wingback chair. Come to think of it, Sarah had always sat stiffly; she'd never taken off *her* shoes. She looked so fragile sitting there in that long black dress with that little black lace cap on her head. This is ridiculous, and for some crazy reason she remembered a silly joke about a man who kept going into the same bar night after night with a carrot sticking out of each ear..."and he would just have one drink and then leave. It was driving the bartender crazy, but he refused to ask the man why he was wearing carrots because he knew that was exactly what the man wanted him to do. Finally, one night the man came in with a stalk of celery sticking out of each ear and the bartender could stand it no longer. "Why do you have a stalk of celery sticking out of each ear?" he asked, and the man replied, "I ran out of carrots."

Beverly started laughing louder than her joke deserved while the others managed a few chuckles for this joke that had popped out of nowhere. That wasn't what they'd expected. Sarah, who had always suffered from only a sporadic sense of humor, smiled politely, obviously having no idea what was even mildly humorous.

"But, Beverly, that doesn't explain why the man had carrots sticking out of his ears?"

Damn, thought Beverly, why in hell did I tell that silly joke? I swore that I'd never tell a joke around Sarah again. She never understands, but that insatiable desire to do so makes her a real pain.

"That's just it, Sarah, it's a ridiculous story with the explanation more foolish than wearing carrots. But there's a point, and that is that sometimes the answer makes no more sense than the question. Sometimes you instinctively know that, but you have to ask, just as the bartender did."

"I guess I understand, but I don't understand what made you think of it now. We were discussing the impending snowstorm, and I had just started quoting from Whittier's *Snowbound*, *The sun that brief December day\Rose cheerless over hills of gra...*"

"You made me think of it, Sarah," Beverly interrupted, "you did, you sitting there so prim and proper in that long black dress and little lacy cap and us needing to know why, but afraid of your answer."

"Don't you like it?" Sarah asked, pertly.

"It isn't that, Sarah, it's just that it's a costume. You look like Queen Victoria in mourning."

"It's not a costume. It was my mother's. We're the same size. See? See how it fits perfectly?" With this, Sarah got up and twirled around to prove her point.

"It certainly does, honey, and it's a beautiful dress—such fine material," acknowledged Sue Ann, "but people don't wear these kinds of clothes anymore. They haven't worn 'em for way over a hundred years."

"Well, I think it's a nice dress and part of a nice custom. It's a morning dress, you see, and it is morning."

"No, Sarah," Beverly corrected, "it is a dress for mourning."

"That's what I said!"

"No, I mean it's a dress for putting on when you're sad like Queen Victoria was after Prince Albert died."

"Well, I'm also in mourning and it's morning, so it is doubly appropriate." Sarah snapped, beginning to show irritation. "I'm in mourning just like Queen Victoria was. I'm in mourning for Charlie. Charlie and I are getting a divorce, you know, and a divorce isn't much different from a death."

As Sarah spoke, she sat down, smoothed her skirt and folded her hands in her lap. Her voice was matter-of-fact as if she were talking about some mere daily occurrence, nothing so overwhelming as her whole marriage.

"It'll all work out. You know how much Charlie loves you," mothered Sue Ann as she went over to hug her, but Sarah put out her hand to ward her off.

"No, it won't, and it's better this way. I never really belonged in Texas. I belong here in this house. There's so much to take care of. My mother must be turning over in her grave at the terrible condition of everything, and her plants, half of them have died. You can't depend on anyone else, you know, only yourself."

"Sarah," said Stacey Lea as she reached over to rest her hand on Sarah's pale folded ones, which were clinched, the knuckles white, "why did you make that speech yesterday? You know how dangerous such talk is and how it would bother Charlie."

"I told you that Charlie and I are going to get a divorce! What Charlie thinks doesn't matter anymore; Charlie was a mistake. All he wants me to do is stay at that ranch with him. I can't do that. I have too much to do. Wait until you see mother's plants, then you'll understand."

"All right then, let's say Charlie doesn't matter, but you matter. Why did you jeopardize yourself the way you did? We'd all agreed that you would keep a low profile."

"We agreed mainly because of Charlie."

"That's not true."

"Why are you scolding me, Stacey Lea? Aren't you pleased with me for speaking up? I did it for you, all of you, for everybody, for my mother too!"

Sarah removed a white lacy handkerchief from the end of her long sleeve and held it with both hands over her face.

"What do you mean, Sarah, that you did it for your mother, too?" Stacey Lea pursued, more puzzled than ever. "She's been gone for sometime."

Sarah lowered the handkerchief from her face and gazed intently at the silent faces of her guests. Finally, she released a soft sigh of resignation, walked over to the large library desk and removed a rosewood-carved box from one of its drawers.

"In this box are letters from my mother to your mother-in-law, Judith Forbes, Stacey Lea. They became friends and corresponded frequently during the years my mother supported the Foundation. These letters have helped me to get to know my mother in a way I never knew her when she was alive."

Sarah opened the box and removed a packet of letters before continuing. "We were never close. I was six years old when my parents divorced, and she returned here with me to live. I hated it here. I'd visit my father and his large, wonderful, second family and never want to leave. The Winthrop house was always full of laughter. I think that's what attracted me to Charlie—his big, boisterous family." Sarah paused for another sigh before continuing.

"When I got older and went away to school, Mother became more and more reclusive. I thought she didn't care for anything but her plants and this big old house until I went through her papers and found her substantial bequests to the Foundation. I realized then that, even though my mother could no longer face the world herself, she reached out to support good things in it. Funny how it's so hard to see one's parents as people just like everybody else with needs and faults and...

It's as if we have blinders on with them, that we take off for others. Anyway, after Mother's death, Mrs. Forbes sent me these letters. I believe they were written with the hope that I'd someday read them. Her last letter haunts me."

Sarah removed the top letter from the neat, pink-ribboned stack. She did not look at it as she took a deep breath and expressed dramatically, *"Thank God, her Sarah was not cursed with her frailties. Her Sarah was strong, and if Mrs. Forbes needed help, she could depend on her Sarah!"*

Just as dramatically, she stopped, looked at her friends, and said, "Don't you see, I have failed my mother in the only thing she ever really asked of me? Sandra Ackerman is dead, the Foundation has been neutralized, the work my mother so believed in has gone for naught, and I make meek little speeches before the AMA."

Sad tears flowed down Sarah's face as her friends surrounded her. Tightly clutching one another, their tears intermingled, a communion of tears.

They cried for Sarah's mother. They cried for their mothers. They cried for all mothers. They cried for Sandra Ackerman. They cried for the Foundation. They cried for Sarah. Sarah cried for Sarah. Beverly even added a few sobs for a broken nail she'd experienced the previous week. They cried in pain, and finally, they cried in pleasure. What a marvelous feeling to just let go and cry. There was definitely a therapeutic value to it, and it was especially gratifying when done with others.

Sue Ann would suggest later that they put regularly scheduled crying sessions into their By-laws, and attendance should be mandatory. She suggested that this was one of the things that was probably wrong with men; they were never allowed to cry, which made them take out their frustrations in less beneficial ways, even bad ways. All agreed that the whole world would be a much better place if it just had a great big organized cry once in a while.

Finally, their cry gave way to light chatter and warm laughter as they enjoyed the considerable Massachusetts' luncheon feast which Sarah had promised.

But soon, Stacey Lea was back at her place of honor, beginning to pour tea after Sarah had suggested that it was now time for a Boston Tea Party.

"I think it's time we get down to business. Is everyone ready for a serious meeting?" Stacey Lea asked as she continued to pour.

"Absolutely," responded Sarah eagerly, "Now that you understand why I had to make my speech yesterday, I know you feel as good about it as I do. In fact, you should look on it as the kick-off for our campaign."

"No, Sarah, I'm afraid I can't agree," Stacey Lea said firmly. "What you did was irresponsible. We can't go off on our own. Our unity is what will make us strong. You above all should understand that."

Sarah's face and body indicated the sinking feeling she was experiencing inside as she looked at the others for support. Even Sue Ann, always charitable, looked down when Sarah's eyes reached for hers.

"You're all against me. You didn't hear a word I said!"

"That's not true. I know just how you feel. My mother and I were never able to reconcile, and she took her own life. It's always been a sadness for me, but I can't let Virginia Stacey anymore than you can let Agatha Snowden interfere with our objective."

"You've gotten hard, Stacey Lea," Sarah judged.

"And you must harden yourself, Sarah. Can you do that?"

Stacey Lea's simple question was gently asked, but it was great with meaning. Everyone understood, and Sarah even in her distressed state was well aware of what Stacey Lea needed to know. Furtive looks showed her that they all needed to know.

"I'm sorry. I'd hoped that you would find my speech fine and brave. I understand now that it was foolish, like me. I also understand why you feel concern for my future within this group. I am the bad apple and must be sorted out."

"You're not the bad apple, Sarah, you're, well, you're more like the weak link, at least until we understand what happened to you."

"The reason is obvious," stated Sue Ann, flatly. "She'd just had a terrible argument with Charlie, her marriage was in shambles, so she lashed out at all the causes for her unhappiness."

"Sarah, where are you going?"

"To check the kitchen; make sure everything is tidied. I won't be long."

The four women looked in amazement at Sarah's receding back. Beverly was the first to respond.

"Well, I guess that's that until Queen Victoria returns."

"Maybe this is a good time to try to get a handle on things, without her here," Ellie suggested. "First, we know that Sarah flew directly from Texas to Boston, waited three days before holding an emotional press conference, and then shut herself up here. Doesn't it seem contrived?"

"Are you suggesting," Beverly articulated slowly, "that Sarah might be putting on an act?"

"Don't get me wrong, I do believe she's under a lot of stress, but it's possible that some of Sarah's actions are linked with her inability to tell us she plans to stay here, that she doesn't have the strength to continue."

"Maybe she did tell us when we first came," noted Sue Ann as they all began to get on the same page. "Remember when I tried to console her about Charlie. She told me that she didn't belong in Texas, that her place was here?"

"And her costume. She's certainly rational enough to know how ludicrous it is, or at least, how ludicrous we would think it is."

"Yes, and her preoccupation with those damn plants."

"And her preoccupation with this house."

"But why put on an act? Why doesn't she just tell us?"

"Because that makes her a quitter. Maybe she would rather be considered unstable."

"Life can certainly get complicated," Sue Ann sighed.

"No," disagreed Stacey Lea, "we make it that way."

Just at that moment, a smiling head topped with a black lace cap peeked through the door with a cheery, "Hello, there! I just wanted to bob in to see how you're doing. I'll be with you shortly. I only have to fold a few clothes from the dryer before they wrinkle."

"Like hell, you will!" Beverly blared as she made a mad rush toward the disappearing head. "You get back here this minute, Sarah Winthrop! We didn't come all the way up here to wait for you to fold clothes or water your goddamn plants or any other little domestic chores!"

Beverly returned shortly, dragging a somewhat recalcitrant Sarah.

"I don't like your attitude, Beverly. This is my home, you are my guest, and you must obey protocol."

Before Beverly could respond, Ellie asked, "Sarah, what do you want from us today?"

"Would anyone like more tea?"

"No, Sarah," Stacey Lea stated firmly, "we'll sit right where we are until we're finished, and we can't even get started until you answer Ellie's question."

Sarah looked around. They were sitting erect, their eyes concentrated on her. They'd wait, she could see that, the same way Ellie and Stacey Lea had waited for her to speak, before that other tea party. They were good at waiting, those two, and Beverly and Sue Ann didn't seem any different. She was alone. The brittle, thin wall she'd erected began to crumble.

"Anytime I'm in Scotland, I try to get to St. Andrews where they have an ancient cemetery that sits high overlooking the North Sea. How grand to spend an eternity with that view!" Sarah's eyes had a distant look as she drifted far away with her thoughts.

"I know the cemetery. It's beautiful there," Ellie encouraged.

"I love cemeteries! I love to walk around the stones and wonder about the lives that ended there. Did you know *Elegy Written in a Country Churchyard* is my favorite poem?"

"Written by Thomas Gray, wasn't it?"

"That's right, Ellie," responded Sarah, enthusiastically. "Yes, I walk among the dead and ponder, *Perhaps in this neglected spot is laid/Some heart once pregnant with celestial fire; Hands, that the rod of empire might have swayed/Or waked to ecstasy the living lyre?* Remember those lines?"

"Uh, I haven't read it in a long time." Ellie's response was apologetic

"There's one grave... *Yet ev'n these bones from insult to protect/Some frail memorial still erected nigh/With uncouth rhymes and shapeless sculpture decked/Implores the passing tribute of a sigh.*" Sarah's eyes filled with tears as she continued, "I'm always filled with an overwhelming sadness when I stand before that grave stuck back near the thick wall that protects it from the sea. The epitaph reads, *She did what she could.*"

"What does this woman's grave have to do with anything?" Beverly asked getting impatient.

"How would you like to spend an eternity with *She did what she could* on your tombstone?"

"I ..uh, I can't say I'd like it but..."

"Don't you understand? That's the epitaph for women. We do what we can, but it never makes much difference. Women are the passing sighs of Gray's poem, and men are the celestial fires, the hands that sway empires. We're the sighs! We do what we can but we're still just sighs. That's the sadness, and I'm the worst of all. I did what I could with my speech and it was only a sigh. That's all I'm capable of—sighs. That's my epitaph, I've accepted it, and I intend it be on my tomb!"

There was a great pause with no one quite sure of how to address Sarah's outburst, although they were careful not to sigh.

"But until then," Sarah finished, breaking the pause with a casual air that belied her previous eruption, "I have much to do. As Candide said, *I must cultivate my own garden*!"

They were full of sighs as they left Snowden Hall late that early December afternoon. They would miss Sarah. Sarah had been battered and bruised, and her fragile constitution could take no more. Stacey Lea couldn't help but be ashamed that Palmer had played any part in this. She was also sorry that Palmer had won again, but she promised herself that it would be the last time. Just before they left, Sarah had whispered into her ear a final quote, a warning, "Always remember, my dear, what our founding father Ben Franklin wrote, *Everyone is a moon, and has a dark-side which he never shows to anybody.* You must be very careful."

They had looked back and not spoken as they watched Sarah's thin frame fade away as their car rolled down the long driveway. In fact, they spoke very little until they were safely aboard *Air Force Junior* and on their return journey. It started with the weather.

"It's lucky we left when we did," Sue Ann observed. "The snow seems to be getting serious."

"Yes, when I spoke with Palmer, he was already concerned that we were still here."

"I'll bet it's mostly because he wants all the gory details of Sarah's demise," Sue Ann responded, bitterly.

"Don't make it sound as if she's dead!" Beverly retorted.

"Please, let's not start!"

"I know," Beverly agreed, "it's just that it's so hard to accept Sarah not being around, and

that she's going to live in that big old house by herself in that mourning dress. I almost wish I had one to put on for her."

"Now who's talkin' as if she's dead," Sue Ann commented. "I've decided to look at it the way Stacey Lea explained it to Sarah. Now she's a strong link, our senior stateswoman. She doesn't have to play like she's something she's not. Her fortress is our fortress, and when we have need of her and it, all we have to do is take the short trip to Boston."

"Did I say all that?"

"No, but that's the way I've interpreted it; besides, that fat check she gave us is gonna buy lots of support, and there's more where that came from."

"Quite true!" agreed Ellie

The conversation stopped as each again had her own thoughts of the day to ponder.

"I never thought," said Sue Ann, "that I'd ever acknowledge that I'd miss Sarah's quotes."

"Yes," agreed Stacey Lea, "or Sarah being able to help with ours."

There was another lull in the conversation.

"You know," Beverly began, "I feel different after today. I feel like I have this great big need. Something I never have felt before, as if my whole life up to now has been waiting to be."

"To be what?"

"I'm not sure. The only thing I'm sure of is that I don't want to be a sigh."

"ME NEITHER!" their voices agreed.

"Well then, my friends," Stacey Lea said, perking up, "I suggest we get to it. We got a lot done at Sarah's, but we still have a lot to do before our campaign starts, and we only have three days until *Day Zero.*"

"I agree that the more things we have happen at one time, the more impact we'll have, but I don't see how we can be ready by the tenth."

"Sue Ann, we must have deadlines. That's how you get things done."

"I don't disagree with that, Stacey Lea, but a reasonable deadline. After all, this is new to us."

"Listen to me, all of you. I did not choose that date at random. I realize that we'll have to work our fannies off to get ready, but we must! You must trust me in this. I know what I'm talkin' about, and I feel so strongly about it that I'm not sure we'll succeed if we don't do it according to my schedule. Now, let's get to work!"

"I don't understand you, Palmer. I thought you'd be pleased that Sarah wasn't going to be around anymore. Frankly, I rather look forward to you not having her to upset you; even though, I do feel sorry for the poor dear."

"It isn't that. You know I'm delighted to be rid of her. I just don't like the bitch dictating her replacement."

"It's her seat. She's won it time and again, fair and square."

"That's because those voters in Massachusetts are crazy. Sometimes I've wondered if there was something in the air or drinking water up there that affects them."

"There's nothing much you can do about that."

"I'd like to show them what a good strong no nonsense Senator could do for them. Maybe I could change their shameless voting history."

"Now come on, darlin'," Stacey Lea teased as she curled her arms around his neck, "you're just annoyed because that's the only state you didn't carry last election."

"Why shouldn't I be?"

"True. I was disappointed too that you didn't carry the whole nation. Now, come on, let's get some sleep. I'm pure exhausted. Not only am I still suffering jet lag from our amazing trip, but you can't imagine what a trial today was, and to top it off, that big *ole* house of Sarah's is absolutely oppressive. I don't know how she can stand it for even a short time, much less live there for the rest of her life which seems to be what she plans."

"She's plain loco, that's why. Just look at that replacement list she tendered."

"We can't all like the same people."

"She's determined that another woman take her place?"

"Yes, I'm afraid so. She said she won't quit unless."

"That's blackmail."

"Think of it this way, dear. If Massachusetts doesn't appoint another woman, there'll be no women in the Senate, and how's that gonna look? You appointed Mildred Dillard to the Court yourself, and you haven't found her troublesome."

"True, but I knew she'd play the game."

"Can't you do that again?"

"I don't know these women that well. That's my problem. Was there one she preferred?"

"Yes, Crater."

"Then, she's definitely out, and I certainly can't see Mulrooney appointing his wife. That was a stupid selection."

"I don't know. Governor Mulrooney might, if he thought you wanted her. You'd have to show your support, of course. That way it wouldn't cause too many cries of nepotism."

"Well, I won't. I don't like her anyway. Frankly, I think she wears the pants in that family, and I don't want her trying to wear them down here."

"That leaves Marygrace O'Brien."

"The name itself is enough to make me nauseous. Isn't she a state senator?"

"Yes, don't you remember at that reception several months ago?"

"Her? Wait a minute, isn't she that ex-nun with the shiny face and Peter Pan collar?"

"That's right. Cute little thing with reddish blond hair and freckles."

"Yes, I remember her. Once a nun always a nun."

"I suppose they don't ever quite lose the look, but I think she's cute." Stacey Lea recalled that she'd tried not to use that word since it had set up such a to-do with Beverly after the luncheon, but she'd just used it twice. Still, some things were cute, and Marygrace was.

"I certainly won't have any *cute* little ex-nun down here if I can help it, and this time I can."

"Really, dear, knowing how you feel about Cardinal Bishop, I should think you'd enjoy supporting an ex-nun. It'd make him blow a fuse, for sure."

Palmer had a good chuckle visualizing the prospect but then shook his head.

"Shame on you, thinking up ways to bedevil the good Cardinal. It's tempting, but even that can't make me champion a do-gooder ex-nun."

"Well, that exhausts Sarah's recommendations, but there might be another possibility."

"What's that?"

"Leslie Farnsworth."

"Who the hell's that?"

"A lawyer in Boston who's very supportive of WOW."

"What kind of lawyer?"

"Corporate, I believe."

"Any political experience?"

"She supported you."

"That only shows she has good taste."

"I like her. She's lots of fun, one of the girls."

"Keep on. She's beginning to develop the proper credentials."

"Good family, old money, successful practice."

"Married?"

"Yes, she and her husband are part of the same law firm."

"How do you know she'd take it?"

"I don't, of course."

"What about Winthrop? Do you think she'd go for her?"

"As a matter of fact, I mentioned her to Sarah today. Let's put it this way, she didn't say *no*.'"

"I don't know. This Farnsworth's a completely unknown factor. You can never predict what someone will do when they get power."

"We're only talking about little more than a year. How much damage can any of them do in one year? She'll hardly have found the Powder Room before she has to go home."

"Maybe it'd work." Palmer contemplated, reaching over to turn out the light. "I'll give it some thought."

"Very well, dear," responded Stacey Lea as she reached over to kiss her husband goodnight, then settled back down to wait an appropriate moment before adding with a yawn, "By the way, I really would suggest that you not think on it too long. Sarah's not in a good way with the breakup of her marriage and all, quite unpredictable. She just might pop right out of this at any moment and be back down here causing you all sorts of misery."

He didn't speak immediately, but she knew he would. She could almost hear him thinking.

"You have a good point there, Stacey Lea. I'll call Mulrooney first thing in the morning, and you call Sarah. We'll see if we can get this thing done by the first of the week."

CHAPTER TWELVE

COUNTDOWN, DAY THREE

It was almost ten before Stacey Lea stirred the next morning. Palmer had been up a long time. She knew, for he'd awakened her early with the impulse to go to Camp David. Every once in a while he got this whim to go up with some of his cronies, and far be it for her to complain. The luxury of at least a day and a half with no demands from him seemed a luscious eternity.

"Get up, slug-a-bed," Ellie summoned, as she walked briskly into Stacey Lea's darkened bedroom unannounced.

"Don't you dare open those drapes," Stacey Lea commanded, "and what is a slug-a-bed?"

"Oh, it's something I picked up from a novel set in the Middle Ages," Ellie answered as she threw the drapes open, paying no attention to her orders.

"Well," Stacey Lea allowed, stretching, "if slug stands for sluggish and the rest for someone who wants to stay in bed then its no misnomer for me this morning."

"Mildred Dillard called, Sue Ann called, and no telling who'll call next. I don't plan to make another excuse for you. Here, drink your orange juice. I brought you dry toast with black coffee. You want anything else?"

"No, that's perfect. It's so good to get what I want. Obviously, Coleman has gone with Palmer?"

"Yes, strutting around here like the *cat's meow* before they left."

"I have to do something about him. I already know he can't stand things out of order. Why don't we mess up his rooms while he's away?"

"Stace, that's ridiculous! You're evil, besides, we might get caught."

"We'd just deny it. My word's better than his any day, and we need to check him out. Sarah whispered a Ben Franklin quote in my ear before we left her, warning me that everyone is a moon and has a dark-side. It's important we know Coleman's."

"Coleman's all dark side. Let me think about it. I'll have to build up my courage."

"By the way, we should check on the whereabouts of Cardinal Bishop and Judge Earle with Palmer slipping away."

"Already have. Cardinal Bishop is in Buffalo. His mother's being buried tomorrow, and Walker is doing his evangelical bit in Germany and isn't scheduled back until tomorrow."

"Who went with Palmer?"

"The same old boys—Secretaries Johnson and Jennings, Senator Fairmont and General McCracken, and Coleman, of course."

"Then it's just one of those *Fact Finding Missions* Palmer enjoys so much because they also play war games at the Bunk...the Bunker! That's where they were. That's where the table is! They were in the Bunker War Room!"

"The table in your vision?" Ellie responded, comprehending.

"Yes, Ellie. That's where they were, around that big table in the Bunker War Room. I knew something about it looked familiar. Beau picked up Earle Walker that day and they went to the Bunker and Palmer met them there. It's hard to get in there except by helicopter."

"This is good news," Ellie responded, quite enthusiastic now. "It draws the net even tighter around their conspiracy, placing them together in a logical place."

"Yes, I don't know why I didn't think of it sooner. I'm so pleased with myself I think I'll soak in a nice hot sudsy bath for at least an hour!"

"You can't. Mildred Dillard will be here at eleven which means you have about thirty minutes to eat breakfast and get dressed."

"Oh, all right," the First Lady said, indicating that she'd resigned herself to the inevitable, even though she was not yet ready for the world's intrusion. "But, while I dress, you order us some coffee to my office. Oh, and Ellie, get them to send some very gooey breakfast rolls with the coffee. My sweet-tooth's giving me fits this morning."

"Before I forget," said Ellie, walking briskly into Stacey Lea's large sunny office and at the same time reaching into her suit pocket, "here's the key you wanted made."

"Good," Stacey Lea responded, transferring it quickly to the pocket of her forest green coat sweater. "What about duplicating Mother Forbes' writing? Have you had luck with that?"

"See for yourself. Darryl guarantees that it'll take an expert to expose any of his work, and even then there'd be doubt."

"I can't tell the difference. Isn't it fortuitous that your old beau wound up at the Archives, an authority on old papers and things?"

"It's certainly our good fortune."

"Are you still attracted to him?"

"More than I was then. He tells me he had a tough time getting over me when I left with you, and I never even thought he was serious."

"You're blushing, Ellie. It's a big event for you to have a beau who makes you blush. Speaking of events, Palmer's calling Gov. Mulrooney this morning to discuss Leslie Farnsworth."

"I knew you could do it."

"Yes, in fact, it was fun. I was in the *Catbird Seat* all the way. Now, let's see. We have Leslie and Casey lined up. What about Alma Tyler?"

"Still on the fence. Earle Walker really put a scare in her. In all fairness, I can't blame her. California is his home office and her constituency is made up of lots of those fanatical Eternists."

"That's unfortunate, but she's gonna have to snap out of it. She has a responsibility, and since she's already in office, we can't afford her resignation. I'm not gonna fool with Palmer's mind on another choice replacement this soon. You better get her here as soon as you can."

"I followed your trip with real American enthusiasm. You did us all proud!" Mildred Dillard exclaimed as she and Stacey Lea completed opening remarks.

"Thank you. And Ellie's been filling me in on your accomplishments during my absence."

"Yes, things have gone well."

Without further ado, Mildred laid Casey's drawings and their companion pictures out on the First Lady's large American walnut desk.

"My friend at the Justice Department was able to identify two of them," announced Mildred. "Unfortunately, the so-called Colombian is still illusive."

"I'm not worried. When we find these two, they should lead us to others."

"Yes, and Janet Cuéves, our field operative, is starting on that now. She's put together an impressive taskforce—all professionals, of course."

"That's wonderful, Mildred! If this force turns out to be what we hope, we'll be able to do almost anything, and women like Alma Tyler won't be so fearful."

"Yes, that's true, but have you given any thought to what we're going to do with them when we find them.

"Casey asked the same thing. No, I don't know, but I believe they have to disappear. We can't just watch them; they're too dangerous; plus, the impact on the powers that motivate them should be considerable if they vanish—like puffs of smoke. Don't you think?"

"I agree, and Janet had a suggestion you might like to consider. She's Cuban, you know, and she said she knows where there's an abandoned prison in Cuba—a hidden one, where Fidel Castro used to keep political prisoners whom he just wanted to disappear temporarily. She has lots of family there who'd be happy to guard them for a small fee, and she could whisk them off in the middle of the night with no one the wiser."

"I wouldn't want them placed in dire conditions, and that's all I associate with Castro's Cuba."

"According to Janet, this one was somewhat upscale and comfortable and could be again, without too much work."

"What do you think, Ellie?" Stacey Lea's brow furrowed with indecision.

"I think this is an extraordinary bit of luck. Besides, what are our options?"

"You're right. It's our only choice at this point, and we don't have a minute to wait, even if there might be a better one. The bait's on the hook, and our adversaries may be getting ready to swarm down on Casey at this very moment."

It was mid-afternoon before Mildred Dillard closed her briefcase and prepared to leave.

"By the way, Mildred," Stacey Lea asked, her voice reflecting the satisfaction of one well pleased with the day's harvest, "what kind of splash do you plan to make on our Opening Day?"

"Oh, didn't Ellie tell you? I plan to begin a push for an early hearing on Montgomery versus St. Bartholomew's Hospital, the Roman Catholic Diocese of Baton Rouge, the State of Louisiana, and God knows who else. It's been stalled but I'm pulling a few strings."

"I'm afraid you'll have to fill me in," Stacey Lea apologized.

"Certainly. A man named Roy Montgomery claims that his wife is dead because the Church, she was in a Catholic Hospital, wouldn't allow a therapeutic abortion and the State would not intervene. Nor would the hospital release his wife so that he could seek help elsewhere, claiming that she was in a too critical condition to be moved. There's a growing faction, even in today's political climate that agree with Montgomery, that in this case the abortion issue was extended too far, past the realm of logic and all right to life."

"I remember it now. Didn't the lower court decide that the State couldn't interfere in Church controlled institutions?" inquired Stacey Lea.

"That's true, but even if one agrees with that, the Montgomerys aren't Catholic. Also, he had no choice where his wife was taken since the ambulances in Baton Rouge rotate emergency deliveries, and it was St. Bartholomew's turn. It's a complicated case under existing laws."

"Yes, it is," agreed Ellie, "and it's another case that points out one of the very things that Pro-Choice groups feared—the extreme and illogical abuses to women if abortion were made illegal.

"Do you think you have much chance?"

"Probably not this time, but I do have one justice who'll stand with me, and I'm working on a second. Also, I'll write the minority position."

"What good will that do?" Stacey Lea questioned, frowning.

"It will begin to give people hope and courage; especially, lower courts where many decisions, for too long now, have been influenced by the knowledge that there's only one side, and decisions otherwise would be futile as well as politically foolhardy."

"Well, you're certainly going to shake Palmer up because he told me just last night that he was sure, when he appointed you, that you'd play the game."

"Yes, I guess he's in for a few surprises all right."

Upon this point, and several others during her very productive meeting with the nation's First Lady, Mildred Dillard had pleasant reflections while returning to her home in Georgetown. How ironic that Palmer Forbes intended to obtain an appropriation from Congress for his wife's project, WOW, and she intended to use it to support her defensive against him and his intrigues.

Palmer Forbes had no idea what he'd married, of this Mildred was sure. She suspected that the ultimate irony lay in that marriage itself. Perhaps, he was president only because Stacey Lea was supposed to be First Lady? Perhaps Stacey Lea was the one on track, fulfilling her destiny, and Palmer Forbes was only her means to it? Fascinating idea, for Mildred Dillard believed in destiny.

A momentous *Battle of the Sexes* was brewing. The excitement of the upcoming confrontations and their repercussions made her feel young again. She imagined it would be like no battle fought on any field of combat since the world began, and whatever the outcome, Justice Dillard decided, she wouldn't have missed being part of it.

Stacey Lea walked through her husband's dressing room and entered his bedroom. She had a pretty good idea what the key fit. She'd asked Palmer once what the key around his neck was for, and he'd jokingly responded that it was the key to his heart. When she'd replied that she thought she had that, he'd brushed it off with his usual, that it was not anything for her to worry her *pretty little head* about. After that, her curiosity had been piqued, so anytime she got the chance, she'd tried cabinets, drawers, and anything else around to see if her entrance was barred. The only thing locked was the cabinet under the fish tank.

Why he had such a passion for those things was beyond her. Fish could be soothing to watch swimming around but not these ugly little flesh-eating piranhas. Palmer had called her in once to watch Coleman give them a chicken leg. They'd cleaned the bone in nothing flat. Coleman liked them too.

The key turned easily in the lock, but she made no move to open it. She realized that opening the door was going to be harder than she'd thought. Palmer had a right to this private place where no one could intrude. Their lives were like the fish-tank to start with; the darkness underneath should be respected. Sure, she was curious about the cabinet, but she knew that if it had not been for his machinations, she would have left it alone.

Yes, she analyzed, it's his fault that I have to do this. If he'd not been doing so many ugly things, this wouldn't be necessary. The more she remembered, the more courage she got; soon, devoid of conscience and fear, she reached over and opened the door.

There were only two shelves. On the bottom one was neatly folded a bright, plush, velvet cloth, which looked very much like an American flag. In the center of the top shelf sat a bronze urn that bore the single engraved word *Mother.* She shrank from it, instinctively. Pulling out the cloth, she carefully examined the neat manner in which it was folded before unfolding it and spreading it out on the floor.

Stacey Lea sat back and stared for a long time at the long hooded robe. A frown gradually formed deep creases in her brow as she counted the fifty stars and the thirteen stripes. She had to lean over on all fours into the thick fabric to investigate the ornately scrolled letters intertwined in the Presidential Seal. Her fingers had outlined the G, the P, and most of the F before she realized that they were Palmer's initials.

"Dear God," she whispered softly, "what dark secret have I revealed?"

Tears stung her eyes as her head turned back toward the open cabinet. The contents of the urn were obvious; perhaps too obvious and certainly too monstrous to be true. Dashing back to her own rooms, she returned wearing gloves and carrying an envelope and a spoon. Gently removing the top from the urn, she placed a small amount of the powdery substance into the envelope, and licked it tight. Then she returned everything the way she'd found them before carefully wiping the cabinet handle and frame of fingerprints. With a sense of urgency, she left the room.

"Ellie," she panted into her intercom, "I have a rush job for you."

"She's what?" Palmer Forbes screeched, pounding his large knuckled hand down on the big, round table in the Bunker War Room. No one moved as the Commander-in-Chief's bulging eyes glared through an angry red face at Beau Fairmont.

"You idiot!" Forbes screeched even louder, grabbing Beau by his shirt collar and pulling him nose-to-nose. "Can't you do anything right? I've carried you all these years, for what? What would you be without me? Now, get the hell out of here and do your job! This time, I want it done right, or I'll take care of it myself, and you!"

At that moment, all hell broke loose in the War Room. Far too interested in the real-life drama unfolding between the President and his right-hand man, no one had noticed the warnings, from the huge, flashing electronic boards, that the enemy was taking the advantage. No one noticed, that is, until it was too late. Now total chaos reigned as missiles screamed before their thunderous blasts devastated targets, passionless, electronic voices spit out commands, and airplanes roared unchallenged through the radar. The attack was grim and merciless.

"Man your stations! Man your stations!" Forbes shrieked, rushing around the room that was now alive with confusion, his hands waving frantically in the air. "We've lost! I never lose! Take my eyes off you for one minute and you lose! You weren't manning your stations!"

Just then the gigantic boards that surrounded the rotunda War Room agreed, as one after the other blackened, tired of it all. On each appeared in big, flashing block letters the taunting and incontestable facts, YOU HAVE BEEN ANNIHILATED. THERE ARE NO SURVIVORS.

All was quiet, as the earlier cacophony was given time to filter into nothingness.

Finally, Palmer Forbes stated, quietly and coldly, "And you, Senator Fairmont, it's all your fault. I don't want to see you again until you've finished your job. I just got rid of one she-devil; I won't have another to deal with because of your incompetence."

It was mid-afternoon when Beau Fairmont arrived home. Sue Ann recognized from his walk and his hunched shoulders that something was very wrong, especially when he told her that he had returned alone. After eavesdropping on his first call, she quietly went into Randal's bedroom and called Stacey Lea on her daughter's private phone.

"This is an unexpected turn of events," Stacey Lea speculated. "I figured we had, at least, until Monday. We'll just have to move faster, that's all, to make sure Casey's protected—not from Beau, mind you, but Palmer might send some of those nasty men down again. They may be on their way right at this very minute."

"Yes, that wouldn't surprise me. Beau's pretty shook up. I don't know what happened, but I have an idea that Palmer's involved."

"Are you sure you want to bother trying to talk to him right now?"

"Yes, I must do this."

"Very well, but remember our discussion this morning."

"I know. You don't think it's worth the bother."

"I never said that. I only said you can't change a leopard's spots, at least, that quickly. After all, I'm the one who suggested you not burn all your bridges, that you should take it easy on him."

"Well, I'm sure gonna try to get him to cancel that plane reservation he just made to Nashville."

"If you do, you be sure he makes one to someplace else. We have to get him away, at least, until we see how the wind blows after Tuesday."

"I'll do my best; also, I'll do my best to make the fences repairable."

"Yes, Beau might become a powerful friend if we do this right. In any case, he's your husband, and you're gonna have to keep an eye on him if he remains our enemy."

"I wish you were doing this, Stacey Lea. I surely don't feel very strong or very smart right now."

"You are, honey, just remember what I've said to you. Just call it up, it's there. You have good blood. Now, you go do what you have to do. I'll be expecting a call from you later one way or the other. In any case, we'll have *Plan B* ready."

When Sue Ann got back downstairs, she noticed that one of the telephone lines was lit. Picking up the hall phone as quietly as she could, she was just in time to hear Beau advise Casey that Palmer was very upset.

"I've lived in fear too long, Beau. I have to do this no matter the…"

"Why, hello. Casey. This is Sue Ann. How are…?"

"What the hell, Sue Ann! What are you doing interrupting my conversation?" her husband exploded.

She ignored him as she spoke again to Casey.

"We're sorry if we've disturbed your Saturday afternoon. Lord knows, when you get on that campaign trail, you're gonna have far too little time to call your own. Now, you don't worry yourself with anything Beaufort may have said. He's had a few too many bourbons this afternoon."

Sue Ann hardly managed a *good-by* as Beau bounded from the study like an angry bull who had been challenged once too often.

"Go back into the study and sit down, Beaufort. We're gonna have to talk."

There was something about her coolness that halted him. Besides, his prior humiliation by Palmer had sapped most of his fight.

They sat on either end of the overstuffed leather sofa that was close enough to the fireplace to catch a little of its warmth.

"Why don't you put another log on the fire, Beaufort, before we get too involved," Sue Ann suggested. "A hearty fire does cheer on a dismal December day."

Beau obeyed, not replying until he returned to the sofa.

"You want to tell me what's goin' on here? Why you took over my telephone call and put words in my mouth? And I wasn't drinking."

"Well, I had a choice. Would you have preferred I told her the truth, that you're not an honorable man, that you're a no-good liar and scoundrel, and you should be horse-whipped all the way back to Mississippi? But I suspect she knows all that."

"Watch out there."

"No, you watch out. I know what you did to Casey. I know that you've been involved in lots of other things, bad things. And I know something else; it's stoppin' right now."

"Casey tell you?"

"No."

"Who did?"

"That's irrelevant. The important thing is you did it, and you're getting ready to hurt her again. What were you going to do to hush her up this time, Beaufort?"

"You don't understand. I don't want to hurt Casey."

"Then tell me? I'm willing to listen."

"I can't. You'll have to trust me."

"Trust you? That's a laugh!" With that, Sue Ann picked up a large manila folder she'd placed on the cocktail table in front of her and tossed it into his lap. "Look at all the trust in there if you want a laugh too!"

Beau opened the envelope and looked at the contents. His shoulders then truly slumped.

"How long have you been having me followed?"

"For a while now."

"Then you know I haven't been with anyone in several months."

"Yes, is that supposed to help?"

"No, I suppose not, but they never really meant anything, Sue Ann, truly they didn't."

"I never thought they did, but that's not the point. Unfortunately, you've lost the point. Somewhere in the ruckus here in Washington, you got lost, your ideals, your morals, all the good things you wanted to do."

"That's not true, Sue Ann. You fail to consider that I keep getting elected. The voters believe in me."

"The voters in Mississippi vote for a Fairmont. They vote out of habit."

"I wasn't aware you had so little confidence in me."

"Don't try to turn this around. You won't twist things and get me on the defensive today. Look at you! Your waistline's gone, and your face is puffy and red from your drinkin' and high livin'. You're only a shell of the man I married. And that's all our marriage is now too—a shell."

He didn't answer for a few moments. When he did, it was with difficulty.

"Are you saying it's over? That our marriage is over?"

"I wish it were that simple. I wish I could just walk right out of this house, Beaufort Fairmont, and end it neatly right there," Sue Ann gave a big, sad sigh before adding, "but I can't."

"I'm not sure I understand your meaning?" Beau questioned, not a bit relieved

"Beaufort, what you did to Casey was a vile thing."

"Stay out of that, Sue Ann. You don't know the circumstances."

"Perhaps you should fill me in—your side."

"It's business; you never meddle in my business."

"You mean it's Palmer Forbes' business because you're nothing more than Palmer Forbes' boy. Just here to do his biddin'."

"That's not fair, but now that you mention it, we've done pretty well stickin' with Palmer. I haven't heard you complain that I have too much power and prestige?"

"That's what's so frightenin'—the power you have that you've misused. Beaufort, you're gonna cancel that trip to Tennessee."

"I can't do that."

"Either you cancel your trip to Tennessee and leave Casey alone, or I'll see that these pictures of you with all your bimbos get in every paper, respectable and otherwise."

"You're bluffing. You wouldn't do that to yourself; you're too proud, and the children, what about them?"

"I wouldn't want to. I'd like to protect our name, whatever we have left, with all your philanderin', and I'd like to protect our children, but I'll do it if I have to. I promise you that."

Beau looked at his wife closely. They'd been married too long for him not to know when she meant what she was saying. This had been some day, first, Palmer, now, Sue Ann. He was silent quite some time before he responded, and Sue Ann, for once, remained quiet too. She still held a small hope that he was not entirely Palmer's, that some part of him was still hers, that he was still capable of thinking for himself.

"Sue Ann, what I'm gonna tell you is very secret, and you must keep it that way. There are powers that do not want Casey in the Senate. If she runs, she'll be in great danger, maybe, even life-threatening. It's far better that I talk her out of running, for her own sake, my way is best."

"What powers, Beaufort?"

"Leave it be. I can't tell you that. If I could, I would. You've got to believe me."

It was Sue Ann's turn to look at her husband closely. They'd been married too long for her not to know he truly believed what he was saying. Beau was quiet too, giving her that chance. He also held a small hope that she still loved him enough and believed in him enough to let him do what he had to do. It was best for everybody.

Sue Ann was silent some time before responding. *I guess Stacey Lea's right,* she decided, *you can't teach an old dog new tricks, at least, this quickly.* Beau had been doing what Palmer wanted him to do for so long that it was not something you could change in one little talk. She could see that he didn't like his mission and that things were beginning to wear on him. This gave her some encouragement.

"Very well, I'll leave it be for now."

"Thank you," he responded, relieved. "I promise you that when I get back, we'll take a good look at everything. My God, look at the time. I'm gonna have to rush to catch my plane. Be a good girl and call the limo service while I get myself ready. We'll talk more when I get back, okay?"

"Okay," Sue Ann confirmed, regretfully.

While Beau went upstairs to get ready, Sue Ann went to the phone and dialed a number from memory.

"You were right. There just wasn't enough time. It'll have to be *Plan B.*"

"All right, honey. It'll all work out. You'll see."

When the limousine came, Sue Ann walked to the door with her husband, even kissed him good-by.

"Trust me, honey," Beau pleaded, sadly, "it's better this way. I'd do just about anything you want, but I can't do this. I'll be gentle with Casey. I'll make her understand."

Beau waved a kiss as he got into the long black car. Sue Ann closed out the icy air and went back to the telephone.

"Hello, yes, I'd like to cancel a plane reservation for Senator Beaufort Fairmont to Nashville, Tennessee this evening. I believe the plane was leaving at 6:18."

CHAPTER THIRTEEN

COUNTDOWN, DAY TWO

"For heaven-sakes, what time is it?" Stacey Lea exclaimed, sleepily.

"It's six twenty . uh, one," came Sue Ann's hesitant response.

"I'm so relieved that you added that *one*." came the sarcastic reply, "that makes all the difference."

"I'm sorry, Stacey Lea, but I haven't slept a wink. I'm so worried about Beau. I expected to hear something."

"Why?"

"What if something's happened to him? Do you realize that it'd be my fault? I don't know anything about these people you let take him. I've betrayed my husband, the father of my children."

"Will you stop with the melodrama. Nothing's happened to Beau. On the contrary, you have perhaps not only saved your husband but your marriage too, if you want it when this is all over."

"How do you figure that?"

"Well, if Beau were allowed to go to Tennessee, could he possibly talk Casey out of running?"

"Of course not."

"And if he couldn't talk Casey out of running then he'd have failed in his mission, right?"

"Yes, that's true."

"Then if he went down there and failed, Palmer would've been very unhappy with him, right?"

"Yes, that's true, for sure."

"So, if he doesn't go down, then he can't fail, and if he doesn't fail then Palmer can't be mad at him. There you are."

"There I am what?"

"You've saved your husband from failure, that's what. Palmer will probably even be concerned for his whereabouts."

"You know, Stacey Lea," Sue Ann surmised in a befuddled manner, "there seems to be something very wrong with your logic. I can't put my finger on it, mind you, but there's something just not right about all this."

"The only thing not right is that you've allowed yourself to worry all night, and you can't think straight. Besides, no one can think straight when it isn't even light outside. Now get some sleep."

"I can't. You told me to go to Tucson as soon as Beau was out of the picture, so I'm going today."

"I forgot. See what early does? It's good that you're on top of things. Anyway, you have a good trip and call after you've had your little talk with Mary Lightfoot."

"Don't hang up! I still want to know where they took Beau."

"I'm not sure, and I'm not going to speculate."

"That's not fair. He's my husband, and I have a right to know where I helped send him."

"Yes, you do, but if you know you'll have to lie if Palmer asks you. It's far easier on you if you can honestly say that you don't know."

"I can lie just as well as you can. Why should you know and I don't?"

"Because, my dear, I won't be asked where your husband is. Now, run along. Just think how nice it's gonna be flying out there where the sun's shinin' and the breeze is nice and warm. How I do envy you for pulling this assignment and getting a break from the chill."

"Yes, it will be nice," Sue Ann acknowledged with a sigh, "and I do feel better. I'm not sure why, but I do. You always make me feel better."

"Good! Keep in touch, Sue Ann, but please, don't call me anytime!"

"Alma, dear," Stacey Lea said in a tone that could not hide her growing frustration, "I admit that I don't have the answers at this very moment of how to keep your son from going to trial on drug charges, nor how to keep that awful evangelist off your back, but I promise you, we'll come up with something."

"No, I'm sorry. I can't take any more chances. I only held out from resigning this long because I promised Ellie that I'd wait until I'd talked with you. Frankly, I don't know why you've developed such an interest in my political life. I'd have sworn that you never had any interest in anything other than Palmer and all the little niceties that go with your position."

"I suppose I deserve that, and I suppose it's hard to take me seriously just because I've decided to be," Stacey Lea acknowledged, taking a long hard look at her obstinate, sharp-tongued guest. Things were not going well. She'd fully expected Alma Tyler to fall right into place in her scheme of things, but that hadn't happened. She'd already exhausted two pots of coffee and all her arguments on this rather dowdy woman sitting on the other side of her desk. She wasn't even dressed in the fashionable monotone look of the day.

You can tell a lot about a person in the way they dress. Alma obviously did not care one whit about how she looked or what anyone thought about her. She wasn't even intimidated personally by that crazy evangelist. No, there was only one way to get to Alma Tyler—her son, and the enemy had done a good job of that. Talking her into staying in Congress was going to take harder tactics than plain *ole* soft-spoken southern wheedling.

Just then, Ellie appeared with Sarah's file in her arms.

"Mrs. Forbes, I thought you'd like Representative Tyler to look through this file? You have an important telephone call, and while you're handling it, she could get an idea of some of your concerns."

"A splendid idea, Ellie," Stacey Lea replied with great relief and a look of enormous gratitude in her eyes.

Ellie handed the file to Alma Tyler as she explained, "This is only a sampling of a much larger file that Senator Sarah Winthrop has been compiling for over four years. We acknowledge that the evidence here is inconclusive and circumstantial at best, but there is too much to be ignored. We only ask that you review this material in the same fair and thoughtful manner that has become your trademark on the Hill."

Alma Tyler was thrown off by this new approach. She'd been annoyed with Stacey Lea's syrupy cajoling, but she appreciated the forthrightness of her secretary, and although she might have preferred to take her leave, she could hardly now ignore this request without being considered inequitable. Plus, her curiosity had been aroused. She had great admiration for Sarah Winthrop and had recently felt an empathy with her since they'd both come under Earle Walker's mordacious attacks.

"Very well, I'll review the file, but don't expect anything to come of it. If you're familiar with my record on the Hill, you also know that I've rarely changed my position."

"We know your distinguished and honorable record," Ellie responded with a cognizant smile, "and we also know we can depend on your discretion, no matter your final decision."

"Thank you," the congresswoman responded, as Ellie turned to Stacey Lea.

"Mrs. Forbes, you want to take your call in my office?"

"I'll do just that…. How I do thank you, Ellie. I was definitely too cocky in my approach to Alma Tyler. She's a tough old biddy!"

"We probably should've talked about her a little more before your meeting. I think I understand her better than you do."

"No doubt about that. Your timing with the file was brilliant."

"Let's hold up on the brilliant part until we see if it works." Ellie laughed. "Oh, we almost forgot your phone call. Bev's on the line."

"I thought that was simply a ruse to regroup," Stacey Lea confessed as she hurried to the phone.

"Hello, Bev?"

"It's about time! You ship me off to Florida and then ignore me when I call! What kind of networking is that?"

"Now Bev, I'm not without duties myself. Besides, you're always going to Florida. I bet there are lots of morning's you awake and aren't sure whether you're here or there. Now, tell me, do you have good news?"

"I sure do. I think Madge Goldman was so excited she peed in her pants when I showed her that check of Sarah's. She'll announce on Tuesday as requested."

"What does she think her chances are?"

"Now that she has money, she believes she can win; at least, she's confident she'll give Gomez a good run. She has a fighter's reputation down here, and his administration has been riddled with scandal. Still, he has a strong machine, and there are lots of Cubans here who'll vote for him for no other reason than that he's one of them. Same old story."

"All we can do is try this time. Just a woman on the ticket for Governor will have a most wanted effect. Congratulations."

"Thank you. I'll be back tomorrow night. Uh, Stace, we need to discuss Walker."

"Yes, I know. Ellie and I'll do some hard thinking on him today."

Stacey Lea had a leftover troubled look when she hung up the phone.

"Walker?" Ellie inquired.

"Yes, she's crazy with worry about him."

"She should be and so should we. He's a cancer in the country. Wonder what his wife's like?"

"He has one?"

"Yes, he has a wife. I think he met her in a seminary in North Carolina. He has her on the stage with him sometimes. She looks mousy."

"Find out what you can about her."

"Okay, but right now, we better get back to Alma."

When they went back into Stacey Lea's office, Alma Tyler was up looking out the window, the file neatly lying on Stacey Lea's large American Walnut desk. She didn't turn immediately and Stacey Lea and Ellie didn't intrude on her thoughts anymore than they already had by entering.

Finally, she spoke, "It's not me I'm worried about. It's my son. They say he'll go to prison unless I resign. He's all I have, and I didn't have him until I was forty-three. He's only nineteen, very young, and very afraid. So am I," she admitted as she turned to face them. "Damn them, and frankly, damn you too." They understood her frustration.

From that point on the three women worked quickly to get Alma filled in as well as sworn in. They accomplished a great deal in a very short time, and when Mildred was called, and two of the prettiest members of the newly formed taskforce were sent to protect Alma's son, Richard Junior, Alma visibly relaxed and began to enjoy a camaraderie with her new allies. But it was not until Ellie pushed the intercom and told the other end to send up Hanna that Alma could see her life taking on an exciting new aura.

When Hanna arrived, she filled the doorway, a consummate Aryan, the way one thinks Hitler's Master Race would've looked if he'd won.

She held every bit of her six feet plus without denial, and had covered it in soft olive green from her toes to her turtleneck.

One always started at the floor when looking at Hanna, slowing moving up her strong, taut body, pausing ever so slightly at firm breasts before proceeding through a fine square jaw and soft blue eyes to a crown of light golden hair which was, today, held loosely in one long thick braid.

"Alma, this is Hanna Gruber, your bodyguard."

Since Alma was still gaping, Stacey Lea continued.

"Hanna, why don't you show Representative Tyler some of the intricacies of your talents?"

Hanna Gruber did not answer but moved into the room and went through an elaborate martial arts routine with the grace of a ballerina. She finished with a backward kick that she held with no noticeable quiver for all of thirty seconds.

"Isn't she marvelous? She's black-belt, you know."

An '*Oh, dear*' was all Alma Tyler could muster as she stared at this goddess who had most assuredly stepped out of Wagner's Ring Cycle.

For the next few years, Alma Tyler would be an enormous thorn in Palmer Forbes' side. All her energies would be directed with great tenacity toward her duties to her California constituency, her country, and WOW. Then as a senior stateswoman, at the peak of her career, she would retire. Taking all those adroit skills she'd developed in the political arena, she would use them with the same tenacity in directing the movie career of her protégé to super-stardom. Yes, the action movies of Heidi Graham alias Hanna Gruber would take martial arts to unparalleled popularity.

And it all started falteringly on that crisp December day, known to those few insiders as *Countdown, Day Two* in Stacey Lea Forbes spacious First-Lady-White-House office.

CHAPTER FOURTEEN

COUNTDOWN, DAY ONE

"Stacey Lea, wake up!"

She did as commanded and peered right into the disturbed face of her husband.

"Palmer, dahlin', you're finally back! What on earth time is it anyway?"

"It's six in the morning."

"Did you just get home?" she inquired, disbelief in her voice, but knowing full well that he'd gotten in last night.

"No, I got home about eleven last night, *ahem*, but you were sound asleep. I thought you were going to wait up?"

"I tried, but the jet lag must still have been on me," she responded, yawning, with an authentic stretch. "From the looks of you, I'll bet you've not caught up on your sleep after our trip either. Come on, get in bed with me and let's snuggle."

The warm, cozy offer she exuded would have been very tempting any other time, but he had much on his mind this morning.

"Stacey Lea, do you know where Sue Ann is?"

"Uh, let me see . . she may have already left for Mississippi. Randal's there, and the rest of her brood's beginning to congregate for the holidays."

"I checked down there."

"What do you want with Sue Ann?"

"I don't, *ahem,* want her," he snapped impatiently. "I'm looking for Beau."

"I thought Beau was with you?"

"Uh, *ahem,* never mind, that's a long story. Go on back to sleep. I'll see you at, *ahem,* breakfast?"

"Yes, I think I'll get a few more winks; it's still early. And Palmer," she suggested to his briskly departing back, "the way you keep clearing your throat, you might be getting sick. Maybe you should get Doctor Brigham over here to check you."

Palmer Forbes not only had a clogged throat, his nose was itchy, and he had a funny feeling right in the pit of his stomach. Any one symptom was enough to make him cautious and concerned, for they'd always been extremely dependable internal signals of gathering external thunderclouds. But what? His planet seemed in order. Sure, he couldn't find Beau, but he would. In fact, Beau was probably in Tennessee right now talking to Casey. No, it was too early. Then where was he?

The President omitted his swim that morning and went directly to the Oval Office. He called his Secretary of State, Secretary of Defense, his Secretary of Interior and even his Vice President, but he could find nothing new and disturbing. The nation and the world seemed to be moving along just fine. Then he dialed a number from memory, and to its response asked, "You heard from the men?"

"Yes sir, they're in Nashville now. Just contacted me around thirty minutes ago."

"Have they been able to locate Senator Fairmont?"

"No sir, but they'll find him, don't worry."

That made him feel a little better and he smiled as he hung up. Curtis was very efficient, a good man. Maybe his symptoms were a false alarm, and Stacey Lea was right? He could be getting sick. He'd call Brigham and get checked out.

Stacey Lea was putting the final touches to her make-up when Ellie buzzed.

"Martha called."

"I have to go down to breakfast with Palmer right now, but I'll get to my office as soon as I can. It can wait that long, can't it?"

"Yes, it doesn't require a decision, but it's too exciting to keep long. Do hurry!"

"Now you do have me roused. I'll likely choke on that egg I know will be on my plate this morning with Coleman back."

"I don't think you have to worry about Coleman serving you this morning. He hasn't been seen out of his rooms since his return. Understand he sent word that he wasn't feeling well."

"I wonder why?" Stacey Lea responded as seriously as she could. "Maybe he's just getting too old for the hubbub around here."

After they broke their connection, both women spent a moment remembering their Sunday afternoon raid on Coleman's rooms. It'd been naughty fun but fruitless, for nothing had been revealed that could be used against him. In fact, his rooms had proved to be as Spartan as any monk's cell except for the walls which were covered with pictures and memorabilia. Coleman had enshrined his life at the White House on his walls—Coleman with this or that President, Coleman with members of the Cabinet, even Coleman with the Marine Band. There was no Coleman as a boy, no Coleman with an old girlfriend or Mom and Dad, not even Coleman on vacation. In fact, there was no evidence that Coleman had existed until his work here. This only gave affirmation to Stacey Lea's earlier theory that he'd come up from earth's center just to make her life miserable, and from the lack of First Ladies on his wall, Stacey Lea surmised she'd probably not been singled out.

Making her way to breakfast, she pondered her Coleman dilemma. Perhaps their little pranks yesterday were revealing much more than they could've ever anticipated? If just rearranging some of his pictures and transplanting his toiletries could cause him to be ill, or feign illness, then he was going to be a much weaker adversary than expected. In fact, it might not take much to push him over the brink and get him out of Palmer's life forever. She'd certainly like to know the state of his health right now. If Palmer called Paul Brigham, then she was going to make sure the doctor paid another house call.

A residue of her Coleman thoughts marred her countenance when she took her place at breakfast.

"What's wrong with you?" Palmer inquired, looking up from the morning paper.

"Nothing, dear. I just seem to be having trouble getting started this morning."

"Sorry I couldn't wait for you," he apologized, nodding toward an almost empty plate. "I, *ahem,* have a busy day."

"That's all right. I'm a little late, anyway. You know, you really should have your throat checked. You can't afford to do without your voice, and you must be irritating it, clearing it all the time. I don't know what good a president is to his country if he can't talk."

"I've already called Brigham."

"What a relief! I stay so anxious about you, dear. This selfless dedication of yours is gonna put you in an early grave. I say, if anyone's ever going to deserve the eulogy *he gave his life for his country,* it's gonna be you."

"Let's don't prepare that eulogy just yet," he chuckled as he reached over and gave her a light kiss on the forehead. "I better get to work. Remember, we have to dedicate that new Jesse Jackson Recreation

Center downtown at three, *ahem*.... We should leave about two thirty."

"I'll be ready. Oh, Palmer, I was thinking. Since Paul Brigham's coming over to see you, maybe you should get him to take a look at Coleman? I hear he's ill."

"That's a good idea, Stacey Lea. I'll have, *ahem*, Paul stop to see him. I must admit, however, I do find this sudden interest in Coleman's welfare suspect, *ahem* . . . knowing how much you dislike him."

"Shame on you, Palmer! I don't wish ill on my worst enemy, you know that. However, if you should have a mind to pension the man off, I'd not be inclined to mourn."

With Palmer gone, Stacey Lea wasted no time getting to her office and the waiting Ellie.

"I've been on pins and needles," she exclaimed

"Mildred Dillard called."

Ellie could get no further. She was able to open her mouth and able to frame words, but she was unable to discharge sound. Utter panic came into her eyes! Here, at this momentous moment, she'd been struck mute!

"All right, Ellie, calm down, take a deep breath and relax. I've never seen you so excited. You'll be just fine in a minute."

Stacey Lea had come around her American Walnut desk to Ellie's chair and had knelt beside her. Taking both Ellie's hands firmly into her own, she looked up at her with clear, cool eyes. Her words with actions had the needed calming effect, for Ellie looked down and whispered, "We've done it. We have found the enemy, and THEY ARE OURS!!!"

As she finished her news, her voice had fully returned. Relieved, she used every bit of it to deliver her message, adding further drama by standing and raising both hands. Unfortunately, her abrupt movements caught Stacey Lea off-balance, and the First Lady found herself sprawled most unladylike on the floor.

"I'm so sorry, Stacey Lea. Are you all right?" Ellie asked as she reached down to help her victim up.

"Yes," Stacey Lea assured with a sigh, as she straightened her skirt and tucked in her blouse, "but I think we should attempt to continue our discussion in a less lively fashion."

"The Federal Agents, Stacey Lea, the men who entrapped Casey. They're in Nashville. Our agents only have them under surveillance at present, but they intend to swoop down on them after dark and whisk them away. The plane's standing ready," Ellie whispered.

"So they did go down to fool around with Casey," Stacey Lea acknowledged, smugly nodding her head.

"Yes. Do you realize what this means? It means that we're doing things, that we're fighting back. It's real now."

"Yes, and what a boost to our morale. It couldn't be more opportune, on the eve of our official *Opening Day*."

"There's no turning back now."

"No, and I take this as an omen that we're doing what we're supposed to do, that we're right, and we'll succeed!"

The two women sat quietly for several long moments, each deep in her own thoughts of what they were about.

Finally, with a big, satisfied sigh, Ellie stated with great profundity, "You know, Stacey Lea, I've always believed in us, but I never really thought before how much we could do. I now truly believe we have the ability to bring about great change in our nation."

But Stacey Lea was the most profound of all.

"We may be doing a lot more than that, Ellie. We may be saving it."

Mission accomplished! Janet Cuéves smiled smugly to herself as she acknowledged clearance from the Nashville tower and prepared for takeoff. Her smile grew as she lifted the small jet gently into the air. It had been a long time since she'd felt such exhilaration. Her plan had worked perfectly, but she'd known it would; she knew her targets, and they hadn't disappointed her.

Summers hated hotel rooms and always went down before dinner, got a paper and sat in the lobby until Marconi joined him some thirty minutes later. Everyone in the Department knew their routine, and some outside. It wasn't smart to be too predictable in their business. Anyone could have taken them easily, one at a time in the elevator, and they had. Then, rushing the other three had been a piece of cake. That was the real reason it'd been so easy—surprise, no, more like astonishment. They'd be even more astonished when they came to; after all, they'd had no reason for caution. Who'd want to take down Feds on such an insignificant mission as intimidating a woman?

"*Habla usted Español?* Shit, those two look like fucking Puerto Ricans. but even they don't seem to know what I'm saying. Who the hell are these people?"

"Sounds as if the sedative's worn off, and the mood's nasty," Lois Valdez, her co-pilot commented, interrupting her reverie.

"Yes, you take over; I'll go back and break our silence. They're due a showdown, and I'm more than happy to oblige; in fact, I've been looking forward to this." Janet took off her seatbelt, turned and stepped into the plane's cabin. "Having a problem, Tony?"

"What the hell! Janet?"

"Don't you see?" Craig said, relieved. "Harold is pissed about Texas and decided to teach us a lesson. Tell me, Janet, how'd you get us on this goddamn plane?"

"Wheelchairs. We put you in neck-braces and other such paraphernalia and wheeled you right out. No one suspected." Janet continued, elaborating on her well-executed plan, "In fact, we wheeled two of my operatives out with you to further cover our tracks. Anyone who investigates will be unsuspecting of seven wheelchairs, five men and two women."

"You haven't lost your touch."

"Aren't you going to release us now that we've caught on?"

"Who's he?"

"You never met Monroe. He's our tenderfoot. Roger Monroe, meet Janet Cuéves, one of the best goddamn operatives we ever had, even if she is a woman," Craig Summers chuckled. "Heard you were down in Little Cuba in the missing person business?"

"I was, but I got a better job."

Summers looked at her speculatively. "This is what I said it is, isn't it—just a lesson?"

"No, it isn't. Craig, or perhaps I should call you Carl Sixbey. I'm afraid we're taking you out of operation."

"What are you talking about?" They were serious now.

"Let's just say that there are some powerful people out there who don't like the way you've been bothering Casey Bartholomew, among others, and they've decided to take drastic action."

It was a moment she would not soon forget.

"Well, what do you think?" Claire asked as she stopped her little green coupe in the long shaded driveway of a modest-looking one level brown shingled house.

"What do you mean, what do I think?" he replied.

"Johnny, the house, do you like it?

"It's a nice house, I suppose. Why?"

She could tell he was getting nervous, no matter how he tried to disguise it. It had been difficult to get him to come out with her at all. Only by saying in front of his sisters that morning at breakfast, that she needed his advice on a financial matter was she able to get him alone at all. His mother's funeral yesterday had been a drain, and she hadn't expected nor cared that he visit her last night, especially with so many people in the house, but he was distant, even now. Well, the best thing to do was to come right out with it.

"It's our house, Johnny. I bought it for us."

There was a long, uneasy pause before he spoke.

"Then I suppose we're welcome in? It's too cold to sit out here in the car, that is, if you have the heat on inside?"

"Oh, yes, and it has a lovely fireplace." She was so glad she'd come over yesterday after the funeral and turned the heat up.

Claire felt a bit heartened as they got out of the car. Once he got in, he'd like it. She was sure of that. She had worked so hard to get it ready, and she knew what he liked.

The house was deceptive, not as modest or as small as he'd originally thought. After stepping from an ample foyer, he entered one great rustic room that contained all the living area and was only broken by a jutting three-way fireplace. The back opened out to a large raised deck and plenty of snow covered woods. For some reason he thought of Frost's *Stopping by Woods* . . . . . . Why did Claire always bring out the poetry in him? She fed the side of him that should not exist in his avowed world. She was his Satan.

"The fire's ready to light. Could we, and stay awhile?"

"No, we'd be missed. They might be wondering even now."

"Well, how do you like it?" she asked, passively.

"It's lovely," he admitted, walking toward the back, "Looks from the outside much smaller than it is. Must be sitting on a hill, the way the trees drop down."

"Yes, but you can't tell that from the front. That's why it looks much smaller from there."

Her reply was as stilted and innocuous as his comment. They couldn't reach each other.

"Try your lounge chair," she requested, patting a big plaid stuffed chair. "I bought it to your measurements. I hope it's right."

"Claire, please, I can't," he answered, turning to face her.

She wasn't surprised, only saddened. She was also hurt, a condition that progressed rapidly to anger. How could he turn his back on what had been so good for both of them?

"Johnny, if you turn your back on me, you'll lose your soul because I'm part of it."

"If I don't turn my back on you, I'll lose my soul."

"You're saying that what we have is wrong? Have you felt that it was, all these years? I don't believe that, not for a minute. Where's this big convenient Catholic conscience coming from all of a sudden?"

He did not answer her question, not exactly.

"Claire, what we've had together must stop. Rome's been breathing down my neck lately. I can't take the chance of our being found out, and now, with Mother gone, there's no cover for my visits. This house, all of it, is a wonderful dream, but I can't share it with you."

"Didn't you promise me the last time you were home that you'd find a way?"

"Things have changed. Look, we've had some splendid years together. We've both profited. Let's don't end it on a sour note."

"Splendid years, you say? Most of mine were spent waiting, waiting for the day we could be together more, and now, now I get nothing?"

"Why, you ungrateful....!" John Marion exploded, his anger doused liberally with a conscience that she seemed only able to call up in him. He didn't like that. He should have ended this long ago. "Nothing, you say? Have you ever stopped to think of what you'd be today if I hadn't taken you in? Married to some big German clod like Albert, that's what, your body turned to fat from too many children and . . uh, too much *Hasenpfeffer*!"

"I thought you liked my *Hasenpfeffer*?"

"I do, but it's peasant food, and that's all you would've ever been, a peasant, if it hadn't been for me. I taught you how to talk, taught you manners; you didn't even know how to eat properly, taught you how to dress…"

"How to dress? You call the housekeeping garbs I've worn day in and day out for thirty years how to dress?"

"You aren't wearing one today, and you look pretty," he admitted, weakening for the moment. He didn't like to fight with Claire, and he couldn't stand the hurt in her eyes. "Come on, let's not fight. I don't want us to end this way."

"I don't want us to end."

"Look," he suggested, ignoring her statement for it wasn't a plea, "why don't I start that fire you wanted, and you make some coffee, better still, hot chocolate, if you have any. I suppose it won't hurt if we stay out a little longer today."

"No, Johnny, I'll not take anymore crumbs from you." She stood straight and tall, proud as he remembered that first day. Now this stubborn pride angered him. How unfair after all he'd done for her.

"Crumbs, you call what I've done for you crumbs? Why, I shared my pleasures with you. I shared my love of music, beautiful poetry— Shakespeare, Byron, even John Donne, and my love of art! Would you have known Michelangelo, Raphael, uh, Caravaggio? Would you have known any of it without me?"

"And a lot of good it's done me. I've never been to a concert; I've never been to a play, and what works of art have I seen except in books?"

He was stunned by her lack of gratitude. No thanks for all the time he'd invested in her. He was hurt, deeply hurt. He'd thought she was different, for he'd molded and refined her himself, but they were all the same. You couldn't trust them.

"Nothing's stopping you, you know," he answered coldly. "I've made sure you are well off, and Mother has left you a generous bequest. You can do anything you please."

"Your mother knew about us, you know."

"She what?"

"Yes, she thought I was good for you."

"The two of you discussed me?" he asked with difficulty, the thought of it choking the words in his haughty throat.

"She said that you never forgave her for remarrying, but it was the right thing for her. She never regretted it."

"I can't believe this. What else did my mother reveal to you?" His question was coated with sarcasm.

She ignored his manner but relished his interest.

"She said that she'd hoped your sisters would finally bring you around, but they'd only made you worse. She said the only one who'd ever been able to do anything for you was me. With me, you were a good man, what you should be, but you were a bad priest."

That was her trump card, but the look on his face almost made her sorry she'd used it. She had never seen him so enraged.

"You malicious viper! I'm a Prince of the Church. Do you have any idea how powerful and important I am? How many people depend on me for spiritual guidance? Obviously not. You have no idea of the things I have to do. You're an idiot, just like my mother, just like all women—Eves, all of you, Eves!

"Powerful and important doesn't make you a good priest," she pressed undisturbed by his outburst. "Don't you see? That's what your mother meant. You weren't meant to be a priest, and you're not content. That's what makes you a bad priest."

"Don't be absurd. She always wanted me to be a priest."

"Yes, if it were God's will, but it wasn't. It's only been your will, Johnny."

"This conversation is absurd. Get your coat on. We're leaving," he commanded, turning the icy voice he'd always used to such good effect throughout his illustrious career on her for the first time.

He watched her begin to comply, her lack of resistance disturbing him far more than her anticipated rebellion would have, for he'd been prepared for that. She was never predictable. Walking over, somewhat chagrined, he helped her other arm through the sleeve of the fox trimmed purple plaid coat he'd given her last Christmas. Turning her around to him, he looked deep into moisture filled eyes ready to overflow. When he again spoke, the ice had melted from his voice.

"Claire, I'm sorry, but you must understand once and for all that it's over. It has to be. Please don't fight me in this. When we get back, I'm going to pack and leave. I think it would be best if you do the same as soon as you can. I don't intend to see you or contact you again, and you must respect that."

As he spoke, he reached inside her coat and gently massaged the ample breasts he'd enjoyed for so many years.

"What the hell," he reconsidered, "let's stay here this afternoon. I'll give the Gallagher seeds a call and..."

"No, Johnny," was all Claire said as she pulled away and started toward the door.

"Very well, if that's what you want," he lashed out angrily, "but what I want is you out of my ancestral home before the end of the week, and I never want to see you or hear from you again. I don't care what you do or where you go. You can go to hell for all I care, but stay out of my way, or I'll make you sorry our paths ever crossed!"

His words did not disturb her; she understood his frustration. He'd come around in time, and if he didn't? She hated to think of that, but if it didn't work out, well then, she was prepared for that too, as well as one could be. Of one thing she was sure, he'd not go untouched, for she'd be his Eve if she had to; after all, that's what he'd called her.

What a pity he hadn't seen their bedroom, she thought as they drove silently back. She'd combined the two bedrooms of the house into one enormous one with a raised hot tub. He would have loved it, and it had been ready for them, towels out and everything. She smiled smugly, his loss.

Despite the good news Ellie had shared with her early in the day, Stacey Lea did not consider it one of her better days. In fact, with the exception of Palmer's news that Leslie Farnsworth would be appointed the next morning to fill Sarah's remaining term, it went downhill rapidly to an all but sleepless night.

The downhill began when she and Palmer returned from the dedication ceremony at the new Jesse Jackson Recreation Center. That was when Ellie brought her the lab analysis of the powdery substance she'd taken from the urn in Palmer's room. Not that she'd been surprised with the results; she had suspected it all along. But the difference between suspecting and knowing was more disturbing than she'd anticipated.

Traces of Human Remains stared up at her from the impersonal sheet. Traces? That meant the rest had to be that American Walnut coffin and the pale blue lace dress Mother Forbes had chosen for the occasion. Yes, that pretty blue lace dress was in here too. She stared quietly down at the small envelope of ashes that had been returned, as if she were trying to figure out which ones represented the blue dress. Finally, she released an unsummoned consuming sigh, her body instinctively venting more than the frustration of the moment.

She felt compelled to take stock of her world to this point. It wasn't that she hadn't made thoughtful decisions up to now, but she'd also not allowed herself to put them together for fear the enormity of it all would make her do as Sarah had. She couldn't quarrel with Sarah's decision. Right now, Sarah's big, cold house seemed warm and inviting. It was a kind of tomb, Sarah's tomb, but it was also safe and secure, and it was only human to want to feel that way.

She'd like to go home, but she couldn't. No, she had to stay here and hunt down bad guys, work against her husband, make Sue Ann deceive hers, help Beverly untangle the mess with Earle Walker, develop a secret networking for women, and now—on top of all that and most bizarre of all—she had to worry about the final remains of her mother-in-law, at least, what was left of her! It sounded like something you'd read about in a book by Stephen King that would probably sell a million copies, become a successful movie, and take home all the Oscars at the Academy Awards. Wry humor, that's what the critics would call it. Well, it wasn't humorous when it was real; she could testify to that!

Stacey Lea felt sorry for herself, and she allowed herself the luxury of it for exactly fifteen minutes, then, literally shaking herself to remove it as if it were a layer of clothing, she now gave a summoned, decisive sigh before speaking softly to the open envelope she still held in her hands.

"Perhaps you're right, Mother Forbes, perhaps Palmer does have this bad side that you always had to control. It surely is bad what he's been doing to you and you not being able to take up for yourself. Here he's always telling me things you told him like it's the last word, and all the time it looks like he's been feeding your ashes to those disgusting fish."

Stacey Lea went over to her large dressing room and opened one of the smaller drawers of her built-in armoire. Reaching into its recesses, she removed the little key from its hiding place, along with the snugly fitting cloth gloves she'd worn the first time she had intruded into her husband's domain. After all, the last thing she needed was her fingerprints found on that fish-tank cabinet. One couldn't be too careful, and after tomorrow, no telling what Palmer might do.

When she returned from her husband's bedroom, she was carrying the bronze urn. Carefully, she dumped its contents into the ivory box that had been given her by the Shah of Iran, the one that also contained the shards of glass and bits of inauguration picture that were symbolically attached to her distress the morning after her nightmare. Watching as the powdery ashes filtered and intermingled, she spoke softly but firmly to its presence.

"Mother Forbes, I'm putting you here amongst Palmer's broken vow. The first chance I get, I'll bury you both underneath the Pondrin' Tree. You'll like it there, and it'll care for you the way it always has me."

Then, Stacey Lea reached into a drawer of her Queen Anne desk and removed the brown manila envelope that Ellie had given her from Mother Forbes. Removing one of the sheets, she rolled it up and placed it into the empty urn. It just fit, reaching the top.

The look on her face was diabolical as she said, louder than necessary, "Palmer darlin', unless I miss my guess, in the morning you're gonna be reachin' into this jar. See how you like it when your Momma talks back!"

She'd just returned from placing the urn back in its resting-place, when Palmer burst in.

"Stacey Lea, I want you to find Sue Ann immediately!" he commanded. "The Fairmonts seem to have dropped off the side of our planet, and I want to know why."

"Well, if you can't find them, I don't know how you expect me to. Maybe they've taken off on one of those little second honeymoons and don't want to be found."

"That's ridiculous! And I don't exactly expect you to find them, I just expect you to try," he snapped. "Call me when you have exhausted all your sources. I must get in contact with Beau. . . . *ahem* . . It's a matter of national security!"

"All right, dear, I'll do my best."

"National Security, indeed!" Stacey Lea whispered angrily, as she reached another decision that would have a direct effect on Palmer Forbes' peace of mind. Walking with purpose through her husband's dressing room and directly to the fish-tank, she reached over and turned a knob as high as it would go.

Palmer Forbes returned to his wife's rooms two more times that evening, each time more agitated than the last in his fruitless pursuit of Beau Fairmont. Stacey Lea hadn't attempted to help him, stating that she had no idea whom to call with Beverly in Florida and Sarah in

Boston. Palmer insisted that she call them both, which she finally did only to find Beverly not home and Sarah not available.

Finally, the great house was quiet except for Stacey Lea's mind that had gone berserk.

Had their agents succeeded in capturing Palmer's agents? Were they on their way to Cuba? Would Palmer open the fish-tank cabinet in the morning? Had she gone too far? How were they going to handle Earle Walker before he hurt Beverly again? Did they dare use Beverly to spy on Walker? What about the Cardinal? How had she ever expected them to bring down these powerful men? What if Palmer found Sue Ann? Worse, what if he found Beau? Was the robe folded properly? Had she left any fingerprints? Had she gone too far? What was she going to do about Coleman? Wish she had mauve to wear tomorrow.

Stacey Lea didn't think she'd slept at all but evidently she had since she was startled awake with the sound of Palmer screeching her name as he rushed to her bed.

"Stacey Lea, Stacey Lea, wake up! She's back, my mother's back, and she's left me commandments and . . and cooked my fish! Wake up!"

Stacey Lea woke up quicker than she ever had in her entire life to see Palmer rushing toward her, his long flowing robe flapping, one hand waving a sheet of paper. It was to her sleepy and confused early morning mind more frightening than absurd since the patriotic embellishments of the great robe could hardly be discerned in an early morn that had only slightly been touched by the sun.

"Palmer, is that you? What are you wearing? You frighten me!"

Her response was genuine as she instinctively stalled for the moments needed to get everything in perspective, but there was no need. Her words brought her husband to a screeching halt with the realization of how he must look and what he'd just said. Without replying, he turned on his heels and swiftly retreated. To his back, Stacey Lea attempted to bring him back with rapid, now alert questions.

"Don't go, Palmer. What do you mean your mother's back? And commandments? What was it you said about your fish? Is that a new robe? I swear, it looks like a flag."

That was the way Stacey Leanne Culberson Forbes' day started behind the walls of the White House on that cold, crisp, momentous tenth day of December. Her husband's day had started a few minutes earlier.

CHAPTER FIFTEEN

DAY ZERO

Goodman Palmer Forbes approached the fish-tank. His tall, taut body was enveloped in a long hooded robe. With only the diffused light cast from the newly awakened waters, the shadows of early morning made him appear an apparition from centuries past.

But Goodman Palmer Forbes was not enjoying a mental analogy with the past this morning, the ancient high priest making sacrifice to the sea. For the first time since he'd started his secret ritual, thirteen months ago now, he did not feel pleasure. He was impatient; in fact, he felt a little silly. This disturbed him even more. Perhaps Brigham was wrong, for he certainly didn't feel well. Granted, he hadn't slept last night, but how could he sleep when Beau was missing? Beau had always been reliable. Maybe a foreign power had taken him hostage? He'd call the C.I.A first thing!

Turning his attention back to the ceremony at hand, he smiled as he recalled how much he had enjoyed last month, her one-year anniversary. This month was simply anticlimactic. That explained it; besides, it was the number thirteen, and that had never been a good number for him.

Feeling better, he lifted the urn out in front of him, his lingering smile now directed toward his fish. For a moment, this pleasant smile seemed frozen on his face. For it took several minutes for him to fully comprehend the scene in front of him—his fish lying on their sides on top of the water and some on the bottom. Panic and frustration combined as he dropped the urn and began to shake the tank, determined to make his gilled carnivores obey his will, flip over, and participate in his monthly ritual. But they did not respond.

Rage impeded thought, but enough filtered through for him to recall that he'd dropped the urn. Twisting down toward it, he was sent sprawling as his feet tangled in the bulk of his long robe. It didn't matter; his only concern now was for the urn's contents. Reaching out, he grabbed at it, his hand finding first a familiar looking piece of paper partially sticking out of the urn's wide opening.

He didn't read it; he didn't have to. Without thinking, he rushed wildly to the only safe place he knew, only to quickly return, leaving his wife with a bleary early morning vision that neither would ever forget and that he dare not explain.

Stacey Lea lay in bed for some time after her husband's hasty departure. Sleep was impossible. Just the thought of experiencing another abrupt awakening as traumatic as just had occurred made the bliss and renewal that sleep could produce hardly worth it. Besides, sleep hadn't been her friend of late, mostly filled with nightmares. She'd even noticed yesterday a touch of darkness under her eyes, the fruit of her restless nights. That darkness would be frightful bags this morning, and she dreaded that first look into the mirror.

Catnaps, she'd catnap during the day and stay awake during the night. That way all the sinister plottings and dastardly deeds that are associated with darkness wouldn't come upon her unaware. One was too vulnerable when asleep. Certainly, she would have been better prepared for Palmer's outburst if he hadn't had to rouse her, if she'd been alert and waiting. Strange, she'd had trouble getting to sleep last night, but when she had, it had been so deep, that she'd had trouble getting awake this morning. Drugged! Could Coleman have drugged her? She'd had a snack with milk last night, and he had easy access to the kitchen. He could even poison her and no one would suspect. Why should they? She was only the First Lady.

Big tears filled Stacey Lea's eyes as she turned over and pressed her face deep into her pillow. Sobs, muffled by the pillow, shook her body, and she gratefully allowed them to replace her thoughts. When she did turn her face from the pillow, her eyes were dry, and her mind was clear.

Paranoiac meandering, she deliberated, just stall tactics her mind had produced while keeping her conscience at bay. For her fear, the fear she'd had last night that she had given Palmer too much to handle at one time, seemed justified this morning. Carved into her memory forever was the flying robe and flailing arms as they rushed toward her bed, but even worse was the one telling moment in that shadowy morning light when she'd seen the wild look in his eyes.

On the other hand, she surmised, everyone must have times when they seesaw back and forth across that line between the rational and irrational. Hadn't she just done it with that silly drugged idea and thinking Coleman might poison her? She was rational now; surely Palmer was too.

Everybody had something that made them react crazy at times, that pushed a button. One thing for her was Coleman; one thing for Palmer was Sarah. But then, her fear filled conscience intruded again. Maybe you could push lots of buttons at one time and take a person so far over that he'd have trouble getting back? She knew from Palmer's early morning burst into her bedroom that he thought his mother was back from the grave. How would she have reacted if she'd actually succeeded in conjuring up her mother at Culberson Cliff?

"Don't be silly, Stacey Lea," she assured herself, "Palmer is surely settled down now and out and about the business of being President of the United States."

Her musings were interrupted by Ellie's voice on the intercom.

"Stace, I hope you're ready to meet the day because Beverly's on the phone and in a terrible state. I've been trying to calm her but with little success."

"Is she still in Miami?"

"No, she got back last night to find that Senator Abelson knew about Earle Walker. They both went to bed upset, and this morning, she can't find him. She can't find their gun either. She's crazy with worry!"

A day had just begun that would make Stacey Lea complain to Ellie that the world was turning at such a dizzying rate, she was finding it hard to stay on.

Later, much later, Stacey Lea and Ellie would reflect on the events beginning that day and conclude that mysterious forces they could not begin to understand had joined their ranks with a fury they'd neither felt nor wanted. Had they always been there quietly waiting for them to get started? Had these forces known all along, plotted their destinies from the beginning? What else could have so opportunely timed that fury? As unrelated as it might seem, would the tragedies of that day have happened if that day had not been ordained DAY ZERO?

Would any of it have happened without the momentum of that day, or did the world have a safety valve? Could something evil grow and fester just so long before matters were taken out of the hands of mortals and handled by powers incomprehensible? Perhaps we were all no more than puppets, controlled and manipulated in some grand design? The idea was not original.

If they had suspected they were being exploited, would they have attempted to halt the day's proceedings? If so, at what point could they have changed the fates that were at work that day? Had there been an ignored sign, something that might have caused them to halt, to do something differently? Could their wills have prevailed against such forces? Stacey Lea even questioned whether their wills should have prevailed; that was much later, however.

Ellie noted that the Ancient Greeks believed that mortals had some control over their destinies even while their fanciful and fickle gods pulled from all sides. Oedipus, who had from the womb been ordained by the Oracle to kill his father, had been given a fleeting moment of free will. If his pride had not kept him from standing aside at the crossroads, he would not have committed the fated patricide that started his world careening.

Maybe, Stacey Lea allowed, but it would've had to be played out by someone, since it had to happen. That would only have given Freud a complex with another name and Oedipus sounded right. Judas sounded right too. Maybe he'd also had that fleeting moment of free will, but if he had not betrayed Jesus someone else would have. The prophecy had to be fulfilled.

This gave them much to ponder in their own search for that fleeting moment of free will when they might have been able to stay the forces that were unleashed that day. They never found it, and maybe it was best they hadn't, or maybe it simply wasn't there.

"My god, Stacey Lea, it took you long enough. Did Ellie tell you what's happened?" Beverly wailed.

"Yes, now calm down. I'm sure it isn't as bad as you think. Howard may walk in any minute, and you'll feel silly. Howard's a very sane man."

"You didn't hear the way he talked last night."

"Was he angry?"

"I wish he had been. I could've handled that. No, he was extremely depressed and blames himself."

"I don't understand."

"I can't explain it now, but there was no changing his mind."

"How did he find out?"

"He hired a private detective."

"What made him do that?"

"He saw some bruises one time, just the way you did."

"You had no idea you were being followed?"

"No, of course not! In fact, if I hadn't been caught off guard, I think I could've persuaded him it wasn't so. He had to just be guessing because how could that detective have followed me down three flights of stairs without my knowing it? I never met Walker anyplace but his apartment in this building, and I never took the elevator."

"I don't think you were caught off guard, Beverly; I think you wanted him to know. It should be a relief to you."

"Never! I never wanted Howard to know, at least not like this! You'll see; only tragedy is going to come out of this. Besides, he took the gun!"

"Are you sure he took the gun?"

"Of course, I'm sure. It was always kept in a secret compartment of my mother's desk. No one knew about it but Howard and me. I've destroyed him, Stacey Lea. I destroy everything. I'm no better than Earle Walker."

Beverly's sobbing was making her speech incoherent, and Stacey Lea realized that soon conversation would become impossible.

"Stop it, stop it right now! You don't have a thing to cry about! As far as we know, nothing's happened! Compose yourself so that we can figure out what to do. If you're so sure something bad's gonna happen, then maybe we can find him before it does. We can't do that until you settle down and start thinking more clearly." A gulp and a silence indicated that Beverly was attempting to do as Stacey Lea commanded.

"There, that's better. Now take a deep breath, hold it, ... that's right, let it out slowly, very slowly. Good! Now, let's take the worst scenario you can think of. What would that be?"

"Just what's happening," Beverly answered between residue sobs. "Howard's taken the gun, and he's either gone to kill Earle Walker or himself or both. . . Just a minute, Stacey Lea, my maid, ...What is it, Joanna?" Beverly's voice when it returned was cold and lifeless. "Martin Willis is here. It's already happened."

"Beverly!" Stacey Lea ordered quickly, "Don't hang up. Put me on speaker."

Beverly did not answer, but from the sound of voices, evidently complied. In the meantime, Stacey Lea pressed her intercom to summon Ellie. "Get up here, Ellie. Beverly may've been right. She's being visited by the FBI."

"Why don't you sit down, Mrs. Abelson," the FBI Chief suggested in his warmest, most solicitous voice.

That was just the proper tone to herald something terrible, Stacey Lea acknowledged, as she shushed Ellie's scurried arrival.

"If you have come to see Howard, he's not here," Beverly responded, ignoring his suggestion.

"No, Mrs. Abelson, I've come to see you. I deeply regret being the bearer of this tragic news, but we were notified by the New York City Police Department a short time ago that Senator Abelson was found dead in your home there."

"How did he die?" Beverly asked, blankly.

"Perhaps you would like to sit down now?"

"I don't want to sit down! Tell me, how did he die?"

"The investigation hasn't been completed, but there's every indication that it was self-inflicted, that he shot himself. A small revolver was found near his hand."

"I see. Thank you for coming personally. I know you didn't have to do this. Now if you will excuse me, I would like to be alone."

Beverly heard her voice speak those stiff, abrupt amenities as she started toward the door. She didn't care; she had to get away.

"I'm glad I was able to come. Uh, could you give me just another minute, please? I do need to ask you a few questions."

"I really don't feel up to it right now."

"I know," Willis replied, gently, "but if I don't do it, someone else will have to," adding, even more gently, "Get it behind you. Okay?"

"Very well," Beverly acquiesced, continuing to stand near the door.

"Do you know if your husband owned a small pearl handled revolver?"

"Yes, that's the Lilliput."

"Lilliput?"

"Yes, it's a small automatic, just 4.5 caliber, uh, German made. Ours is a fine edition with a decorated pearl handle and ornate etching on the metal. We keep it in a secret compartment of my mother's desk."

Beverly went toward the desk as she spoke, for all of a sudden that seemed to be all she could do—speak.

"I call it my mother's desk although it was in my family long before my mother. Isn't it beautiful? It's made of English Oak, and once belonged to Rasputin, . . the Russian Monk, Rasputin." Opening the secret drawer, she announced in a matter-of-fact-tone, as if she were reading, "The gun is not here."

"From the description given to me by the New York police, I believe that's the gun found by his body."

She said nothing but turned back toward the door.

"One more thing, please. The Senator didn't leave a note. Do you know any reason your husband might have to kill himself?"

"Martin! Oh, Martin!" Stacey Lea's voice called loudly. "This is Stacey Lea Forbes. Beverly Abelson and I were having a little chat when you arrived, and since she's been worried about her husband, I asked her to leave me on."

"Hello, Stacey Lea. This is a pleasant surprise, even under such circumstances. It's good you stayed on. Mrs. Abelson is going to need all of her friends right now," said Willis as he hurried to the phone, and Beverly, evidently glad to leave things in the First Lady's hands, made her escape.

"I want you to know that I shan't forget how kind and compassionate you were in relaying to Beverly this horrible news. I certainly intend that Palmer know. I'm overwhelmed! She'd only just told me how the Senator was so worried about his dear mother that she'd suggested he get right on a plane and hurry back to New York to check on her. It seems he had some kind of premonition, but upset enough to kill himself? He was a rational man."

"I know what you mean," Willis acknowledged, "but we see this all the time. Unfortunately, it always seems to happen to the ones you'd least expect."

"It's just about the last thing I'd expect to hear about him. The world's gonna be shocked."

"Yes, I agree. He was a respected senator and will be sorely missed. This is an unfortunate situation."

"You took the words right out of my mouth," Stacey Lea responded sweetly. "Isn't it unfortunate that we must mar the good Senator's fine record and memory by the scandal that always comes with these messy violent ends, not to mention what all this'll put his poor wife through at a time when she has such personal loss to deal with?"

"Yes, It's going to be hard, no doubt about it."

"And here she is my very dearest friend. The President will be upset too, especially when he sees how much Beverly's pain will distress me." Stacey Lea sighed dramatically.

"It's always hard on the ones left behind." Willis acknowledged, becoming uncomfortable with the direction this conversation seemed to be heading.

"Then I know you'd want to spare the Senator's widow and all of us as much as you could, if you could, that is?"

"I'm not sure what you're getting at, Stacey Lea, but there really isn't much I can do."

"I am surprised! I always thought the FBI could do just about anything, especially with you at its head. Palmer's told me many times that you're a metaphor for gold—the best Chief the Bureau's ever had. There's nothing you couldn't do."

There was a long pause before Bureau Chief Martin Willis replied.

"What did you have in mind, Stacey Lea?"

"Palmer, please let me in. I'm worried about you. Are you all right?"

"Yes, just go on to the Abelson's. I can't leave now. Tell Beverly that I'm sorry about Howard, and I'll extend my condolences in person later."

"I can't leave you like this, dear. You've never refused to come out of your room. I have to see for myself that you're all right."

"I need to be alone right now. Go do your duty and respect my wishes. Find out when and where the funeral is going to be, and I'll try to make it."

She could tell from his voice that the subject was closed, and she was concerned. He wouldn't see anyone, even Coleman; he hadn't eaten breakfast, and there seemed to be no way of budging him out of that room. What if he were that way tomorrow, and the day after, and the day after that? What had she done?

On second thought, why should she blame herself? If he hadn't been doing so many ugly things, she wouldn't have been placed in her present position. Besides, she'd only done what Mother Forbes told her to do, and the fish, well, whatever had been going on with those fish had had to be stopped for his own good. Furthermore, he sounded much better than earlier. He would probably be quite himself when she returned and very passionate tonight, as he always was on the tenth of the month.

Stacey Lea was not entirely able to dismiss her concern for Palmer with this assessment, but her thought process was able to consign him to no more than a worrisome flutter in the pit of her stomach. If she hadn't been able to do so, she might not have been able to cope with the incredible events of the day, and right now, for starters, Beverly needed her badly.

She gave a troubled look back at the windows that marked Palmer's rooms as her car went through the iron gates of the White House.

"It's surely a sad day, Ellie, and furthermore, it looks like more snow."

"It's been forecasted. We've already had more snow this winter than I can recall for a long time."

"That's so, and it's hardly winter, but you know, I'm glad it's the way it is today. I've far more trouble dealing with sadness when the sun is shining. It's as if nature's laughing. She always bests us, but I hate to see her flauntin' herself. I prefer the outside matching my inside."

"I firmly believe, Stacey Lea, that you're the incarnation of a wood nymph or some such nature spirit." Ellie laughed. "You're so attune to it."

"Not it, Ellie, *Her.* My daddy's the same. We were born from Mississippi mud. Did you get hold of Sue Ann?"

"Yes, she's on her way back to Washington and would like to go with you to the funeral tomorrow. I better warn you now that she's uptight about her husband and wants him home."

"I expected that, and I think it's time too. After all, you can't keep an important figure like Senator Fairmont hidden for too long. Besides, he should be at Howard Abelson's funeral."

"That's tomorrow though."

"Yes, we'll have to work quickly. When you get to Beverly's, call and make arrangements for Sue Ann to be taken to him as soon as she gets in. Be sure you also talk to her and make it clear that unless she can make him behave, he'll have to stay on that boat until hell freezes over. I don't care how many Federal Agents are out looking for him! The agents?"

"Everything went off smoothly in Nashville, and they're already in their Cuban home. Janet Cuéves told Mildred Dillard that they were so surprised, that it still hadn't sunk in when they got to Cuba."

"Can you imagine the shock-waves when it sinks in that they're missing?"

"Yes, Janet said the same thing. She went directly back to Nashville in case someone else showed up, but she doesn't think it's a good idea for her to stay past today. She suspects the place will be swarming with Feds when they catch on."

"Wonder if Martin Willis knows about all this?"

"I'd think he'd pretty much have to. By the way, you did handle him well."

"I'm beginning to realize that one can do almost anything with a bit of flattery."

"And a devious mind."

"Maybe so," Stacey Lea nodded, cheerfully, "this cloak-and-dagger stuff isn't as difficult as I thought it would be."

"You do seem to have a knack for it. Look, there's Beverly now, waiting outside."

"Beverly, honey, get in here and get warm. It's freezing out there."

"I only came outside when I saw your armada. Besides, I can't feel the cold. I'll probably never be able to feel anything again." Beverly's tone was woe-filled as tears started trickling down her cheeks.

"How you do talk. You know Howard wouldn't want you to mourn that way. And look at your pretty face—no make-up, and the tears in the cold are going to chap it; that'll never do. Howard bought you pretty things because he wanted to show off your beauty, and you're going to say your farewells like this? Shame on you!"

"It still hasn't penetrated, has it Stacey Lea?" Beverly snapped angrily, almost forgetting her tears. "This is a great tragedy I bear. I've killed my own husband just as surely as I pulled the trigger. His blood's on my hands. I'll never be able to wash it off."

"What's that wonderful quote by Lady MacBeth, Ellie, something to do with the perfumes of Arabia?"

"I don't remember exactly, something about the smell of blood sweetened by perfumes of Arabia."

"No, that's not right, nothing can sweeten the smell of blood. I should know; I played Lady MacBeth in college. *Here's the smell of blood still; all the perfumes of Arabia will not sweeten this little hand.* I can't believe us! We're actually quoting Shakespeare at a time like this!" Beverly blustered, her eyes wide with revulsion.

"No, it was you quoting the Bard, and very well, I might add," Stacey Lea, observed.

"Let's change the subject since there's obviously no understanding to be found here! Did you get hold of Sue Ann and Sarah?"

"Yes," Ellie answered, "Sue Ann's on her way home from Arizona , but Sarah said she couldn't possibly come. She wanted you to know how sorry she is, and that she would call you soon. She's also sending flowers."

"Flowers aren't exactly the proper thing for a Jewish funeral; however, I guess I should be relieved she isn't sending one of those goddamn plants of hers. I really didn't expect her to come, Stacey Lea, but I'll be hurt if Palmer doesn't come tomorrow. After all, Senator Abelson was a dedicated public servant and gave many years of exceptional service to his country. Its President should give a few moments to him."

"Now, Beverly, I understand how you feel, and Palmer will be there if he possibly can. I only said earlier that he might not make it, just in case he doesn't. Your people bury so quickly that you should realize that not everyone can drop everything at a moment's notice, especially the President of the United States. And I'll be there tomorrow. Wouldn't you rather have me?"

"I'd rather have Palmer for Howard. God, I almost feel as if I'm already in the funeral procession, we're going so slow. Can't you tell the Secret Service to get the lead out of their asses? My brother will beat us there at this pace, and he's coming from Florida."

"If you'd been willin' to come to the White House, we could've taken the helicopter over and been in the air now," Stacey Lea snapped as she opened the limousine's intercom. "Spencer, would you please move along more quickly. We're in a bit of a hurry."

Speeding along behind a siren, they quickly got to Andrews Air Force Base, and were soon comfortably settled aboard *Air Force Junior* and on their way to New York City.

"I believe that I'll always think of this plane with sadness. Both times I've flown in it, we've taken a melancholy journey. I don't choose to ride it again," Beverly moaned, beginning to get herself worked up anew.

Stacey Lea ignored her, as she requested Ellie to turn on the television. "Martin Willis said he'd release the news of Howard's death to the media at twelve o'clock, and it's one minute after."

"I can't bear to watch it," Beverly cried as she settled herself closer to the television, so she wouldn't miss any of the details that were part of her life.

All of a sudden, it seemed very important to see the media pronounce Howard dead. Perhaps then there would begin to be some reality to all this. It had only been last week that they'd been in this same airplane going to say good-by to Sarah. Now they were going to say good-by to Howard. Both had been Senators, and both would never be back to Washington. Would they mention that? Would they tell about Howard's accomplishments, that he had been Mayor of New York City before he was Governor, before he was Senator? That he'd been honest, intelligent and fair? That he'd loved her and protected her and spoiled her?

"We have just received word that United States Senator Howard Abelson, Senior Senator from the state of New York and powerful Chairman of the House Ways and Means Committee, was found dead this morning in his New York City home. The cause of death has not been made official, but he apparently died of a heart attack. More information will follow on the five o'clock news."

"Just that, and that awful picture? I thought the media had an obituary prepared for famous people, and they simply had to fill in last minute details?"

"They do, Beverly," Ellie consoled, "but you must keep in mind that the announcement was just given out. I'm sure there will be plenty about Howard later in the day. Let's try another station."

Ellie switched channels just in time for a very detailed announcement, but not the one they'd expected. In fact, Howard was all but forgotten in the drama that was about to unfold.

"We take you now to Eternal City, California, home office of the Church Eternal, where it was just announced that Judge Earle Salvation Walker, the Church's founder and dynamic leader, died this morning from an apparent heart attack."

As the three women stared at the screen and attempted to digest what was happening, they knew instinctively that they were part of it, more than they could at the moment comprehend.

They watched in awed silence as Harlan Parker proclaimed that Earle Walker's body would lie in state in the great Temple and that he would be buried under the great dome. Then Beverly, Stacey Lea and Ellie leaned over, their eyes opening wide for the grand finale.

Stepping forward, gracefully, her long white gown draping gently, her straight brown hair wistfully brushing her waist, and her pale unembellished face filled with an otherworldly glow, Carolyn Walker spread her arms ever so slightly, her palms out. Then, gazing steadily and innocently at her worldwide waiting audience until she was confident that she had drawn them to her, she spoke.

"My dear friends in Christ, I know and share your sorrow, but my husband wouldn't want us to be sad. The good Lord told him sometime ago that this day was upon us."

"What a lot of crap," Beverly inserted.

"Yes, the Lord told him that it was time for him to come home. He had earned his Kingdom in Heaven. Judge Earle was filled with joy that he would soon be standing by the Father.

"His father has two horns, a tail and a pitch fork."

"Shush, Beverly," Stacey Lea chided.

"He said, 'Carolyn, think of how grand it will be. I'll be right up there opening those pearly gates for our faithful flock.' His eyes filled with tears of joy as he told me that he'd already seen in a vision how he'd reach down his hands and pull us up. 'Praise God,' he said, 'I'm being taken on ahead, just like Jesus was, to prepare the way. Prepare ye the way saith the Lord!'

And Judge Earle turned to me and said, 'It's going to be left up to you, Carolyn, dear wife, to lead our flock home.' He said he and Jesus would always be by my side, and I can feel their presence with me now, with all of us. Praise the Lord! Oh, I pleaded, and I cried, and I prayed that this cross be taken from me, for I am only a woman, frail and weak."

"Not with those balls."

"I can never take my husband's place; I can never fill his shoes, but we know that when we're called to service we must obey. So, dear friends in Christ, you must help me with my mission, help me in the way Earle taught us, help me and I know we'll reach our Eternal Home. We'll be with our dear Leader and our beloved Lord up there in the sky forever and ever. Praise the Lord!"

By the time Carolyn Walker had finished, her hands had risen slowly above her head and the tears were flowing freely down her upturned face. She was faint, or at least that's how it seemed, and Harlan Parker, Walker's favored disciple, came forward to assist her departure.

"Enough's enough, turn the damn thing off," Beverly ordered. "I can't watch anything after all that bullshit. That's what it was, you know, just bullshit."

"I know, but I couldn't help but admire her. She's incredible!" acknowledged Stacey Lea.

"What's incredible is that Howard and Earle both died of heart attacks on the same day."

"Howard didn't die of a heart attack," corrected Stacey Lea.

"That's my point. Earle didn't either, anymore than Howard did."

"You can't say that! It's a coincidence, that's all."

"Don't you see? Howard went to California, killed Earle, then came back to New York and shot himself."

"That's ridiculous! He was with you last night, and he couldn't have gotten out there and back to New York early enough to kill himself before the housekeeper arrived!"

"And why not? You can get to California in three hours if you are on one of those fast jets. I'm surprised you even question that, Stacey Lea, the way Air Force One zips you around, and I was in bed by nine. We'd had a terrible argument, and I had a terrible headache, so I took a sleeping pill and went to bed."

"Okay. Say you went to bed by nine, Howard left the house by ten, in the air by eleven, in California by two, at Walkers by three, kills him by four, back on the plane by five, in New York by eight, home by nine—what time does the housekeeper come?"

"Between ten and eleven on days we aren't home."

"Then he only has a little over an hour to kill himself. That's really too pat . . ."

"Remember, it takes less time coming west to east," Beverly nudged, reinforcing her point.

"In any case," Stacey Lea blustered, still resistant, "they would have no reason to conceal Walker's murder. That would martyr the man!"

"They've already done that but in a neater way. Think of the scandal they'd have if it ever came out that Earle Walker was murdered, not to mention the reason. Such a scandal might topple that silly church. This way, Carolyn Walker moves right in, and they have a jolly good time mourning."

"It could work," Ellie granted, thoughtfully, "that is, if your husband shot Earle Walker. We have nothing to support that."

"It's simply common sense; besides I have this," Beverly snapped as she removed a small ivory envelope from her bag and handed it to Ellie.

"What's this?"

"A note from Howard, a last note."

"You mean you've had a note all this time, and you didn't mention it?"

"I don't know what you mean by all this time. I didn't find it until I went back upstairs this morning while you were talking to Martin Willis. It was on my bed-stand."

"What does it say?"

Ellie opened the envelope and read,

Dear Beverly,

I am sorry for the pain you've suffered. I don't want you to blame yourself, for none of this is your fault. I promised to always take care of you and keep you safe, and I've failed. I promise you this, however, that Earle Walker will never again hurt you. I'm sorry if these last acts of mine may cause you any more pain, but they're necessary if you are to get on with your life. You have been the finest wife anyone would ever want, and I thank you for our years together.

Forgive me for what I must do today. I am at peace.

Your loving husband,
Howard

"That's beautiful," Ellie sighed, her eyes moist.

"Yes, it is," Stacey Lea agreed, "but it must be destroyed immediately."

"I can't destroy my last note from my husband!"

"Then I'll do it for you. If it ever fell into the wrong hands...."

"It won't."

"As long as it exists there's a possibility that someone else could see it. The very fact that your husband and your lover..."

"Don't call Earle Walker my lover!"

"That's exactly what he was, whether you like it or not! Now, as I was saying before I was so rudely interrupted, the mere coincidence of their deaths is going to cause some early comparisons. You know how people like to connect dots. The fact that two of our founding fathers, Thomas Jefferson and John Adams' died on the same day and it was Independence Day to boot tops the list in American History's "Believe it or nots."

"They did?" Beverly quizzed, raising one eyebrow.

"Yes, and I even read a book comparing the two men inspired by that uncanny fact." You don't want that kind of speculation to inspire a book comparing Walker and your husband, do you?"

"God no," Beverly moaned with both eyebrows raised.

"The very taint of scandal was what I was trying to ward off when I talked Martin Willis into covering up Howard's suicide. You want his memory honored, don't you, Bev?"

"Of course, I do. It's hard to know what to do. I don't handle misery well, but this is especially hard because it's all my fault. How am I going to live with this?"

"You'll live with it, and you'll deal with it, just as we all have to deal with sorrows and problems, nobody escapes. Just remember that there are lots of ways of dealing with things, and no one pulled that trigger but Howard."

Stacey Lea's comforting words and the compassion on her friends' faces finally opened the floodgate for Beverly, as her prior sobs turned into the cry she so desperately needed. Stacey Lea and Ellie hugged her tight and joined in.

It was Stacey Lea's second cry that day, but she had plenty of tears with some to spare. Wonder if anyone ever ran out of tears? Strange question to have, she thought, as she watched Beverly and Ellie walk down the steps toward the waiting limo, especially strange, when there were so many really important questions running through her head. Could Beverly be right? Could Howard, sweet, mild-mannered Howard, have committed a crime so violent as murder? Could he have left Washington, gone to California and then gotten back to New York to be found dead by the housekeeper late the same morning? One could get to California in little more than three hournow, it was possible.

Would they ever know what happened last night? This thought took her eyes down to the ivory envelope in her lap. Slowly and searchingly she read, as if she believed that underneath its black inked message another, more complete one, would be revealed.

Howard Abelson put down his pen, folded the sheet of ivory paper and tucked it into a matching envelope. Resting it on the desk, he stared at it for a moment before retrieving his pen to scroll *Beverly* across the front.

Would this truly be his last words to his wife? If so, they weren't profound or eloquent. Somehow, a man's last words should be both. They should also be noble and memorable like *Give me liberty or give me death, I regret that I have but one life to give for my country,* or Voltaire's, *I die adoring God, loving my friends, not hating my enemies....* No, he stopped abruptly, *I could never use that one, for I hate Earle Walker.*

Perhaps he shouldn't leave a note if he couldn't leave a grand one? Besides, what if he wasn't able to pull it off? He wasn't worried about being able to kill himself. God knows, he'd thought about that enough times now that Paddy was gone, and he was sure Beverly would be better off rid of him, especially after their talk earlier. But he couldn't make that departure until he'd rid Beverly of Earle Walker. Here was his problem. Was he capable of killing another human being, even one as contemptible as Walker?

He'd soon know. His travel plans were made, Earle Walker was expecting him, and a limo had been ordered. He bristled as he remembered the sneer in Walker's voice.

Abelson quickly went up the stairs to his wife's bedroom where he gave her a light kiss on top of her sleeping head and placed his farewell note on her bed-stand. Standing back, it occurred to him that both were unsatisfactory, only whispers. It also occurred to him that perhaps that was all their marriage had been, never more than a whisper.

Senator Abelson's flight to Southern California was filled with memories and questions, most of the latter beginning with 'if'. For example, if he hadn't made love to Paddy first, would he have been able to make love to Beverly? He hadn't expected there to be a problem. Since his early lovers had been women; he assumed he was bisexual like a lot of men he knew.

Beverly was the eternal woman, earthy and elegant. She still aroused him, but now he understood. In the beginning, he'd just misread the signals. He'd tried. When they first got married, he'd gotten hard just watching her move, dressed in one of those marvelous costumes he still helped her choose, but turn out the light or leave the light on, the moment Beverly started taking off those beautiful clothes, he limped out. Abelson chuckled at the pun.

Finally, they had both accepted the truth. It had taken him longer than it had his wife, for he'd even tried a one-night stand with another man just to prove he could, but he couldn't. No, it seemed that once he'd met Paddy, he was destined to remain faithful.

Professor Padraic Monaghan, English Literature 101 at NYU, had only been ten years his senior. He had been drawn to him immediately, this small and delicate man with a voice and speech that gave proof to the silver-tongued peculiarity of the Celtic race. They had been lovers over forty years, but he was dead now, his body wasted by disease. His death had been a whisper. *We are such stuff as dreams are made on, and our little life is rounded with a sleep.*

Why hadn't he thought of Shakespeare when he'd wanted something for his note to Beverly? Paddy would have thought of him. *Rounded by a sleep* was soft and gentle like a whisper. Not a bad way to be remembered. Paddy would have liked that one, and Beverly would have too.

To be or not to be! Shakespeare fit every occasion. However, unlike Hamlet, he was too tired to be afraid of the unknown—tired of feeling guilty, tired of dividing his time, tired of being in the middle, just simply tired of being the right angle of their persistent triangle. Beverly had resented Paddy; Paddy had resented Beverly. The only arguments he and Paddy had ever had were about Beverly, and then Paddy could be a real bitch. But God, the making up was worth it. The taste and feel of Paddy's soft, salty skin against him, their sweat intermingling in fiery passion, their hands moving over one another with wild abandon, building and building until neither could stand it any more and then,...just the thought of it filled his groin with excruciating pain.

When Howard got back from the lavatory, his thoughts switched to Beverly.

He had thought that with Paddy gone he could concentrate on his wife. He felt strong; there should be nothing standing in the way of their making love now. He would have planned that first evening with all those romantic things—champagne, candlelight, flowers, her favorite, orchids. He'd have had her wear stockings, long dark sheer stockings that he would with great deliberation remove, inch by inch, warming her uncovered skin with his hand and tongue, gravitating upward to tease the warm, moist nest between her legs, then he'd move down to suck each toe as his hands delicately stroked each foot. Beverly had elegant feet, long, narrow and always well groomed. He would have her wear her hair up so that he could gently and slowly take it down, his kisses becoming now more passionate against her neck and shoulders as he opened that silky, marvelous Chinese kimono he'd recently given her, the only barrier to her soft rounded body. He'd take his time with her breasts, kneading, sucking, his tongue dancing over them until she was panting and writhing, her body begging for release. But he would be in charge, his will dominating her, refusing her relief as his hands and tongue worked their way down and deep until he knew she could stand it no longer, and then,...just the thought of it filled his groin with excruciating pain.

When Howard got back from the lavatory, his thoughts switched to Earle Walker.

Had Earle Walker done those things to Beverly before he'd started brutalizing her? Closing his eyes, he tried to picture the two of them in bed, but all he could see was Beverly's tear-stained face last night when it became clear that it was too late for them, that Paddy would always be there, between them, and Earle Walker too.

"Stop, there's not a thing for you to cry about. If I'd been here for you, you'd never have gotten mixed up with Joe DeLucca or that displaced Polish Count, whatever his name was, much less, Earle Walker."

"He was Hungarian. You know about them?"

"Of course, I do."

"You've had me watched?"

"I've only had you watched when you start twisting that little pinkie ring. That's a dead give-away."

"I never realized it. Sounds almost Freudian. My mother gave me that ring."

"I believe it would've had to have been your father for Freud."

"I don't guess I mean Freud; all of his problems were sexual."

"So are ours."

"Not really."

"No? Wouldn't things have been fine if we could have made love?"

"If that's what you believe, Howard, then you must really think I'm a slut."

"Don't call yourself that."

"Why not? If you think the only reason I went to bed with other men was because I had to have it, then what else am I?"

"Then why did you?"

"You're no different from other men; you think with your prick."

"What does that mean?"

"It means, Howard, that being with other men was my way of dealing with the fact that you were with Paddy."

"You knew about Paddy before we were married."

"Yes, and in my foolish, illogical mind, I believed that once we'd made love, that would be the end of Paddy."

"That *was* foolish. Even if I'd been able to make love to you, I could never have given up Paddy."

"Yes, I found that out."

"However, perhaps now that Paddy's gone...?"

"You're unbelievable! How could you possibly think that I'd ever share your bed now?"

"You've shared my home all these years."

"Yes, I have, because, in spite of Paddy, you're my best friend. I love you and depend on you, but go to bed with you, never. Another woman, I'd know how to fight; a man, I don't know how to compete with a man."

"Paddy's dead."

"And so's anything we might've had, a long time ago; besides, he'll always be between us. I think you know that."

Howard Abelson's thoughts were full of those last moments with his wife as he stepped into the waiting limo. Opening his briefcase, he removed the gun case and took the Lilliput from its velvet lining. Loading it and placing it in his pocket, he then looked at his watch—a bit short of two a.m. His first thought was to change it, to move it back the three hours that separated East from West, but then he reconsidered. After all, he wouldn't be here long.

Carolyn Walker slipped quietly into the small viewing room behind the library when she heard her husband answer the late night doorbell. Earle could spy on almost everyone and everything in Eternal City from this room. He didn't know she had a key. She'd rarely dared use it, but tonight, she couldn't contain her curiosity. Earle had been too secretive after the phone call.

No matter how confident Earle was that he had her completely under his thumb, she'd never stop hoping and praying for a way out.

He never said a kind word to her anymore. All he did now was treat her ugly and…she couldn't even say it, it was so terrible, but it was wrong; she told him so. God had punished the people at Sodom, and God would punish him, but when? She couldn't wait much longer.

She was right, it was important because Earle was recording tonight. All she had to do was switch on the view screen to bring the library into full view just as Earle returned with ….

"You sure you won't take off that coat, Senator? You're gonna get pretty warm in here."

"I don't plan to be here long."

"You have time for a drink?"

"No, thank you."

"Well, I'm gonna have one," Walker said as he pushed a button to reveal an elaborate, concealed bar and poured himself a whiskey, a man's drink. "Have to keep it secret, you know. Don't want the faithful to get any ideas that what's good for the gander is good for the geese."

Earle chuckled over that one. He was in great spirits, especially after meeting his formidable opponent. Couldn't believe this pale-faced little fag had such a good reputation for getting things done in the Senate. Look at him standing there, squirming, nervous as hell. This was going to be a pleasure. Why, he'd wiped his ass with better men, but then, this wasn't a man. In fact, this was going to be too easy. He'd take it slow, torment him, before he squashed him like he was nothing more than a worm under his shoe.

"You know, Abelson, I can't figure out why you're here, unless you came to thank me for doing your job for you. Maybe you're just curious to know how that Jew bitch of yours is in the sack. Is that it?"

"No, Walker, I didn't come to talk," Howard replied getting calmer as he removed the Lilliput from his coat pocket.

Walker laughed nastily before he spoke again.

"You think you can frighten me? Why, you fuckin' fag, the day'll never come when I can be intimidated by whore scum like you. You can't hurt me. Put that fuckin' toy away and...."

The shot hit Earle point-blank in the chest. His drink went crashing to the floor as his hand instinctively grabbed the edge of the desk. A look of bewilderment spread over his face as he brought his other hand to his chest where a deep red spot was gradually spreading. He stared down in disbelief at his blood-covered hand that could not stem the flow.

"You fuckin' fool, she's not worth it," he gasped as he lurched toward his assailant.

The second shot rang out as it again entered his chest but this time ripped downward. Earle buckled to his knees. Howard stood quietly watching, recognizing that it hadn't been hard at all. In fact, he'd rather enjoyed it. He had no desire to rush away, wanting with genuine curiosity, he realized, to watch Walker die. He'd never watched anyone die. He'd been with Paddy at the end, but Paddy had been so weak for so long that he had just faded away, just a whisper. There hadn't even been the death rattle that he'd always heard accompanied such events. This was different. This was the violent death of a violent man, and surely, it could be an interesting experience; maybe even a mirror to his own end since that too would be violent.

Walker was down now and had managed to roll slightly to his side. Abelson still hadn't moved and didn't look up when Carolyn Walker entered and spoke. Her voice was quiet and controlled.

"Senator Abelson, you go now. Senator, Senator Abelson!" Her voice got louder as she tried to break into his thoughts. "Senator Abelson," she repeated as she took his arm firmly and turned him toward the door, "put your gun back into your pocket. Yes, that's right. Now, I want you to go home. Go out and get in your car and go home. Don't say anything to anyone about this. I'll give you one hour to be away from here. Come, I'll walk you to the door."

He didn't speak as she guided him out.

When Carolyn returned to the library, her husband had turned himself completely on his back.

"Carolyn," his voice was low, weak as he called, "Carolyn, get help. Did you get help?"

"No, dear."

"You idiot, I'm bleeding to death."

"I know, dear," She agreed pleasantly as she began to pick up the pieces of broken glass from his last drink.

"You fuckin' bitch, get help, I say."

"That was ugly, Earle. You apologize and ask sweetly; a please might be nice to hear."

There was a long pause before Earle spoke again, this time more slowly and with greater difficulty.

"I'm sorry, Carolyn, now will you please get me some help?"

"That was much better, dear. I don't think I've heard you say please to me since Seminary. You rest there, I'll be right back."

Carolyn Walker gave her husband a warm smile as she took the broken glass and walked briskly from the room. When she returned, she was carrying a large, plastic trash bag—the thirty gallon size.

"I'm sorry to have to move you, dear, but I must put this under you. You're bleeding all over our beautiful carpet. You might ruin it, for blood is hard to get out of anything."

She knelt down and raised her husband's head efficiently. When she did, he reached back and took her arm pulling her toward his face.

"Now listen, bitch," he spoke, mustering all his strength, those magnificent eyes only slightly diminished, "you go sound the alarm right this minute. I must have help."

"You don't seem to understand, Earle," she answered, staring back, steadily. "Senator Abelson was sent by God. He was God's instrument. You have sinned, and *Vengeance is mine, saith the Lord.* You know I can't interfere with God's wishes; besides, I promised Senator Abelson

I would give him one hour, and it hasn't even been ten minutes. What kind of person would I be if I went back on my word?"

"Carolyn, please…"

She interrupted, "I've got it, dear, I'll help take your mind off everything. You used to love to hear me sing. I'll sit right here with you, stroke your hair—you used to like that too—and sing to you. Now let me see, what shall I sing? I know."

Carolyn Walker's voice had never sounded quite so good.

There's a garden where Jesus is waiting,
There's a place that is wondrously fair;
For it glows with the light of His presence,
'Tis the beautiful garden of prayer.
O the beautiful garden, (her voice rose, strong and lilting, for she loved the chorus)
the garden of prayer,
O the beautiful garden of prayer;
There the Savior awaits, and He opens the gates…

Walker interrupted. He hadn't attempted to move or speak throughout her solo. Perhaps, he knew it was useless; perhaps, he also realized it was too late; perhaps, he'd been saving his strength, hoping to prolong the inevitable. But now, he raised his arm. It was so unexpected that Carolyn jerked back, thinking instinctively that he was trying to slap her or grab her neck in an attempt to take her with him, but that wasn't it.

He raised his arm straight up, as if reaching for something only his dimming eyes were privy to. At the same time, the room filled with agitation, a turbulence that Carolyn knew must be the death rattle that accompanies violent ends. That was when it happened. Just as Earle raised one arm with what must have been sheer will, he spoke his last word as a mortal human being, his wife, her song, and her world forgotten.

Freud would have danced with delight for Earle did not say, *Spare me, Lord, God have mercy,* even *Praise the Lord;* Earle did not say farewell to his faithful, his apostles, even his wife; Earle did not say shit, fuck, even damn. No, Judge Earle's last word in this world, where he had used words so easily to control and manipulate, was to the only person who had ever controlled him, the one he thought he'd vanquished when he was twelve, the one whose marvelous, mesmerizing, steel-gray eyes matched his own.

In that split second before those eyes glazed over, never to be seen on this earth again, Earle Sylvester Walker probably gave the only sincere plea he had ever made in his life when he reached out and cried, "*Mother.*"

Carolyn Walker did not allow her song to intrude on this final moment. She sat quietly, respecting death and the solitary task of dying. Finally, confident that she was now alone, she began again to stroke her husband's thick wavy hair, and again, her light, clear soprano filled the room. She completed every verse of *In the Garden*, then modulated into *There is a Green Hill Far Away,* to *In the Sweet By and By,* then *Are You Washed in the Blood?* to *Ivory Palaces,* ending with a rousing chorus of *Bringing in the Sheaves.* It was an inspired medley and she felt renewed when it was over.

It was almost two when Carolyn Walker gave her husband a light wistful kiss on the forehead. She allowed herself a moment of sadness with this final farewell, not because he was gone—she was happy for that—but for the youthful dreams that she'd thought they had once shared. Rising, she went to the phone, pushed a button and spoke softly to the sleepy response on the other end.

"Harlan, this is Carolyn. You must dress and get up to the house quickly and quietly. Earle's dead, and we have planning to do."

When Howard Abelson stepped out of the cab and started up the steps of his Lexington Avenue brownstone, the great city was already alive with promise.   Normally, he would have stopped to absorb its energy, but not today.   He was very tired.   It was best to be tired at a time like this.   He couldn't imagine anyone being able to kill himself if he'd had a good night's sleep and was full of energy.   He also thought that it would be more difficult if it were a sunny day; he loved sunny days.   Today, however, was perfect for his task, cold and dreary, a day made for dying.

The trip home was a blur.   He couldn't even remember leaving Walker's.   Somewhere in his mind the voice of a woman kept telling him to go home.   He had no idea what she looked like or who she was.   It didn't matter.   All he could see was Earle Walker lying on the floor, the blood beginning to soak into a very pretty carpet.   He was sorry about that.

Gun wounds were messy; at least, they were in the chest.   He'd have to come up with a neater way of going.   He had always been neat.   He considered getting into the bathtub.   That way, the blood could be scrubbed out.   But that was undignified.   He pictured himself at his desk in the great library, but that beautiful old Kirman from Beverly's family was on the floor there.   He didn't want to stain it.

Finally, making a decision, he went to the kitchen and got a large plastic trash bag—the thirty-gallon size.   Spreading it out on his desk, he opened his briefcase and took out the Lilliput, which he placed on the plastic.   He sat down and turned the gun over in his hands admiring its craftsmanship.   It was a thing of beauty.   He liked beautiful things but understood that even beautiful things could be deadly.

It occurred to him that Beverly might still be asleep, probably very much as he'd left her at what seemed so very long ago.

Leaning over and turning the Lilliput upside down into the roof of his mouth, he pulled the trigger.

Stacey Lea's return to the White House after escorting Beverly to New York was just ahead of the forecasted snowstorm. She didn't speak to anyone as she rushed upstairs in her concern for her husband. It was a relief to find that he had emerged from his rooms, and in his place, there were workman busily dismantling the large fish-tank that had sadistically pleasured him for over a year.

This was good news, indeed! Whatever Palmer's condition was, he'd at least recouped enough to remove the literal source of his early morning trauma. The weary-filled dread that had permeated her return was somewhat lifted, for she had imagined all sorts of things from his being curled up beside his fish tank, his mother's note clutched tightly in his hands; to finding him rushing around the White House, his cape flaring in back of him. This last vision had haunted her throughout the day as she'd groped to make some sense out of the rest of it. DAY ZERO was to have been a beginning, a day that began to set things right. It wasn't supposed to have gotten out of hand; it wasn't supposed to have gotten bloody.

Freshening up quickly, Stacey Lea bounded down the stairs eager to find her husband and assure herself of his condition. She walked purposely toward the West Wing, the site of the Oval Office, a bounce beginning to develop in her step. It was on her way there, just as she rounded the corner to the busy area around the President's famous office that Coleman appeared.

"May I help you, Madam?"

"As a matter-of-fact, you may. I just got back from the sad mission of escorting Senator Abelson's new widow to New York, and I'm looking for my husband. Do you happen to know where he is?"

"He's in the Oval Office, Madam."

"That's where I thought he might be. Thank you, Coleman," Stacey Lea replied, pleasantly, as she started to walk on.

"I'm sorry, Madam, but you can't go in there. At present, he's quite busy and does not wish to be disturbed."

With his words, Coleman had placed himself firmly in front of her, barring her passage; his usually dour facade replaced by a blatant expression of challenge. Had he known that she was already near the end of endurance, perhaps, he would have stepped aside; had he known that this would be the great battle, perhaps, he would have stiffened himself in anticipation; had he known that this field of combat would be a fight to the death, perhaps, he would have made hasty retreat to fight again another day, but such gifts to foresee the future were not his. He stood his ground.

"Did he give you specific orders to keep his wife from him?" Stacey Lea questioned, her pleasant mask dropping away as the smoldering embers within her began to stir and ignite.

"No, Madam, but I always know his wishes, and I know he'd not wish to be disturbed at this moment. He hasn't had an easy day."

Stacey Lea noted mentally that she hadn't had an easy day, either. She didn't speak as her anger mounted, nor did she look up as she started around him, announcing that she would speak to Harriet, his secretary. Coleman moved with her, the bulk of him again impeding her passage, his determination further revealed in his raised hands and firm voice.

"Madam, you cannot disturb...."

That's all he had time to say. Coleman was a big man, broad of chest and large framed. He wasn't fat but solid and a bit stocky with age. In fact, he was large enough and strong enough to have stood his ground; that is, if he'd anticipated Stacey Lea's next move, but it would never have crossed his mind. Until recently, she had allowed him to best her in many small ways, hardly shown her annoyance, nor had she allowed her animosity to emerge. The deliberate coffee spill on his sleeve as well as the ransacking of his rooms were actions that disturbed him, but neither was so great that he wasn't confident that he could amply handle everything in good time. He did not know his adversary.

Stacey Lea lunged, she lunged with all her might, and Coleman went smashing back, hitting his head against the corner of a hall side-table. The table, its contents, and Coleman collapsed to the floor. She didn't stop there. Picking up a small hall chair, she threw it at him; she threw a nearby lamp, a vase that opened his already damaged head; everything she could find she threw with almost superhuman force.

People emerged from everywhere—security guards, Secret Service, the household staff, the Presidential Staff, even a few sightseers got in from the public rooms in all the confusion. It was chaos, and no one knew what to do.

Do they restrain the First Lady? Dare they touch her? What procedure did this fall under? There was nothing in their manuals to cover such an event. Finally, a quick thinking security guard placed himself in front of Coleman just as Stacey Lea was about to throw a brass umbrella stand. No one will ever know if that courageous deed checked her hands, for at about the same moment the doors of the Oval Office were thrown open to reveal a red-faced President of the United States supported on either side by the heads of the FBI and the CIA.

Stacey Lea's back was to them as she raised the stand high over her head and at the same time loudly admonished the guard to get out of the way, but her husband's voice penetrated through her own.

"What the hell's going on here?" Palmer bellowed.

Stacey Lea turned toward his voice, her arms still raised, balancing the umbrella stand.

"I'm glad you're here, Palmer. Coleman barred me passage in my own home! I want him out of here. I'll not spend another night under the same roof with him! I want him out by, uh, sundown!"

With that, Stacey Lea turned, put down the umbrella stand, and retraced her steps, while the gathered throng separated as she passed through. When she reached the contorted body of Coleman, she stopped and looked down at his bloody head. The blood had now oozed down his cheek and drops were beginning to spread over his starched white jacket. With disdain, her foot kicked a nearby piece of porcelain from the flesh-opening vase toward him just before she walked quickly and deliberately away.

Stacey Lea walked directly to her bedroom and sat down at her dresser. For a while, all she did was look blankly at herself in the mirror as she allowed her blood to settle back in its veins and her heart to regain its familiar beat. Finally, she allowed thought.

"Well, Stacey Leanne Culberson Forbes, that was some show you just put on."

"Yes," her reflection responded, *"but it was worth it. We got rid of Coleman and got even at the same time!"*

"Yes, but Palmer's had enough happen to him today without my little exhibition."

"So,... he's a big boy!"

"There's a limit even for big boys! I didn't need to add to it by going into one of those obsolete rages of mine—something he's never seen, and attack his favorite employee!"

Stacey Lea got up, twirled around, and collapsed backward onto her bed.

She'd done it this time. How was Palmer going to react to her exhibition? She needed to talk to Daddy and Annie.

Just as Stacey Lea reached for her private line, Palmer strode in. He looked beat, she noted, as he walked toward her. She couldn't read his face.

"I think we need to talk," he said as he pulled a chair over to the bed.

Stacey Lea sat up and waited.

"I'm aware that you're under a great deal of stress with Howard Abelson's suicide. Yes, Martin told me what really happened and what you asked him to do."

"I did try to talk to you about it this morning."

"It's okay. I thanked Martin for helping you. I know how you feel about Beverly, and frankly, I'm glad you did it. The notoriety his suicide would receive serves no purpose."

"Thank you for understanding, Palmer. I was afraid it might displease you."

"No, but what happened downstairs a few moments ago certainly did."

She didn't speak. She knew he'd get to this, and it was best to wait. Palmer was quiet and different, and she could in no way anticipate his next move.

"You might be pleased to know that Coleman's wound was only superficial."

She still didn't speak as it occurred to her that she would have much preferred for him to rant and rave.

"Coleman told me that he only barred your way as he urged you not to disturb me."

"That's correct."

"Then why did you react as you did?"

"I'm not even sure I can answer that. I've been up here trying to figure it out myself. All this stuff with Beverly, and then, my worry about you…." Her voice trailed off for a moment. "I was so eager to see you and see how you were, and then Coleman stepped in. He was determined to thwart me. He gets some sadistic pleasure out of undermining me."

"I believe you imagine that, Stacey Lea."

"Do I? Do I imagine the secret looks you two sometimes share? Do I imagine his possessive attitude, his unabashed presumptuousness that he knows better than I what's best for you? Do I imagine that he's in some kind of competition with me, inserting himself at every opportunity? Do I imagine that he's confident enough of your feelings for him that he dares to treat me with impertinence and haughtiness?"

"Sounds to me like you're jealous of Coleman."

"That's an ugly thing to say, Palmer. I've never questioned your appointees. Your staff's around all the time, and we've gotten on just fine, but Coleman's different; he's inherited, and he's not your staff; he's our staff in our home. Should I have to share our home with someone who makes me uncomfortable and enjoys doing it? I'm supposed to be the dutiful little wife, who never complains, who goes along with anything and everything you say and do. Well, there's a limit, and I have reached it."

"You've just correctly explained the difference between my staff and our staff. However, you're incorrect in your understanding of where Coleman fits. Coleman may be on our house staff, but he's my man."

"No, Coleman's your monster. Perhaps it's you I should've been throwing things at."

"Stacey Lea!" Palmer's voice rose as he raised himself quickly from the chair, "I don't know what's come over you, but this has been a long day, and I have too much that needs my attention without having to spend my time on domestic nonsense. Understand this! Coleman is not yours to fire; therefore, you will apologize to him for your outrageous actions and consider the matter closed."

"Never!" Staccy Lea rejoined as she also rose, her tone and body rigid.

Palmer looked down at his wife, dumbfounded. She was immovable; he didn't know her anymore. He'd be glad when this day was over for nothing had gone right. His ordered world had shattered as if a major nuclear explosion had been set off at its core. Did it have anything to do with his mother? Crazy, but what else could explain today?

There was no question that in one day his *Grand Design* had received crushing blows from all directions. Women seemed to be declaring for every office in the land; Alma Tyler wasn't leaving after all, and Mildred Dillard was rebelling on the Court. He couldn't call a Bunker meeting—who was left? Beau was missing, and he'd had to send a taskforce out looking for his taskforce because it was gone too. Walker was dead, his fish were dead, and now Stacey Lea, his always cool, collected wife, had gone berserk, half-killing his most trusted employee. Palmer sank slowly back into his chair. He despaired; he wished he weren't president anymore. It was truly the low point in his illustrious career.

And this was unfortunate because Goodman Palmer Forbes was a good president; that is, he wasn't aggressive or weak, liberal or conservative, intelligent or sensitive. In short, he'd become the most popular American since Ronald Reagan. Everyone everywhere loved and admired him, and he had always done what was best for everyone everywhere. Everyone knew that in order to do this, the Presidency had to be above laws that applied to others—this was an unwritten law. He was not the first to use this power. So, what was wrong? All he knew was that he couldn't lose Coleman today too. He looked at his wife who still stood rigid.

"Stacey Lea, I need Coleman right now. I beg you to end this feud for my sake."

"And I beg you to respect my feelings and not ask such a thing of me."

Palmer didn't reply as he turned and walked toward his own rooms.

Palmer Forbes went directly to the cabinet where he had placed the *Mother* engraved urn. After removing the rolled paper it concealed, he sat in the nearest chair and gazed at it for a long time, as if he did not know by memory its familiar contents.

GOODMAN'S DAILY TEN COMMANDMENTS

1. You will rise and shine!
   The early bird gets the worm.

2. You will bathe and brush your teeth.
   Cleanliness is next to Godliness.

3. You will eat a hardy breakfast.
   Breakfast is the most important meal of the day.

4. You will approach each task pleasantly and with industry.
   Don't put off until tomorrow, what you can do today.

5. You will keep busy throughout the day.
   An idle mind is a devil's workshop.

6. You will carefully lay out your clothes for tomorrow.
   Your Scout Motto "Be Prepared."

7. You will kneel and pray before retiring.
   Prayers are the stair-steps to heaven.

8. You will get eight hours sleep every night.
   Early to bed and early to rise/Makes a man happy,
   wealthy and wise.

9. You will *get a haircut.*
   Focus for the day.

10. You will Be a good boy,
    Be a Good-man,
    If Mother can't see you,
    Remember God can.

Finally, Palmer Forbes crumpled the paper in his large hand, rose, threw it into the bright burning fireplace as he said, "No, Judith Anne Goodman Forbes, you will not best me so easily. I'll not go down without a fight!"

He turned and walked swiftly to the Oval Office, stopping only for a short but thoughtful moment at the big hall mirror by Stacey Lea's door.

Just before entering his office he turned to his secretary and commanded, "Harriet, please call Coleman and have him come to my office, and," he added with a sigh of resignation, "call Domenic and tell him I want a haircut in the morning, about seven. I believe I could use one before the Abelson funeral."

Sue Ann had hardly had time to freshen up after her return from Tucson when the long black limousine pulled into her driveway. She had never been so excited or so nervous, for she'd not seen or spoken to her husband in three days. Not only that, she had absolutely no idea where he was. He could be hanging by his feet somewhere, in a cellar with rats crawling around, or where it was so cold that frostbite could cause him to lose his toes, even a whole foot, and she would be responsible. These and similar thoughts had been running through her head ever since she let that long black limousine take him away. She bet this was the same one.

Hmm, she considered, looks like we're going north toward Baltimore. Maybe the driver will tell me now that we're on our way? I don't know who Stacey Lea and Ellie thought I might tell anyway. I'm supposed to trust them, but they don't trust me.

"Yes ma'am, we're going to Baltimore. He's on a big boat in Baltimore Harbor."

What a clever idea! Beau likes his creature comforts and some of those ocean liners have beautiful accommodations. He's probably in one of those grand staterooms right this minute drinking his bourbon and watching television. It was silly of me to worry, especially with Stacey Lea in charge. She'd see that Beau was well taken care of.

With her conscience somewhat eased, Sue Ann rested her head against the back of the cushion and closed her eyes. She must have dozed, for it seemed only moments later that she was being helped out of the car.

"What's this?" she asked, looking at the rusty old scow in front of which she had just been deposited.

"It's the *Bella Delores*, ma'am, the Cuban freighter where your husband is being detained."

Damn! This isn't at all what I expected. This is a fine kettle of fish Stacey Lea's gotten me into. She could have, at least, put him on one of those fancy ocean liners!

Sue Ann followed her escort up the gangplank and down into the ship to a locked door. Her heart was pounding rapidly and her palms were sweaty.

"Hello, Beau," she said, as she stepped into a large spartan bedroom.

"Sue Ann," Beau acknowledged, startled, rushing toward her to hug her tightly, "Oh, Sue Ann, they've got you too. How could they do such a thing? I can't bear the thought that I've gotten you into this mess…the mother of my children!"

"Into what mess, Beau?"

"I don't know; that's the worst part of it. They won't tell me. But I've figured out that it must be some foreign power, some terrorist organization. One thing for certain, something really big is startin'. I can feel it. My god, it's wonderful to see you," Beau continued as he held her at arms length, his eyes devouring her. "I thought I might never see you again!"

Sue Ann was touched at the genuine concern his profuse welcome exhibited. For a moment, she even felt a twinge of that prior conscience for putting him through this ordeal, but then the hurt started welling up again, and the bitterness over his past escapades consumed all sympathetic emotions.

She thought of the times she'd gone to bed knowing he was in bed with someone else; she thought of the times that she'd had to muster the courage to face women that knew him intimately, the way she did; she thought of how she'd had to exhibit a proud face to a world that knew her husband cheated on her; she thought of what he'd done to Casey; she thought of God knows what else he'd done that she didn't know about and didn't want to, and with each thought, her heart hardened.

"Have you been treated well, Beau?" her coolly questioning voice cut through his exuberance.

"Yes, but I know it's only a matter of time before that changes. I haven't seen their leader yet. When he shows up, no telling what's gonna happen…."

The last part of Beau's expressed thought faded. He looked thoughtfully at his wife while slowly and incredulously a new reality confounded him.

"You aren't a prisoner, are you, Sue Ann?"

"No, Beau, I'm not."

"You mean to tell me that you're part of this conspiracy against me? That you knew? That you had something to do with my being on this goddamn banana boat?"

"What kind of boat?"

"BANANA, BANANA BOAT! Can't you smell 'em? I'll never be able to get the stench of rotten bananas out of my nostrils as long as I live!"

She tried very hard. She bit her lips, rolled her eyes, straightened her back, took a deep, deep breath and held it, but it exploded from her under its own volition as her back collapsed, her eyes teared, and her face became distorted with uncontrollable laughter.

Her husband didn't join her. As she curled over in the only really comfortable chair in the room, giving in to uninhibited glee, Beau stiffly stood, a befuddled look on his face as he nursed his hurt and his pride.

The world was insane, Sue Ann decided at that moment. It seemed that nothing could be serious or sad without also having some pure crazy part that took the dignity right out—Sarah had left the Senate to water plants; Stacey Lea had visions while sitting in a tree; Beverly had lost her husband and her lover the same day from the same thing; Beau was held captive on a banana boat! Could anything be sillier than that? Could any of them have planned all this?

No, there was no question in Sue Ann's head at this moment that there were higher powers, sitting up there right now having a wonderful time pushing and pulling, setting up obstacles and daring any mortals who might get out of line. They were laughing at them, and she was determined to join in. We humans take things much too seriously, she decided. She'd not make that mistake again!

"Are you about through?" Beau inquired stiffly.

"Yes," Sue Ann answered, sitting up and trying to settle down.

"You think it's funny, uh, that your husband has been held captive? I assure you I don't join in your sadistic humor."

"No, Beau, I just find it ironic that it's a banana boat, knowing how you hate bananas."

"You didn't know where I was?"

"No, I didn't."

"You let someone take me off, God knows where, and you didn't care? Well, I assure you I'd have never let anyone do that to you."

"I was worried about you, but if you recall, I tried my best to keep you from going to Nashville. You didn't leave me any choice."

"You didn't give me any choice. How did I know that if I tried to go to Nashville, I'd be kidnapped?"

"What you should have known was that going to Nashville was wrong."

"I told you then that I didn't relish the job, but I also told you that I didn't have any choice. You've got me in a helluva mess with Palmer, and you also haven't helped Casey. I would've been much gentler than who they must have down there in place of me."

"Casey announced for the Senate today."

Beau did not speak, only looked at her thoughtfully.

"How did you arrange this, Sue Ann?"

"I didn't have a thing to do with Casey runnin'; you know that."

"No, how did you arrange for me to be brought here?"

"I didn't."

"Who did?"

"It doesn't matter."

"It matters a great deal. I want to know what's going on. Isn't Palmer looking for me?"

"Yes, I understand he is."

"You haven't talked to him?"

"No, I've been away."

"And he couldn't find you?" Beaufort looked befuddled.

"No."

"Where've you been?"

"It doesn't matter."

"What does matter?" he asked, looking more befuddled.

"Beaufort, I've been advised to tell you that you can be released if you swear to say nothing about your captivity."

"I have no intention of doing any such thing."

"I hope you'll change your mind; otherwise, I've been told to inform you that you'll stay here until hell freezes over."

"I couldn't be kept here. Someone would discover me."

"I wouldn't bank on that. In fact, you could probably stay on the high seas like the *man without a country* just going back and forth from Cuba with loads of bananas."

"Who are you speaking for?"

"That doesn't matter. What does matter is your Gentleman Swear."

"How do you know I'd keep my coerced word?"

"That's a well taken point and one that was considered. Unfortunately, if you should break your word, those pictures I had compromising you with other women will be given to the tabloids."

"You wouldn't do that even if just because of the children."

"I agree that I'd have trouble. It would destroy our family and our reputation, so I gave them to someone else."

"You what? That's blackmail, you know?"

"You have to make a decision, Beaufort."

"Sue Ann, don't you have any feelings for me at all?"

"Yes, but I can't let them interfere anymore than you could let me interfere with your going to Nashville or a lot of the other things that's been goin' on."

"What do you mean by that?"

"Howard Abelson and Earle Walker both died of heart attacks today."

Beau didn't say anything. He just waited for whatever Sue Ann might come up with next. Earle Walker dead?

"I've been told that you shouldn't have the problem with Palmer you might expect, but even if you should, I think that it's about time you started being your own man again. What can he do to you? Can he take your seat away from you? Can he take your children away from you?"

"What about my wife?"

Sue Ann sighed, "I don't know about us, Beau. So much has happened to us, even this, my allowing you to be kidnapped. We've so many scars on our marriage, and many are still open wounds that may never heal. But, at least, do for yourself; take back your dignity, Beaufort. Nothing can come right unless you do."

"If I swear, what happens then?"

"Well, for starters, we go home; then we go with the Forbeses to Abelson's funeral tomorrow."

"And what do I tell Palmer?"

"Tell him that you and I were on a second honeymoon, and that was more important to you than going to Nashville to blackmail Casey."

Beau Fairmont walked over to the small porthole and looked out at the now familiar sea. He had a good feeling beginning somewhere deep inside. It was unfamiliar, but he liked it. He hadn't felt good about himself in a long time, but if Sue Ann would help him, maybe he could again.

Sue Ann was spunky, that's for sure, but she could never have pulled this off on her own. Stacey Lea could do it, and if she'd gotten on to Palmer's little game....? Hell, what did he have to lose? His bridges were already burnt with Palmer when he hadn't shown up in Nashville; besides, he could hardly desert the South, his roots. What would his forebears think? He didn't relish taking on Stacey Lea anyway, especially after what he had been through the past few days. He'd play it cool, sit back and watch. Sue Ann didn't want to tell him who her leader was, fine. He didn't want to officially know; it would be easier this way.

Beau turned around to face his wife, who was now standing, waiting impatiently for his answer.

"You think we can get out of here, the way the snow's coming down?" he asked smiling.

"We can't try until you swear."

"I swear. As a gentleman, I give you my word of honor."

"I'm not sure that's good enough under the circumstances. Do you *cross your heart and hope to die\stick a needle in your eye?*"

"C'mon, Sue Ann, don't be silly. That's kid stuff."

"But that's when swears meant something. Say it, Beaufort, and do it right."

Senator Beaufort Randal Fairmont looked at the serious countenance of his wife and did as she required. As he made the sign on his heart that sealed the oath, he realized that he didn't feel silly at all. There was something pure and uncomplicated about what he'd just done, and he felt part of a secret place where words were kept and honor had true meaning. It was a place where villains lost, wrong was righted, and dragons were slain. He liked it there.

As the lights of the great Capitol twinkled and died, DAY ZERO had taken its toll on most of its participants.

The Fairmonts had slowly made their way back to their Georgetown home from the harbor in Baltimore; a late candlelight dinner by a brightly burning fire could not bring to rest the concern both felt over the next day's Presidential encounter.

Beverly Jean Abelson on the East Coast and Carolyn Walker on the West Coast had never met, but this day had joined them in a sleepless night, their thoughts united by the same two men whose untimely deaths had changed their destinies.

And in the great White House, Coleman slowly removed and packed carefully each picture that represented the only life he cared to remember. He then waited for the snow to end, so the helicopter could take him to Camp David, his temporary home.

Palmer did not join Stacey Lea as he usually did on the tenth night of each month. They were separated this night by more than the walls between their rooms. Palmer Forbes lay alone, watchful, overwhelmed by the wreckage that had befallen his controlled, ordered existence. Stacey Lea lay helpless in a world that, she too found, had rushed boldly out of control. She could no more check it than she could reach out to the man whom she instinctively knew needed her for the first time in their marriage. It was the opportunity to build something for them, but she was powerless, for she'd been the major cause of his woe.

Throughout the nation a sleeping giant began to stir, ever so slightly. It had started that day with Casey Bartholomew, Mildred Dillard, and others who'd thrown their hats into the ring, who had announced that they would no longer be bridled.

Only President Forbes and Cardinal Bishop remained to hold the line, and President Forbes didn't at this moment have appetite for the contest. In one fell swoop, The Bunker, that mighty fortress, had lost its great purpose and was nothing more than what it should have been all along—a haven for the *ole boys club* to play *old war games*.

CHAPTER SIXTEEN

AFTERMATH, DAY ONE

The blizzard of yesterday had left Washington bathed in white, the air crisp, the sun bright. There was also a pervading coldness both inside and outside the First House of the nation.

Even though there seemed to be no tension in the soft swallow-bite Stacey Lea could hear from across the breakfast table, she could feel it. Calm before the storm? She would have welcomed his rage to this frigid silence. She might have even welcomed Coleman, for just the sight of her old adversary always sent the blood coursing through her veins, a more natural feeling than this.

Stacey Lea had already talked to Ellie this morning to find Beverly was somewhat improved now that her brother had arrived. He had a steadying influence on her. It made her think of Travis. Could they have had a good relationship if he had lived? They'd been as distant as strangers after he'd ruined her playhouse under the Pondrin' Tree. All those lost years when they had the same blood rushing through their veins. Blood was the most important thing, but you didn't realize it when you were young. Yes, she reflected, Disraeli was right—*youth was a blunder.*

Yesterday was a blunder too. She hadn't planned to attack Coleman. She guessed all that pent-up anger she felt for him was just too much with everything else that had been going on. Physical rage had always hurt her in the end. It'd destroyed her relationship with her brother; now, it had hurt her marriage, how much, still remained to be seen.

Palmer was unreadable this morning, not talking at all. He wouldn't even talk to Beau. When Sue Ann had called earlier to tell her what happened and say she was back, Beau had already tried to talk to Palmer, but Palmer wouldn't take his call.

Well, she could not put it off any longer if Sue Ann and Beau were going to go with them to the funeral.

"Thomas, would you please get me some hot coffee. Not a refill, this has gotten cold. Get me a new cup."

"Yes, Mrs. Forbes," Thomas replied quietly as he complied with her request.

"Is that a new hair cut, dear?"

"Yes," her husband answered, not looking up from his paper.

"It looks very nice," she complimented, wondering if the haircut was just a coincidence.

"Thank you," he acknowledged, nodding but still not looking up.

"Sue Ann called."

"Yes, I understand the Fairmonts are back among the living."

He still did not look at her.

"I invited them to join us today for the funeral."

Palmer did not answer immediately. Slowly, he folded the paper and placed it beside his plate before looking across at her.

"You had no right to do that."

"I don't understand why not. We're taking a whole entourage of people with us, and the Fairmonts are our oldest and dearest friends. You've never taken exception to my inviting them anyplace before."

"I'm sure you know very well from Sue Ann why not."

"You mean because you wouldn't talk to Beau this morning?"

"Exactly."

"Had you informed me that they were *personae non grata* around here?"

"No, but you should have realized that since I've been unable to reach the Senator or his wife for several days, and since I wouldn't take his call, there was something wrong."

"You mean that because Beau wasn't at your beck and call earlier in the week you're miffed with him?"

"It's not that simple. He had a job to do, and he didn't do it."

"What job?"

"That's none of your business."

"You know, Palmer, I feel somewhat *persona non grata* around here this morning too. Perhaps I should join the Fairmonts in another form of transportation to the Abelson funeral."

"Where are you going?" Palmer asked sharply, watching his wife rise.

"I'm gonna call the Fairmonts and retract my invitation."

"Sit down. I'm surprised that you agreed so quickly given your temperament yesterday."

"So we're back to that, are we? I thought we settled that last night. Is your *man* waiting in some dark corner for me to come 'round?"

"If you're referring to Coleman, he's gone."

"I would say that's good riddance to bad rubbish!"

"You should know. That's your area of expertise, isn't it, the thing you want to be remembered for—rubbish? Isn't that what you want me to get you an appropriation for—rubbish?"

Stacey Lea did not respond as the color drained from her face; she could not find words to answer this hurtful challenge. Big tears welled up in her eyes as she rose with effort, feeling the debris that represented her marriage impeding her progress from the room.

But that wasn't all that impeded her progress, for her husband, now red-faced with rage, rushed around the table to grab her arm as she started toward the door. He pulled her close to him with one arm as the other shoved the morning paper into her chest.

"You may go to your room now, Mrs. Forbes," he sneered, glaring down into her eyes, "but not without the morning paper. I wouldn't want you to miss another indelibly recorded chapter in the Forbes' Presidential History, this one called *Domestic Tranquility.*"

With that, Palmer released her roughly and left the room.

Stacey Lea followed, holding back the tears as best she could. Once inside her door, she leaned against it and allowed them to flow freely. She was afraid of what she might see when she looked at the paper. Security had sworn that no pictures escaped to support yesterday's confrontation, and without pictures, her past flawless reputation would quickly put to rest the worst rumors. Sitting down at her desk, she opened the paper to see Coleman sprawled across the front page. The caption read *Domestic Tranquility at the White House.*

Coleman, desolate and alone, did not settle into his room at Camp David. He didn't see the morning paper until much later, but he did see the picture of him sprawled on the floor of the White House quite early on the morning television news.

By the time his body was found, the presidential entourage was just setting down at Andrews on its return from the Abelson funeral. On a table beside his cold, dangling feet was a copy of the *Washington Post*, neatly folded to expose his infamy. There was no other message.

"SHE WHAT?"

"Shh," cautioned Ellie, "you don't want everyone to hear, do you?"

"Why not? We could all use a big laugh this morning. I've never heard such an idiotic idea. Stacey Lea must've completely lost it."

Beverly's voice was still a few decibels too high to assure secrecy, and Ellie was distressed that someone might hear. She understood exactly where Beverly was coming from, for she'd had a similar reaction earlier this morning when Stacey Lea had proposed it.

"I know what you mean, Beverly, and frankly, I felt the same way when Stacey Lea told me."

"Well, I'm glad you're not both crazy. I can't even imagine such a thing coming into her mind. You know, I've been tolerant and cooperative throughout some difficult situations. I've allowed myself to take a vision seriously, to take that kid swear without much objection, and I dashed off to Florida to successfully persuade Madge Goldman to make a run for Governor. I didn't complain. I helped form a secret organization, used its password, wore its color. I even ordered wisteria for the house one day, but Stacey Lea wanting me to seek Howard's empty seat in the Senate is much too much to ask. I'd be the laughing stock."

"I believe you should think about it."

"I thought you said you agreed with me that it was crazy?"

"I did when she first told me, but after thinking about it, I'm not so sure."

"Tell me, Ellie, luv, how'd you think this out?"

"Well, in the first place, you have a good education. Correct me if I'm wrong, but you did get you Masters in English while Senator Abelson was still Governor."

"That's right, but don't get the idea I got it for some self-improving purpose. I did it simply to keep my sanity during those first years of marriage when I was thrust so bluntly onto the Albany political scene. Being a new wife, much less a governor's wife, was very traumatic for me."

"You still got it. Maybe it's time you started using it, and maybe you've got it in other ways, too. I'd consider it a great honor that Stacey Lea even thought of it. She's a good judge of character."

"But how could she believe that I could fill Harold's shoes?"

"I don't know. I don't have her insight, but I do believe that we all have a time, and that if we turn our backs on opportunities, they're lost forever. Maybe this is your opportunity to be what you can be; maybe all this tragedy with Howard was meant to end with this opportunity for you. Perhaps, you should go with the flow; give it a chance. We might not be able to pull it off anyway. Governor DeLucca's pretty much his own man."

Beverly sat quietly. She could hardly believe that she was giving any thought to such an outrageous proposal. *Her*? Miss Mess-up, personified? Then, she remembered what her mother had said that fateful day when she'd told her she was a love child, touched by God. Her mother had had confidence that she'd find herself someday. Was this her chance? Could she do good for a change? What was she going to do anyway? One thing she liked about Ellie was that Ellie knew when to be quiet.

"I'll have to do some serious thinking, Ellie, and I hardly have time for it now with Howard not even in his grave. Maybe you're right. Maybe I should get serious about my life, and if not Howard's seat, something worthwhile. Tell Stacey Lea that I'll give it thought, and, uh, tell her that if I decide that I can handle Howard's seat with honor, I believe I can get the appointment myself. Okay?"

"She'll sure be happy to hear that. We both agree that Governor DeLucca's going to be tough."

"Joe and I go back a long way. He's not so tough."

"I hope I haven't broken anything up," Beverly's brother said as he walked in and over to give his sister a warm kiss, "but you have important visitors, my dear. Governor and Mrs. DeLucca have arrived to pay their respects."

"Let's don't keep the governor waiting. I wouldn't want to get on his bad side," she said as she winked at Ellie, and took a last look in the mirror, "besides, I never could get those few hairs to stay put. I don't know why I should expect them to now."

Stacey Lea dressed carefully for Howard Abelson's funeral. Black from neck to toe, she faced herself in the long mirror in a quandary whether or not to make it head to toe. The black floppy felt hat looked nice and would look even better when she got on her long black coat, but should she cover her face? She'd made it a practice not to do so; people had a right to get a good look at her. On the other hand, she needed a cover today, her eyes were red and so was her nose. No, she decided, taking the hat off for the third time. If I wear a hat when I don't usually, those awful reporters will probably accuse me of trying to hide behind it? She threw the hat on a chair.

Reporters were having a field day with her. She had prided herself on her relationship with the media and had gone out of her way to give them delightful little things to report. She had even appeared on a number of talk shows and allowed their cameras to follow her around in the White House a few times, just as they had Jacqueline Kennedy. Not many First Ladies had been that open.

Still, she had given them cause. If she were a reporter, she would have a field day too, especially with her ultimatum. She had seen what they were doing with that on television this morning—*Showdown at the White House, Get out of Town by Sundown, Draw, Mr. President,....* That Coleman! Would he ever stop causing trouble in her life?

The telephone interrupted her misery.

"Stacey Lea?"

"Oh, Annie, I've really done it this time.

"Are you all right?" Her father asked, joining in.

"I'm all right. Well, I'm not all right, right now, but I will be."

"How's Palmer takin' this?"

"Not well, but he does have a lot of other things bothering him. My little exhibition came at the worst possible time."

"What happened to get you so upset?" Annie asked.

"It was a lot of things. I'd just come back from the sad mission of escorting Beverly Abelson to New York after her husband's sui . . uh, death, and I was already upset. I wanted to see Palmer, and Coleman was determined that I not see him. He blocked my way. He simply pushed me too far when I was already at the brink."

"He had no right tryin' to stop you." Annie consoled "That wasn't his place."

"I agree, but I didn't have to push him down and throw everything I could find at him. I promised you, Daddy, and I promised me a long time ago that I'd never lose my temper the way I used to. Now look what I've done!"

"Yes, but havin' control and submergin' your feelin's are two different things. I've seen you hide yourself more and more over the years to the point that, sometimes, when I see you on television, I hardly know you. I find myself askin' if that cool, distant woman is my Stacey Leanne?"

"I'm always your Stacey Leanne, Daddy," she laughed, then sobered, "and you're my source."

"No, no person can be that for another. I won't always be here for you, but your source is the same as mine, right here on the River. I think you know that. And if things don't go right for you there, you turn your back on it and come home. That's not quittin', that's survivin'."

Stacey Lea's tears flowed for a long time, not for herself and her present predicament but for the frail man who was her valiant champion. What would she do when he was gone?

Wylie Culberson was thinking the same thing; he'd been thinking it for some time. If she hadn't married Palmer Forbes, it wouldn't bother him so much, but Palmer didn't understand her, never had and never had tried. Forrest Thornton had been such a fool.

"Good morning, Wylie," Forrest said as he strode in unannounced, "I was out riding and thought I could use some good company and a cup of Annie's strong coffee."

"Speak of the devil! I was just thinkin' about you."

"I hope *devil* is just a figure of speech. I wouldn't want it to fit too snugly."

"I just talked to Stacey Leanne."

"I figured you would. How's she doing under fire?"

"I wish she'd come home for a few days, but I guess she's right. You can't run from a storm; you have to ride it out."

"She always knew about storms," Forrest said with a chuckle. "Frankly, I don't think it's that big a thing. I'll bet most people are glad to see she's human. The Stace I know always plunged in."

"Why didn't you marry her?"

"I wondered if the day would ever come when you'd ask me that. I suppose it's the privilege of age to ask such questions?"

"I know you were pretty mixed-up for a while. Losin' both parents in one year can do it, especially the way your father died. Something like that's hard to deal with. You go through wonderin' why you didn't see, what you'd have done to stop it, and then while you're blaming yourself, you're also grievin'. No one has the right to put another through that."

"You should know. I've often thought how strange it was that Stace's mother and my father both killed themselves, and here we live side by side."

"Yes, I guess it's strange, at that. Did I ever tell you that I had dinner with your father the night before?"

"Yes sir, I believe you did, but we didn't discuss it. I couldn't talk about it then."

"Yes, I went over to dinner, excellent dinner, wild duck. He'd been hunting that day, so they weren't frozen, hardly cold before they were cooked.

"No one can cook wild duck like Caana."

"I agree with that. Anyway, we had a fine dinner, prolonged by old bourbon and good conversation. It was a man's evenin'. That's the only way to put it—the kind of camaraderie you can only find in male company. It should have lingered as one of my pleasant memories, but the next morning your dad went purposely into the woods with that same gun he'd shot those ducks with. I had no inklin' of his intent."

They didn't talk for a while, each buried in his own distant memories.

"Late that afternoon of the funeral, Stace and I met at the Cliff. We hadn't had a chance to talk since we'd come from the funeral."

"It's about time," Stacey Lea said, looking at her watch.

"I'm sorry," Forrest replied, tying his horse off and walking quickly to the Gazebo, "we had more people come in just as I was leavin'. I'll be glad when it's all over."

"What are you planning?"

"I don't know yet. I know I'm gonna get away from here."

"Don't say that. This is where you belong, me too. You can't get away no matter how hard you try."

"I don't feel about this place the way you do, never did."

"You just won't allow yourself to realize it. You can't leave here, Forrest, and you can't leave me."

"You're not going to be here. You're away at college."

"I'm tired of going to school."

"And what do you want to be? Just a pretty little blue-eyed blonde with nothin' in her head?"

"You should know what I want." With that, Stacey Lea put her hands gently on his cheeks before bringing them up around his neck. Reaching her face up, she brought her lips onto his where they clung silently.

He stood there for a moment, unmoving, as his body began to wake to a passion that was not unfamiliar, but new in this relationship. This new marvelous feeling hurtled quickly out of control, and they became pure sensation.

"I'd gone up there," he admitted, " still looking on Stace as the little girl I used to wipe tears from and protect. It turned out she'd become total woman, and I couldn't make the transition. Dad's death was just on me, Thornhill was strangling me, now Stace had exerted a hold on me that I wasn't prepared for. So I went directly back to the house, packed and left."

"That much I know. There was no consoling her except I think she did believe you'd come back."

"I started to, many times, but each time I was kept from it by the feeling that I'd suffocate here, and I knew Stace would suffocate anyplace else. Finally, I wound up in Paris where I met Emilie, and thought that was that."

"When did you know it wasn't?"

"When I brought Emilie back here shortly after our marriage. I realized my mistake, but it was too late."

They were both quiet again, filled anew with distant memories and shared regrets.

"I knew I'd find you here," Forrest said, as he tied his horse off and walked toward the Gazebo.

"I understand you're back with a French wife. Are you stayin'?" Stacey Lea asked rudely.

"There's no reason for that tone."

"And there's no reason for you to hurt us this way."

"There is no us, there never was—not that way."

She hadn't looked at him, standing with her eyes looking out over the water, needing a familiar view when her feet were on unfamiliar ground. When she turned, she was white with rage made more formidable by the early evening shadows.

Walking close to him, she said quietly, "Forrest Thornton, you're a coward and a liar. You've lied to yourself and you're lying to me; you'll rue the day you crossed your fate."

She then tucked her body neatly into his, folded her arms around his neck and kissed him slowly and deliberately. She coaxed with her whole self, willing his response, as passionate as that last time.

Then, she pulled away, turned and walked directly to her horse. He watched her, realizing he had been pulled into a well-rehearsed melodrama. It was a suspenseful moment, her moment, which he acknowledged was hers to orchestrate as she wished. Finally, she stepped her horse up closer to the Gazebo, the color was back in her cheeks and a smile played on her lips.

"That's all the wedding present I have for you, Forrest. Take that home to your cute little French woman, and remember this Southern Belle, who surely has better things to do."

Yanking her horse around, she rode off.

"Stace's sense of the dramatic was always overdone, but that day she was outrageous," Forrest grinned as he related some of that day's memories to his host.

"That was her way of dealin'."

"I understood, and I also understood that I deserved anything she had to dish out. I made my life more complicated by running away. If I'd faced my problems, everything would've fallen into place, into its proper place. Stace had tried to tell me where I belonged, but I wouldn't listen. That afternoon on the Cliff I understood, but it was too late."

Forrest looked over as he finished to find the old man had his eyes closed. He got up to slip out, realizing that he'd never gotten that cup of coffee. He could hear Annie singing somewhere upstairs. Oh well, it was only a visiting excuse anyway, to see how Wylie was and how Stacey Lea was doing under all the publicity.

Wylie Culberson spoke to his departing back.

"It's still not over between you two. There's something that still has to be played out. She'll be back someday; she'll be back to stay. I'm glad you'll be here."

The trip to New York on *Air Force One* was as icy as the land they had left below. Palmer sat up with the Burkes and gave them his undivided attention for both the going and the returning journeys. Stacey Lea estimated that he spent more time talking to the Vice-President and his wife on this sad trip than all the times put together since their first mutual campaign over five years ago. He was even looking at the latest Burke grandbaby pictures, a pitfall he always avoided.

Bob and Blanche Burke had been the perfect balance for the Forbeses, one the nation heartily appreciated. While they didn't sparkle and dazzle, they did exude stability and confidence. Both in their sixties, gray-haired, and comfortably mature, their marriage was the old-fashioned kind filled with children, grandchildren, and great-grandchildren. Their fatherly and motherly figures represented home, hearth, and apple pie, all those traditions that Americans prize most. They brought, in their secondary position, a secure feeling to a nation wary and weary of the parade of Burke's inept, insignificant, or immature predecessors. Unfortunately, they were deadly dull.

Today, however, Stacey Lea welcomed their friendly smiles. For if it hadn't been for them and the Fairmonts, she would have been caught between Palmer's ice and everyone else's uneasy pleasantries. Media coverage of her Coleman incident had caused an uncomfortable divide between her and people she'd known for years. She didn't think that most were passing judgment or even being critical, but no one seemed to know how to get by it. That Coleman! Would he ever stop causing problems in her life?

She could even imagine that underneath the Burke's friendly greeting, there was a raised eyebrow, but she was wrong. It was this matronly Blanche Burke who, at the very first opportunity, reached out to commiserate. It was right after the graveside service.

"Stacey Lea, I've been hoping to get a minute alone with you. I want you to know that I'm sorry that Coleman incident got blown up so. There isn't one person who's spent any time at the White House who isn't glad to see him gone, at least, any woman. He was arrogant and disrespectful besides being sort of spooky. Men don't usually see these things, especially when they don't receive the same treatment. Sometimes we women have to take the bull by the horns."

"Thank you, Blanche. That's very kind of you, and a kind word today is particularly welcome."

What a nice woman, Stacey Lea acknowledged as she, Palmer and the Burkes got back in their limousine after the service. She'd have to invite her to lunch soon. Maybe she had misjudged the Burkes for even Sue Ann had been critical of what she'd done to Coleman. In fact, the first thing Sue Ann had asked was what had come over her?

"The papers and television are havin' a field day with you, Stacey Lea. What on earth happened?"

"I want to know every single one who takes advantage of me on this. I assure you, they'll be blacklisted in my domain."

"That'll be about everybody. I heard on the radio comin' over some of them laughin' about how you gave Palmer until sundown."

"I didn't give Palmer until sundown; I said I wanted Coleman out by sundown. That's different."

"Doesn't sound much different to me, but it's so like you to get melodramatic. If you had to say anything publicly, why couldn't you have just said you'd like him out as soon as possible, something normal people would say, but sundown?"

"Maybe I'm not normal," Stacey Lea snapped, "because I also expect a friend to like me the way I am and take up for me, not criticize me when I need consoling."

"I'm sorry. I didn't know you were that touchy about it. As far as getting rid of Coleman, it's good riddance, but you did do it with flare. You have to admit that."

Stacey Lea cringed when Sue Ann had said good riddance. It brought back that horrible explosion by Palmer. It was the ugliest he'd ever been to her, and he didn't seem the slightest repentant, even now.

"I lost my temper, Sue Ann."

"You know, honey," Sue Ann did console this time, with genuine feeling, "I've an idea that the reason the media is havin' such fun with you is because they find it refreshin' that the First Lady might not be that perfect creature they've been covering for so long. Your perfection was unnatural amongst the rest of us."

"I wish Palmer felt that way."

"It's obvious he isn't any happier with you than he is with us. How long do you think we're gonna be banished?"

"Who knows. A lot's happened, much more than you know, and certainly, much more than we had planned. I think we need to have a meeting to assess the progress, as well as, the damage. Why don't you have a luncheon?"

"When? We're leaving soon for home."

"I'll have Ellie call you tomorrow with plans and a guest list."

"All right. Look at Beau. He looks like a lost soul sittin' there with Lewis Stratton."

"Spare me, Sue Ann. Just make sure he keeps his word."

"He will, but it's new to him."

"What? Being honest?"

"That's a nasty jab, Stacey Lea. You know I meant his not being up there with Palmer; Palmer not talking to him."

"He's not talking to me either."

"Seems to me, he's overreacting about Coleman. Was he that fond of him?"

"He depended a great deal on Coleman and a lot happened yesterday. Right now, I suspect he's feeling somewhat overwhelmed. I'm somewhat overwhelmed myself."

Stacey Lea wondered what Sue Ann would say if she knew about the fish and Mother Forbes, and Palmer's haircut. On the other hand, Palmer's haircut may have just been coincidental. A part of her wished it were, but she knew she could never again trust Palmer to do the right thing. He also no longer trusted her. If Mother Forbes was right, she needed that leverage, as bizarre as it was.

They had reached the doors to their private suites before Palmer spoke to her. At first, it seemed an afterthought, but she soon realized that it was totally and cruelly calculated.

"Oh, by the way," he said, pausing with his hand on the knob to his rooms, "you'll be happy to know that Coleman won't be bothering you any further. I was informed just as we landed that he hung himself late this morning. A newspaper with that picture was on a table near him."

He left her standing in the hall.

Although it was late afternoon, Stacey Lea didn't turn on the lights, call down for dinner, or speak to the returned Ellie. Somehow, she did get inside her door and into her bed, the only place she could think to go with her life crashing in on her. How she wished for her Pondrin' Tree!

She wouldn't even answer Ellie's frequent intercom calls. Finally, Ellie fixed a light dinner tray and took it to the First Lady's apartment. She was concerned. She'd returned from Senator Abelson's funeral on Air Force One, and had seen for herself the coldness between the First Lady and the President, and now, the whole House was abuzz with the news of Coleman's suicide. She understood why Stacey Lea wanted to pull the covers over her head, but this was not the time, too much depended on her.

Ellie tapped lightly on the First Lady's bedroom door before entering.

"Stacey Lea, you might as well get your head out from under those covers," she said as she turned on a small table light. "It's going to do you no good."

"Turn out that light and leave me be. When I didn't respond to your call, you knew I didn't want to see you."

"You are going to eat something, and we're going to talk."

"I'm not hungry, and I have nothing to say."

"Stace, you had no control over what happened to Coleman."

"He'd be alive today but for me."

"And so would Howard Abelson if Beverly hadn't gone to bed with Earle Walker."

"It's not the same."

"Yes, it is. Remember what you said to Beverly? You told her that there are many ways to solve problems and that her husband, alone, chose to solve his by pulling the trigger. It helped her because it made sense. Now you must use the same logic on yourself. Coleman's death is not your fault; it is his."

"No, it's my fault; you know it."

"All right then, let's say that it is your fault. Wasn't it you who told all of us that there would be risks, that we weren't playing a little game, that we'd do what we had to do to succeed no matter what the consequences to our safe little worlds?"

"Yes, but I didn't expect disaster everywhere. It was a mistake, and I can't go on with it."

"Wasn't it you who told all of us that if all Sarah lost was her marriage then maybe she was lucky?"

"Yes, and look at her. She's part of the disaster."

"I don't agree. Maybe she couldn't handle it, but she's not sorry. She hasn't given up on what we're doing."

"Sarah's crazy, for godsakes, she's up in Boston watering plants!"

Ellie didn't speak for a long moment. When she did, her voice didn't attempt to hide its rage.

"Maybe so, but I'd rather be her than you any day. You're spoiled and self-centered, Stacey Lea. It's all right for other people to make sacrifices, but when it makes you unhappy, penetrates your little world, then it's time to stop. Maybe you should go home and stick your head in that wonderful Mississippi mud of yours, wallow in it the way you're wallowing in self pity."

"Don't you go after talking to me that way," Stacey Lea ordered as she saw Ellie turn to leave.

"No, I'm going. Frankly, I'm beginning to doubt that you and I have some great destiny together. Besides, I wouldn't care to be around when you tell the others you don't want to play anymore, not after the way Sue Ann's been sticking her neck out, and Millie, and Alma Tyler and Casey…and Beverly, why she was willing to use her affair with Walker to help, and now she's actually thinking of Howard's seat because you want her to. No, thank you, I have no desire to be around."

"Come back, Ellie, you've made your point," Stacey Lea admitted, exasperation in her voice, "but I did kill Coleman, just as sure as I put the noose around his neck. You'd have difficulty too if such a burden were on your shoulders."

"Yes, but let's look at this burden honestly. You didn't wish him dead; but you did wish him gone, right?"

"Yes."

"And you're glad he's gone?"

Stacey Lea thought for a moment.

"No, I thought I'd be, but it's caused a terrible rift with Palmer even before the news of Coleman's death. I don't know what the damage will be."

"There's your problem. You don't truly blame yourself for Coleman's death. You know full well that suicide's an irrational act. You can't blame yourself for something you never could have bargained for, but you can blame yourself for something you could have bargained for."

"What do you mean?"

"I think you could have bargained for the problem it has caused for you with your husband. He blames you, and that's going to be a tough thing for you to make right. You took your Coleman obsession too far. In some respects, he's won or will if you let him. Remember what you told Sarah after she made that irrational speech on her own?"

Stacey Lea's brow furrowed as she digested Ellie's criticism.

"Yes, I went off on my own when I attacked Coleman. It was just as irrational as Sarah's speech, and did no more good. In fact, it did a lot more harm."

"I'm afraid you may be right about that."

"You told me I should leave Coleman alone, that I had enough to do." Stacey sighed, a big heavy one.

"Don't beat yourself up. Maybe you couldn't help yourself. This thing with Coleman had been building for a long time. In any case, it's done now, and can't be undone. We're just gonna have to pick up the pieces and figure out how to deal with the aftermath."

CHAPTER SEVENTEEN

AFTERMATH, DAY TWO

"Beau, do you have a tux in Mississippi?" Sue Ann called from her husband's closet.

"Yes, but I think I'll take that new plaid dinner jacket. It'll be nice for the holidays."

"All right. Anything else you can think of while I'm in here?"

"Yes, you," Beau's voice answered as he walked in behind her. "Sue Ann, I still don't know why you're so head-set to stay here in Washington to give some silly luncheon that you haven't even planned yet."

"We've been through this already, Beau. I have to stay."

"There's something you're not telling me, but then, there's a lot about you I don't know anymore," his voice caressed as his hands tried to follow suit. He found himself turned on more than usual by this new mysterious aspect of his wife.

"Leave me alone, Beaufort. I'm still off limits."

"That's another reason you should go with me. We made a deal. I'd keep my nose even out of my own kidnapping, but you'd give us another chance. How are we gonna get started on that if you stay here? We need to be together."

"Where did you put the cummerbund for that jacket?"

"Don't change the subject. I'll stay away from you if that's what you want, but I would feel much better if you'd go home with me. I don't have the slightest idea what you and Stacey Lea and God knows who else are up to, but don't sell Palmer Forbes short. He's nobody's fool."

"I don't know where that cummerbund is, Beau."

Beau sighed, shaking his head. Sue Ann was sure pig-headed. Women could be more pig-headed than men.

"Well, since we're so snug in here, bribe me with a little kiss, and I'll find it for you."

The little kiss became so involved that neither heard the telephone.

"Senator Fairmont," their housekeeper, Mrs. Bridges, called on the intercom, "Harriet Sawyer is on the line from the White House."

A look of utter panic came on Beau's face.

"I won't speak to her, Sue Ann. I'm not ready to be humiliated by Palmer again before Christmas."

"Is it going to be any better after Christmas?"

"Probably not, but I don't want to talk to him now. Will you tell her that I've already left?"

"No, Beaufort, I won't do your dirty work for you; besides, I don't care to have a Presidential Pall hanging over our holidays."

"Damn!" he exclaimed as he plodded over to the phone, shaking his head, "there may be more than Presidential Pall hanging over our holidays if I have to confront Goodie today."

"Wait a minute, Beau. Maybe you're right," Sue Ann reconsidered, a little frown creasing her nodding head. "Palmer was in a foul mood with us yesterday, and he can't be any improved with that Coleman thing. I don't relish him takin' his upset with Stacey Lea out on us. Yes, we'll let them handle their differences first; besides, it might do him good to stew."

"Mrs. Bridges, please tell Harriet Sawyer that the Senator has gone to Mississippi to be with his family for the holidays."

Turning back toward her husband with an impish grin and a sparkle in her eyes, she asked, "Now, where were we before the President interrupted?"

A Presidential Pall had permeated every aspect of White House life this morning. Even though the great house glittered and sparkled in the merry array of the season, those who worked in and around were not gladdened, a condition that would have warmed the heart of Dickens' *Scrooge*, for the President was smiling none, talking little, and seeing few. This state was grievously aggravated when he couldn't reach his old friend, Beau.

He had never felt the lack of friends until now. In fact, he'd never thought on the word, but it was more important than he had realized, especially when he was caught without one. Who had been his friend? All he could remember was Beau, only Beau. It was only Beau with whom he could be himself; it was only Beau who really knew him, and only Beau who'd been involved in most of his secrets.

Could Beau be upset about that last time up at the Bunker? True, he'd been a little hard on him, had even blamed him for losing the war game. Beau should have understood that there are times the President gets weary of having to make decisions for everyone. He should understand that it gets lonesome at the top.

He was lonesome right now. He wanted Beau here to go to Coleman's funeral with him. He couldn't take Stacey Lea; it had been her fault. Coleman had been a friend too, not the same as Beau, but he had always been there for him. Who was going to handle the Bunker meetings now? Who was left to go? He and Beau weren't talking, Walker was dead, Coleman was dead, and Vondergraven was an idiot. Only the Cardinal was left.

"Harriet," he requested over his intercom, "get me Cardinal Bishop in New York."

"Hello, Mr. President. It's a pleasure to hear from you."

"Good to speak with you. I'm calling because of some recent unfortunate situations that have directly affected our mutual endeavor. Obviously, you know of Walker's death."

"Yes, and Coleman's."

Palmer's face reddened as he got the feeling that the churchman had pronounced the name of his faithful manservant with a forked tongue.

"I thought we should consider Walker's replacement."

"I'll admit I feel no sorrow for the man, but he's left a void that will be impossible to fill. His wife certainly won't do, and she seems to have taken over his power."

"Women, however, don't have staying power. She won't last long even if we have to aid her departure. In any case, we're going to have to replace Walker."

"I'm skittish about newcomers."

"I'll be sure that anybody we consider will be checked out from head to toe, inside and out." Why was he cajoling this man? He was President; he should simply tell him. However, he wasn't going to tell him the taskforce was missing. That would send the good Cardinal into a tizzy.

"Mr. President, my opinion at our last meeting, that we should move with extreme caution, hasn't changed. In fact, now with Walker's death, perhaps we should let things sit for a while. After Sandra Ackerman, I have real concern about continuing with our mutual endeavor."

There was a long pause before Palmer answered, and when he did, his voice was cold and filled with rage.

"Now you listen to me. Get your fuckin' head out of your pompous ass because I'm weary of hearing your cowardly excuses. You're up to your high-and-mighty nose in our mutual endeavor, and you're not out until I say you are."

It was the Cardinal's turn to pause. When he did speak, his voice was also cold, but controlled.

"Mr. President, it would be best if we continued this conversation at a less stressful time. This is a busy season for me, and I need to focus all my attention on Church and God. Perhaps after the first of the year, we could get together. In the meantime, I'll give a replacement serious thought."

"Very well, . uh, I guess I lost my temper just then. There's been a lot going on. You know what it's like at the top."

"Indeed, I do. You seemed tired at Senator Abelson's funeral. I want you to know that I'm sorry about Coleman. I know how much you thought of him. Suicides are unsettling because they are mortal sins. You should get yourself some rest. Take a vacation to a warm climate over the holidays, relax, enjoy yourself. You'll come back a new man!"

"Maybe you're right at that. However, there seems to be a lot of women getting involved in politics lately. We're going to have our work cut out for us in the new year."

"Merry Christmas, Mr. President!"

"Merry Christmas, Your Eminence!"

Palmer Forbes left his big official desk and walked over to gaze out the window, his thoughts inward. Merry Christmas? How was he going to have a Merry Christmas with so much wrong in his life? His best friends gone—Beau, Coleman, Stacey Lea? How could he have a good Christmas if he wasn't talking to Stacey Lea? But Stacey Lea had taken Coleman away. She was no friend. He had never trusted women anyway; they were all irrational.

His mother had been the worst of all, Forbes acknowledged, as he left the Oval Office view of the white landscape and walked back to his desk. Sitting down, he picked up the familiar stationery and reread the *Focus for the Day*. This in itself was clearly all the proof he'd have needed in Court to put her away. She'd just told him Tuesday to get a haircut, and now she was telling him to get another one. How rational was that? Maybe she was annoyed that he had deliberately waited a day. Rebellion had always displeased her.

Getting up, he walked over to the adjacent bathroom and stood before the mirror. Hmm, maybe it was a little long over the ears. It wouldn't hurt to take a few snips here and there. Going back to his desk, he again opened his intercom.

"Harriet, please call Domenic and schedule a haircut. I want a few more snips before I leave for Camp David."

Stacey Lea was irritated. Palmer would still not talk to her. How long was he going to sulk? There was such a big chasm between them they might as well be in different states!

This thought was still in her mind when Ellie called to say that Palmer was leaving for Camp David this afternoon, and Coleman was going to be buried up there tomorrow.

"Who's going with him?"

"I don't know for sure. I think just a few members of the staff. Thomas, I know, is going."

"Well, that does it! Can't take me? How's that gonna look? Palmer may not be willin' to talk to me, but I've a few things he's gonna hear, and right now!"

By the time Stacey Lea got to the Oval Office, she'd calmed and decided it was best she didn't go to Coleman's funeral. How should she act if she went? She couldn't act grieved 'cause Palmer would never believe that she was sorry. She could throw herself across Coleman's bier, sobbing, and he still wouldn't believe. And think what the press would do with that!!.

"Harriet, is my husband in?"

"I'm sorry, Mrs. Forbes, you just missed him. He's gone to get a haircut."

"He just got one yesterday."

"Yes, I know. I don't think he was altogether pleased with it."

Stacey Lea walked to her office in silence. She and Ellie had agreed that if Palmer went for another haircut right on top of the other one then the first one had not been a fluke—he was obeying his mother. She took no satisfaction in this confirmation. In fact, it upset her that this man she'd married could be controlled in this childish manner. She didn't mind tears now and then to bring him around, and sex often worked well too, but this *Ten Commandment* thing was distasteful. In the first place, the rules were corny, and she did not like that silly little poem at the end. But Mother Forbes insisted that they gave him stability when he began to skid too far across the line, and he had sure done that.

"Did you see the President?" Ellie asked, when she arrived at her office, concerned that there may have been more angry words.

"No, he was getting a haircut."

They had never shared a more profound sentence. As both women attempted to deal with the full import of their mutual intelligence, Ellie was reminded of Disraeli and Queen Victoria; Stacey Lea thought of Woodrow and Edith Wilson. Had Edith Wilson stood in this great house long ago and had the same fears? She was frightened, for she realized, as did Ellie, that she had the power of the Presidency in the Ninth Commandment. It was an awesome responsibility.

"Well, Ellie," Stacey Lea said with resignation, "I suppose you better pay a visit to your friend, Darryl, later today. It seems we're gonna have more work for him."

"I need to call Sue Ann about the luncheon first. Have you decided when you want it?"

"Tomorrow, 'cause Palmer will be at Camp David."

"I don't relish calling her if you want it tomorrow. She's probably going to have a fit at the short notice."

"No, I think she'll welcome it once she gets over the initial shock. She's eager to go to Mississippi with Randal already there and the rest beginning to congregate for the holidays. Uh, tell her to call the others, starting with Beverly. I want you free to go see Darryl."

"Anything else?"

"No, but while you're getting the luncheon underway, I'll sit here and make up a list of *Number Nines*. I'll let you know when they're ready."

"Would you mind if I didn't come back tonight?"

Stacey Lea laughed for the first time that day. "By all means, stay with your Darryl. I'm glad to know that someone may be having fun. It's a lot better than staying in this house which seems to be totally covered in a Presidential Pall."

Stacey Lea sat down at her desk and took out a pen and a pad of lined paper. She already had the first one, so she quickly wrote,

9. You will destroy the robe.

She smiled. That will rid us of the last vestiges of whatever he was doing with Mother Forbes' ashes. She could never approve of such a macabre thing; however, she wasn't sure the Commandments weren't just as unhealthy. It almost seemed tit for tat.

Hmm, tell him to close the Bunker? No, Mother Forbes had cautioned that it had to be kept simple, something that could be done in a day. That way, it became part of the whole and made all of the Commandments work together to keep her son's mind orderly and focused in a positive manner. What was simple anymore, she questioned, chewing on the top of her pen? Certainly not, be nice to Stacey Lea! No, that wasn't simple for him right now, but...

9. You will ask Stacey Lea to help you.

Help him what? This wasn't as easy as she had thought it would be. Then an idea developed.

9. You will ask Stacey Lea to help you pick your tie.

That was simple enough. She would get nine copies. Palmer was such a creature of habit, after nine of them, he would not have to be told anymore, would just expect her to do it forever. She continued, now, her pen dancing rapidly across the lined page.

9. You will ask Stacey Lea to pick your tie.

9. You will ask Stacey Lea to help you pick your suit.

9. You will ask Stacey Lea to pick your suit.

Nine of each, she decided as she smiled smugly. After that, Palmer would start depending on her, and she could move on to bigger things like *You will go over your schedule for the day with Stacey Lea.* That could very well be the next one she could slip in, and that would just about do it. If she could get control of his day, then she could control where he went and what he did. That way, he wouldn't get into any trouble, and they could finish out their presidency pleasantly.

And maybe, if he started depending on her enough, they could get rid of those silly commandments and that awful poem, and let this thing between him and his mother rest in peace. That would be her goal.

A frown knitted her brow as she looked back over her list. No, it would probably be a mistake to start these *Ask Stacey Lea's* too soon.

After all, he wasn't even speaking to her right now. She could give him the *Robe* one right away and then she would use a few Mother Forbes had left behind. She'd send him to the dentist next week. He hadn't been in a while.

And not one a day. Have them show up sporadically, keep him off guard; besides if he got one a day, he would expect them even when he was away, like tomorrow. She couldn't very well stuff a supply in his suitcase.

Completing these thoughts, she toyed with the idea of having Darryl make one as a reminder that the twenty-third was her birthday. He always forgot; it was so close to Christmas. This brought her thoughts hurtling back to that fateful luncheon and Beverly and Sue Ann's hurtful jesting that perhaps he would get her a fish-tank too. She was glad when Ellie interrupted these thoughts.

"Sue Ann just called to say Beverly can't make it tomorrow, but she can make it Sunday."

"I suppose that would be all right, but make it early. Palmer might come back early afternoon. Why can't she make it tomorrow?"

"She said she has a meeting with the Governor of New York."

CHAPTER EIGHTEEN

AFTERMATH, DAY THREE

Joseph Sean DeLucca strode into the Abelson study unannounced and confident. He was always confident. As the son of an Italian father and an Irish mother, he represented the peace that now existed between two great and competitive emigrant societies that enhance this nation. He was proud of it. However, when the genes had completed their competition, the Italians seemed to be the sole survivor, for Joe had no outward characteristics to identify him with the *Sons of Hibernia*. His hair was dark, skin olive, and eyes soft brown. In all other aspects he also resembled his father's family with his craggy face, slightly above average height, and stout frame.

There was an animal magnetism in all this that most women found hard to resist, but when combined with the subtle gifts from his mother, Joe DeLucca was formidable. Gentle creases framed eyes leading to a poetic soul which manifested itself in a tongue that had surely been dipped in Erin's morning dew. He could have charmed the snakes out of Ireland himself, and Beverly, aware of this, braced herself.

"Let me look at you," he said, taking her by the shoulders and turning her face to look deeply into her eyes. She pulled back, careful for any possible maneuver that might give him the advantage.

He allowed her to move away without resistance. A wary relationship had always existed between them. It was part of that mystique that kept the fire ignited. He liked the game. Beverly was never predictable, and he doubted if she'd changed anymore than had his feelings for her.

"I never should have let you go. Maybe we should fly off to some carefree island where we can spend our days sparring and our nights making up?"

He sounded somewhat wistful.

"Stop it, Joe. You know we'd last thirty minutes tops. You want to be President more than you want me or anyone else in this shitty world."

"You always had such a delicate way of putting things, love. Is this coffee hot?" he asked, as he picked up a carafe from the table.

"Yes, but would you rather have a drink?"

"Are you going to let me relax enough to enjoy it?"

"I thought you were always relaxed with me? You did tell me that once."

"Only when you are."

"You mean I'm not?"

"What is it Beverly? You have something on your mind and until you get it off, there's going to be no peace here. Frankly, I'd like to enjoy these few minutes with you. It's been a long time."

She went over to make them both a scotch. While busy with the drinks, she inquired casually, "Have you decided who you plan to appoint to Howard's seat?"

"I was thinking of Lou Diaz. Do you know him?"

"Isn't he a state congressman from Manhattan?"

"That's right. He's been doing a good job for me, and he's popular, not just with the Spanish constituency either."

"You still drink your Scotch neat?" she asked as she handed him the short glass.

He took the drink as answer, then inquired, "How're you holding up?"

"That should've been one of the first things you asked."

"Hell, that was a busy question anyway," he answered, grinning. "I'm still waiting for you to tell me what's on your mind. Then I'll tell you what's on mine."

"Stop playing games with me."

"I'm not. I've missed you."

There was a pause full of memories.

"Isn't Dave Perez in the U.S. Congress?"

"You know he is. What's your point?"

"Well, Perez in Congress, then Diaz in the Senate. Seems to me, you'd appoint another Jew."

"I thought of that, but this appointment is critical to me right now. I need someone I'm sure of if I'm going to make a bid for the Presidency. Hell, I wasn't even that sure of Howard, but I knew I could depend on you with him."

This is the perfect lead in, she realized, but she couldn't bring herself to ask him yet.

"You hungry?"

"Starved."

She recognized the look in his eyes.

"That's got to be over."

"Maybe not, now that Howard's gone. It'd be easier?"

"You know, Joe, you have the ability to go all the way, but a woman's going to be your downfall."

"Just you."

"And I want more than that now. I want Howard's seat."

It was out and received with a long pause, a very long one as he looked at her.

"You're not kidding, are you?"

"No."

"That's absurd, Beverly. You don't know anything about politics."

"I don't want to be the Old Bev anymore. I want to do something worthwhile. Sure, you can ask why I have to start in the Senate, but why not?"

She was talking rapidly now, making her sell.

"Look, I've been on the Hill with Howard. I know just about everyone, even the ones who aren't anyone. Stacey Lea Forbes is one of my best friends, also Sue Ann Fairmont."

"They are wives, just as you were. That's different. It's behind the scenes.

"And politics isn't?"

"You'd be spending a lot of time in the public eye. You'd have to watch yourself constantly."

"I know; in fact, you might be surprised at how much I do know. Remember, Sarah Winthrop was my best friend until she got ill. We talked a lot, and I have a good education; besides, who the hell knows much up there anyway? Any aide knows more. All I need to do is get filled in."

"Where the hell did you get this crazy idea?" he asked as he got up and started walking the floor.

She didn't answer, just waited.

Finally, he walked over and pulled her up to face him.

"Do you realize the flak we'd both take if I appointed you?"

"It wouldn't last, and if we announce during Christmas week there'll be less. Everyone's away or busy."

"You have this all figured out, don't you?"

"I want this, Joe, I want it bad. Look, who could you possibly get up there whom you could depend on more?"

"This isn't a game, Beverly."

"Yes, it is. That's all politics is, a game, and you know it."

"What if I agree? I'm not saying I'm going to, mind you, but what if I did? Would you do what I told you to do?"

"No, and you shouldn't expect me to. I'd listen to your advice, and if I thought you were right, I would, but I won't be your *yes-man*."

He grinned and his Irish charm penetrated his Italian suave.

"But what about my *wo-man?*"

"I can't believe you'd want me to fuck you for it."

"But would you?"

"No, of course not. That's the same as my telling you that if I didn't get it, I'd tell the world about us."

"You took us right to my next question, my dear, which makes me believe that the thought has crossed your mind."

"As a matter of fact, it has."

"You make a lot of sense," he answered, his grasp tighter, "you won't fuck me for it, but you'd consider blackmail."

"In the first place, Joe, going to bed with you isn't going to make you give me the appointment, we both know that. As for blackmail, I honestly don't know. I'd hoped it wouldn't go that far."

"I should wring your pretty neck and be done with you. You've never brought me anything but misery. My heart breaks for you and then you turn and break my heart."

"God, Joe," Beverly laughed, "will you ever change? That Irish charm of yours is wasted on me."

"No, it isn't."

And she realized that he was holding her closer now, his hands that had held her so tightly were now gentle. Cupping her chin, he kissed her. They kissed a long time.

When he let her breathe, a little frown was playing on his brow. "I'm not sure the Hill's a good place for women right now. Look what happened to Sarah Winthrop. I feel bad about that. I wouldn't want anything happening to you."

"Then you think something is going on to hurt women there?"

"I didn't say that. All I know is there aren't many there now, none in the Senate with Sarah gone."

"Leslie Farnsworth is taking her place."

"She's green, like you, and she'll only be there a year. Howard had three years left."

"And Casey Bartholomew of Tennessee will be there after elections next year."

"How do you know she'll win?"

"I just do, that's all."

A quizzical frown spread over DeLucca's face.

"What else do you know?"

"As I said before, you might be surprised."

"You're the one playing games now."

"I want that appointment."

"You know, I came here today hoping that now with Howard gone, we could see each other occasionally?"

"We can see each other more if I'm a Senator."

"You know what I mean."

Beverly sighed and touched his face gently before she spoke, "You tempt me. You tempt me much. It'd be so easy to be a shadow in your life, but I've been a shadow far too long. I want to be what I know I can be. I have to do this, and you, well," she threw her head back and gave that husky, irresistible laugh of hers that filled the room, "you, my love, better concentrate on keeping those pants zipped if you want to become the best goddamn president this country's ever had."

He laughed. She always made him laugh.

"God knows, I'd like to try," he continued seriously, "but I'm afraid I may get tired of waiting for Palmer Forbes to tire of the position."

"I don't think Palmer Forbes will seek to change the term limit."

"Don't kid about something like that." He searched her face.

"I'm not absolutely sure, mind you, but I can tell you that Beau Fairmont won't be back."

"He's already declared."

"He's going to undeclare before the first of the year."

"Forbes' right hand is going to leave? What's going on, Beverly?"

She hesitated. What could she say without giving something away? How little would he accept? A lot would have to do with how much he respected her. Maybe this was a good test. She chose her words carefully, a new thing for her.

"Joe, there are a lot of things going on, but I'm not at liberty to say much more than that. I will say that the idea of my filling Howard's seat did not originate with me. I'd never have had the confidence to consider it by myself. I have it now, though, because others have it in me. I promise you that you can only come out a winner if you send me to the Senate. I know that's hard to believe, and I know that you're not used to taking half answers, but I ask you to respect me in this. If I could tell you anything more, I would."

He didn't finish his drink, just stood and looked at her long and hard, then he looked around.

"Is this the room Howard died in? I think I read he died in the study?"

"Yes."

"Are you planning to make this your New York residence?"

"Does this mean you're going to let me have it?"

"Do I have much choice?"

"I've never seen you in any situation, Joe, that you couldn't find an option."

"As long as you remember that, Beverly Jean, we'll be fine. Now, I believe you promised me lunch."

Beverly sat curled up in a big armchair long after Joe DeLucca had left. She felt warm and delicious inside, the way she used to feel when she and Joe had made love, but they hadn't made love today, and they wouldn't be making love again, at least, not soon. When they got through playing politics then they would be together. Maybe they'd be old, decrepit, and cantankerous, but they'd be together, even if just for their twilight years. For now, however, they'd have a proper, respectable relationship—The Governor and The Senator.

Senator Beverly Jean Abelson. What a ring it had!

Going over to Howard's desk, she took a pad of paper and wrote it down time and again, still disbelieving. Finally, she picked up the phone and dialed Ellie.

"It's done."

"What's done?"

"What I was supposed to do." Thinking it and writing it hadn't been too hard, but she still could not bring herself to say it. Joe had said it, but she hadn't. Maybe she wasn't ready to share it? She felt silly; besides, she was going to see them later, she should have waited.

"Uh, did you see Governor DeLucca today?"

"Yes, I got it." She still couldn't say it, even though she'd called because she wanted to tell them.

The line was quiet for a long moment, while Ellie pondered this strange conversation.

"You got the appointment?"

Stacey Lea, who was evidently right at hand, grabbed the phone.

"You got Howard's seat?"

"Yes."

"How on earth did you manage it?"

"I just did, that's all."

"Maybe you *just did,* Beverly, because you were supposed to."

"Maybe so. I feel good about it, but I'm not comfortable with it yet."

"Senator Beverly Jean Abelson. I like it."

"So do I."

"When will it be announced?"

"We've chosen December 24th. I had thought right after Christmas, but Joe thought it would go more smoothly if we announced Christmas Eve. The timing's going to be paramount. There'll be enough controversy, as it is, but maybe I'll be settled in a little by the time people get through with the holidays."

"That's smart. We'll be away by then too, so that will be good for me. Palmer's not gonna like it."

"No, I'm sure he won't."

"The main thing is you believe in yourself. It may not be easy at first, but I know you'll be a good Senator, and others will see that as time goes by."

"Thank you. I know I'm going to have a storm to weather for a while. Strangely enough, however, once Joe had gotten used to the idea, he said something very similar."

"I'm sure DeLucca would never have given you the appointment if he hadn't believed you could do it."

"He said that too."

When Beverly got off the telephone, she curled back into the big chair to consider her future and the immediate storm ahead. She'd never liked this house, she considered. Fortunately, she and Allan had held on to their family home off Park Avenue although Howard had insisted on their living here. She would sell this house now and move home. She would bring the desk back from Washington too—the one that had once belonged to Rasputin, and the wonderful chair, and she would take this Kirman home to place under them. They would all be together again where they belonged.

They made her think of that fateful day long ago and her mother. She wished she could share this moment with her. She knew she was beginning to find herself, and that she would now be what she could be, but then, her mother had always known this day would come.

She thought of Howard's mother. She'd been too senile to understand anything for over a year now. She was glad she wouldn't have to know about Howard or that the house was being sold.

She thought of Howard. If she could undo their tragedy, she would, but as Stacey Lea had said, it had been his choice. Maybe he hadn't really cared once Paddy was gone. Maybe she had just been a decoration in Howard's life. Sometimes she'd wondered if that was all. She would prove she was more. She realized that she needed to do that desperately.

Getting up, she went over and took the drink in her hands that Joe had not finished. It seemed appropriate for her toast. It had been Joe's drink.

She spoke in a firm, confident voice.

"Here's to you, Senator Beverly Jean Rabin Abelson. Here's to you and your grand new world! And Sarah," she added quietly, as she put down the glass, "I promise you, I won't be a sigh."

Stacey Lea slipped out of the White House as quietly as a First Lady can slip out of the White House, only one car and two Secret Service men. She arrived at Highgate at exactly seven p.m., which made her slightly late since her appointment was for seven. Sue Ann had picked up Beverly at the airport and they were impatiently waiting.

"You're late!" Beverly exploded in greeting, as she dashed to the phone. "Here, I'll dial and you catch your breath, deep ones, like you told me that time. I hope you know what you're doing!"

"Don't worry. I'll not hurt your senatorial position, but it must be done. We need her cooperation. By the way, Sue Ann, what do you think of our new Senator?"

"I think it's wonderful. She's gonna be a grand senator; although, I admit it caught me by surprise."

"I hope the rest of the world takes it as well," Beverly wished seriously.

"It won't be bad, you'll see," Sue Ann encouraged, and Stacey Lea was brought to wonder if the mutual respect that had been developing between her two friends wasn't a little nauseating. The old meowing was much more fun.

"Okay, it's ringing."

"Hello, Mizz Walker, I'm running a little late, but I'll be at your door in five minutes, okay?"

"Yes, I'm waiting for you."

Sue Ann and Beverly walked Stacey Lea down the three flights of stairs to what Beverly could only remember as the *Devil's Den*. They watched her enter the door before they retraced their steps to wait. Both were nervous.

"It's surely easier goin' down steps than comin' up," Sue Ann panted when they reached the top.

"Yes, and it's going to be hard waiting. I'm afraid of this meeting. I hope Stacey Lea hasn't underestimated Carolyn Walker."

"Don't worry about that. After watching her performance on television the day Walker died, anyone would be a fool to take her lightly, and Stacey Lea's no fool. Come on, let's watch television."

"First, I'll mix a batch of Margaritas and pop some corn in the microwave."

"You have any dirty movies?"

"A few."

"Then that's what we'll watch. That should relax us plenty."

As Sue Ann and Beverly prepared to pass the time, Stacey Lea was being introduced to Harlan Parker.

"I've known Harlan longer that I knew Earle. In fact, Harlan introduced us. I don't know what I'd do without him right now." Tears filled the eyes of Earle Walker's widow as she spoke. It was a nice touch but wasted on Stacey Lea.

"A pleasure to meet you, Mr. Parker. Mizz Walker's fortunate to have you. None of us can do without friends in times of great tragedy. That's why I'm so glad I'm able to be a source of comfort for my dear friend, Beverly Abelson, Senator Abelson's widow? It was quite a coincidence that he died the very same day as your Earle. Two new widows the very same morning whose husbands died of the very same thing. A profound thought."

"Yes, I . . uh, guess it is," Carolyn Walker responded, thrown off guard by Stacey Lea's boldness. She had been curious enough to accept when Ellie Farmer had called requesting this secret meeting. Now she wasn't so sure.

"I think it would be best if we speak alone," Stacey Lea said, smiling sweetly.

"I have no secrets from Harlan." No way, Carolyn thought, you're a first-class shrew, Mrs. Forbes, and I have no intention of being alone with you.

"Mizz Walker, may I call you Carolyn? Fine. Please call me Stacey Lea. Carolyn, what I have to talk to you about is woman-to-woman stuff, and I'd feel awkward talkin' such things in front of a man, even if he is your best friend. I know you understand, Mr. Parker. I promise to return your Carolyn unscathed."

As Stacey Lea spoke, she had taken Harlan Parker's arm and gently begun steering him from the room toward the kitchen, she assumed, since they were passing through the dining area.

Harlan Parker looked back weakly as he was ushered away, "I'll fix a snack and a drink," he called back, as if assuring Carolyn that he'd only be a few steps away.

"That's a wonderful idea," responded Stacey Lea, enthusiastically. "I'll have a glass of wine, please. White or red, it doesn't matter."

"We don't drink," Carolyn informed coldly from behind.

"Very well, whatever you're having."

While Stacey Lea dispensed with Harlan, Carolyn Walker had a chance to rally from her challenger's initial onslaught. Whatever this little *tete-a-tete* was going to be, the first moves Carolyn intended to leave to her guest. After all, she'd wanted this meeting, and she evidently wanted something else. Let her work for it. She had always found it much easier defending, and married to Earle Walker, she had become skilled at the nuances of it.

Carolyn and Stacey Lea were now sizing one another up with each syllable, wary adversaries.

"Now, Carolyn, the reason for my visit. I'm here because I wish to know the direction of your ministry. Your husband had very strong views where women are concerned. Are you going to continue with his archaic attitude?"

"My husband was, uh, is a saint. I'll continue as he knew God wished. If that's old-fashioned, so be it. Earle knew and taught the ways of God whose ways are sometimes hard to accept. I am fortunate to have his example."

"Oh, spare me," Stacey Lea responded, casting the art of repartee aside. "Earle Walker was a vile, contemptible man. He touched me personally because he hurt three of my friends directly with his hate-filled speech and personal decadence. I also know that he treated you abominably, but we both would prefer all this be our little secret, wouldn't we?"

"What color wine do you prefer?" Carolyn asked, starting toward the kitchen.

"Red. I read one time that a person who appreciates wine always prefers red," Stacey Lea added grinning.

"I like it better, but it gives me a headache," Carolyn replied, also grinning.

"Then make mine white too."

When Carolyn returned, she was followed by Harlan carrying a small tray of cheese and crackers. Carolyn carried a chilled bottle of good Chablis and two glasses.

"I'd like to wish you good evening, Mrs. Forbes," Harlan said after he placed the tray down on the glass-top cocktail table. "I'm going back to my hotel room for the night. It is a pleasure to meet you; you are every bit as lovely as your pictures."

The two women sat on either end of the sofa, both more relaxed, but still with reservations and not sure where to start again. Finally, Stacey Lea spoke, after all, it was at her behest that they were together.

"So, how do you feel about all this Eternist stuff of women having to stay at home?"

"Sarah Winthrop your friend?"

"Good friend."

"Alma Tyler?"

"Not as much as Sarah."

"How much of a friend is Beverly Abelson?"

"One of my best."

"That's who he was sleeping with, you know?"

"You haven't answered my question?"

"About women and the home?"

"Yes."

"Let me put what I put earlier another way. Earle had a successful formula. I'm still untried, so I don't want to rock the boat."

"Did you know that your husband had been involved in a secret plot to literally get rid of women in important positions, maybe going as far as condoning murder?"

"No, but I'm not surprised. He hated women, starting with the woman he always called his *saintly mother.*"

"I guess you wouldn't like to see what I just told you get out?"

"I have an idea you wouldn't want it to either."

Stacey Lea liked Carolyn Walker more with each counter.

"I've heard speculation that your husband didn't die of natural causes."

"You always hear that kind of thing when an important person dies suddenly. I wouldn't be surprised if they were saying the same thing about Howard Abelson."

Each wondered what the other knew, but wondered at the logic of pursuing it further.

"A secret organization has been formed to support and encourage women in politics and other important positions. What would you tell your people about any of these women this organization might encourage?"

"Nothing. I'm sorry, but that's the best I can do for now."

They looked at each other and understood.

When Stacey Lea got home that night, she took Howard Abelson's suicide note out of her purse and ripped it into many little pieces. She hadn't needed it, after all. Carolyn Walker would not be their enemy.

CHAPTER NINETEEN

THE LADIES LUNCHEON

The First Lady's limousine pulled out of the White House drive promptly at nine that morning. After her visit to Carolyn Walker last evening, she and Ellie had worked well into the night planning this day's agenda. They had more loose ends after Day Zero than she had realized. It was going to be a monumental task getting WOW's operation started, and she would also need to do a monumental amount of traveling for the Cause. She and Ellie had already begun to plan some of those camouflaged junkets. Wonder how Palmer was going to take to her traveling? She would have to cross each bridge when she came to it. Palmer? She had a lot of bridge building to do there, and it wasn't going to help if he returned and she was out. She did hope everyone was on time.

And they were. It was a small select group that gathered that morning at Sue Ann's. Mildred, Casey, Alma Tyler, and Beverly—even she was on time and didn't have her eyes closed against early morning bags. In fact, her enthusiastic voice was the first sound to greet them when Mrs. Bridges opened Sue Ann's big red front door.

"Stacey Lea, you and Ellie get in here quick! She's spectacular!"

They entered the large drawing room to find the marvelous Hanna, Alma's bodyguard, in the middle of a martial arts exhibition. She was taut and poised, her face lined with serious concentration as she waited for the new arrivals to get settled. She'd been impressive in olive green, but today, covered in black, she was formidable. Her masterful movements lasted exactly nine minutes and fifty seconds, perfectly timed and choreographed to the Overture of Wagner's *Der Fliegende Hollander.* She ended with the back-kick that had won Alma Tyler's heart that day in Stacey Lea's large sunny office at the White House. It would become her trademark

When it was over, everyone breathed a deep sigh of pleasure and presented Hanna with the ovation she deserved.

"My God, Alma," Beverly exploded, "you should bottle her; you'd make a fortune! At the very least, you should get her in the movies."

The jolt that Beverly's words produced could not have been duplicated even if Hanna's spectacular kick had been delivered to the California Congresswoman's mid-section. A delicious look began to spread across Alma's face as the idea began to germinate. And Beverly would later legitimately boast—a rare thing for a politician, that if it hadn't been for her, Hanna Gruber would probably never have become Heidi Graham, the martial art goddess of the silver screen.

Keeping Alma's attention after that was difficult, since her life had now taken on a new focus, but Stacey Lea, a determined taskmistress that day, got them all down to business.

"What Ellie's giving you is your area assignments. We'll all have to do our part."

"Not if you're going to send me to the Southwest all the time!" Sue Ann snapped, looking at hers. "I live in the South; besides, that sun out there isn't good for my skin."

"Casey also lives in the South, and she has more need to keep closer to home with her campaigning. Besides, you did such a fine job with Mary Lightfoot back in Tucson, I couldn't resist sending you back,"

Stacey Lea responded calmly while dismissing the matter. "I want each of you to take your list and come up with, at least, one woman in each state that we might consider for membership. Each nomination must be accepted unanimously."

Their progress was slow. Finally, in frustration, Alma Tyler suggested they stop where they were, contact the women already decided upon and let them help propose other prospects. "Besides, time's flying, and I'd like to get my son's problem handled before I go. I don't plan to stay for lunch. Here are the pictures you wanted. I even got one of the man who approached me with the deal."

"Good! Just give them to Mildred, and we'll do the rest."

"That's all there is to it?"

"Yes."

"What are you going to do?"

"Don't worry, Alma. Just rest assured that it'll be taken care of."

"What names did they use?" Mildred asked, looking hard at the pictures.

"Raymond Gonzalez and this one is Harold Curtis. He seemed to be in charge."

"Harold Curtis!" Casey shouted, "That's the name of the man who blackmailed me! Let me see those pictures. That's him. He's brazen to use the same name, and the other, why, the other is my Colombian, Señor Martinez. He's one of them! This is unbelievable!" Casey's eyes bulged with the incredulity of it all, but she recovered quickly. "What are we going to do about them? If we don't plan something really bad, I'll take care of them myself."

"Stop it, Casey. You can't go off on your own, none of us can," admonished Stacey Lea, with fervor, since she'd learned the hard way with Coleman.

"I want them punished. They hurt me. Now they're hurting Alma and her son. How many others have they hurt, and how many others will they hurt if they aren't stopped? I want them hurt."

"They'll be taken care of. Don't worry about it."

"You know, Stacey Lea," observed Sue Ann, "you're going around promisin' Alma you'll take care of this, then promisin' Casey you'll take care of that, but none of us know a thing about what you do, you and Mildred and Ellie. Frankly, I'm surprised you let the rest of us attend this luncheon, especially me. You wouldn't even tell me where Beau was."

"What do you mean, where Beau was?" pounced a surprised Beverly.

"Oh . . uh, nothing."

"That's one of the reasons right there, Sue Ann," Stacey Lea noted with satisfaction. "The more who know everything, the more likely someone is to slip."

"Maybe so," concluded Casey, "but I agree with Sue Ann. I insist on having some input into the future of these culprits."

"As I see it," announced Beverly, "it's like a trust test, at least for us. We're supposed to trust you to do whatever you think should be done; even though, we're responsible for whatever you do"

"You already sound like a politician," Stacey Lea reproached.

"That's what I want to be, and I'd sure hate to wake up some morning and find that I'd lost it all because one of your schemes backfired."

"My schemes aren't going to backfire!"

"It's true that secrets are better kept if fewer know," placated Mildred, "but they do have the right to make decisions if they're expected to take the risks."

"Besides," supported Ellie, "we could use more input."

"Very well," Stacey Lea acquiesced. "Are you leaving or staying, Alma?"

"I'm leaving. I'm going to depend on the five of you to take care of this mess. I'm confident that with Casey's zeal, and Beverly's caution, I have nothing to worry about now."

With that, Alma left, Hanna in tow.

And then there were five, and during lunch, this new equality they shared brought great enthusiasm to the business at hand. They had nothing but praise for Mildred, the secret taskforce, and the Cuban Commune, a name they'd quickly given their Cuban prison operation. They'd also quickly authorized the use of the Commune for Alma and Casey's two culprits, and they were now considering it for Dr. Carl Vondergraven.

"As I said before, I think Vondergraven needs to be interrogated regarding Sandra Ackerman," Beverly pressed.

"I agree," supported Ellie.

"I guess I shouldn't feel this way," admitted Sue Ann, "but I'm afraid to know."

"What do you mean, my dear?" Mildred asked.

"I mean that the knowledge could destroy me. If Sandra Ackerman was murdered and Beau was involved, how am I going to deal with that?"

"But what if he isn't, then you don't have it hanging over your head?" Mildred encouraged.

"I've thought about that, too. But knowing there may be something I don't know isn't difficult for me when I know that knowing might be worse. I've had to deal with what Beau did to Casey, but I don't know what I'd do if I had to deal with his involvement in Sandra Ackerman's death. He'd have to be punished, but how? I can't mete out punishment for something that serious, besides, Beau isn't the only one to be dealt with."

If the enormity of the situation had not hit all of them before, it did now.

"Sue Ann's right," Beverly decided. "I hadn't thought of it that way. We're going to have one helluva mess if we open this can of worms. We all know it goes right to the President of the United States. Sorry, Stacey Lea."

"Yes," acknowledged Mildred, "and what will we have accomplished? We would have exposed our cover, and we could hardly hope to win. In fact, we'd have everything to lose."

"And it could cause wounds in the nation that might never heal." Ellie added. "I wonder if this is what Gerald Ford felt when he decided to pardon Richard Nixon? I have more sympathy for him now than I ever had. It's not easy being in those kinds of shoes."

"True, but we're better off than Ford; at least, we have each other." Casey was attuned to this point. Since she'd been alone in her misery for so long, the fact that these women were with her now made all the difference.

Stacey Lea remained quiet. She had considered the consequences of questioning Vondergraven. That was one reason she had hoped to make these decisions alone, for to have to deal with what an interrogation might uncover might be more than she too could handle. She was relieved that Sue Ann had voiced her own fears. Sandra Ackerman's death should be avenged, but there is all kinds of justice.

"I see nothing to gain," decided Mildred. "If we do find that Sandra Ackerman was murdered, what do we do with that knowledge—expose the President of the United States, the Senate Majority Leader, and the most powerful Catholic Cardinal in the world? Could we expect to win? Besides, their operation is already neutralized."

"Yes," Stacey Lea, relieved by their conclusion, recapped. "Earle Walker conveniently died; Beau won't be going back to the Senate after the end of his term next year; their Federal taskforce has been all but removed, and I assure you, Palmer will not attempt a third term. We've wanted to establish a network for women, and that has begun. A new day is dawning for us, and we have much to do."

"Yes, let's start the New Year with positive attitudes, leave all this crap behind," agreed Beverly.

"Then we send Carl Vondergraven to Cuba and be done with it?" asked Ellie.

"Yes," announced Sue Ann, smiling, feeling much like a queen who has successfully dispensed with a major detractor, "send Carl Vondergraven to Cuba with the rest of the pack, and let's get on with our lives."

"Has anyone considered what we're going to do with these men we keep so easily sending off to Cuba?" Ellie questioned.

Everyone paused. It was only a short pause, for Beverly took the matter into her soon to be senatorial hands to address in what some would say perfect senatorial fashion.

"Who the hell cares? We'll cross that bridge when we have to. Right now, let's just get rid of the bastards." Raising her glass high in the air, she added, "Here's to the Cuban Commune!"

"Not so fast," admonished Stacey Lea. "We still have Cardinal Bishop to dispense with."

"Well, we certainly can't send him to our Cuban Commune. Can we?"

"No, but he isn't a threat anymore with their operation neutralized. Why don't we simply leave him alone."

"We can't do that. If we do, he and Palmer might start up again. Besides, he shouldn't get off free. No, we have to topple him."

"Well," pondered Mildred, "we could get some operatives to poke around and see what they can come up with."

"And if they don't come up with anything, we can set him up, the way they did me," supplied Casey.

"He's formidable. I've had to be around him a lot with Howard representing New York. I would hate to tangle with him."

"We don't. We take it right to the top, to the Pope," Sue Ann submitted with more enthusiasm than she felt.

The air was heavy as they considered their onerous opponent. Little did they know that their concerns over Cardinal Bishop were unnecessary? At that very moment, his Eve was preparing to serve up some *apple streudel.*

Claire dressed carefully and the results was quite fashionable. The only relief to her all-over purple look were the tiny white flowers at the collar of her crepe dress, although her stockings also added contrast as they lightened with their sheerness.

She had a lot of purple since it was Johnny's favorite color. Today, she found it almost too appropriate given its symbolic use in the Church where it represented a time of waiting, joyfully in Advent and sorrowfully in Lent. Today, she wore it to represent her own waiting, and for her, it also symbolized joy, past joy that had now turned into sorrow. *Would these be her widow weeds?*

Johnny had left as he had vowed, promptly after they'd returned from their little house, and she had obeyed his wishes and moved from his family's estate. It had not been easy. His sisters had wanted her to stay. They, at least, appreciated her, but she knew that Johnny would never return if she stayed on as the family housekeeper. They needed more common ground if it was going to work. This seemed less likely now.

She had waited at their house for him, but there had been no word. Perhaps she expected too much. After all, she'd only been a small part of his life. Johnny was stubborn. He would not allow himself to dwell on her or think about what she had said that last day. He'd go about that ordered, sterile world in which he existed and not allow her entrance. She must act quickly if there was a chance she could save him, quickly, before he had time to settle in and cut her from his memory forever.

Claire bundled herself in the purple plaid coat that Johnny had given her last Christmas, and taking one last look in the foyer mirror, she delivered an enormous sigh before braving brisk Buffalo December winds.

"His Eminence is waiting for you in the study, Mrs. Zimmer," the Chancery housekeeper announced as she took Claire's coat. "You may go right in."

Claire knew where *right in* was. After all, she'd spent her happiest days here with Johnny; perhaps it was appropriate that it end here too, if that was the way it was going to be.

I assure you, Claire, what you've told me will be handled with the utmost delicacy." The Bishop comforted. "I don't see any reason for the Holy Father to know about this as long as John quietly retires, and certainly no reason for scandal. I love John like a brother. Don't you worry, for I'll be discreet,"

Claire looked at the clock as the Bishop escorted her to the door. It had only taken an hour.

"Did you get it all, Jack?" Bishop O'Donnell questioned the rapid footsteps that followed Claire's departure.

"Yes," Monsignor Jack Wordman replied as he came smiling into the foyer. "I told you something was going on there, but I don't think that we would ever have gotten him on our own."

"I agree. We've had a real stroke of luck. No one has John Marion's ear the way you have, and still, he never let you too close. Get Rome on the line. Cardinal Scolari will be overjoyed."

"I hope they don't underestimate his power and popularity."

"Don't worry. That's the main reason they want to get rid of him. Remember this, my good man, no one's irreplaceable, especially a Prince of the Church who thinks he is.

"What do you think they'll do about him?"

"Are you getting cold feet?"

"No, but I don't relish a confrontation. He's tough; besides, he has trusted me."

"So, what does that matter, we're both getting what we want? I go to New York, and you take over for me here."

"I agree, but I don't want to have to worry about him getting even."

"The way I understand it, he won't be in any position to do that. Cardinal Bishop will be rewarded for his tireless service to Mother Church and be allowed to enter one of her ancient Monasteries, probably that one up in the Italian Alps, which has such a stellar alumnae of wayward sons. Yes, he'll be relieved of his duties so that he can pursue a much longed-for life of prayer and contemplation. Who knows, when Scolari's through with him that may be exactly what he'll want."

Bishop O'Donnell's voice had literally dripped with equal amounts of pleasure and sarcasm, enough to allay the fears of his younger associate.

"That sounds good enough to toast. Care to join me in a glass of the vine, 'Cardinal' O'Donnell?"

"Delighted, 'Bishop' Wordman! And let this be a lesson to both of us, messing with a woman can only get you a one-way ticket to Rome."

By the time Mrs. Bridges began to serve her famous Mississippi Mud Pie, all the old business had been crossed off the list Stacey Lea and Ellie had spent the prior night preparing.

"I'd appreciate it if you'd hold off on dessert for just a few minutes, Mizz Bridges. We have one more matter to discuss, and I need everyone's undivided attention. That wouldn't be possible if you're serving up one of those wonderful desserts of yours."

"Oh, come on, Stacey Lea, we're tired of decision making. Enough's enough." Casey complained. The others began to grumble in agreement; only Ellie, who knew the matter to be discussed, smiled her approval.

"I know. I feel the same way, but everything we've done today was Old Business, sweeping up the mess and bringing order back to our lives. Every meeting should have New Business, something that's looking ahead, something refreshing on the table. Frankly, after all we've had to deal with today, we deserve it; WOW deserves it."

There were no further complaints, for now everyone's curiosity was aroused; besides, they were rational women and agreed that after the distasteful things they'd had to deal with today, they did deserve something new and refreshing, and so did WOW.

"All right, Stacey Leanne," Sue Ann nudged, "out with it. I have a plane to catch."

"Yes," Beverly sighed, "You're beginning to make me wonder if I'm going to be able to take all that meeting stuff Senators have to deal with."

"Very well. As you all know, it's our goal to support women running for office. So, if that's our focus, I propose that we take as our ultimate goal the task of preparing a woman to become President of the United States."

Beverly was the first to break a lengthy silence. "Don't you think that's premature?"

"Not at all. Don't you see? Considering the fact that we're starting at a minus, it's going to take at least twenty-five years."

"If that's the case," Beverly now responded wryly, "then we better get started, or none of us will be around to see it."

"This is not a joke, Beverly," Stacey Lea snapped.

"What do you have in mind, Stacey Lea?" Sue Ann asked. "What do you mean, 'prepare a woman'?"

"Just what it sounds like. We take a young woman and orchestrate her education and career until we make her president."

"She'd already have to be in her twenties," Casey surmised.

"Yes, even late twenties," Mildred Dillard added.

"And how do we find this candidate? Run a contest?"

"Of course not. We can hardly do that," Stacey Lea replied laughing.

Liking the idea, they began talking amongst themselves, molding the character and the qualifications of this future and first woman president, even to her looks and her ability to wear mauve.

"Harvard. She should have a law degree from Harvard."

"Then she would already have to have it or be there."

"It would have to be someone whom we could have easy access to."

"Would we tell her right away? Let her know her destiny?"

"Of course, she'd have to be in on it."

"What if she told others about us and our plan?"

"We'd have to be sure of her, sure that she would work with us and be discreet."

Finally, Beverly, in her new senatorial voice, got everyone's attention.

"I don't know why we've wasted time discussing this, for I'm sure that if Stacey Lea brought it up, she has already picked the *Chosen One.*"

"There's no need to be sarcastic, Bev," Stacey Lea replied tartly.

"I'm right, though, aren't I?"

They waited.

"Well, I have given it some thought" she admitted and quickly continued. "I'd like to submit for your consideration, Randal Fairmont, Sue Ann's daughter. As most of you know, she just turned twenty-one, is in her first year of law school at Harvard, and comes from a family illustrious for its dedication to public service."

Sue Ann gasped while the others sat quietly digesting Stacey Lea's proposal.

"Does she know?"

"No, of course not. I don't even know if she's willing."

"She's a little young."

"Yes, I agree, but she already has political experience, and a name…"

"Stacey Lea, I don't believe you know how difficult Randal is. We'll not be able to control her. In fact, she can be very stubborn."

"But we don't want to control her, Sue Ann. We want her strong and her own woman. We simply want her to want to be president and work with us for it."

Sue Ann frowned, thinking of her only daughter.

"What do you think, Sue Ann?" Casey asked. "Do you think she might go for it?"

"I don't know," Sue Ann replied, shaking her head. "I never know about Randal, but I do know that if she goes for it, she'll stick. That's her way."

"President Randal Fairmont," Beverly said, remembering the first time she'd placed Senator before her name. "It does have a ring to it."

"Yes, it does," agreed Mildred. "I move that Randal Fairmont be the first Woman President of these United States, that is, if she's willing."

At last, to everyone's delight, Mrs. Bridge's served her famous Mississippi Mud Pie, and Casey announced that there must be no more decision making, anything to divert the mind, for one did not eat that many calories without giving strict attention to it. Sin should be enjoyed.

"It's sinful, all right," groaned Beverly.

"If you lived here with Mizz Bridges cookin' very long, maybe you'd have trouble fittin' into all that mauve you have," goaded Sue Ann, good-naturedly.

"That reminds me, I have Christmas gifts for all of you."

Beverly went to the hall, and when she returned, she was carrying a large shopping bag. Reaching in, she distributed identical gaily-wrapped packages.

"Well, open them."

"Isn't it ironic that the only Jew in our midst, the only one who doesn't celebrate Christmas, is the only one who remembered it?" stated Sue Ann, quite touched by Beverly's gesture.

They agreed as they opened identical boxes to find identical heavy silk-fringed scarves with an all-over mauve-on-mauve wisteria-flowered pattern. Once all the 'ohs' and 'ahs' and 'thank yous' had been enthusiastically delivered, they gave themselves up to Christmas cheer. Mildred gave the moment greater dignity by using her spoon as a gavel to announce the season officially open.

Their hearts were full as they said their farewells that cold December afternoon. It was the season of goodwill, and they had never felt it so strongly. They had never felt so connected to this universe, this earth, this nation, and to one another as they did at this very last moment when each put on her coat, put on her gloves and wrapped around her neck Beverly's marvelous gift.

It was a new beginning for them, the kind that happens only *once upon a time.*

THE END OF THE BEGINNING

Randal stood again at the window, her mind bounding from the past to the present, and it seemed as if it had happened exactly that way, one big leap for there to here. Now, she was in a holding pattern, a limbo, neither here nor there, waiting to be. She recalled a maze the Hopi Indians wove into mats and baskets, life's journey with its bends and turns until near the end there was a little niche where the soul rested to reflect back on that journey before stepping into the maze's center. That's where she was now. Soon, it would be over, and she would be where she had focused all her energies to be. Did every president-to-be stand gazing into space on inauguration morning with feelings of both wonderment and apprehension? She humbly prayed that she would serve with honor and distinction, that she would be good for her country and make it proud of her.

As her thoughts jumped around, a cab pulled to the curb at Blair House and wherever her thoughts may have been brought them immediately to the present. She bounded out the front door to fling her arms around the occupant's neck, hardly giving him time to remove himself from the vehicle, much less identify himself to the Secret Service swooping down.

"Oh, Eli, thank you for this."

"I could hardly miss your big day; besides, I'm proud of you for realizing your dream, for becoming what you were determined to be."

That was all he had time to say before their twins, Suzy and Abe, gathered around.

The Marine Band was playing *Hail to the Chief* as President Matthews preceded her down the stairs to the platform. She wondered how he felt knowing that it was the last time it was being played for him. He had walked ahead of her reluctantly, and only after she'd given him an impatient little nudge; this 'ladies first' stuff was often tiresome to deal with.

They both spent a few moments shaking hands and hugging supporters and friends who had earned the right to be there. Randal embraced her family, Eli first, and then stepped to her mother and the Aunts. Her mother and Aunt Sarah were octogenarians now and the others weren't far behind. With the exception of Aunt Sarah who was in a wheelchair, they stood straight and tall, validating good genes and privileged lives. Mildred Dillard had been dead over ten years and Casey Bartholomew had been too ill to attend, but she knew they were here; she could feel their presence. Two past presidents were here too, Goodman Palmer Forbes and Joseph Sean Delucca.

Forbes was still lean and lanky like Lincoln but the once pretty face no longer masked the unstable character that was inside, at least, not to her and those who knew him, and Delucca had a greater girth than during his presidency, but still exuded a magnetism that the years had been incapable of diminishing. She could see why he and Auntie Bev had kept their promise to spend their golden years together, no matter the scandal.

Aunt Ellie, the youngest of them all, did not look it, as her bent frame, crippled by arthritis, walked forward almost lost in the black robe that identified her as Chief Justice of the Supreme Court. This would be her last official act, and Randal knew that she had waited painfully for this grand finale to a distinguished career.

Suzy and Abe walked forward too. They held the Fairmont Bible that documented the lives of Fairmonts since before the Civil War. Opening it discreetly, she placed the soft burgundy Moroccan leather notebook tenderly inside. As she did, her eyes touched Aunt Ellie's and they shared a moment filled with memories of this book, the last gift to Eleanor Fanny Farmer from her father. In it, she had documented that first meeting in Aunt Stace's magnolia covered First Lady apartment in the White House when they had chosen their secret name, and in it, she had also documented that Christmas luncheon at the Fairmont's Georgetown home when they'd chosen her.

"I, Randal Stacey Fairmont, do solemnly swear . . . ."

She knew it by heart; she'd practiced it many times the past years. It ran through her head like a favorite song that seemed to always be near the surface ready to spill out; it was part of her. Every day she said it like the Lord's Prayer, the twenty-third Psalm—her grandmother's favorite—and with the same reverence. It had become a litany like the Rosary, but it was never rote nor stale, always fresh and invigorating.

When it was over, she kissed her son and daughter and thanked them, knowing they understood that she was thanking them for supporting her destiny; then she hugged Aunt Ellie so tightly she felt her wince, but her smile belied pain. The world waited as she looked at her mother and the Aunts. Her eyes met Stacey Lea's, and she realized that Aunt Stace knew exactly the unprecedented thing she planned to do on this solemn occasion and was amused. But why not, she was also unprecedented.

Randal turned to the vast crowd in front of her, stepped to the edge of the platform, looked directly into the scrutinizing eyes of the cameras which had not always been kind to her, and raised her arms high, her hands open, as her voice emitted a resounding, "YES!"

The cheers were heard around the world.

ABOUT THE AUTHOR

JEAN CANDLISH KELCHNER taught English and Humanities at Kean University of New Jersey before devoting herself full-time to writing. She is a member of the American Association of University Women and the International Women's Writing Guild. Born and raised in Augusta, Arkansas, she now makes her home in West Paterson, New Jersey. Contact her through her website www.jckelchner.com, or through AuthorHouse at www.jckelchnerwhitehouse.com.

OTHER BOOKS BY THE AUTHOR

Assignment: Trophy Art, ISBN: 1-58345-064-5, published by Domhan Books, 2001.

Meet Maxine Cantrell, the spy with a heart! Join her as she copes with terrorists, dashing villains, egocentric art collectors, an ex-husband, her straight-laced mother, JOB, her hush-hush agency, and the sleepy Texas hometown where she goes when she is overwhelmed.

What About Me? ISBN: Paperback: 141400592X, ebook: 1414005938, published by AuthorHouse.com, 2003.

When Jessie Boland's lawyer husband, Douglas, has an affair, she moves to their New York apartment, gets herself a job at the Metropolitan Museum, and a psychiatrist on Fifth Avenue. Jessie, who has spent all of her life being what she thought she was supposed to be, is finally challenged to awaken to who she really is and what she truly can be.

Daughters of Eve, a Herstory Book, Paperbook: 1-4140-4356-2, e-book: 1 4140-4357-0, published by AuthorHouse.com, 2004.

Fiction and Fact combine as five women tell their stories— Nitocris, an Egyptian Queen who would be Pharaoh; Bathsheba, a Biblical Queen who bathed on a roof and caused King David to sin; Devorgilla, a Medieval Lady, whose wild Celtic blood caused her to often clash with her Norman husband and the border between Scotland and England; Christine, a

Renaissance Poet who made her livelihood with her pen and wrote, for the first time about widowhood, rape, and other subjects that affected women of her day; and Artemisia, a Baroque artist, who for the first time drew women bigger than life with passions to fit.